No Regrets

Tattoos and Tears
Book 4

By Amiee Louise

NO REGRETS

First edition. October 2, 2025.

ISBN: 978-1968759285

Written by Amiee Louise.

1

Sam

I pull up to the kerb and Peyton stumbles on the pavement as a scum bag photographer continues to take her picture. I grip the steering wheel tighter, until my knuckles turn white. *Rein it in Newbolt, stay calm.* She ignores me, and I crawl slowly along the kerbside as the *click, click, click* of the photographer's camera causes me to clench my jaw and grind my teeth.

"Angel, please get in the car, you're going to be all over the goddamn motherfucking newspaper tomorrow," I retort, and she narrows her eyes at me like a sulky fucking teenager.

"I don't fucking care! Leave me alone, Sam," she slurs rebelliously and stumbles on her heels.

Fuck me, she's drunk.

"Get in the fucking car."

My voice is low and commanding, but she carries on walking, ignoring my request. The *click, click* of her heels on the pavement, grating on every last fucking nerve in my body.

"So, help me God, do *not* make me get out of this fucking car, angel," I rasp and my nostrils flare with anger. *Breathe Newbolt, one, two, three, four, five.*

"Fuck off!" she hisses defiantly, and I close my eyes.

Sometimes I think she enjoys taunting me.

"Angel, please, just get in the car," I say, as calmly as I can muster, and she rolls her eyes. *God give me fucking strength.*

I pull to a stop at the kerb, she opens the passenger door and unsteadily gets in. I take in the sight of her; she looks dishevelled, but still manages to look beautiful, all at the same time. I pull smoothly out into the traffic and start to speed down the street, the silence hanging thickly in the air between us is deafening.

"I've been going out of my fucking mind," I say through clenched teeth. "Who the fuck was that bloke on the phone?"

She leans her head back on the headrest.

"How many fucking times, Sam? It's none of your fucking business and I'm fine! I'm not your problem; you need to stop acting like we're still together. Truth is, it's fucking creepy."

With those words I feel my chest constrict and I can't stand to see her acting this way.

"I fucking care about you, angel. I still love you, you're the mother of my child. I need you more than I need my next breath," I admit softly, and she turns her head away from me. "Look at me, angel."

She turns back to me.

"Do you want to know what I've been doing tonight? *Do you?*" she spits angrily. "I was in a bar and I had sex with the owner over the pool table. That was who was on the phone. It was dirty and seedy, and I *loved* every fucking minute of it!"

She laughs bitterly, and I feel like my heart has been ripped clean from my chest. It cuts me deep that she's been with another man and I feel the boiling jealousy running through my veins, even though I know I have no right to be jealous.

Another man has had his filthy, motherfucking hands on her.

"He fucked me hard and rough, he treated me like the whore that I've turned into," she screams, and she starts sobbing hysterically.

What the fuck happened to her to make her act this way? She's hiding something from me, it's like she's returned a completely different person to the woman I fell in love with.

"Take me home, please," she says with a sniff, and I shake my head.

"No, I'm taking you back to my place, angel. I'm going to feed you and make you some coffee, you're going to shower and then you're sleeping in my bed."

She shakes her head and screams at me.

"WHY ARE YOU BEING SO FUCKING NICE TO ME? I FUCKED SOMEONE ELSE!" She lowers her voice and I grip the steering wheel so tight, my knuckles turn white. "Why aren't you shouting and screaming at me for being so reckless and cold?"

The truth is, I don't know. I know I should be shouting and cursing her to hell, but I can't. We aren't technically together right now, but she's the mother of my child and this past month has made me realise what I already knew, I still have feelings for her. Hell, I *love* her, so god damn much.

"Please, just take me home, Sam."

She sobs. I reach over the centre console to her, but she flinches back from me, as if I have burned her. I clench my jaw at her reaction and move my hand away. The moment is interrupted by my phone ringing and I push the button on the steering wheel to activate the hands free.

"Hey, I'm driving, and you're on hands free, dude."

Brody's voice comes through the cars sound system, "Did you find her, mate?"

His voice is filled with trepidation and I take a deep, cleansing breath.

"Yeah, man, I've got her; she's in my car. I'm bringing her back now."

He breathes out a sigh of relief before he speaks again, "Is-Is she ok?"

I close my eyes briefly and she scowls.

"Let me out," she says softly, as she reaches for the door.

"*Shit!* Brody, I'm going to have to call you back, man, I need to pull over."

"Sam, what's going on?" His voice sounds panicked.

I reach over to stop her from opening the door, while the car is moving, and I swerve to avoid an oncoming car, the honking of the horn startling both of us.

"*Fuck! Jesus Christ!* Angel, will you stop please! Stop for a fucking second! You're going to get us both killed!" I raise my voice.

"LET ME OUT OF THIS FUCKING CAR, RIGHT NOW, SAM!" she screams.

"Peyton, babe, it's me Brody. Listen to me, sweets; I need you to calm down for me, yeah? We all just want what's best for you, that's all I promise."

His voice is soft as he tries to placate her. She pulls her hand back from the door and rests it in her lap.

"Would it help if Sam bought you to me? I live with him, but I've got my own living space in the opposite wing to him. I've got some beers in, we can talk, just you and me, no judgement. How does that sound, babe?" he says softly, and her eyes look so haunted.

It breaks my heart to see her this way. She nods, and her wide, blue eyes are brimming with tears.

"I'm bringing her home, Brody."

"No worries, man, I'll see you in a little while, dude, see you soon, sweetness."

He hangs up the phone and I signal to pull over at the side of the road. The car crawls to a stop, and I put the handbrake on. I lean over the steering wheel.

Why won't she fucking talk to me? Why can't she just tell me what was so bad that she's hit the self-destruct button?

"I didn't ask you to come and find me, I was fine," she says indifferently and swipes angrily at the tears that have tracked their way down her cheek.

I scrub my hands down my face. *Fuck me.*

"Freddie needs you, I fucking *need* you, Peyton."

Another tear escapes from the corner of her eye and she squeezes her eyes shut.

"No, you don't need me, Sam; I made you think I was dead. That's unforgivable; I see it every time you look at me."

I reach for her hand, but this time she lets me take it and I hold it in mine. She is trembling uncontrollably; I bring her hand up to my mouth and place a gentle kiss on the back to try and calm her.

"I'll never forget the way you looked at me when you first saw me in your hospital room. That image is burned into my fucking consciousness."

I shake my head and slam my hand harshly against the steering wheel.

"I was in fucking shock! I'd spent a whole year mourning you, grieving for you; I would wake up in the morning and think *'what's the fucking point'.* I tried to take my own life, for fucks sake! I opened a vein just to make the fucking pain stop! I wanted it all to stop."

She grimaces at my honest words and snatches her hand away.

"Let me out of this fucking car now, Sam," she says coldly.

She opens the car door and gets out, stumbling, as her heels hit the floor. I slam my hands on the steering wheel and shout, "*FUCKKKKK!*"

I watch as she staggers down the road. I open the car door and pace down the street after her. It takes me a few long strides to catch up with her; I grab her wrist and she spins around, slapping me hard across the face. Her eyes widen as she realises what she has just done. She puts her hand to her mouth and starts to sob.

"I'm sorry, I'm so sorry Sam, I'm sorry, I'm sorry, I'm so sorry," she repeats over and over.

Her knees buckle underneath her, and I catch her in my arms. We both sink down to the floor and I hold her in my arms tightly at the side of the road.

"Sh, sh, sh, it's alright, let it all out. I've got you, angel, you're safe."

I kiss the top of her head. I just let her cry, holding her tight, stroking her back and reassuring her as best as I can.

I am not sure how long we sit at the side of the road, but her tears have finally subsided. I scoop her up in my arms and take her back to the car. I sit her in the passenger seat and click her seatbelt into place. She is still trembling uncontrollably, and it fucking breaks my heart. I make my way to the driver seat; I climb in, close the door, fasten my seatbelt and pull away from the kerb.

For the remainder of the journey to my house in Hertfordshire, we are both silent and left to our thoughts. As we drive through the security gate and pull into my gravelled driveway, I notice she has fallen asleep, she must have been exhausted. Brody is sitting on the stone steps, wearing a pair of dark blue and grey plaid pyjama bottoms, a white vest and black skull slippers. I get out of the car and go around to the passenger side, smirking at the sight of Brody in his pyjamas.

"What's so funny?" Brody asks.

I chuckle.

"You on the doorstep in your pyjamas!"

Brody narrows his eyes and folds his arms across his chest.

"Funny fucker," he mutters grumpily.

As I open the passenger door, I scoop her into my arms, kick the car door shut with my boot, and make my way to the front door. Brody locks my car and helps me inside. As I step inside, the hallway is flooded with light. *The pros of modern technology!*

"I'm going to go and put her in my bed, I'll sleep in one of the spare rooms," I tell him.

Brody brushes my arm reassuringly.

"Are you sure this is a good idea, dude?"

I shake my head.

"No, it's a fucking awful idea, but what other fucking choice did I have? Leave her out there on her own, vulnerable, upset, scared? I love her with everything I am, Brody. We were going to get married and have our happily ever after. But we never got that, now she's the mother of my child, but she's so haunted and..." I close my eyes and stop myself, before I say too much. "I'll be right back."

Brody nods in understanding and I make my way up the stairs to my bedroom. I lay her down on my bed, pull off her shoes and undress her carefully, leaving her underwear on, and pull the covers up over her. She looks so peaceful when she's asleep, but I know that is far from the truth. I spend a moment admiring her. She is so beautiful, but her beauty is marred with the dark circles under her eyes. I push a strand of her dark hair away from her face and kiss her gently on her forehead.

"Goodnight, angel," I whisper and leave the room.

I go back downstairs and into the kitchen where Brody is perched on the worktop, with a glass of amber liquid in his hand. He pushes a glass over to me.

"You look like you need it, dude." We both smile at each other as I take the glass and take a long drink. "So, shoot, you look like you could do with a chat."

I shake my head.

"Cole tracked the GPS on her phone and I found her stumbling drunk outside that new bar, JJ's Inferno. She wouldn't get in the car. It was like she wasn't even there, and it was fucking scaring the shit out of me. She eventually got in the car and she started screaming at me, telling me she wasn't my problem anymore. Then she proceeded to tell me she fucked someone else tonight; it broke my fucking heart, Brody. She's the only woman I've ever loved, and she tore my heart clean out of my chest."

Brody pours me another drink and I knock it back.

"*Fuck*, what isn't she telling me, Brody? Why is she acting this way?"

Brody shrugs.

"I have no idea, dude; she's hit the self-destruct button, that's the way it sounds to me, anyway. I've been in rehab a few times to know the signs,

I think she's been through a trauma, a trauma so bad that she's switched everything off and she's determined to punish herself and everyone around her. I'm no shrink, but you need to either help her, or give her the space she needs."

I scrub my hands down my face.

"She's the mother of my kid, for fuck's sake."

Brody knocks back his drink.

"So, you think just because she's someone's mum, she hasn't got the right to break down? *Jesus Christ,* don't be a fucking prick, Sam."

I can always rely on Brody to be honest with me, brutally so. He tells it like it is, I need that sometimes and now is one of those moments.

"*Fuck*, I don't know how to fix this...mess, Brody," I say dejectedly and Brody smirks.

"So, you expected what? To go out there tonight, find her, she would be eternally grateful for you rescuing her? Like a knight in shining armour and she would fall back into your arms? Fucking hell, dude, what do you think this is Mills and fucking Boon?"

I take a sip of my drink as Brody throws his head back and laughs.

I'm glad my love life amuses you, Hart.

"Look, man, I'm sorry, I don't fucking mean to take the piss, but you need to realise she's not the same girl she was a year ago."

I fucking hate it when he's right.

***

Brody went to bed a while ago, after a long chat. Even though I knew it was wrong at the time, I couldn't resist the magnetic pull I felt when I went to check on her. She looked so peaceful and vulnerable asleep in my bed. Before I could get my thoughts in check, I was stripping down to my boxers and climbing into bed next to her. Feeling the warmth of her body next to mine and inhaling her unique scent and touching her soft skin, after a whole year, was more than I could handle. She is my home, even after her absence, and she owns me. That thought caused me to drift off into the best sleep I'd had in a long time.

I'm not sure how long I have been asleep, but I am woken by Peyton writhing next to me. I rub the sleep from my eyes and move over to her.

"Stay with me, angel," I soothe. She thrashes against me, and I try to envelope her in my arms. But she's definitely been working out; her tattooed biceps are taut and stronger than I remember. "Focus on my voice, angel, you need to stay with me." I use my husky voice, urging her to come back to me from her nightmare, but it doesn't seem to be working.

"Angel."

I can feel her heart beat banging in her chest and the strangled whimpers coming from her make me feel as if my own heart is being ripped from my chest.

"Shhh, I've got you angel, come back to me, stay with me."

She starts bunching the sheets in her tiny hands and she bucks up off the bed, her back arching into me. I try to hold her, and she struggles against me.

"Angel, it's Sam, focus on my voice. It's just a nightmare, you're safe."

She lets out a scream and my heartbeat quickens. I feel like my heart is breaking seeing her like this, seeing her react to a vivid nightmare like this.

"NO! NO! GET OFF ME! NOOO! PLEASE DON'T," she pleads. She is soaked with sweat and her beautiful face is contorted with fear, I can't fucking bear it. "NO! NO! NOOOOO!" she screams.

I grip her wrists in my hands and gently shake her, begging her to come back to me. She thrashes violently against me, whipping her head from side to side. Seeing her like this is killing me. I swallow past the lump that's formed in my throat.

"Angel," I rasp.

I let go of her wrists and pull her to my warm chest, trying to offer her comfort, something familiar and safe. She screams again, and I feel her fist connect with my cheek. She punches me hard enough that my head snaps to the side. *Fuck me; she's definitely stronger than I remember.*

"*Fuck,*" I curse, and she opens her eyes.

She looks confused, and she struggles to focus on her surroundings. Her pained sapphire eyes, look into my green ones and she starts to sob hard.

"Oh God, oh God, oh God, fuck, fuck, fuck."

She jumps from my arms and scrambles out of bed. She is in her underwear and her skin is glistening with sweat. She drags her hand through her hair and her breathing is erratic. I can see her visibly trembling from my position on the bed. What could possibly make her react like this? *What the fuck was she dreaming about?*

"Angel," I whisper, and she shakes her head.

She is clammy with sweat and she looks so pale; she looks like she has seen a ghost.

"Please, Sam, just don't," she chokes out and runs into the adjoining bathroom, she locks it behind her.

I sit on the edge of the bed, wondering what the fuck just happened. I pad across the bedroom and tap softly on the bathroom door.

"Are you ok, angel?"

I hear her sobbing softly and I rattle the door handle.

"Let me in, babe, talk to me, please."

There is a silence and I hear her start to violently vomit. I bang the door hard with my fist.

"Peyton, angel, open the door, or I'm going to have to break it the fuck down."

Fuck!

"Angel, please open the door."

I start pacing the floor and run my hands frantically through my hair. I need to talk to someone. I reach for my phone and swipe my finger across the screen, selecting the person I need to speak to.

"Do you know what fucking time it is, Sam? These late-night phone calls need to stop, mate, the Mrs is beginning to get a complex!" Jax's calm voice comes down the phone.

"She had a nightmare, dude. I don't know what the fuck I'm doing. I'm out of my depth and I don't know how to handle this. She's scaring the living fuck out of me, Jax," I say in a desperate, panicked voice and I hear him curse.

"Do you need me to come over, mate? I can be there in ten minutes, five, if I put my foot down."

I run my free hand through my hair.

"*Fuck*, I don't know. She's locked herself in the bathroom. She's throwing up, and she's refusing to come out, I don't know what to do, man."

Jax curses on the other end of the phone, for a second time.

"Who's that, baby?" I hear Ruby's voice, thick with sleep on the other end.

"It's just Sam, sweetheart, go back to sleep," Jax soothes her.

"Doesn't that boy ever fucking sleep?" she says sleepily, and I suddenly feel bad for calling.

"Look, dude, I'm sorry I shouldn't have called, I'll talk to you in the morning."

"No, it's fine honestly, mate."

With those words, Peyton comes flying out of the bathroom like a tornado, and she starts frantically collecting her clothes. She starts getting dressed and fumbles her way into her clothes, as if she can't wait to get out of here.

"*Shit!* Jax, I need to go."

I hear Ruby curse.

"Where are my fucking clothes?" she asks, with an infuriated edge to her voice and she rushes past me, but I catch her by the wrist before she can run off. She flinches away from me and struggles against my grip.

"*Fuck!* Jax, look, I'll talk to you tomorrow, mate."

I quickly end the call and throw my phone down on the bed. She spins around, slapping me hard across the face.

"FUCKING LET GO OF ME!" she screams, and I growl. *Fucking women!*

"Not until you tell me what you were dreaming about, angel. You scared the fucking shit out of me."

She carries on struggling.

"Ugly things. I don't need them in my head, and I'm damn sure you don't fucking need them in yours." She starts pounding my chest and hitting me. "Just fucking let me go! Why won't you let me go? Why Sam? WHY!"

She lets out a sob, and the noise breaks my heart. She collapses in a heap on the floor at my feet and sobs hard and hysterically. I sink to my knees and gather her in my arms as she begins to relax in my hold.

"Shhh, I've got you, angel," I soothe, as I hear the front door close.

"Sam, babe, it's me. Where are you?"

Ruby's voice echoes through the house.

"Up here, babe, in my bedroom," I call out as Peyton's head snaps up, and she scrambles away from me, like a frightened, wounded animal.

"I need to go home."

She gets to her feet and runs straight into Ruby on the way out.

"Oh, babe," Ruby soothes and wraps her arms around her. "Shush, it's alright, I'm here."

Peyton sobs so hard it makes my heart clench.

"Please, take me home, Ruby."

I sit on the edge of the bed and scrub my hands down my face. *This definitely isn't the way I imagined my day ending.*

"Take me home, Rubes, please. I can't be here, I just can't," she sobs and Ruby rubs her back reassuringly.

"Ok, babe, keep calm for me, yeah? I'll take you home, it's going to be alright."

I stand up and pull my jogging bottoms on.

"You can take one of my cars, honey. Take the Aston."

She nods, and a grin crosses her face. She is wearing a leopard print onesie, and she jumps up and down clapping excitedly. I smirk at her enthusiasm.

"Yay! Thanks, Sam!"

She kisses me on the cheek and takes Peyton downstairs. I follow them both and take the set of keys for my fire engine red Aston Martin V8 Vantage from the hook in the hallway.

"Be fucking careful, babe, or Jax will have my balls; and I happen to be quite fond of my balls!" I warn and Ruby laughs.

"Cross my heart. Careful is my middle name, Newbolt."

Ruby winks as I toss the keys to her and she catches them. Peyton's head is down and my heart breaks for her. I take one of my hoodies from the coat rack and start to pull it over her head. She complies as I pull it on for her.

"Thank you," she whispers. I smile as she pulls the sleeves over her hands.

"You're welcome, angel."

She doesn't look at me and Ruby looks from me to Peyton.

"Do you two need a minute?"

Ruby's voice breaks the silence and Peyton shakes her head.

"No, I'm done."

I can't help but think that her phrase has more than one meaning.

2

Peyton

I wake up the next morning and I have the hangover from hell. *Ugh...whose idea was it to get completely shit faced? Oh yeah, mine.* I pull the duvet back over my head and a hand reaches to pull it back.

"Oh no you fucking don't, missy," Ruby says sternly. "Coffee's in the machine. Shower, get dressed, and then you and me are going to have a long fucking talk," she snaps abruptly.

I peel the duvet away and get up to make my way to the bathroom. I feel like a chastised teenager. I look at my reflection in the mirror and gasp. I look like shit, my eye makeup is smudged, I have dark circles under my eyes, my face is pale, and my hair looks like the rats have been at it. *Great.* I peel off the Rancid Vengeance hoodie, which smells of Sam, and drop it on the floor. I step in the shower and turn the water to scolding hot. The hot water feels so good against my skin and I sink down to the floor. I hug my knees to my chest and try to remember what happened last night. I close my eyes.

The bar...vodka...Jack...Sambuca...Sam. Shit, Sam. *Fuck!*

Half an hour later, I am out of the shower, and I feel so much better. I feel almost human; I get dressed and opt for denim shorts, a Superman vest and my Converse trainers. I dry and straighten my hair, wearing it down. I go into the kitchen and Ruby is sitting at the breakfast bar. She scowls at me and pushes a cup of coffee towards me. I take it from her and take a long sip, relishing the hot, sweet black liquid, as it slides down my throat.

"You and Jack Scott, really, babe?"

I look puzzled over my coffee cup and she narrows her eyes at me.

"How did...?"

She stops me by holding up her finger.

"Sam's not stupid, he only said the name of the bar to me and I knew instantly. What the fuck, Peyton? I mean Jack Scott, of all people; if you thought Sam was a slut, this guy takes the cake. Then page five, pictures of you and Sam. What the fuck were you thinking?"

I take another welcome sip of coffee. *I really don't need this shit right now.*

"Sam needs to mind his own fucking business. As for me and Jack, it was no big deal, just a bit of fun. I needed to let my hair down and blow off some steam."

I shrug, and she cocks her perfectly groomed eyebrow at me.

"Or blow him, by the looks of it," she says sardonically.

I put my coffee mug down forcefully and narrow my eyes at her.

"So, what if I did? I'm single and just because I'm a mum now and I'm not with Sam, I need to become a born again fucking virgin?" I shout.

"I'm not saying that, I'm just looking out for you, babe, that's all. I know you and Sam still love each other, any fool with a pair of fucking eyes can see that," she says softly, and I shake my head.

"So, what, he's been innocent and kept his dick in his pants the whole time I was gone? Don't insult my fucking intelligence, babe. You know me better than that."

She stands up and strokes her bump.

"What the fuck has happened to you, Peyton? Have you no regard for his feelings at all?"

I scrub my hand down my face. *His feelings? What the fuck?*

"Whose side are you on? You've got no fucking idea what I've been through! I'm fucking broken, Ruby! You don't fucking get it! I ended things with Sam because he doesn't deserve this broken version of me!"

My voice breaks, and Ruby's face is marred with concern.

"Then talk to me, you know I'm here for you. I'm on your side."

I shake my head. *I can't, not now.*

"Just fucking forget it, Rubes. It doesn't matter."

I pick up my coffee and finish the remains of the cup.

"Of course it fucking matters, Peyton!" she says exasperated.

I love Ruby to death, but I won't subject her to that.

I put the cup on the breakfast bar, go into my bedroom and change into my running gear. I need to run; pounding the pavement at six thirty in the morning is exactly what I need. I pull on my cropped jogging bottoms, purple and grey Nike Shox trainers, my sports bra and a tight black vest. I pull on a grey hoodie and pull my short hair into a small ponytail.

"Where are you going?"

I pick up my phone and grab my Beats headphones. *Music and an early morning run are just what I need to clear my head.*

"I need to run, Ruby. Please, just give me this."

She nods.

"Ok, whatever you need, babe, call me when you're back. I'll drop Freddie off and we can talk properly?"

I nod; maybe talking to Ruby will help.

She leaves, kissing me on the cheek and promising to come back later. I leave shortly after her, connect my headphones to my phone, and do some stretches outside the flat before setting off on an early morning run. I set a steady pace and before I know it, I am entering the Green Parks. I am in a world of my own, lost to my thoughts, as I am greeted by the smiling face of Jack Scott.

Shit.

I pull out my Beats earphones and smile at him. He looks especially gorgeous this morning, wearing long black shorts, a black t-shirt that clings to his tight tattooed muscles, and his iPhone on an armband. There is another man beside him, and he resembles Jack. They have the same silver-grey eyes and the same smiles.

"Good morning, petal."

Jack grins and I smile.

"Good morning, Jack." I suddenly feel awkward. *Ground please open up and swallow me.* "Erm..."

I look to the floor and my heart is thundering in my chest.

"Peyton, this is my brother, Nate."

I look up at him and he beams. The only difference between the two, is that Nate has dark collar length hair falling in his eyes and is greying at the temples. He is obviously older, clean shaven, and he is as handsome as his brother.

"Peyton, I'm so pleased to meet you. Jackers has told me a lot about you since last night."

Nate smiles warmly, and we shake hands. If he feels my clammy palms, he doesn't say anything.

"Pleased to meet you, Nate."

I have never felt so awkward in my whole life. *Is this really how actual one-night stands go?* I'm relieved I didn't go back to his place; I would have had to endure the infamous walk of shame.

"Erm...I should...go."

Jack stops me.

"Don't go, petal. We didn't get a chance to swap numbers last night, you just took off. Was my company really that riveting?"

I look to the floor, extremely embarrassed at my pathetic drunken behaviour.

"I'm sorry, it wasn't you..."

Jack throws his head back and laughs bitterly.

"Don't finish that sentence. Let me guess, it wasn't you it was me, right? That's how the notorious blow off goes, isn't it?"

I shake my head. *Shit, how do I explain without sounding like a complete psycho?*

"Jack, it wasn't like that at all, I'm in a bad place right now. I never act like this, ever."

My voice is barely a whisper and Nate regards us both intently.

"Please, let me make it up to you, give me your number at least. I know I said I wouldn't call, but Nate is my witness, you absolutely have my word."

Nate holds his hands up.

"I solemnly swear, I will make sure this dickhead calls you, treasure, I promise. Even if I have to dial the number for him myself."

I nod in defeat. He takes out his phone and I recite my number off to him. He punches it into his phone.

"I promise I'll call you, better yet, let me take you for a coffee, petal."

He looks at his watch.

"I've got time now before work, I don't have to be at the bar for a while yet."

My heart starts pounding, and it isn't because I've done too much running. I have to get out of here. I don't answer him and take off at full speed around the perimeter of the park.

"Peyton! Peyton! *Shit!* Don't run away from me."

He sprints to catch up with me and runs backwards in front of me.

"Please stop."

I look at him and his grey eyes are full of conflict.

"I'm not like this with women, ever! *Fuck*, please will you just stop for a second?"

I stop running and he comes to a stop in front of me. He smiles a megawatt smile, and I look up at him. My blue eyes lock with his grey ones.

"See, that was fairly painless, wasn't it? *Wow*, you look even more stunning than last night; your eyes are...absolutely breath taking."

He reaches towards me to tuck a strand of hair that has come loose from my ponytail, and I reluctantly let him.

"Do you want to tell me why you left last night? I was starting to think it was something I did."

I avoid his gaze and stay silent.

"Was it my imagination, or did we have mind blowing sex and then you ran out on me? You couldn't get away from me fast enough, what did I do?" he pleads.

I shake my head and bite my nail nervously.

"Look at me, petal; we were both drunk, but I'm not the bad guy. Contrary to popular belief, I'm one of the good guys, depending on who you talk to." His attempt at a joke falls on deaf ears as I look up into his eyes. "I'm a saint compared to say, Samson Newbolt," he says sarcastically.

I place my hands on my hips, slowly losing my patience with this infuriating man.

"Don't you fucking dare mention him, Jack, you've got no right! He's..." I say defensively, and he stops me.

"You're still fucking in love with him. Yeah, I get that, but I'm still willing to take a chance on you, Peyton. Doesn't that say something about me?"

I shake my head and my eyes glaze over. *I will not cry, I will not cry.*

"I'm fucking broken, Jack; don't you get that?"

He takes a step closer to me, and with every step forward he takes, I step back.

"*FUUUCKKK!*" he roars.

My heart beat kicks up a notch and I take a few deep breaths.

"Are you scared of me, is that it?" he says softly and I hang my head in shame. "Do I scare you, petal?" he presses.

A stray tear slips down my cheek and I quickly swipe it away, hating that I look so pathetic.

"*Christ.*"

He moves forward, and I move backward. As I take my final step backward, I collide with a hard wall of muscle, causing me to gasp out loud.

"*Fuck me,* what the hell have you said to her, Jackers?" Nate says sternly.

I look from Nate then back to Jack and shake my head.

"I'm so sorry, I can't fucking do this, Jack."

I turn and sprint as fast as I can, away from Jack and away from the park. *Right now, I think I am living in a nightmare.*

3

Sam

I need to run, to get some of my pent-up frustration out. So, I set the treadmill in my gym to a steep incline and begin to pound a steady pace, until I experience that delicious ache in my calf muscles.

"Fuck me, dude, you must be desperate to get that frustration out." Brody chuckles from the doorway, and since his stint in rehab, we've rebuilt our relationship.

To replace his drug addiction, he uses regular intense exercise to keep his brilliant mind occupied, and he's become my work out buddy. He speaks when he has something to say, calls me out when I'm being a dick, and he questions me when he thinks I have something I want to share. He has kind of taken Jax's place as my best friend. Jax has been preoccupied with Ruby and his impending fatherhood lately, which is understandable. Brody and I have come to a mutual understanding: he is there if I need him and I'm forever grateful to him for that.

"Do you want to talk about it?"

I slow down to a walk.

"She had a bad nightmare, dude. She punched me in the cheek; it scared the fucking shit out of me." I point to the faint purple bruise forming on my right cheek. "I asked her about it, but she just...clammed up and point blank refused to talk to me about it."

He lets out a breath.

"*Fuck,*" he curses.

I know he cares about her, just as much as I do. He got close to her, and I'll never really know what happened that night on the bus, but I'll be eternally in his debt for the friendship and the unbreakable bond it created.

"She had this...haunted look in her eyes, and it broke my fucking heart, Brody."

I stop the treadmill completely and go over to my rowing machine and sit down. I scrub my hands down my face and shake my head.

"She's a mess man, and it's fucking terrifying me. She left here at three this morning, Ruby took her home. I've hardly slept, I'm fucking exhausted."

Brody is sitting down on the bench press lifting weights, and he places the dumbbell in the rack.

"Fuck me, dude, that's some heavy shit."

Typical Brody, says it like it is.

"What do I do? how can I make it right?"

He stands to his full height and looks at me.

"You don't. I get that she destroyed you, Sam, but you have to look at this from her point of view. She's broken too, and you going in there, all guns blazing, isn't going to help her. It's going to push her further away."

I remain silent, knowing he's one hundred percent right.

"Our relationship is so fragile right now, I'm fucking terrified she's going to run from me again," I speak candidly, and it feels good to finally get it off my chest.

"Number one, don't give her reason to fucking run. And number two, stop pushing her away. You're both as bad as each other. The way I see it, women aren't the complicated fucking creatures we make them out to be, they're simple once you figure it out, dude," he says with a self-satisfied grin plastered across his face and I cock my pierced eyebrow at him.

"Since when have you been an expert with women, Hart?"

He grins wickedly.

"Since this dog started getting regular fucking pussy!"

He laughs, and he has my attention. *When did Brody find a girlfriend?*

"What's her name, dude?"

He looks coyly away, and he seems almost shy.

"It's early days. I don't want to jinx it, she's...she's just someone I've known for a while."

He looks away and tucks his hands in his pockets.

"I've been seeing her...for a few years, on and off."

I nod and I'm grateful that he's finally opening up to me.

"It's nothing, it's not serious," he says quickly, and I smirk.

The sly dog.

"You love her, don't you?"

He actually blushes! Then, it's as if he catches himself, and he shrugs nonchalantly.

"It's complicated," he says softly.

"You just said women weren't complicated. *Christ,* dude, make up your fucking mind!"

I laugh, trying to lighten the mood and he blurts out.

"She's fucking married, ok?"

His voice cracks and I've never seen this side of Brody before. *Is this the side that Peyton talked about, the vulnerable side?*

"*Fuck me,* this is all such a fucking mess, Sam. I thought I could handle sharing her, but I can't fucking stand it."

He runs his hands anxiously over his short, cropped hair and squats down in front of me.

"I can't fucking stand it, Sam! Thinking of his fucking hands all over her, her sleeping next to him. It should be me!"

He gets to his feet and starts furiously pacing.

"*FUCCKKKKK!*" he shouts. "*Fuck me;* I need to get fucking high."

He takes a few deep breaths, as if he is trying to steady himself.

"At least when I was high, I couldn't feel anything. Fuck me, what I'd give not to feel anything now. I don't do feelings and all that girly bollocks. If I allow myself to feel, then it's...*real,* ya know?"

He's pacing the floor now, frantically running his hands over his hair.

"*Fuck, fuck, fuck, fuck.*"

I slow the treadmill down to a stop and make my way across the gym to him. He stops pacing as I come to a halt in front of him. He looks so vulnerable and scared. His eyes are glazed and as I squeeze his shoulder in a gesture of reassurance, he breaks down. He sobs, heart breaking wails of pure anguish and all I can do is pull him into a bear hug. As he sobs, all my worries pale into significance.

4

Peyton

I make my way back to the flat and I feel a little calmer after my run and my early morning encounter with Jack Scott. I walk up the stairs into the reception area of the building and Jimmy, the security guard and concierge, smiles warmly as his way of greeting me. He is around sixty years old, and he reminds me of a cuddly bear. His salt and pepper hair is thinning on top and he has piercing ice-blue eyes. He also has a slight paunch, but his tall frame makes it look in proportion with the rest of his body.

"Good morning, Peyton."

I put on my best fake smile.

"Morning Jimmy."

He rounds the desk and hands me a package. It is a tall, white, oblong shaped box, with a silver ribbon wrapped around it.

"This came about five minutes ago for you, sweetheart."

I take it from him and smile, intrigued at who would be sending me gifts.

"Thanks Jimmy, I appreciate it. Did you see who delivered it?" I enquire, and he shakes his head.

"No, it came by a courier on one of those swish motorbikes; the man riding it was wearing a helmet. I didn't see his face; sorry I can't be more help, love."

I nod and pat his arm.

"It's ok, Jimmy, no worries, thanks again. I'll see you later, enjoy your day."

I make my way up back up to the flat, open the door and kick my trainers off. I close the door behind me and go into the kitchen to open the mysterious package. I sit it down on the worktop and untie the ribbon. I open the box tentatively, and what's inside makes me smile. A cup of Starbucks coffee and a rocky road brownie. There is a business card at the bottom of the box; it is a plain black card, with embossed silver lettering. It reads: *Jack J. Scott, owner and proprietor JJ's Inferno, freelance writer, blogger, underwear and fashion model.* There are three phone numbers for him, a website, an email address and the address of the bar. There is also a note; his writing is elegant, flowing script.

Petal

Seeing as you wouldn't come for a coffee with me. I thought I would bring the coffee to you. All women like coffee and chocolate. It's an unwritten rule. Please call me, let me make it right.

Jack x

I only left him around half an hour ago. *How could he have got this to me so quickly?* More importantly, how did he know where I live? I take the lid off my steaming coffee and take a sip. It is perfect, just the way I like it. It instantly makes me feel better, like a miracle elixir. My phone starts to ring, and I don't recognise the number. I pick up hesitantly.

"Hello, petal."

Jack's deep honey voice fills my ears.

"Hey," I say softly.

"Did you get my gift?"

I can hear the smile in his voice, which makes me smile too.

"I did, thank you. It was very thoughtful of you, Jack."

I take a small bite of the rocky road brownie and the richness of the chocolate instantly melts in my mouth.

"Mmm," I moan with delight and he chuckles softly.

"I take it you like the brownie?"

"It's gorgeous," I say with my mouth full and he pauses for a few seconds.

"Glad you like it, I made them myself with my niece."

My eyes widen at his admission and I instantly feel bad for rushing out on him.

"I...I'm sorry about last night, Jack, I really am. I don't make a habit of acting like a complete bunny boiler in front of potential suitors."

He laughs.

"Glad to hear it. Now, will you at least allow me to take you to dinner? I don't do romance but let me show you that I can be a gentleman, on occasion."

I pause, contemplating his question. *Can I really go out on a date with Jack when I'm still so hung up on Sam?*

"Don't leaving me hanging, petal."

I hesitate.

"Jack..."

He cuts me off.

"I get you're still hung up on Newbolt, but at least consider it. I'm not proposing marriage, just dinner. We can take it as slow as you need to."

I pause, seriously considering whether I can go on a date with Jack Scott. *Am I ready to get back onto the dating scene?* He's in a whole different league to Sam, but if I'm going to do this, I need to at least give Jack a chance. Before I know what I'm saying, I blurt out, "Ok, yes, I'll go on a date with you. One date and we'll see how it goes."

He chuckles softly.

What have I got to lose?

"One date. How does Saturday sound?" he asks, and I find myself agreeing, all too easily.

"Saturday sounds perfect."

"Perfect, I'll pick you up at seven thirty; I have to go now, I've done my good deed for the day, petal."

We both laugh, and the door taps softly.

"Ok, see you Saturday, Jack. Bye."

I hang up the phone and open the door. Ruby is standing at the door, with Freddie in her arms.

"Hey babe."

She kisses me on the cheek and hands Freddie to me.

"Hey rock star, mummy's missed you."

Ruby comes inside and shuts the door behind her, leaving a trail of *Ed Hardy* perfume in her midst. Freddie shrieks excitedly and claps his hands.

"Someone's in a good mood this morning, baby boy," I coo and Ruby laughs.

"I just hope this one is as easy to cope with as he is."

She strokes her growing bump and I laugh.

"It wasn't so easy in the beginning. He was up every hour, on the hour, screaming the house down. I was convinced I was a terrible mother, until

Rem explained that he was screaming because he expected me to go in and pick him up. After that, it was pretty much plain sailing. I was so lucky to have Remy."

She cocks her eyebrow, in her typical Ruby Logan way.

"Did you make the beast with two backs with my big brother?"

I avoid her gaze and busy myself with laying Freddie down on a beanbag.

"Oh, my fucking God, you did! You slut! You and my brother...did the horizontal hula," she screeches and puts her hand to her mouth. "OH MY GOD, PEYTON!"

I narrow my eyes at her.

"Stop with the theatrics, Rubes, it was just sex. It was a onetime thing, *never* to be repeated," I say to try to placate her, but she sees right through me.

"Just sex? There's something you're not telling me, babe; I can see it in your eyes."

I pull off my top and shake my hair loose, hoping to distract her from her question.

"Do you mind not undressing in front of me, Peyton? It's not going to make me stop the questions."

She stands with her hands on her hips and pouts. I smirk.

"It's not as if you haven't seen my tits before, babe. Since I've had Freddie though, they've definitely got bigger, don't you think? I certainly had no complaints from Remy!"

I push my breasts together and we both burst out laughing like a pair of naughty schoolgirls.

God I've missed this so much.

"Come on, babe, spill, you're *so* dying to tell me."

I finish my coffee and throw the cup in the bin.

"I'm going be late for work," I try desperately to change the subject.

"Stop fucking stalling and tell me, you silly tart!"

I huff out a breath.

"He told me he loved me, alright? He said he never stopped loving me, we had sex, he begged me to stay. The next morning was...weird. I got up, and I was going to leave without saying goodbye."

Her eyes widen.

"I fucking knew it! He was...*weird* when we last FaceTimed, distant, almost pining. Now I know why. He was acting really un-Remy-like, he wouldn't stop asking about you, and said you'd been avoiding his calls."

She narrows her eyes.

"He was my rock in the year I was away. Remy was always the one I imagined myself ending up with, getting married, settling down, having a few kids, but it never could have worked. Look at my track record with men, Rubes. My childhood sweetheart turned out to be gay, the man I lost my virginity to, namely your brother, left me and put a whole ocean between us. I dabbled in internet dating, which was an absolute mitigated disaster, and then there was Callum. We all know how that one turned out."

Her eyes soften, and she moves closer to me, enveloping me in her arms. The sweet familiar smell of her perfume washing over me, instantly calming me.

"Maybe it was good that you finally shagged Remy out of your system, because you and Sam are *obviously* meant to be together."

She sighs dreamily, and I pull away from her. I roll my eyes.

Ruby just can't fucking help herself, meddling in my love life.

"This whole mess with Sam is just another reason why I shouldn't be anywhere fucking near him, Ruby," I say miserably, and she tuts melodramatically.

"Oh *please,* you're like...Taylor and Burton, Kurt and Courtney, Katie and Peter, Kim and Kanye."

I cock my eyebrow and she chuckles softly.

"Ok, those *were* bad examples, but you get what I mean, I can't help it if I'm in love with love, babe. I finally got my Prince Charming! We're having a baby, and it might not be an ideal situation with him being on the road, but this past year has been so perfect. He's attentive, and he understands me. I'm convinced he's the one my soul's been searching for, just like you and Sam. You two are meant to be."

I shake my head.

"No, you don't get it, Ruby. I don't deserve a happy ever after, and I'm not that person anymore. J.D....he fucking *broke* me. That night changed me. He brainwashed me into thinking Sam had asked him to kidnap me and hurt me. I was in that room for hours and I was fucking *terrified.* I spent the past year hating Sam with everything in me, because I was fucking dumb enough to believe a lie."

My voice shakes, thick with tears and Ruby throws her arms around me.

"That fucking boy is a mess without you, babe."

I shake my head and I swallow back the lump in my throat. She squeezes me tighter and strokes my hair.

"It's going to be alright, I promise. Look, there's a BBQ at his parents' house next weekend. I would love it if you would come and I know the boys would love to see you. I need my wing woman with me, back where she belongs."

I pull away from her and shake my head.

"I can't face them. It was bad enough in the hospital, I couldn't look either of them in the eye and Lori looked as if she wanted to claw my throat out."

Ruby chuckles.

"She's not that bad, she's a pussycat. Besides, I'll be there. I'll have your back, I promise. Please just think about it?"

She gives me the famous Logan puppy dog eyes, and she knows she's got me. *Bitch.* I nod reluctantly.

"Ok, I'll think about it."

She claps her hands excitedly and I begin to wonder just what I'm letting myself in for.

5

Peyton

The rest of the week passes in a blur. The shop has really taken off with the news of the new series *of 'Inked @ Saint Sinner'* spreading like wild fire. We are booked from the time the shop opens until we close in preparation for the start of filming next week. By the time the end of the week comes, I am grateful when we flip the closed sign on the shop at seven p.m. on Friday evening.

I am relaxing on the sofa, with a long overdue glass of wine, after I made the journey back from work. Freddie is asleep, and Kai is patrolling the building outside, after a few stray photographers kept attempting to get past the security desk without being seen. I am alone and relishing in some me time while watching re-runs of Sons of Anarchy on the T.V. I suddenly hear a loud pounding on the door and my heartbeat starts to quicken, I'm not expecting anyone.

Relax Harper, Kai is outside, and if he saw anyone suspicious trying to get up here, he would intercept them, before they got within ten feet of me. You're safe.

I open the door cautiously and I am greeted by Brody. I let out the breath I didn't know I was holding as I take him in.

"GOOD FUCKING MORNING, VIETNAM!" he shouts and starts to laugh to himself.

A very drunk Brody. I look at him more closely, his skin is sweaty and clammy, his eyes are wide, glossy and wild and his complexion is pale. *Fuck me*, he's not drunk, he's high. *What could have happened for him to fall off the wagon after six months of being clean?*

"Keep your voice down please, babe, my little rock star is sleeping."

He puts his finger to his lips.

"Shhh! I'll be as quiet as a fucking mouse, I promise."

He tries to wink, but he ends up losing his balance and stumbling into me. I stop him from falling flat on his face and pull him inside the flat, closing the door behind us.

"Sit down before you fall down, babe; I'll go and make you some coffee."

He sways and plops ungracefully down on the sofa.

"I don't want coffee. Do you have any Nutella? I'm fucking starving. What about crisps? Cereal? I know, I want cereal," he babbles.

Fuck me, what do I do?

"I'll find you some cereal, babe. But first, you need to tell me what you've taken."

He rolls his eyes petulantly and makes a snoring sound.

"Are you going to fucking lecture me and drag me back to rehab? I thought you were different to the rest of them, sweets."

I stand in front of him. He looks awful; he is twitchy, and he smells of cheap perfume.

"No lectures from me, I promise."

I hold my hands up in defence and he smirks cheekily.

"How about a fuck then, sweets? I'm so horny."

He adjusts himself in his jeans and I roll my eyes.

"Not in this lifetime, rock star!"

He smiles boyishly.

"I like it when you call me rock star, it makes me feel important," he says in a melancholy tone and my heart breaks for him.

This is vulnerable Brody, the poor defenceless boy who just craves to be loved. I need to call Sam to let him know that Brody has fallen off the wagon.

"I just need use the bathroom for a second, babe, make yourself at home. I'll be right back."

He salutes, and I go into the bathroom. I run the tap, a trick I picked up from Cole. I dial Sam's number and he answers on the second ring.

"Angel," he rasps, but I have no time to acknowledge the slickness between my thighs.

"Sam, I need your help," I whisper and start to pace the floor in the bathroom.

"Is everything ok, angel? Are you ok? Is it Freddie?" he says, in a gruff panicked voice.

"Freddie's fine, he's asleep, but Brody just turned up out of the blue at my flat. He's drunk and high, Sam; I'm really worried about him."

He growls.

"*FUCK!* Don't let him leave, angel, keep him there. I'll be there as soon as I can," he says softly.

"Thank you, I didn't know who else to call."

There is a slight pause.

"No need to thank me, angel, you did the right thing calling me. He disappeared with a stripper a few hours ago, we just assumed he was still with her. I'll bring Lenny, his sober sponsor, he trusts him. Just in case he gets out of hand, Lenny will know what to do."

I hear a female in the background.

"Don't go, hot stuff, I wasn't finished."

I hear the faint sound of a zip.

"Here, take this and fuck off, we're done here, sweetheart."

I hear the rustle of paper and the sound of heels clicking across the floor. My heart slams against my rib cage. I will never get used to Sam with another woman.

Another woman's hand touching what was once mine. The thought makes my stomach roil.

"I'll be thirty minutes tops."

His voice cuts through my thoughts and I swallow back the lump in my throat.

"Ok, I'll see you soon."

I hang up, not giving him the opportunity to say goodbye. I flush the toilet, turn off the tap and go back out into the living room. Brody isn't on the sofa where I left him, and I start to panic that he's done a disappearing act. I walk across the living room floor and I find him in the kitchen. He is sitting on my worktop, barefoot, with his feet swinging back and forth, eating a bowl of cereal. He has the biggest grin on his face, it makes my heart slam violently against my ribcage. He reminds me of a child. I start to think that Brody never really had a proper childhood, being pushed from one care home to another, never really having a place to call home, never really staying anywhere long enough to belong to a family. To a certain extent, Brody is a perpetual child, never really growing up, rebelling against authority, and always getting into trouble. He picks up my open bottle of wine and swigs from the bottle. He regards me intently and I chuckle softly.

"What?" he says around a mouthful of cereal.

"What happened, babe, you were doing so well."

I brush his arm reassuringly and he flinches away from my touch.

"I don't want to fucking talk about it," he says flatly, and I busy myself putting the washing up away.

"Are you not going to push me? Make me tell you, give me a fucking ultimatum?" he says with a bored, monotonous tone to his voice. I turn around and cock my eyebrow at him.

"If that's what you think, then you obviously don't know me at all, Brody. I would never force you to tell me anything, or give you an ultimatum. True friends don't do that. I'm here if you need me, babe, that's all I can offer. If you want to vent, shout, cry, whatever, I'm here."

He cocks his head to the side and puts his bowl down next to him on the worktop.

"How the fuck did I deserve a friend like you, sweets? I've never been a good person. I'm destructive, I destroy everything I touch, and I destroy the people who mean the most to me. I'm surprised the boys have stuck around as long as they have."

My heart breaks for him and I move closer to him.

"You are the sweetest person I know. You're kind, you're gentle, you're funny, and you deserve so much more than what you give yourself credit for."

He smiles, and I stroke his face. He leans into my touch and places his hand on top of mine.

"Thanks, sweets, but I know none of that is true. You're just trying to placate me and make me feel better."

I go to speak, but he jumps unsteadily down from the worktop and moves closer to me. His lean frame towers over me.

"Sam is a fucking idiot," he whispers and tucks a strand of my hair behind my ear.

I chuckle softly.

"Don't change the subject, babe, this isn't about me."

He backs me up against the worktop.

"It's all about you, sweets, don't you know? Sam's a fucking mess without you," he states matter-of-factly, and I shake my head.

"What about you? Why are *you* such a mess, Brody?"

He hangs his head and I regard him intently, waiting for his reply.

"Because today is the anniversary of my mum's death. On this day twenty-one years ago, I found the junkie whore that bought me into the world dead, with a fucking needle in her arm. She never cared about me, I was just a fucking inconvenience to her; she told me often enough. I was a mistake, an embarrassment, and she wished she'd aborted me. She loved the drugs more than she loved me. How fucked up is that?"

He laughs bitterly. All I want to do is cuddle him and tell him that everything is different now. He has people around him that love him and care about him.

"I hate that she fucking did that to me, Peyton. I fucking hate that my own mother didn't want me. She didn't give enough of a fuck about me to get clean. And my dad, he left us before I was even born; I don't even know who he is. I can't accept peoples love because I'm terrified they'll fucking leave me too."

He puts his arms either side of me, trapping me between him and the worktop. He leans his head down on my shoulder and that's when he breaks down. He sobs, gut wrenching, hiccupping sobs, and I start to wonder if it is the first time in twenty years that he has let his emotions free. I put my arms around his neck and pull him closer to me.

"I'm here, babe. I'm not going anywhere, I promise. It's going to be alright."

He moves his arms and pulls me tight to him. I stroke his back soothingly and his whole body vibrates with sadness. Unexpectedly, I hear someone clear their throat.

"Angel," I hear Sam rasp.

Fucking hell.

"Sorry to interrupt, I should have knocked," he apologises, without an ounce of sincerity to his voice.

I look at him, and the burning jealousy in his eyes is evident, even though he is trying his hardest to mask it.

"I'll give you two some space," he says flatly and leaves the room.

Brody pulls away from me and I cup his face in my hands.

"It's ok to let go of your emotions, babe. No one would think any less of you, it just proves you've been strong for too long. Never be ashamed to cry, *ever.*"

He sniffs and swipes his hand across his nose.

"*Fuck me*, I'm such a girl." He smiles. "You could have told me you had called Sam."

I avoid his gaze and he tips my chin up to face him.

"Hey, it's ok, I'm not mad, sweets. You did the right thing."

He kisses me on the end of my nose and grabs my hand, pulling me into the living room, where a tall, wiry man, with grey slicked back hair is standing with his hands behind his back. Sam is awkwardly standing nearby with his hands in his pockets, chewing some gum.

"What sort of fucking trouble did you get yourself into this time, son?"

The man, who I'm assuming is Lenny, chastises Brody in a paternal, fatherly way, and it makes me wonder what their story is.

"It was just a temporary relapse; just a blip. I don't need to go to a meeting, or back to fucking rehab, Len," he says, with an uninterested tone to his voice and rolls his eyes.

Brody's phone vibrates in his pocket and he takes it out. He studies the screen and I see his expression change from almost carefree, to boiling, intense rage. His whole body is vibrating with the anger that is emanating from him in large waves.

"*FUCK!*" he bellows and throws his phone across the room. It hits the wall with such force; it shatters into tiny pieces. He runs his hands over his head and starts pacing the room, like a caged animal. His jaw is tight, and his eyes are blazing with fury. It is a whole new side of Brody I haven't seen before and another layer I have yet to discover.

"Son?"

He stops and looks Lenny in the eye.

"DON'T YOU DARE FUCKING CALL ME THAT! YOU HAVE NO FUCKING RIGHT! YOU'RE NOT MY FUCKING DAD! STOP TRYING TO PRETEND YOU ARE, OLD MAN!" he shouts and Lenny stalks closer to him.

"Oi, you little shit, don't you *ever* fucking talk to me like that. I'm not above giving you a clip round the fucking ear, Brody Hart."

Brody laughs sullenly.

"My dad left me and my mum before I was even fucking born. My mum died with a needle in her arm and abandoned me. Now my girl doesn't want me, am I really that fucking unlovable?"

He continues pacing and his shoulders start to shake as he begins to cry. My heart breaks for this broken man and all I want to do is give him a hug.

"*Jesus fucking Christ,* I can't fucking do this anymore," he chokes out and starts pacing the floor with his hands behind his head. "*Fuck me.*"

He shakes his head and Lenny steps behind him, placing his hand gently on his shoulder.

"You don't have to pretend to be strong with us, son, we understand, me more than most. You're like a son to me and Nance. After Daryl died, we never thought we would get another chance. It's ok to admit you're struggling, you're not the only man to fall off the wagon. It's ok to ask for help."

He sinks down to the floor, and with each of his sobs, my heart breaks a little more. Lenny sits down next to him and pulls him into his arms.

"I'm too fucking old for this shit, son, but I'm always here for you."

He kisses the top of Brody's head as he cries uncontrollably, and I feel so helpless watching Brody break down like that. Sam's eyes lock with mine as we both watch this situation unfold in front of us. The sound of Freddie crying on the baby monitor interrupts our moment, and Sam holds his finger up.

"I've got him, angel."

He winks and goes off into Freddie's nursery. I hear Sam quietly singing to him on the baby monitor while Brody is still sobbing softly. Lenny looks up at me with soft, azure eyes and smiles. I smile back and move into the kitchen, giving both men some privacy to talk. I lean on the worktop and begin to wonder how my night got so full of drama. The sound of footsteps echoes across the floor and startles me.

"Sorry, darlin', I didn't mean to scare ya," Lenny says in a deep, gruff East London voice. "My boy tells me he came here first, sweetheart. I want to say thank you for being there for him. He tends to revert back to the drugs when he's in this mood, so I wanted to thank you for not letting him leave before we got here."

I smile cordially.

"I consider Brody one of my best friends, so there's no thanks needed."

I drop my gaze to the floor, feeling intimidated by the large, brusque old man in my kitchen, and he chuckles throatily.

"He talks about you a lot. He thinks the world of you, and he trusts you. It's nice to finally meet you, sweetheart, and put a face to the name."

He reaches out his hand and formally introduces himself.

"I'm Lenny Nicholas, but you can call me Len," he says gruffly, and I take his hand.

"Peyton, it's really nice to meet you, Len."

I smile warmly, and he kisses the back of my hand.

"Pleasures all mine, sweetheart."

He smiles and his blue eyes dance with amusement. I hear a soft chuckle behind me and spin round to see Brody with his eyebrow cocked.

"Leave it out, Len! Stop trying to chat up my best friend, you filthy old perv!" Brody jokes and Lenny moves closer to him, grabbing him in a playful headlock.

"I'll give you old, you little fucker!"

I laugh softly, enjoying seeing their interaction. I have never seen Brody this way before. It makes my heart swell with love and happiness to know that he has someone outside of me and the boys to turn to when he needs to talk. Brody and Len leave the room, and I can hear their hushed conversation. I busy myself by tidying the kitchen and wiping the work surfaces until I am satisfied with it.

Ten minutes pass and Brody saunters back into the kitchen, looking relaxed. It is almost as if tonight never happened. His hands are tucked into his pockets, and he has a roguish look about him. He moves towards me, hugs me, and kisses me on the cheek.

"Thanks for being there for me, sweets." He winks. "I'm going to stay with Len and Nance, just for tonight."

I nod and they both leave, closing the door behind them, leaving Sam and me in my flat, alone.

"Something you need to tell me, angel? You and Brody?"

I shake my head.

"What the fuck is wrong with you? Had you bothered to ask him, he would have told you today is the anniversary of his mum's death. That was the cause of his relapse, and you're welcome, don't fucking mention it," I say sharply and go to pass him, but he grabs my wrist.

"Angel," he rasps.

"Fucking let go of me, why don't you just go back to whatever whore you're sticking your dick into these days?" I spit venomously, and he drops my wrist, as if I have burned him.

"Is that what you really fucking think of me, angel?"

He runs his hand through his already mussed hair and I shrug. *I honestly don't know what to think anymore.*

"Just go, Sam, I can't be around you right now."

He moves fluidly towards me and backs me into the wall. My heart beat kicks up a notch.

"I'm not going anywhere. Not until you talk to me."

As he brushes a strand of hair away from face, I flinch involuntarily. I can feel my body tremble at his closeness.

"Are you scared of me, angel?"

I bite my lip, drop my gaze to the floor, and fidget with my hands.

"No, of course not I-I'm fine," I lie, as he lifts my chin up to face him. His green eyes turn serious.

"You seem to forget I spent almost a year memorising every single inch of you, every contour of your sexy little body, every look, every smile and every reaction. When you just told me, you weren't scared of me, it was a total lie, absolute bull-fucking-shit; you gave yourself away. You looked down, bit your lip, and fidgeted with your hands."

He smirks as I still my hands and drop them to my side. I hate that even after all this time, he still knows how my mind works and he can read me like a book.

"Every thought, every single fucking inch of you, still belongs to me. You *own* me, Peyton, just like I own you."

I steal a glance at his strong, chiselled features. His strong jaw, his blazing green eyes, his sculpted cheekbones and his plump full lips. He is so handsome.

"Why are you scared of me, angel? I won't hurt you. *Christ,* I would never fucking hurt you."

He shakes his head, and his voice wavers as he cups my face in his hands.

"Tell me why," he rasps.

I can't find my voice as I attempt to swallow past the lump that has formed in my throat.

"Because out of everyone, you have the power to break me, Sam. You have the power to tear down every wall, every barrier, every fucking defence I've spent the past year building around myself. You have the power to tear it all down in a second and that terrifies the shit out of me. I don't have the strength to fight anymore; I'm so bloody tired of fighting," I say wearily.

Sam steps forward and forces me to look at him. I see the determination and hidden lust in his eyes.

"Then don't, angel. Don't fight it, give in to it. You and me are meant to be. I can feel your heart beating, I see that glazed look in your eyes, the bead of sweat at your temple. You want me, Peyton, admit it. You want to be spread beneath me. You want my cock buried deep inside you while you make those soft little whimpering sounds, begging me to let you come. Until you're gripping my biceps so hard, you almost draw blood," he says hoarsely, and I swallow hard as I feel the slickness pool between my thighs.

I shiver at the thought and he smiles wickedly.

"See, you want me. Let it go, angel. I need you under me, screaming my name."

I moan softly as he thrusts his hips into me.

"Feel how hard I am for you, angel?"

He nuzzles my neck and I feel his hot breath on my skin. He smells faintly of alcohol, Joop, mint, and his familiar, intoxicating Sam smell.

"Touch me, angel, put your hands on me. I need to feel you."

Our eyes lock, and he lifts my hands. He places them on his firm, muscular chest. I run my hands across the planes of his chest and down to his solid abs. He growls.

"That's it, angel. That feels so fucking good."

I move across to his biceps. I grip them hard and run my nails lightly down his arms. When I look up, his eyes are glazed, and the green is so prominent; they almost sparkle like emeralds. I move my hands up, around his back, and caress his broad shoulders. He moans softly and abruptly spins me around. He lifts me up effortlessly and sits me on the kitchen worktop before nudging my thighs apart. He positions himself between them and I can feel his solid erection pressing into my inner thigh.

"I'm going to kiss you now."

He leans forward and softly brushes my lips with his. He wraps his hand in my hair and gently tugs me towards him, deepening the kiss. His tongue caresses mine, and he slowly strokes the roof of my mouth. I continue my journey across his back and shoulders, alternating from soft, gentle touches to harsh, rough grasps. He continues to kiss me with such passion and moves his free hand to cup my breast. He gently kneads it in his large hand and pulls away from our kiss. I feel bereft as his lips leave mine, and he rests his forehead against mine.

"What the fuck are we doing, angel?" he whispers with an edge of uncertainty in his voice.

I shake my head.

"I don't know, but I know I want this with you. Make love to me, Sam, Take me like you used to. Please, I need you," I say almost anxiously.

He squeezes his eyes shut, as if waging an internal war with himself.

"*Fuck!*" he curses.

It is in that moment that Sam completely detaches himself from me. He steps back from me, as if he wants to be as far away as possible.

"Why the fuck did you come here, Sam?" I say flatly, and he runs his hands through his hair.

"Because you called...Because of Brody... I don't know. *Jesus Christ,* I really have no fucking idea, babe," he says huskily.

I swallow back the lump that has formed in the back of my throat.

"I get so many mixed signals from you, Sam. You show up here with your muscles and your god damn charm. You fuck with my head until I can't think straight, lead me on and then blow me off like I mean nothing. What the fuck?!" I raise my voice.

He hangs his head, and I jump down from the worktop. I move towards him until we are toe to toe, and I jab him in the chest.

"You are un-fucking-believable, Newbolt. Just get out and go back to whatever slut you had on her knees for you."

He smirks, and I want to slap his smug fucking face.

"I see that green is still a colour that suits you, angel," he rasps as I attempt to shove him backwards, but he doesn't budge.

"Get the fuck out, Sam."

How fucking *dare* he come into my flat and treat me like that. *Fucking prick.*

"You don't really want me to leave, you're just...frustrated and desperate for a release. You've been craving my cock since that day in the hospital," he says boldly, and I slap him across his cheek.

How fucking dare he make assumptions about me?

He laughs and clutches his cheek.

"Now that wasn't nice was it?"

I go to walk out of the kitchen, but he stops me by softly gripping my wrist.

"Don't forget you can't lie to me, angel. I know you better than you know yourself."

He towers over me and backs me up into the worktop. He places his hands either side of me, trapping me.

"You can't keep fucking doing this to me, Sam," I say with an acidity to my voice.

He smiles his panty-dropping smile, and I feel the familiar heat between my legs.

"Doing what, angel? Unravelling you? Driving you fucking crazy? I'm pretty sure if I put my hand in your knickers you would be soaking wet, hence proving my point. You want me, no matter how much you fucking deny it," he says gruffly, with a self-assured tone to his sexy as sin voice.

"You're enjoying this, aren't you? You enjoy fucking with my head and torturing me with your leather and your tattoos."

I hate the tremor in my voice as I say those words. He tilts my chin up and I avoid his eyes.

"Look at me, angel," he says in a commanding voice, and I look up into his eyes.

Unexpectedly, he crashes his lips against mine feverishly. His large hands roaming over my body. I moan softly into his mouth, and he lifts me into his strong arms. I automatically wrap my legs around his waist, and he strides across the flat without breaking our kiss. His stubble scratching my cheek is a contrast to the soft velvet of his tongue. He kicks the door of my bedroom open with his boot and deposits me in the middle of my California King bed. He breaks our kiss, and his green eyes are blazing. He stands at the foot of the bed and unbuckles his belt on his jeans.

"I want you naked, now, angel; no arguments," he rasps, and I do as he says.

I take off my yoga pants and my vest top, until I am lying on the bed in my underwear. He hasn't taken his eyes off me once. He strips off his black shirt, and the sight of his naked torso never fails to momentarily disarm me.

"You need to start eating again, you're too thin," he says matter-of-factly, and I smile at his concern.

He kicks his boots off and takes his jeans off, until he is standing in a pair of tight blue Superman boxers, which emphasise his impressive package. I chuckle softly, and he cocks his pierced eyebrow.

"I haven't done my washing in a while," he says gruffly, and I nod.

"Ok, I believe you. Thousands of others wouldn't."

I wink, and he laughs as he stalks towards me. He slowly climbs on the bed and positions himself between my thighs. As he looks down at me, I am reminded of J.D's cruel words once again.

"*Oh, you're so deluded, sweetheart, Sam's in love with me; he has been for years. Ever since that night we spent together! He uses women because he can't come to terms with his sexuality, but he always comes back to me. Now after all these years, he's seen that no matter how many women he has in his bed, I'll always be here, I'll be the one who he comes back to in the end. He asked me to punish you, to do with as I please and you know what? He doesn't fucking care!*"

This can't be happening, not now. Sam and I are both naked on my bed, and I'm freaking the fuck out. *What the hell is wrong with me?* I can feel a panic attack threatening. My chest feels tight, my breathing is erratic, my heart is pounding, and my blood is roaring in my ears. Sam is kneeling between my thighs with a look of concern marring his chiselled, model worthy features. Hidden in his furrowed brow is a look that tells me he feels way out of his depth.

"Angel, stay with me. You're safe, I've got you," he says softly as he pinches my chin between his thumb and forefinger.

I look into his green eyes, and I try to regulate my breathing.

"We can go slowly, as slow as you need to. I don't want you to feel uncomfortable with me. I just want to give you pleasure and make love to you to chase away whatever demons are in that beautiful mind of yours."

He gently strokes my cheek with the back of his hand and smiles his panty dropping smile. His dimple jumps into place as I feel my breathing return to normal. The fucked-up part of my brain thinks about where he was when I called him: in a strip club, probably getting his cock sucked and his needs taken care of. The fierce possessiveness I feel towards him comes to the forefront of my mind and pangs deep in my chest. Suddenly, I feel the jealous side of me spring to life with a force larger than anything I have ever felt. I get to my knees and climb over him, so I am straddling him. He smirks and circles my waist with his large hands. I undo my bra and my breasts spring free as I fling my bra onto the chaise lounge in the corner of the room.

"I'm in charge now, Newbolt. All those other women, they're *nothing* compared to how I can make you feel," I say with conviction in my voice.

He cocks his eyebrow, and he removes his hands from my waist, allowing me to take charge.

"That fire I loved about you, it's burning so bright it's blinding, angel. I can't see anyone else but you, it's always been you," he rasps, and I lean forward, brushing my breasts against his chest.

I nip his earlobe between my teeth, and the deep rumble of his chuckle vibrates through my body, causing goose bumps to form across my skin. I lick a trail from his neck down his shoulder and trace the letters of his tattoo across his collar bones. I allow my hands to roam over his chest, and I move down, keeping my breasts pressed against him. I circle his pierced nipple with my tongue, and he moans softly.

"*Fuck,* angel."

I lean back on my haunches and admire this beautiful man underneath me. The man who owns every inch of me, the man who I love with all my heart, but I can't allow him back into my life. So much has changed. For now, this is all I can give him. His green eyes are sparkling and blazing with a fiery heat. He licks his lips as his eyes travel over my body and examines the top half of my torso, which is marred with scars. He reaches up and traces the thick, white scar on my shoulder blade, running his calloused finger over the scar that spans from one collar bone, to the other. This was exactly the reason that I didn't want him to see me naked.

As he is looking at me and regarding me intently, I know he sees the ugly scars that J.D inflicted on me. He sees the pain and torture I endured for him, *because of him*. The body he once worshipped is now marred and tainted, a constant reminder of a time in my life I would rather forget. I see the second he registers, and I turn my face away so he can't see the shame and embarrassment in my eyes. He reaches up and tucks a stray strand of hair behind my hair.

"Angel, look at me."

He turns my face forwards, and I reluctantly look into his eyes.

"Is this-is this what that mother fucker did to you?" he says, with a clenched jaw.

I nod and feel my eyes brimming with tears.

"Hey, you're still the most beautiful woman in the world to me, angel. You're still perfect. I'll take whatever I can get with you, scars and all. I should have fucking ended him when I had the chance."

His eyes are full of fury, but I don't want J.D to ruin this moment between us. So I reach back boldly and cup his straining erection. He growls as my hand makes contact with his cock.

"Angel," he warns, but I shake my head.

"I'm still in charge, Newbolt, and I say no more talk of the past. We're just focusing on the here and now and how much pleasure I can give you."

He grins and spreads his arms out to the sides.

"I'm all yours, angel."

I climb off him and pull off my knickers, discarding them over my shoulder and set about stripping Sam's boxers off him. He lifts his hips, allowing me to pull them down his muscular thighs and down his legs. I throw them onto the floor, and I crawl between his legs, making my intentions clear. I fist his cock once and take it deep into my throat. He bucks his hips, causing me to gag, but I don't stop.

"*Fuck*, what are you doing to me, angel?"

I lick up and down the length of his cock as I take him deep in my throat and run my tongue over the bell-shaped tip, flicking his piercing.

"You have a rather beautiful cock, Mr. Newbolt."

He chuckles softly as I repeat the words I said to him all those months ago. I bob my head up and down as I take him further into my mouth, licking and sucking as I go. I flick his piercing with my tongue, and he growls.

"The piercing is so fucking hot."

I can feel his cock twitching with his pending release as I cup his balls.

"*Fuck,* baby, that feels so good, *Jesus!*"

I keep sucking and open my throat, taking him as far into my mouth as I can go.

"*Bollocks! Fuck!* I'm going to come, angel. Move if you don't want me to come in your mouth."

I continue sucking, ignoring his warning as he spurts his seed into my mouth, yelling as he finds his release.

"OH FUCK! PEYTON! I'M COMING! JESUS! FUCK!"

I swallow and lick my lips. I look up at him with a satisfied grin plastered on my face.

"Are you ready for round two, Mr Newbolt?" I purr seductively, and he guides my hand to his still solid erection.

"Does that answer your question, angel?" he says huskily.

I move to straddle him once again, guiding his cock into my already soaking wet pussy. I drop down onto him and he growls as he circles my waist with his large hands. I lift myself up and drop back down, controlling the rhythm. I increase the pace, and I pinch my nipple between my thumb and forefinger.

"*Fuck me*, you're so beautiful, you're a god damn work of art, angel," he rasps, and I grin wickedly.

"You're not so bad yourself, rock star!"

I wink cheekily, and he cocks his eyebrow as he rolls both of us so he's on top.

"As good as it felt having you in charge, angel; I think it's time to remind you who's really in charge."

With his muscular thighs either side of me. He takes both wrists in one of his hands and pins them above my head. I relish him being in control as he presses his body against mine, and I have missed the feel of his skin against mine. He kisses my neck and I wrap my leg around his waist. He moves his head down my chest, suckles my nipple with his teeth, and kisses a trail from my breasts to my navel. I am writhing underneath him as he touches every part of me. I had almost forgotten what it was like to feel his weight on top of me, pressing me into the bed. An expert swivel of his hips reminds me that he is still inside me as his piercing rubs deliciously against my inner walls, until I feel the friction stroking my g-spot. He moves in and out at a leisurely pace, driving me higher and higher towards my orgasm.

"*Sam!* Oh God! Sam! Sam!"

He increases his thrusts, impaling me so deeply, I feel his cock bang against my cervix.

"God, your cunt feels like fucking heaven, angel."

His dirty talk causes me to mewl softly, and he chuckles throatily.

"I'd forgotten how much you loved my dirty talk, angel."

He quickens his pace and I cry out.

"SAM! Oh God! Please don't stop, don't stop! I'm so fucking close," I plead desperately and writhe beneath him as he is pumping in and out of me in frantic strokes.

I can feel my orgasm rising to the surface, and as he thrusts forward once more, that's all it takes to tip us both over the edge. I let out a scream, and I explode around his throbbing shaft. My orgasm washes over me, causing my sex to ripple around his cock. Wave after wave of my orgasm crests and rolls over me, like I'm floating on a sea of pure carnal bliss, total and utter ecstasy. That is just what Sam does to me; he makes me lose all sense of control and I can't say no. He's my weakness, my kryptonite, a habit I just can't kick. He came into my life like a hurricane, a totally unexpected tidal wave, and turned everything upside down.

At the same time, he growls out his release, coating my insides with his seed. I cling to him and look into his clear green eyes, as if I'm experiencing it for the very first time. He smiles his famous dimpled smile, and I immediately forget my own name and why I shouldn't have let this happen again in the first place. He pulls out, and I start to shake with tiny aftershocks. He collapses on top of me and sags against me. Both of us are panting out laboured breaths.

"*Fuck me,* that was amazing, angel."

I chuckle softly and press a kiss to his wide shoulder.

"Pleasure was all mine, Mr. Newbolt."

He laughs silently against my neck before finding the strength to pull out of me and roll over so he is lying next to me. I crawl over to him, needing to be close to him. He wraps his thick, corded, tattooed arm around me and places my hand over his heart. We are both content to just lie there, relishing the feel of skin on skin in absolute silence, for what seems like an eternity. I felt truly connected to him for the first time in a year.

6

Sam

The truth is, I don't know why the fuck I came here. Some twisted part of me wanted to be the hero and come to the rescue after she called me to tell me Brody was here. Another part of me just needed an excuse to see her again. Even though it's only been a few days, it feels like a lifetime since I saw her, and the painful reality of it is, I missed her. When I came here earlier this evening, I never thought that we would end up in bed together.

I'm lying in the dark, in bed next to her, and I can't sleep. I'm lying awake, with my hands behind my head, just watching her sleep. She looks so peaceful and serene when she's at rest, she's so beautiful. My heart slams against my ribcage as she shifts in her sleep, and an overwhelming sense of guilt washes over me. I have no idea where it came from. I have this uncontrollable urge to run, run as far away as possible. I slowly pull the duvet off myself and get out of bed. I pull on my jeans, my boxers and my shirt. I jam my feet into my Doc Martens, without tying the laces and the leave the bedroom as quietly as I can. I grab my keys, my phone, and my wallet and slip silently out of her flat. Momentarily feeling ashamed and full of remorse, I know deep down that it's a dick move on my part, sneaking out in the middle of the night. But every instinct I had inside of me was screaming at me to run. Run away from the woman I love more than life itself. It doesn't make sense. *None of it makes any fucking sense.*

I take the stairs two at a time and leave the building. As I exit through the front doors, Jimmy, the security guard from my old building in Greenwich, greets me. Jimmy Frazer is an ex-boxer and was a big deal in the boxing world in the sixties. After I sold the building, instead of putting Jimmy out of a job, I moved him here, along with three security guys from Cole's team. He smiles warmly and tips his hat.

"Mr Newbolt."

He nods, and I smile, tucking my hands into my pockets.

"I've been telling you for years, Jimmy, call me Sam. How are you?"

He leans against the door.

"You know, good thanks, son, I'm in tip top form."

I pat his shoulder.

"Good, good. How's the Mrs?"

He smiles tenderly at the mention of his wife Pru. They have been married for almost fifty years, and they're still so in love.

"She's magic thanks, Sam. Still complaining, so I know she's alright."

We both laugh, and I feel a pang of jealousy. Jealous of his perfect relationship, his perfect marriage. *Fuck me, get it together Newbolt.* I pull my phone out of my pocket and call Cole.

"Cole, yeah, it's me."

His deep growl comes through the phone.

"Do you know what fucking time it is?"

I look at the time, it says one fifty-seven a.m. and I suddenly feel bad for calling him so late.

"Man, I'm sorry, I wasn't thinking. It's cool," I say sincerely, and he pauses briefly.

I hear a creak and footsteps walking across the floor.

"It's ok; it's fine. I'm up now anyway, where the fuck are you?" he says grumpily, and I run my free hand through my hair, suddenly wracked with guilt for running out on her.

It has to be this way, it has to be.

"I'm at Peyton's," I say quickly, bracing myself for a lecture, Cole Benedict style.

"What the fuck were you thinking, Sam? She doesn't deserve that, she's the mother of your child, you prick."

I squeeze my eyes shut; knowing that every word he says is true.

"Look, I know, I know. Spare me the lecture, please. At least until tomorrow. I just need to get out of here, Cole."

As he says those words, I see Kai sitting in a black 4x4 Land Rover with tinted windows.

"It's ok, Kai's outside. I'll get him to drive me."

I hear Cole curse.

"*Fuck me,* Kai's on my payroll; he's there to protect her, not to drive your lazy arse around!" he barks, and I puff out my cheeks, feeling exhausted.

"Just this once, Cole, please? I need to get home. I can't drive, I've been drinking."

He growls.

"This is the last fucking time, Sam. Next time, you either drive yourself, or you're on your own."

I wink at Jimmy, saluting him goodbye and rush across the street.

"Thanks Cole, I owe you one mate. Kisses to Addy and Amy."

I hang up to Cole cursing and I bang on the window, startling Kai from his game of The Sims. He pushes a button to let the window down.

"Mr. Newbolt," he says in his Texan drawl and nods coolly.

"Is this what Cole pays you for? Sitting outside Peyton's flat, playing The Sims when you're meant to be watching out for anyone suspicious?" I say sarcastically as his face flushes red at being caught.

He gestures with his chin for me to get in the back. I climb in and lean my head back on the headrest as Kai pulls away from the kerb. My head is fucked with a capital F and I'm an absolute mess. That is exactly the reason why I shouldn't be anywhere near her, and that is the thought I cling to as I drift off somewhere between Camden and Hertfordshire.

7

Peyton

I am glad I agreed to go on a date with Jack tonight since I woke up this morning to an empty bed. If I wasn't so deliciously sore when I move, I'd be almost sure that I dreamt that Sam was here.

Fucking stupid infuriating man.

I cling to the molten rage I feel towards Sam as I set about my day. I call Ruby and Danny to arrange a shopping trip for my date tonight, anything to take my mind off Sam. I take my morning shower and bathe Freddie. I dry off and dress quickly, opting for black skinny jeans, a turquoise bat wing top and green Converse. I pull a black beanie hat on, apply natural make up, and slick on some clear lip gloss. I admire my handiwork in the mirror in the living room and decide I look good. *Take that, Newbolt, I don't need you.* As I'm getting Freddie dressed, Kai pads out of his room wearing long black basketball shorts and a white vest which clings to his deeply tanned muscles.

"Mornin', doll," he says in his American drawl, which has become familiar to me.

I smile as he sets about making himself a cup of coffee. I pull Freddie's jeans up and nuzzle his nose with mine.

"Aren't you a handsome boy? Yes, you are."

Just like your daddy. But I don't say those words out loud. *I will not allow Sam to ruin my day.* He chuckles, and I tickle his belly, causing him to squeal with delight.

"The little guys in a good mood this morning, darlin'."

I nod.

"Yeah, he is. I'm taking him shopping with Danny and Ruby in a little while, just giving you a heads-up."

He nods curtly and takes a welcome sip of coffee.

"All good with me, doll. Give me twenty, I'll go take a shower."

Kai finishes his coffee in two mouthfuls and makes his way to the bathroom. The door closes, and as I finish dressing Freddie, the door knocks. I pick him up and pad over to the door.

"Is this Uncle Dan Dan, ready for our shopping trip?"

I swing the door open expecting Danny, but I am greeted by my brother, Dexter. His eyes are rimmed red and his usual highlighted hair is now back to his original dark brown. It is unstyled, flat, and dishevelled.

"Sis."

His voice is thick with tears, and I look down at the suitcase at his feet.

"Oh, Dex, come in."

I pull in his suitcase. He steps into my flat, and I close the door behind him. He plucks Freddie from my arms and holds him close.

"Hey dude, look at you. Come to Uncle Dex."

I look at Dexter with such concern in my eyes. It's clear that he's hurting, otherwise he wouldn't have shown up here out of the blue.

"Dex, do you want to talk about it?" I say softly, and as I say those words, he lets out a stifled sob.

"*Shit,* sis I'm sorry. I'm sorry to just show up like this."

I shake my head.

"You know my door's always open for you, you're my brother and I love you. I'm here for you."

He hangs his head, and a tear rolls down his cheek.

"I promised myself I wouldn't do this. *Fuck.*"

He sniffs and hands Freddie back to me. I take him and strap him in his buggy. I sit down on the sofa and pat the space next to me.

"Come and sit down."

He sits down, and he scrubs his hands down his face.

"Grace left me, we split up."

My eyes widen at his revelation. My brother Dexter and his fiancée Grace have been together for around eight years now. They met in college and have been together ever since. I always thought they were solid. Grace grounds Dexter and he's a calming influence on her feisty nature. Their personalities perfectly complement each other, he's the quiet one and Grace is definitely the outspoken one. Grace is the same age as Dexter at twenty-five. She is a tall, slim, and feisty redhead, with curves in all the right places and a fiery personality to match the shade of her hair. Dexter and Grace are like a Hollywood couple in the looks stakes, with Dexter's chiselled cheekbones, tall, lithe, and muscular physique, blue eyes and his dark hair. When they are out in public they definitely turn heads, they are literally made for each other...or so I thought.

"What happened, Dex? I always thought you two would be together forever."

He shakes his head.

"She said the wedding was off, she needed some time apart and told me we were over. No word of warning, just totally out the blue."

I'm about to speak, when the bathroom door opens, and Kai steps out, still wet from his shower, with a towel around his waist and a folded towel around his neck.

"Is everything ok, doll?"

I nod, trying not to gawk at him.

"Everything's fine, Kai, this is my brother, Dexter. Dex, this is Kai."

He nods and makes a dash for his bedroom, closing the door behind him. Dexter cocks his eyebrow.

"Something you want to tell me, sis?"

I roll my eyes and Dexter smirks.

"Get your mind out of the fucking gutter, Dexter James Harper!"

I hit him playfully, and Dexter laughs.

"You've got to admit, it does look a bit dodgy sis, a half-naked man stepping out of your bathroom, looking like he should be modelling Armani."

I cock my eyebrow.

"I'll pretend you didn't just say that! Kai works for Cole, Sam's bodyguard. he's my security detail."

I air-quote *'security detail'* and Dexter nods.

"Right, we've definitely got some catching up to do, sis!"

I spend an hour filling Dexter in on the events of the past few weeks, and by the time I'm finished, I feel like a load has been lifted off my shoulders.

"Sam fucking Newbolt needs to watch his back. His face won't be so pretty when I've finished with him, the fucking selfish son of a bitch."

Even though he is three years younger than me, Dex has always been fiercely protective of me.

"He can't go around fucking treating you like that, sis; he's got no right. Where the fuck does he get off?"

I touch Dexter's arm, and he opens his arm out to the side, inviting me in for a hug. I crawl into the space, and he pulls me closer to him.

"I had no idea, sis. Why didn't you call me or mum and dad? They're really worried about you."

I smile softly. The truth is, I didn't call my family because I hate it when they worry about me. I know it's what families do, but I hate being the cause of their upset.

"Call mum to check in, sis, put her mind at rest. I've already had six missed calls from her."

He reaches into his pocket and shows me his phone. I suddenly feel bad for not calling sooner. He hands me his phone.

"Go on, call her. I'll stick that fancy pants coffee machine on and watch F-Dog."

I roll my eyes at his ridiculous nickname for my son as he smiles and winks. *God, I've missed my over-protective, pain in the arse, baby brother.* I kiss him on the cheek and take his phone. I dial my mum and she answers the phone on the first ring. I go into my bedroom and look absentmindedly through the window, observing the hustle and bustle of a regular day in Camden.

"Hello? Dexter? Please tell me your sister's ok. I've called six bloody times! It's common courtesy that you answer the phone to your mother, Dexter James Harper!" she reprimands, and I chuckle softly at her outburst.

"Mum, it's me," I say tenderly, and she sighs.

"Peyton, is that you, my darling girl? Oh, thank the bloody Lord!"

Her soft, soothing voice instantly calms my racing thoughts.

"I'm fine, honestly, mum. I've just been busy, that's all. Work's been mental, and I haven't had a spare minute," I lie, not wanting her to worry.

"That's a pathetic excuse, Peyton Leigh Harper. I know you don't want us to worry, but no matter how old you get, me and your dad still worry about you. How's our beautiful grandson, darling?"

I smile as she swiftly changes the subject to Freddie.

"He's fine, thanks, mum. Growing every day. He's sitting up on his own now, and he reminds me so much of Sam."

I sigh and drop down heavily onto my bed.

"How's he doing? Do you see much of him now you're not together?" she asks probingly. I bite my lip, and for some reason, I *can't* lie to my mum. She sees right through me.

"On and off; he makes an effort to see Freddie when he can," I say vaguely, and she laughs.

"You're still sleeping with him aren't you, sweetie?"

My eyes widen, and I slap my hand to my mouth.

"Mum!" I squeal.

I do *not* need my mum quizzing me about my sex life. *That's embarrassing.*

"You can't lie to me, I know that tone when I hear it, Peyton. Just because I'm your mum, doesn't mean..."

I stop her.

"Mum, please! I don't need that image in my head!"

We both laugh.

"I take it you've heard about Dexter and Gracie?"

I look up at the ceiling.

"Yeah, he looked heartbroken when he showed up on my doorstep."

My mum sighs heavily, and I hear Dexter call through the slightly open door.

"Close the door if you don't want me to know you're gossiping about me!"

I throw one of Freddie's teddies at the door.

"Dex!"

He laughs.

"Hi mum, ask her about her date tonight," he shouts, and my mum shrieks excitedly.

Bastard.

"Date? You have a date? Who's the lucky man? It's not Sam is it?"

I squeeze my eyes shut and bite my lip.

"No, his name's Jack. He owns a bar; we met, hit it off, and he asked me out on a date. It's no big deal, mum."

If only she knew.

"Don't go rushing into things, my darling girl. I know you still love Sam; any idiot can see that. You don't need any other complications; you have that beautiful boy of yours to look after now."

I roll over onto my stomach and kick my legs up behind me.

"I know mum, I...love Sam, so much, but it's different now. How does the saying go? If you love someone enough, you have to let them go."

My mum scoffs.

"That's utter bullshit, Peyton, and you know it! Any daughter of mine would know that if he means that much to you, you'd bloody well fight for him."

I try to stifle my laugh at my mums' blunt and to-the-point tirade. God bless her. *Talking with her is just what I needed, to set things into perspective.*

"I'm not saying jump into a relationship with him again. Just...get to know him again, let him spend time with his son. Last time, it was such a whirlwind; I don't think either of you knew what you were getting into. The next thing I knew you were engaged and pregnant, slow things down. If you love each other, it'll work itself out, darling, I promise you. Listen to your old mum; I know I blabber on, but it's just because I love you, and I worry about you."

I press my lips together and swallow back the lump that has formed in my throat. *God, I've missed her and my dad so fucking much. No parent should think that they've outlived their child.* That thought breaks my heart.

"Mum," I sob.

"Hey, enough with the tears, darling. I know, come home, Peyton. Spend some time with me and your dad. London isn't going anywhere. Think about it, and you make sure you look after that brother of yours," she says, and it is as if she just gets it.

Since I gave birth to Freddie, I finally understand the phrase *'a mother's instinct'.* My mum isn't just my mum, she's my best friend too. There's nothing stronger than the bond between a parent and a child. A knock on the door pulls me from my thoughts.

"Sis, Danny and Ruby are here."

Dexter pokes his head briefly around the door. I sit up and wipe the tears away from my eyes.

"Thanks, Dex," I call out.

"Look mum, I have to go. I'm going shopping with Ruby and Danny. I'll definitely think about coming home for a while, thank you for talking sense into me. I love you."

I hear her sniff. *I hate it when my mum cries.*

"Ok, darling girl. If it's meant to be, it'll work itself out, I promise you. Don't do anything I wouldn't do! Call soon, love you, Peyton, bye."

I hang up the phone with renewed hope that maybe things will work themselves out after all.

***

After an afternoon of shopping with Ruby and Danny, my feet are sore, but I have an outfit for my date with Jack Scott. Dexter insisted on babysitting Freddie, so I enjoyed spending the afternoon with my two best friends, despite being tailed by Kai. He kept the press at bay, and we shopped in relative peace. I have showered, styled my hair, and applied my makeup. I am standing in my bedroom wearing a loose, oversized, long sleeved, grey jumper dress and grey socks pulled up to my knees. All of my clothes are spread out across the bed and I am debating whether the outfit I bought for tonight sends the right message.

"It looks like someone raided an Oxfam shop in here!"

Dexter laughs, and I spin around, narrowing my eyes at him.

"Funny."

He leans against the door frame.

"I thought so. I'm Dexter Harper, and I'm here all week."

He winks cheekily and bows dramatically. I roll my eyes and try to hide my amusement. Dexter is naturally funny and always used to cheer me up when I was sad when we were younger. He was always the one to get up and entertain at family parties. If he wasn't a policeman, he would have been an entertainer of some sort. Like Sam, he was born to perform, but somehow, he didn't pursue it further.

"You're so funny you should be on the stage. Sweeping it!" I say wryly.

He throws his head back and laughs. I start to chew furiously on my nails, suddenly feeling nervous about my pending date with Jack.

"*Jesus* sis, you look as if you're about to shit a kitten! It's just a date, he's not proposing marriage!"

Dexter smiles, and I look at him.

"What if he realises I'm too fucked up and not worth the effort, Dex?"

Dexter moves forward and pulls me close to him, enveloping me in his arms.

"There's that fucking self-doubt creeping in again. You're beautiful, you're funny, intelligent, and I'm not just saying that because you're my sister. Sam's a fucking idiot."

I chuckle softly against his chest. *That seems to be the general consensus on Sam these days.*

"He needs to build a bridge and get the fuck over it. Surely he can see you did it for the right reasons, you did it with the best intentions."

I sigh heavily against him, and he rests his chin on the top of my head.

"If he can't see that, then he isn't worth your time or your tears, sis. Just go on this date with Jack Shit, or whatever his name is. Let him wine, dine and sixty-nine you, or whatever it is you do on dates these days. See how it goes and take it from there."

I laugh at Dexter's dry sense of humour and pull away from his embrace.

"The leopard print and leather playsuit, you'll knock him dead."

He winks, leans down to kiss my forehead, and leaves the room. I pick up the leopard print and leather playsuit that Ruby begged me to buy and hold it up against myself in the mirror. My brother has *extremely* good taste in women's fashion. He must have picked it up from being with Grace, who is a fashion designer. I pull it on, and Dexter was right, it looks amazing on me. The shorts accentuate my short-tattooed legs and make them look longer. The low cut of the neck makes my boobs look fantastic, and the waist cinches in to make my slim figure look curvy. I team it with some silver bangles, silver hoop earrings, and a long, silver, skull necklace. I look in the mirror and I have to admit, I look good. I pull on a pair of leopard and skull print Iron Fist heels and fluff my hair in the mirror. I slick on some red lip gloss, smack my lips together, and I'm good to go. I grab my skull clutch bag with my phone, keys, and purse. As I go into the living room, Dexter wolf whistles.

"What have you done with my sister? You look foxy!"

We both laugh.

"Thanks, Dex. You have extremely good taste in women's clothing. Ever thought of a career change?"

He cocks his eyebrow.

"I think I'll stick to my day job, thanks, sis."

I pick Freddie up and kiss him gently on his head.

"Mummy loves you, sexy boy. Yes she does," I coo and turn to Dexter.

"He can't sleep without Keith, his penguin. His bottles are made up, they just need warming. And if he wakes up and won't settle, call me immediately and I'll come straight home."

He takes Freddie from me and gives me a one-handed salute.

"How hard can it be looking after a baby? I've got this, sis. Go and enjoy yourself, you deserve it; let your hair down."

Kai steps out of his room, looking like he could literally model for Armani. The cut of his black suit is tailored to the height and shape of his body perfectly. He nods coolly, and I can't believe that I have to take a security guard on a date. *Is this what my life has become?* The door knocks, as if on cue, and I take a deep breath.

"Wish me luck."

Dexter kisses my cheek, and I stroke Freddie's face.

"Good luck, sis. Even though you definitely don't need it."

Dexter smiles, and I swing the door open. Standing outside my door is Jack Scott, in all his glory. He is wearing dark jeans, a black blazer, a black and white checked shirt, and black shoes. The first two buttons are undone to reveal his tanned and tattooed chest. He isn't wearing his glasses, is clean shaven, and he looks delicious. His silver-grey eyes widen as he takes me in. He swallows, and his throat visibly bobs.

"Fuck me, petal. You...you look amazing," he compliments me, and I smile shyly.

"You don't look so bad yourself, Mr. Scott."

He straightens to his full height and offers me his arm, grinning widely.

"May I?"

I nod at his gentlemanly gesture and take his arm, stepping out of my flat and closing the door behind me. We walk down the corridor, and Kai is at least ten yards behind us.

"Is Andre the Giant really necessary? Three is definitely a crowd. This is meant to be a date, not an interrogation."

He says it as a joke, but I can't help thinking that he is serious. I drop my gaze to the floor.

"The press seem to follow me around a lot lately; it's...just a precaution," I try to explain as Danny breezes past us, cocking his perfectly groomed eyebrow and winking.

I think Jack just got the Danny Debonair seal of approval.

I smirk, and I catch him checking out Jack's bum as we reach the lift. Jack pushes the call button and we wait in silence for a few seconds. The lift pings and the door slide smoothly open. We step inside, and Jack crowds in behind me, pressing the button for the ground floor. The doors slide closed as Kai reaches the lift, and I swear I hear him curse as Jack backs me into the wall.

"*Fuck me,* you look stunning. I need to control myself around you. You could be bad for my health and my sanity."

I laugh, and he tucks a strand of hair behind my ear. I suddenly feel nervous and so out of my depth with this intimidating man who exudes everything masculine. He tips my chin up.

"Look at me, I'm trying *for you.*"

His silver-grey eyes are blazing with sincerity and something which resembles lust.

"I can't get the image of you underneath me out of my head, it's all I've thought about. I'm hoping if I play my cards right, I can have a repeat performance."

His voice is rich and cultured, with the hint of an accent, which I didn't notice when I first met him. I can't quite place the whereabouts.

"You're simply...exquisite, I'm looking forward to getting to know you better," he compliments, and I smile.

Jack Scott can be charming, maybe I judged him a little too harshly. I decide there and then that I am going to give him a chance. We're both adults, what harm can it do?

We arrive at a small and intimate fusion restaurant, called Paradox, in the heart of Mayfair. As we exit the car, I see Kai leaning against his 4x4. He cocks an eyebrow and touches his hand to his chest; he looks as if he is speaking to someone.

How the fuck did he know where we were heading?

Jack and I both step inside, with his hand at the small of my back. I suddenly feel way out of my depth and definitely underdressed. The low ceiling and white drapes give a romantic feel to the place. There are around ten tables, which are low to the ground and have jewel accented coloured cushions either side, instead of chairs. The walls are a vibrant magenta and gold, with multi-coloured lights over each table. Jack greets the hostess with familiarity, and the way he kisses her on the cheek makes me think there's history between them. She greets us in accented English. She is very beautiful, Asian, with long black hair and has unusual pale green eyes. She is wearing a white silk blouse, black pencil skirt, and black Christian Louboutin's.

"Jack, it's so good to see you. Nate requested I seat you and your guest immediately, come."

She completely ignores me and leads us to the back of the room in the corner. I sit down on the low purple cushion, and Jack sits opposite me, on the turquoise cushion.

"I will bring you a bottle of champagne; on the house, of course."

She strides off, leaving Jack and me alone.

"This place is amazing."

Jack smiles.

"Thanks, my brother Nate owns it. He's also the chef. It's his baby; I'm proud of him. Anyway, enough about my brother, tell me more about you, petal. You're looking very beautiful tonight."

I smile bashfully at his praise and idly tuck my hair behind my ear. I am about to speak when we are interrupted by the arrival of the hostess with a bottle of champagne. She is about to uncork it, when Jack stops her with a gentle brush of her hand.

"Some privacy, please," he says, with an air of authority in his voice.

She nods curtly and leaves us alone. Jack smiles and cocks his head to the side, regarding me intently.

"Now, where were we?"

He picks up the bottle and begins to pour the champagne. He places the bottle back on the table after he finishes pouring and hands me a glass. He picks up his own glass and clinks it against mine.

"To good company and to getting to know each other better."
I clink my glass to his and take a sip of the bubbly liquid.
So far so good.

8

Sam

We are about to go on stage at Earl's Court in London in front of twenty thousand, die hard, Rancid Vengeance fans. Our loyal fans have supported us for eleven years, and we sometimes see the same faces in the crowd. It is extremely humbling. But, just lately, I don't know what the fuck is wrong with me. I never get nervous before a gig, *fucking never*. I'm usually pumped full of excitement, eagerly anticipating going out on stage and rocking the place to the ground.

Instead, I'm in my dressing room, staring absently at my reflection in the mirror. I look like crap, my face is deathly pale, my skin is clammy, and the green in my eyes isn't the same green that Peyton fell in love with. *I'm a total fucking mess*. The night I got up and left her keeps replaying over and over on a loop in my mind.

My hands are trembling, my heart is pounding like a fucking freight train, and I feel like I need to throw up. I take in a few deep breaths, *in...out, in...out,* and try to give myself a pep talk.

"Come on, Newbolt, pull yourself together."

I slap my cheek hard, and I hear a soft chuckle behind me.

"*Fuck me*, Sam Newbolt giving himself a pep talk before a gig? Wonders will never cease!"

I turn and meet Brody's amused gaze.

"I don't know what the fuck is wrong with me, Brody," I say wearily.

His face drops, and a look of concern washes over his features.

"Want to talk about it, dude?"

I shake my head.

"Same shit, different day, man," I sigh.

He folds his arms across his chest and leans his hip against the dressing table as he regards me intently.

"*Fuck me,* you look like shit."

I cock my pierced eyebrow at him.

"Cheers, mate. That fills me with such confidence, *dick*," I say sarcastically, and he shrugs nonchalantly.

"I'm not going to fucking lie to you. When was the last time you had a decent night's sleep, man?"

I shrug. I don't actually know the answer to his question, because I can't actually remember the last time I slept properly. I survive on four hours a night these days, if I'm lucky.

"Fuck knows, dude." I scrub my hands down my face and squeeze my eyes shut. "I'm fucking exhausted, mate."

Brody goes to speak, but he is interrupted by a robotic, female voice coming through the P.A system.

"Five minutes to show time, five minutes to show time."

I take a deep breath, and Brody pats me on the back.

"Come on, Bolt; let's give these fuckers a show!"

I laugh at his words and follow him into the corridor where Jax and Lucas are waiting for us. Jax has his guitar loosely slung across his back and his blonde hair is pulled into a low ponytail. He looks at me with concerned eyes, and he is about to speak when we are joined by our manager, Alistair.

"Boys." He grins. "I know you won't let me down but go out there and fucking own it tonight."

He slaps me on the back and salutes the rest of the boys as he strides off down the corridor. Jax swings his guitar round to the front of his body so it hangs off his shoulders. Lucas expertly spins his sticks, throws them elaborately up in the air and catches them like a pro. Brody is leaning casually against the wall with his arms folded while chatting up a girl with short red hair.

She is running her long, blood-red nails up his arm and giggling at his jokes. She annoyingly smacks her lips together as she chews some gum. I suddenly start to think how blessed I am having these boys in my life, *my brothers, my family,* even though they aren't blood. But how does that saying go? You don't have to be blood to be family, right? These boys have been with me through thick and thin and everything in between. I'm extremely lucky to have them in my life; it's a rare thing to have people like that that I can turn to.

"Sam?" Jax's concerned voice cuts through my thoughts. "Everything alright, mate?"

I swallow harshly and manage a smile. *Get it the fuck together, Newbolt.*

"Yeah, yeah, all good, man." I squeeze his arm and pat his shoulder affectionately. "Let's do this."

Lucas' voice echoes down the corridor, as we all begin our journey to the stage. Brody catches me up and looks me with troubled eyes.

"Are you sure you're ok, dude?"

I go to speak, and Brody cocks his eyebrow.

"Before you answer that, think about who you're fucking talking to. I can spot a bull shitter from one hundred yards away, it's one of my many fucking talents!"

He laughs, and I smirk.

"Shame you can't spot a gold-digging whore at ten paces!"

I wink, and he rolls his eyes.

"Everyone's allowed a fucking weakness, Newbolt; we all know that yours happens to be a certain brunette, tattooed goddess."

As he mentions her, *my Peyton*, I start to feel less like going on stage and more like going to a bar and just getting absolutely fucking shit-faced.

"I get it, dude, I do, but you can't let her stop you from going out there and fucking doing what you do best."

I smile and pull him in for a manly hug. He laughs as I pull away.

"*Wow,* I didn't know you felt that fucking way about me, dude!"

We both laugh and continue our walk to the stage. We stop near the doors and I can hear the fans chanting.

"Vengeance, Vengeance, Vengeance."

The roar fills the venue and the walls are vibrating with stomping feet. The boys all pat my shoulder as they run onto the stage, leaving me in the corridor to make my grand entrance. Donovan hands me a microphone and clips the mic pack to the pocket of my jeans.

"Good luck, Bolt."

I wink.

"Cheers, man."

I make my way to the stage, and as soon as I take my usual spot I take a deep breath. *In through the nose, out through the mouth.* I feel my muscles start to relax, and all the tension I felt moments before has vanished. That feeling has been replaced with pure adrenaline. *I feel fucking invincible.* Jax's signature guitar riff fills the venue, and I growl into the microphone. This is what it's all about, this right here, performing, giving the fans a show, losing myself in the music. There's nothing like it, it's fucking priceless. The spotlight moves towards me until I am bathed in soft light. *This is my moment.*

"Hello Earl's Court, how the fuck are we doing tonight? You're all looking fucking beautiful out there."

The crowd scream and stomp their feet. I chuckle softly and turn to Jax.

"Flash, are you fucking ready to give these beautiful people an ear-gasm?"

He moves to his microphone stand.

"Hell fucking yeah!"

I salute.

"YEAHHHHHH!"

I roar, and the crowds' screams seem to get so loud that it's almost deafening.

"Give me a riff, Flash."

Jax winks, and his face breaks out into an ear-splitting grin as he starts an impressive guitar solo to a song called *'Hell's Angel'* off our *'Hurricane Vengeance'* album. His flawless guitar skills never fail to impress me; he is truly gifted. He gives me a wink of encouragement as Brody accompanies him with an equally impressive riff and moves fluidly across the stage to stand back to back with Jax. Lucas pounds an energetic drum beat, and I start to sing.

"Hell ain't a place for this hero, or a rocker with a microphone. Heaven is reserved for the angel on my shoulder, without you in my life, this world gets colder and fucking colder."

As I sing those lyrics, I lose myself in the music and close my eyes.

"I see your reflection as I pass a pane of glass, never realised how long this shattering pain would last."

Jax steps out and takes the spotlight, expertly making love to his fret board. I can tell by the look in his eyes that he is in his element. I grin broadly, and Brody starts to bounce up and down. His energy is contagious. As I bob my head to the beat, I move to Lucas and rest my one foot on an amp in front of his drum kit. I put both hands to my ears.

"FUCK YEAHHHH, AXEMAN!"

We make it to the end of the song, and soon, we are at the end of the first half of our show. *If I could bottle up this feeling and sell it, I would be a very fucking rich man.* There's no feeling like it, having an audience eat from the palm of your hand. *I was born to do this, it's in my blood.*

As the second half of the show begins, we pull out all the stops and I bring out Bolt the showman. We perform some of our hits, old and new, we share some anecdotes with the fans and interact with them, as if they are our long-lost friends. Their enthusiasm has my adrenaline pumping, and I feed off the crowd's raw energy. It drives me to give the best performance I can. We all give a thousand and one percent and perform each song as if it will be our last. As the show nears the end, I move to the front of the stage and sit down on the edge of the stage with my long legs dangling in front of me. The front row of fans are screaming and reaching out to me.

"How are we doing tonight, London? It's so fucking good to be here! Have you missed us?"

The crowd whoops and cheers. I chuckle softly.

"That's what we like to fucking hear; can we get the lights up for a minute?"

I gesture to the side of the stage and the room lights up. I can see the sea of fans before me and the sight never fails to amaze me. All these people are here for us. *Wow.*

"*Wow,* we would like to take this opportunity to thank you all so much for your ongoing and continued support, coming to our gigs, buying our music. It humbles each and every one of us; it makes all those shitty garage sessions seem fucking worth it!"

The rest of the boys join me, and Lucas leans over to speak into the microphone.

"Hey, guys, for our last song of the night, we need a volunteer."

The crowd scream so loud and the overexcited fans in the front row all yell: "ME, ME, ME, BOLT! PICK ME!"

I smile my dimpled grin, and I swear at least two girls in the front row, burst into tears. *Good to know I can still have that effect on women!* I turn to the side of the stage.

"Can I get a chair, please?"

From the corner of my eye I can see our roadies at the side of stage scrambling to get a chair at my request. Donovan runs onto the stage with a wooden chair and puts it down. I give him a thumbs up, and he winks, as he rushes off stage. *Our roadies definitely deserve a pay rise.* I get to my feet, and the boys resume their positions. I catch the eye of a brown-haired girl in the front row, with a short pixie cut and elfin features. I can't tell what colour her eyes are, but they almost look too big for her face. She bites her lip and my cock starts to stir. I point to her.

"Come on, darlin', come up here and join us on stage."

She points to herself as if to say '*Me?*' and I nod.

"Yeah you, babe, come on up."

Cole and Skip help her up from the front of the stage. I lift her up, and she clings to my biceps. She looks even more gorgeous close up. Her eyes are a deep chocolate brown colour. She is wearing a short denim skirt, a cropped Rancid Vengeance t-shirt tied at the waist to show off her flat stomach and pierced belly button. I catch a glimpse of a cherry blossom branch tattoo, which looks like it extends up her ribs. The crowd goes wild, and I take the girls hand.

"What's your name, sweetheart?" I say into the microphone.

"Donna," she says in a nervous Black Country accent, and I smile wide. She looks terrified.

"Do you want to sit down there for me, sweetheart?"

She nods as I take her hand and help her sit down on the chair. I cheekily kiss the back of her hand as I let go of her.

"Right, are we ready to rock this motherfucking place to the ground? Let me hear you scream, London!"

The crowd screams, and I turn to the boys.

"Ready boys? Let me hear Corrupted, fucking give it to me, Flash!"

Jax turns to Lucas, and he begins the complex intro to one of our biggest hits to date, '*Corrupted*'. Lucas pounds twice on his drums, and Brody joins in. I straddle the chair with Donna underneath me and steady myself with my hand on the back.

"There's a girl I know called Donna, she rocked my world, she blew my mind, with her rockin' body and her crazy lies."

I change the words to include her name and start to grind my hips on her. Her face breaks out into a smile. I can see her hands itching to touch me, so I grab her hand and place it on my stomach. *I feel like a fucking stripper.* I cock my head to the side, giving her the green light to move her hand.

"She shook her hips, grabbed her tits and rocked me until the sun came up; she's corrupted, from her head down to her feet."

She moves my shirt up and moves her hand underneath it. Her hand feels soft against the ridges of my abs. I gyrate my hips, and she gasps out loud as she feels my erection dig into her stomach. She scratches her nails down my stomach and round my back as Jax moves to the front of the stage with Brody to play their guitar solos. I straighten myself, and in one fluid move, I lift her up effortlessly. I then sit myself down on the chair and sit her in my lap. She puts her arm around my neck, and I wrap my free hand around her waist.

"That girl is corrupted; she drives me wild when she's screaming out my name in pure fucking ecstasy."

We get to the end of the song, and I lift her off my lap. I elaborately bow in front of her and kiss her hand.

"I'd like to thank Donna for being such a great sport and joining us up here tonight; it was my pleasure, babe."

I wink and twirl her around then lean down to make sure the microphone can't pick up what I'm about to say.

"Meet me after the show, babe? I'll put your name on the V.I.P list. I'll be waiting," I whisper low in her ear and flash her my dimpled grin.

She nods as she bites her lip seductively and makes her way back down to the audience. We perform an encore and soon the show is over in a blaze of expensive and elaborate pyrotechnics. I feel exhausted, but after a show, I like to let off some steam. And there's no better way to release that pent-up energy than to have some hot, nasty, sweaty sex. After a show, sex is like a form of therapy for me. I know it's fucked up; I'm literally a psychiatrist's wet dream. *Pleasure to bury the pain? Sounds like a fucking good plan to me.*

9

Peyton

The meal goes by swiftly, with Jack and I getting to know each other better. I feel like I have known him for years and the conversation flows easily. We find out we have more in common than I once thought. We like the same films, and we share a passion for art and tattoos. He makes me laugh, and he regards me with rapt attention throughout, never once taking his eyes off me. After our decadent dessert is cleared away, we are half way through our second bottle of champagne when he reaches across the low table for my hand. I let him take it, and as he caresses his thumb gently over my knuckles, my eyes lock with his. He lifts my hand to his lips and places a feather-light kiss on the back.

"This thing between us, whatever this is." He gestures between us before he continues to speak. "It scares the piss out of me, petal. I don't *do* relationships. I mean *never,* but I wasn't banking on meeting you. It's amazing what chance meetings do. They throw you off completely and your life ends up taking a totally different direction than the one you had meticulously planned out in your head. Do you know what I mean?"

I try to process his words as I regard him with guarded eyes.

"You see here's the thing, I fuck, but I don't do commitment. I don't do exclusivity. It's not in my nature. My brother Nate and I, we are complete polar opposites. He was married at twenty-three, and he has a kid. Our parents were over the moon when he and Hope said they were having a baby. I think they were relieved, because they wanted grandchildren desperately, but they were never going to get me to settle down, have the perfect life, a loving woman, and a couple of kids running around."

I raise my eyebrows at his blatant nonchalance of monogamous relationships.

"Is that what this is about, Jack? Your inability to commit? You're fucking unbelievable!" I say a little more harshly than I intend.

He puts his hand to his forehead and audibly sighs.

"It's not like that. I didn't mean for it to come out like that. I don't know what you want from me, Peyton. I like you...I *really* like you, more than I've liked anyone in years. You're feisty and you don't take my bullshit. Neither of us are looking for a long-term relationship, why dance around that fact?"

I fold my arms, and I find myself at a loss of what to say.

"Then why the fuck did you ask me to go out with you? Because you think I'm a sure thing? Because I'm a guaranteed lay? And to think I was actually beginning to like you."

I laugh bitterly.

"I'm not capable of giving you any more than just sex! Don't you get that? I'm not into the whole hearts and flowers thing. I asked you out because I like you... and the sex, well... that was *incredible,* but I'm not the type of guy you take home to your parent's, petal. I'm the one they warn you about. I'm the villain in this piece; I've done things I'm not proud of. You're too...pure and precious for that. I just can't offer you anything more than regular sex. I'm sorry, I'm not capable of it. I've seen how being in love screwed Nate up. I know it's selfish of me to even ask, but I like you, Peyton, more than I've liked a woman in years..."

I hold my finger up to stop him from continuing. My head is telling me to be reckless, to just go with it, to live in the moment, to accept his offer of being his '*fuck buddy*'. But the rational part of me wins out. It screams in my face that nothing good ever comes with being reckless.

"You know what, just stop fucking talking!" I say rudely as I stand up, grab my bag and do what any sane person would do; I turn around, leave, and I don't look back.

10

Sam

We have just come off stage after performing a gig at Earl's Court, in our hometown of London, and I am in the dressing room, like I am after every show. I'm fresh from a shower and am wearing a grey distressed Iron Maiden t-shirt. My jeans are riding low on my hips, and my hair is still damp from my shower. I am sitting on the sofa drinking whiskey neat from the bottle and Donna, the girl who I picked from the crowd, is waiting for me, as per my request.

I smile my panty-dropping smile, and she literally swoons on the spot. She is hot, her short brown hair emphasises her high cheekbones, her big brown eyes are so expressive, her tits are pert, and her waist is tiny. I adjust myself in my jeans; I'm fucking aching and desperate for a release. I need to feel the softness of a pair of breasts in my hands, the wet heat of her mouth as she deep throats my cock and the velvet of her internal walls as she grips my dick when I enter her.

Get a fucking grip, Newbolt; you're acting like a horny teenager.

"Your reputation precedes you, Sam," she purrs.

I cock my pierced eyebrow at her as she drapes herself over my lap.

"Number one, only my close friends and my family call me Sam. Since we're neither, it's Bolt. Number two, my reputation, as you put it, is whatever the press says it is, sweetheart."

I smile, bringing out the famous Newbolt dimples, and she practically creams her knickers. I spread my arms out across the back of the sofa and uncross my legs.

"Now get those gorgeous lips around my cock, darlin', there's a good girl," I rasp and chuckle softly.

She practically jumps from my lap, as if I've burned her, and throws me a look of pure disgust.

"God, you are such a fucking pig!" she shrieks.

I take a long pull on my whiskey with a bored expression on my face.

"Your loss, babe. I would have fucking *rocked* your world."

I shrug nonchalantly, and she leaves the room, practically colliding with Cole. He shakes his head.

"What the fuck did you do this time, Romeo?" he says in his deep baritone voice.

"Must be that old Newbolt charm, mate," I joke, and he strides into the room, sitting himself down next to me.

I gulp whiskey from the bottle; it burns as it slides down my throat, and Cole folds his arms.

"What the fuck is going on with you, Sam? You've got a second chance with the woman you love and you're pissing it up the wall. I don't get it."

I shake my head and scrub my hands down my face.

"I need more fucking whiskey if we're going to continue this conversation, man."

Cole chuckles low and throaty. I take another swig of whiskey and hang my head.

"She's fucking with my head man. She's adamant she doesn't want to be with me, but in the next breath, she's fucking me like a porn star. She's just one massive contradiction after another."

Cole goes to speak, but he is interrupted by my phone ringing. I see her name flash up on my phone. I swipe the screen and connect the call.

"Hello?" I say gruffly.

"I'm at a club called #W1K in Mayfair. If you want to fuck me, come now."

Before she gives me a chance to answer, the line goes dead.

Fuck me.

11

Peyton

I can't get away from the restaurant fast enough, and before I know it, I have removed my heels and I'm running as fast as my legs can carry me, heading for no particular destination. I stop for a second, and I take in my surroundings. I am in Mayfair, which is a place that is unfamiliar to me. I look up and down the street; I seem to have successfully ditched Jack Scott and Kai, my security detail. I take a breath and try to calm my racing thoughts. I need to drink, dance, fuck and forget all about this awful night. One which started off so perfectly. I lean against an estate agents window to put my heels back on and begin to walk down the street.

I come to a club called '*#W1K*'. The music is pumping, and it seems like a good a place as any to drink and dance. I walk confidently to the entrance, and the large bouncer at the door nods and smiles in my direction, dropping the royal blue rope to allow me inside. I pay my entry fee and step into the main vestibule of the club. It is as elegant as it looks from the outside, with its royal blue and light grey theme. The seating area is filled with blue velvet booths, and the bar fills the left side of the club with its white marble bar top and soft blue lighting. I order a vodka and cranberry and down it almost in one gulp.

Fuck, I needed that after the night I've had.

I don't know what comes over me, call it Dutch courage from the vodka I just drank, but before I can get my thoughts together, I pull my phone out and dial Sam. It rings twice before he answers.

"Hello?"

I order another drink and I boldly say, "I'm at a club called #W1K in Mayfair. If you want to fuck me, come now."

Then I hang up.

***

I'm not sure how much time passes, but as I'm perched on a bar stool, my skin starts to prickle and the hairs on the back of my neck stand on end. That's when I know Sam is here. As one song fades into the next, one of my favourite songs starts to play. I get down from my bar stool and make my way through the crowd of people and onto the dance floor. I can feel his eyes on me as soon as I start to move my hips to the pumping beat of the remix version of *Mirrors by* Justin Timberlake. The beat is surging through my veins, lighting me up from the inside, making me feel alive. I swing my hips suggestively in my leopard print and leather playsuit, which highlights my impressive assets and accentuates my figure. I feel sexy and powerful as my skin starts to heat.

That's when I spot him. He exudes sexiness, and he is wearing loose jeans, an Iron Maiden t-shirt, and a black leather jacket. His hair is styled into soft raven spikes and he looks delicious; definitely the epitome of a bad boy rock star. His strong jaw is tight and his plump pink lips are set into a straight line. I notice he isn't smiling as I lower myself to the floor and back up again, running my hands erotically down my sides. His blazing green eyes are focused firmly on my body, and I can feel his eyes licking flames against my skin. I close my eyes and let the music wash over me, twisting my head and my shoulders easily to the left and the back to the right. I have to admit, I am secretly enjoying teasing him from across the crowded dance floor.

As I slowly open my eyes, I feel a large, strong hand slide around my waist and press flat against my stomach. I am instantly aware that it isn't Sam.

"Dance with me, beautiful," a male voice with a broad Manchester accent says close to my ear, and I start to bump and grind with Mr. Manc.

My back is to his chest as we move in time to the music. He is moving fluidly with me as my eyes lock with Sam's. His green eyes are fierce, and he looks positively murderous. As Mr. Manc and I continue our sensual dance to the pulsing rhythm of Justin Timberlake, I can sense the rage coming off Sam in large tsunami like waves. I grind my arse against the obvious bulge tenting in Mr. Manc's trousers and step up my game. I spin around until I am facing Mr. Manc, and I look up into his eyes. The lighting in the club makes it difficult for me to make out the colour. He smiles a bright, cheesy grin that wouldn't look out of place in a toothpaste advert. He is tall, lean, and has laughter lines around his eyes, which add to his attractiveness. His blonde hair is pulled into a neat man bun, and his black V-neck t-shirt clings to his body, as do his deep burgundy jeans. He is extremely handsome.

"Hey gorgeous," he says with that wide grin.

I smile back and lean in close to his ear.

"Hey yourself."

He chuckles as he wraps his lean arm around me and pulls me closer to him. He grinds his hips into me to the beat of the music. I hear someone clear their throat behind us. The hairs on the back of my neck stand to attention, and my body instantly recognises him, sensing his presence before I see his face. *Sam.*

"Do you mind if I cut in, mate?" he rasps, and Mr. Manc raises his eyebrows.

"I don't think so, mate. Find your own, this one's mine. There's plenty to choose from."

Shit. Definitely the wrong thing to say. It's like dangling a piece of meat in front of a hungry lion.

"I don't think I heard you right, mate."

I want to say something to stop the inevitable fight, but I am frozen to the spot. All I can do is watch the proverbial dick-swinging contest unfolding in front of me.

"I said find your own, *mate.*"

Mr. Manc emphasises the word *'mate'* and Sam nods, smirking cockily.

"That's what I thought you said," Sam says calmly.

"Look, what's your fucking problem, mate?" Mr. Manc says with an edge to his voice.

Sam smirks.

"Number one, I'm not your fucking *mate,* and number two, you've got your filthy hands all over something that *belongs* to me."

Mr. Manc regards me intently.

Belong to him? What the fuck?

"Is that true, babe? Do you belong to him?"

Before I can protest, Sam grabs me by the wrist and pulls me away.

"Do not say a fucking word," Sam says low and menacingly as he leads me towards the exit.

Except we don't leave, he takes a sharp turn jerking me to the side and pulling me into the ladies' toilets. *He's obviously been here before.* He checks each cubicle for occupants by kicking the doors open with his boot. When he is happy we're alone, he pulls me forcefully into a cubicle and locks it behind us. His large frame takes up the majority of the space, and I am effectively trapped between the wall and Sam's hard chest. His scent is enveloping me, intoxicating me, and pulling me deeper under his spell. He puts his large hand around my throat and squeezes. He doesn't squeeze hard, but he puts just enough pressure to let me know he's in charge.

"Did you enjoy fucking teasing me? Did you?" he says through clenched teeth. "You called me to come here and fuck you, and then I watched you grinding your arse against that bloke, fucking taunting me. Were you deliberately trying to make me jealous?"

I go to speak, but he moves his hand from around my throat and places his finger against my lips.

"Think very fucking carefully about your answer, angel. Because right now, my self-control is hanging on by a fucking thread."

The possessive look in his green eyes actually scares me, and I have never seen Sam so out of control. His eyes are wide, dark, and menacing as he looks down at me.

"I..."

I am at a loss for what to say and come to a sudden realisation. I *do not* belong to Sam, not anymore.

"You know what, Sam? *Fuck you!* I don't have to answer to you. You don't fucking own me! Yeah, I called you to come and fuck me, and yeah, maybe I *was* making you jealous. And what? That guy actually *wanted* me, and yeah, I would have let him take me home and let him fuck me until it was *his* name I was screaming!" I shout, and he punches the door with his fist, growling loudly.

"ENOUGH WITH THE FUCKING MIND GAMES, PEYTON! YOU ARE FUCKING MINE! DON'T YOU GET THAT? *MINE!*" he roars and thrusts his hips into me, showing me the evidence of his arousal.

"*Jesus*, you fucking grind my gears like no one else, angel," he says huskily before he reaches round the back of my playsuit and unzips it, exposing my lacy underwear.

He yanks the playsuit down my body and expertly undoes my bra one-handed. I palm his hardness through his jeans and he growls.

"FUCKKK!"

He drops my clothes to the floor and tears my knickers off, the ripping sound echoing around the cubicle. I feel exposed and naked, in more ways than one. My breasts feel heavy and ache to have his hands on them. He expertly laps my nipple with his talented tongue. I cry out at the delicious torture. The throbbing between my thighs is so unbearable. I'm close to begging him to shove his cock in me, just to sate my greedy pussy's needs. My sex floods as he continues his assault on my nipples, and I feel wanton, squirming in agony waiting for him to fill me. This virile, God-like creature, who owns every inch of me, who worships me. The look in his green eyes almost pushes me over the edge as I urge him with my baby blues to take me, to fuck me primally and animalistically. He releases my nipple with a pop and spins me around to face the cubicle wall. I can feel his warm breath on my neck, and I shiver at the way his hard body feels pressed against mine.

"Palm the wall, angel, this is going to be quick and hard. Do you fucking understand me?" he says gruffly, and I nod, oddly turned on by his dominance.

I do as he says, and I hear him unzip his jeans, lowering his boxer briefs just enough to give me access to his already hard cock. My thighs feel slick with my arousal; I have never been this turned on. He reaches around and squeezes my neck in his large hand. He leans forward and I can feel his warm breath on my neck as his scent envelopes me. Every nerve in my body is on fire as he nips my neck with his teeth. The scrape of his stubble on my already too sensitive skin causes me to shiver. His other hand snakes down my stomach and he finds my swollen clit. I moan out loud as his finger swipes up my wetness.

"*Jesus fucking Christ!* You're always wet for me, angel," he growls.

"Sam," I whimper, and he squeezes my neck.

"Shhh, angel, you need to be quiet. I'll take care of you."

He moves his hand away from my aching cleft, and I feel him fist his cock behind me. He rubs the head against me, and I push back towards him.

"Ah, ah, angel. You might have been the one to call me, but I'm the one in charge now. I say when. Don't fucking push me; you need to be taught that if you play games with me, you will fucking lose," he bites out.

I go to spin round, but he pushes me face forward to the wall with a firm grip. I feel him lean down, and I turn my head slightly to see what he is doing. He picks up my torn knickers from the floor and reaches up to grab my hands. He holds both of my wrists in one of his hands and expertly ties my hands behind my back with my discarded underwear.

"Turn around, I won't fucking tell you again. I'm in charge, and you need to learn that you own me, just as I own you. You know every corner of my heart, just as I know every corner of yours, angel."

I shiver at his sweet words, and before I can speak, he pushes me against the wall and enters me. I gasp at the sudden invasion and push back to meet his every thrust. He uses my tied hands to gain leverage, to establish a rhythm. He starts to pick up his pace, and he pounds me into the cubicle wall.

"Angel," he growls low and huskily in my ear.

I mewl quietly as I hear the door open and the click of heels against the floor tiles. I turn my head to the side and Sam puts his finger to his lips as he expertly swivels his hips, teasing me. With every thrust, I feel his piercing rub against my g-spot; it feels so good, I want to cry out. I hear the idle chatter of the women in the toilet.

"Did you see Sam Newbolt? Fuck me, how fit does he look tonight? It should be illegal to look that good. I swear my ovaries exploded when I saw him!"

An eruption of giggles alerts me that there is at least three women out there. I turn to Sam and raise my eyebrows. Sam smirks cockily, and unexpectedly, he moves us backwards without his cock leaving my pussy. He sits down on the toilet seat so that I am sitting on his lap, facing away from him. He lifts me up and impales me on his waiting hardness; I bite my lip to stop myself from screaming out. He's enjoying torturing me. *Bastard.* As soon as I hear the toilet door close and the room fall completely silent, I let out the breath I didn't know I was holding.

"It's my cock that's inside you, angel. Those women, they're...inconsequential," he rasps as he reaches around to play with my swollen nub.

I feel the familiar ache of longing, coupled with the feel of his cock inside me. The ripples of pleasure are sparking behind my eyelids, between my thighs, and down to my toes.

"Oh God Sam! Please, I need to come," I plead almost desperately, and my voice doesn't sound like my own.

He chuckles darkly.

"I can feel your pussy clenching around my cock, angel. You're close."

He increases his pace and reaches around with his other hand to play with my nipple. He rolls it between his thumb and forefinger. I moan softly.

"Oh Sam, please, please, don't stop."

I pant as he drives his cock in and out at a relentless, punishing pace. His fast rhythm is making me crazy, and I feel myself trembling with desire. I can feel my orgasm building somewhere deep within my core. He rams his cock up inside me, keeping the pace fast and frantic as we both near climax. My breath is coming out in ragged pants as I feel my orgasm thunder through my whole body.

"Sam, Oh Sam! Sam! I'm coming!"

He leans forward to nip my earlobe between his teeth.

"That's it, angel, come all over my cock," he rasps breathlessly as he growls out his climax. "*FUCKKKKK!* Oh shit! Angel, I'm coming!"

I feel him as he pumps his hot seed inside me. I squeeze my pelvic muscles around him, milking every last drop, and he growls in my ear. He stills, and I fall back lax against him. I wait for my breathing to return to normal before I go to speak.

"What the fuck was that, Sam?"

He laughs gruffly, and he begins untying my makeshift underwear restraints.

"That, angel, was me claiming what's mine," he rasps and lets my discarded underwear fall to the floor.

I lift myself off him, and as I spin around to face him, I stumble into him. He catches me in his muscular arms, and as my skin makes contact with his, all my nerves light up and stand to attention. It feels as if it is my body instantly recognises his.

"You fucking belong with me, angel. What's it going to take for you to accept that?"

He reaches up to tuck a strand of my hair behind my ear, and I close my eyes, leaning into his touch. He's right, I do belong with him. But how can it work when everything is so different to the way it used to be?

"Come home with me, angel. I fucking need you. I'm sorry I ran out; my head was all over the place, but I promise you, it won't happen again."

My blue eyes lock with his and the look in his eyes is so sincere, it almost breaks my heart to say no. I pull away from him and start to get dressed. I fasten my bra and step into my playsuit.

"Fuck!" Sam growls and stands up, his large frame crowding the small space.

He runs his hand through his raven hair, and I drop my gaze to the floor. "Angel, please, don't do this."

He tips my chin up, and I can't look at him.

"Fucking look at me, angel. I need you to tell me that you don't want me. Look me in the eyes, tell me we're done, and I'll fucking walk away. It will kill me, but I'll walk away, I swear."

I shake my head.

"Sam, please."

My voice is shaky and thick with unshed tears. *Can I tell the only man I've ever loved that it's over? Do I really want him to walk away?*

"Fucking tell me it's over, angel. I need to hear the fucking words," he says hardheartedly.

Everything is so different now. I'm someone's mum, and I kept his son from him, for six whole months. I won't apologise for that, but it kills me that I can never take it back. He tried to take his own life because of my actions, and now I have to deal with the consequences. *It has to be this way.* I take a deep breath and reach into my bag. I go to pull out the engagement ring he gave me all those months ago, but I can't bring myself to be so cruel.

I look up at him. *Pull up those big girl pants, Harper.*

"It's...over. I'm sorry, it *has* to be this way, Sam."

I pick up my heels and my bag. I shove past him and swing the toilet door open. He grabs my wrist and pulls me back.

"Angel."

A stray tear slips down my cheek.

"Sam, let go of me."

He lets go of my arm, as if I've burned him, and I run out of the toilet to the distinct sound of a mirror shattering and Sam roaring in pain.

12

Peyton

Monday morning rolls around way too fast, and today is the first day of filming for the new series of *Inked @ Saint Sinner*. After a lengthy chat with Seb yesterday, I find out that the first person to feature in the series is, Nicholas Slade. After a couple of hours spent on Google, I find out that Nicholas Slade is a British actor, and he is one of the U.K's *hottest* exports in Hollywood. He started off acting in low budget Brit flicks and moved to the States, where he landed various roles in *Into the Fire, Fix Me* and *The Photograph*. At thirty-three, he is a huge star, despite his background.

He grew up on a council estate in Camberwell and attended an acting school called 'London Academy of Music and Dramatic Arts' on a scholarship. He earned the scholarship by taking the lead in various performances in school productions and was spotted by a talent scout. He landed a prestigious role in a play called 'Domino' at the Old Vic theatre, where he was discovered by Damien Valentine. Damien Valentine was dubbed the 'British Tarantino' and Nicholas got his big break in British gangster flick, *Chelsea Smile,* which was a huge success and rocketed his career into oblivion. Nicholas is also considered 'The British George Clooney'; he is one of Hollywood's richest, most eligible bachelors, and has women queuing up and vying for his attention. Today, I'm going to be tattooing him. *Shit.*

I take my time getting ready for work; taking longer than usual in the shower. I step out of the shower, brush my teeth, and head to my bedroom. I dry off quickly and get dressed. Today, I opt for a pair of black leather shorts, a black and white striped t-shirt with a black rose stitched above the left breast, black knee-high Converse, and a necklace shaped like a music note. I have styled and straightened my dark hair into a neat bob and apply my usual natural make up. I give Freddie his breakfast, kiss him goodbye, and leave him with my brother, Dexter. Dexter has taken some annual leave from the police force following his split with his fiancée, and he has decided to stay with me for a while. Kai follows me out, dressed in his usual *Men in Black* attire, and we make our way down to the parking garage to begin our Monday morning.

As soon as I step into the shop, it is a hive of activity. There are camera men all over the shop floor, lighting rigs set up in each corner, and people with clipboards meandering around. I have never seen the shop so busy; it reminds me of Piccadilly Circus. I spot Seb straight away amongst the sea of people. His six-foot six frame eclipses everyone in his wake.

"Good morning, honey bunny."

I smile at his familiar term of endearment, taken straight from the film *Pulp Fiction.*

"Good morning, pumpkin," I reply, and he grins.

In the ten years I have known him, I have never seen Seb grin like that. His whole face lights up, and I swear I see a dimple in his cheek. I nod to Parker and Harley, and there is a young woman who I don't recognise. She is medium height, around five feet five, full sleeves on both arms, tattoos up her neck and across her chest. She has violet eyes, has stars tattooed in an arc around her left eye, and she is wearing thick black-rimmed glasses. Her turquoise hair is pulled up on top of her head in a bun. She is wearing a red and white polka dot corset, black cropped skinny jeans, and New Rock boots. She regards me intently and Seb places his hand at the base of my spine in an intimate, but reassuring gesture.

"Babe, this is Harlow Martinez, she's our new temporary shop receptionist. Harlow, this Peyton, she's one of my best friends and one of the best artists I've got."

She smiles, and I return the gesture as I shake her hand.

"Nice to meet you, Harlow."

She nods.

"Likewise, Peyton, call me H," she says in a Geordie accent as Seb looks between us.

"You can gossip and all that girly shit in a bit. I need a quick chat, babe, if that's good with you?"

I nod, and we make our way into the back. I put the kettle on and go about making the coffees. Seb leans against the worktop with his arms folded across his broad chest.

"Nick is on his way as we speak. The producers want to do a brief introduction with us, then with Nick. They want a bit of background on why he wants the tattoo and general bullshit. He's specifically requested you, so just treat him as you would any other client, babe. I've got every faith in you."

I suddenly start to feel nervous.

"*Whoa!* Way to throw me in at the deep end, babe!" I joke, but Seb doesn't laugh.

"Don't you dare doubt yourself, babe. You're the best fucking tattoo artist I know. I know you're having problems with Sam, but I also know you would never let it interfere with your work."

He envelops me in his tattooed arms, and I cling to him tightly.

"Thank you," I whisper, and he kisses the top of my head.

"What for, babe?"

I take a breath.

"For giving me my job back; you didn't have to. And for believing in me...for having my back and always being in my corner."

He pulls away from our embrace and pinches my chin between his thumb and forefinger.

"Listen to me, babe, and you listen fucking good, you've got absolutely nothing to thank me for. I gave you your job back because you're the fucking best in the business. I took a chance, and it paid off because I saw you had potential. I've always believed in you; you've got skill. It killed me listening to you say you served coffee for a living while you were gone, you were born to tattoo. I'm fairly sure you were born with a tattoo machine in your hand!"

I smile softly, and he moves his hand from my face.

"What I'm saying is, everyone deserves a second chance, babe. And yeah, I was mad as hell when Willow told me you were alive, but she explained what happened and even though I was pissed, I understood. I care about you, Peyton, you're like my little sister. We're family, and I'm here for you, even if it is just to stroke your ego!"

We both laugh. I hear the shop bell ring and a commotion coming from the shop.

I think our star guest, Nick, has arrived.

I recognise him as soon as he walks confidently into the shop. He holds himself in a casual manner as he walks with an air of regality and elegance. Nicholas Slade. His entourage consisting of a woman with chocolate coloured skin. She is curvy, tall, and looks as if she is around Sam's height. She has long straight black hair with blue streaks all over and unusual green cat-like eyes. She is wearing a white trouser suit, with a green top underneath, which make her green eyes pop, and classic black Louboutin heels. From the way she carries herself, I am assuming she is his agent.

The other person with Nicholas is a burly looking man of Oriental descent, with ice-blue eyes, and blonde hair in a crew cut. I assume he is Nick's bodyguard. Seb turns to greet our star guest, and as Nicholas smiles brightly, I take in every inch of him. He is around six-foot-tall, extremely muscular, has lean, narrow hips and his dark brown almost black eyes remind me of Minstrels; his dark brown hair is neatly styled into a soft quiff. A tattoo of a set of dice, playing cards, a lucky '8' ball and the words 'You make your own luck', peeks out of the open neck of his shirt and extends up his throat and neck.

He is wearing a pair of tight-fitting jeans, which seem to mould to his pert arse and lean muscular legs, a black Henley shirt with lime green piping, which stretches across his shoulders, and he wears a pair of bright white Adidas shell toe trainers. The camera crew from the TV company flock around him as the door closes behind him.

"Cheers for the welcome guys, but it really isn't necessary," he says light heartedly, in his soft South East London accent.

The camera crew disperse, leaving Nicholas standing with his hands tucked casually into his pockets. He is as charming as I have seen him in interviews. His smile is infectious, and his personality is magnetic. He crosses the room and stops in front of me. His deep brown eyes roam the length of my body, and I suddenly feel exposed in front of this gorgeous, virile man.

"Breathe, love."

He leans in to whisper in my ear, and I let out the breath I didn't know I was holding as he offers me his hand. I take it and he kisses the back of my hand softly.

"Nicholas Slade, but I'd prefer it if you called me Nick."

I clear my throat and manage to find my voice.

"Peyton Harper."

He smiles a bright white megawatt Hollywood smile.

"Ah yes, the beautiful creature that snared and tamed our very own Mr. Newbolt."

I blush at his words, and I feel my face grow flushed as he chuckles softly.

"No need to be embarrassed, love."

I bite my lip, and I can see why millions of women fall for his old English charm.

"I can see I'm going to have to keep an eye on you, Nicholas," I say as he cocks his dark eyebrow and smirks.

"I was counting on it, and please, call me Nick."

He winks, and I smile, suddenly feeling extremely nervous and awkward around this huge Hollywood super star.

"Relax, love, you look tense."

I subconsciously wipe my sweaty palms on my jeans, and he regards me intently with his inquisitive brown eyes.

"They say an orgasm can relieve some tension, you look like you could use several," he purrs seductively.

Cocky bastard.

The old me would have shot back a sharp, witty one liner, like on the day I first met Sam. But the new me has absolutely nothing to say, no flirty banter, no cheeky one liner, *nothing.*

He brushes my arm gently, and I flinch violently as his hand makes contact with me. He immediately pulls his hand back and holds both of his hands up defensively. A look of genuine concern crosses his chiselled and handsome face.

I need to stop reacting that way. Maybe Remy did too good of a job teaching me self-defence.

Peyton

Past

Freddie is a few weeks old and I'm itching to get my figure back to the way it was before I got pregnant. Remy is a part-time self-defence trainer and uses his military training to teach basic defence. I refuse to be the victim that J.D almost destroyed. Remy has a home gym in the basement of his house and it is kitted out with a punching bag, bench press, treadmill, and a cross trainer. I am ready for my first defence lesson, and I'm raring to go. I am dressed in black yoga pants, a hot pink vest, and trainers. My hair is pulled up into a short ponytail. Remy is wearing white Adidas jogging bottoms, a grey vest, and trainers. His hair is tied back into a loose ponytail. Freddie is asleep upstairs, and we have bought the baby monitor down with us.

"Right, first lesson in self-defence: what are you going to do if someone grabs you from behind?"

I am suddenly assaulted with memories of J.D grabbing me from behind, drugging me, and dragging me off helplessly. I shake away the thoughts and look at Remy.

"I know it's difficult for you, beaut, but to prevent this from happening again, you need to do this. Not for just you, but for that little boy upstairs."

I nod and smile.

"So, first lesson in self-defence: if someone grabs you from behind, you drop all your weight to the floor. The point of it is to drop your weight below your attackers' centre of gravity. This gives them less chance of succeeding."

He moves behind me and the anticipation of him grabbing me from behind sets my nerves on edge and my whole body on full alert. He grabs me from behind and I struggle at first. Once I'm over the initial shock of being grabbed, he whispers in my ear, "Relax, beaut, it's just me. Drop your weight."

He tightens his hold, and I try to drop my weight to the floor, failing miserably as I fall in a heap on the floor. Remy offers me his hand and helps me up. I get to my feet and dust myself off.

"Again!" Remy barks.

He moves behind me again, and I take a few calming breaths before he grabs me. I drop my weight, but my arms are restrained.

"Good girl. Now, attack me. Step on my foot, or hit me in the groin, whichever you feel comfortable with."

I reluctantly stomp on his foot, repeatedly, but his grip doesn't loosen.

"Beaut, that's my prosthetic, I can't feel anything!" he says in an amused voice and I bite my lip to hide my smirk.

I'm such a fucking idiot! I stomp on his other foot and his grip loosens until my arms are slightly free.

"Good, now, rear your elbow back into my stomach, but make sure it's repetitive, jab, jab, jab."

I rear my elbow back into his hard stomach, and he lets go of me.

"Now what? Use that beautiful head of yours. Am I just going to give up and go home? Or am I going to try to attack you again?"

He lunges forward, and I remember my training from my boxing class. I put both hands up in front of my face and stand with my feet shoulder width apart. He smiles and nods.

"Well done! Now assess me. Have I got a weapon? Is it concealed? Have I got my hands out ready to attack you?"

I assess him, and his hands are out in front of him.

"Your hands are in front of you."

He nods.

"Well spotted."

He rushes forward, and before I know it, he has tackled me to the floor. He rolls us both, and he gets to his feet, offering me his hand to help me up.

"Too slow. Never drop your guard, never turn your back, and never let yourself get distracted, not even for a second."

I nod and get to my feet.

"Thanks for agreeing to teach me, Rem. I really am grateful."

I smile, and he smiles back.

"Don't thank me yet, beaut. We've got a long fucking way to go."

Peyton

Present

I am jolted back to the present by the concerned voice of Nick Slade.

"I apologise, love. I meant no harm, and it was never my intention to frighten you."

I wrap my arms around myself, burning with pure embarrassment at my reaction to such an innocent touch.

Fucking J.D.

"I abhor men who put their hands on women purely with the intent to harm them; how one could hurt a creature as beautiful as you is beyond me."

I smile shyly at his compliment, and he returns the gesture.

"Such a pretty smile, love."

I slowly begin to relax, but the slight tremor to my hands is still visible, even to the less observant of people. I swallow hard to clear the lump in my throat.

"If you would like to follow me to my station, Nick."

He nods and follows me back to my workstation. He hops up onto the chair in one fluid movement, and I drop down into my leather chair, sinking down onto it as it hugs me like a pair of strong arms.

"Subtly changing the subject is certainly a clever way of deflecting your problems, Miss Harper, but I'm a very observant man. I can see the slight shake of your hands. I scared you, and for that, I am eternally sorry. I don't know what happened to you, because I tend to stay away from those bloody awful rag mags. I know we've just met, but sometimes talking to someone who is considerably impartial can be a great help to lift that crushing burden," he says softly in his crisp accent, and I feel instantly soothed by his words. "Underneath this somewhat handsome facade, I'm just a normal, ordinary fella from a dodgy council estate who got lucky. If Hollywood has taught me one thing, it's never judge a book by its cover."

He lifts his leg and crosses it to rest casually on his knee. He leans back, making himself comfortable. His presence is overwhelming and everything about him commands you to look up and take notice of him. He really is the whole package: stunning good looks, charming personality, and he is a natural flirt. Although, something about him doesn't scream your typical Hollywood star. He seems to just *see* people for who they really are, which is an extremely rare quality.

"You have the most stunning blue eyes I've ever seen."

I smile.

"Do you flirt with every woman you meet, Nick?"

He throws his head back and laughs, attracting the attention of his entourage and piquing the curiosity of the camera crew.

"Just the beautiful ones, love!"

He smirks.

"You're a charmer, I'll give you that," I joke.

I look up at him and my blue eyes lock with his deep brown ones.

"People say the eyes are windows to the soul, and yours say a lot about you, even the things you don't say out loud. I can tell just by looking at you."

He cocks his head to the side and regards me intently. We sit in silence for a moment before he speaks again.

"I can tell that you were quite different before the light was extinguished from those stunning eyes. Sam was quite smitten with the feisty hell cat he met when you tattooed him, but this girl facing me is someone completely the opposite of what Sam told me of you."

He leans back in the chair and folds his muscular arms across his chest, watching me with great interest.

"Whatever happened to you changed you completely, and I'm sensing that you're craving desperately to be that person again."

I look up at him open mouthed. He definitely has an uncanny knack of reading people and seeing into their very souls. He smiles his dazzlingly bright Hollywood smile, and from across the room, Seb catches my gaze. He frowns and narrows his eyes, mouthing, *"Are you ok, babe?"* I nod and smile a fake smile. Nick chuckles softly.

"If you want people to actually believe that you're ok, you have to be a little more convincing than that."

I narrow my eyes at him, and he sweeps his tongue across his bottom lip.

"Do you have a filter?"

His brown eyes sparkle with amusement and he laughs throatily.

"It seems to be broken, love."

I spin around to my desk and pull out my sketchpad. I don't have to turn around to know that Nick has moved to stand right behind me. I can feel his warm peppermint breath close to my ear.

"I'm an actor, love, a bloody good one; I know how to manipulate people into believing whatever I tell them. I can teach you, I'm a *master* at what I do."

His voice is a low gruff whisper. The camera crew, Seb, and Nick's entourage are watching our every move with a piqued curiosity. *That's all I need.*

"We're going to be front page news tomorrow, Mr. Slade," I say with a hint of annoyance to my voice.

"I've told you, it's Nick."

I spin around, and he leans down, resting both of his hands on the armrests of my chair, trapping me beneath him.

"You know, that annoyed tone you used back there, is the most believable feeling I've heard from you since I stepped in here. Good girl, I'm impressed."

I lift my chin in defiance.

"Have you quite finished analysing me, Nick?" I snap, and he smirks, subtly changing the subject.

"Directors love to work with me, because I bring out the best in the other actors, especially the ones who have to work closely with me. I can definitely see what Sam sees in you."

I roll my eyes.

"Did Sam send you here to plead his case? If he did, you're wasting your time, Nick."

He smiles and nods.

"I merely came here because I want a new tattoo. I heard you had returned from your...*hiatus* and word on the street, as the kids these days say, is you're the best in the business, so here I am. I did speak with Sam about my visit, and he did nothing but sing your praises as regards to your work. He didn't mention anything of your relationship, or lack thereof. I know Sam, I know he's hurting, and I chose not to push the issue. If he wants to tell me then he will, in his own time."

He straightens himself and stands at his full height, then moves to the leather chair and sits himself down. All the time, the camera is trained on the situation unfolding between us.

"Do you have a particular design in mind, Mr. Slade?"

He throws his head back and laughs.

"So, we're back to the formalities, Miss Harper? As you wish. I want a pin-up girl, full colour, to represent Lady Luck and to match the theme of the rest of my tattoos. I was thinking of a brunette, tattooed, blue eyes, large breasts, stockings...rather like yourself," he says boldly, and I cock my eyebrow as I pick up my pencil.

"Flattery will get you nowhere, Nick."

I bite my lip to hide my smirk.

"I want her to represent luck, beauty, and everything Hollywood. Think Audrey Hepburn, Marilyn Monroe, Bette Davis, Greta Garbo, and Elizabeth Taylor, but with a modern twist for the twenty-first century. I want her holding playing cards, aces, and I want the phrase 'Luck Be a Lady Tonight' incorporated into the design."

As he continues to speak, my pencil dances across the page and it's times like these that I absolutely love my job. Sketching, drawing, creating, and then finally getting to tattoo it onto someone's skin as a permanent reminder. For me, it's art in it truest form.

"You've got this adorable crease right between your eyes when you're concentrating, it's really quite charming," Nick says softly, and I smile at his compliment.

"Hair up or down?" I question, and he reaches over to tuck a strand of my hair behind my ear.

"Definitely down, love."

Nick Slade is definitely a natural flirt. Everything he says sounds so smooth and charming.

Enough Harper, you've had your fill of famous men.

Half an hour passes, and after some idle chit chat with Nick, I am finished sketching his tattoo. I turn the sketchpad round to show him and he cocks his eyebrow.

"This is exquisite; if I could draw, this would be exactly what I would have drawn."

My eyes widen, and my mouth forms a perfect '*O*' shape.

"You mean there's something that the great Nicholas Slade isn't good at? Alert the press!"

We both laugh, and I find myself totally relaxed around this man.

"Yes, unfortunately, I'm a stickman kind of guy. Although I make up for it in other activities."

He winks cheekily.

"Where on your body is this going, Nick?"

He lifts his shirt up and points to a blank space up the right side of his ribs. I nod and try to hide the pink flush on my cheeks.

"I won't be a sec."

I move across the shop towards the thermal copier machine, and I put my design onto the glass. Seb comes over and brushes my arm.

"Everything alright, babe? I forgot to mention that Slade is a shameless flirt, but you seem to have him under control," he says suggestively and smirks. I hit him playfully.

"Get your mind out of the gutter, Henry! He's just another client. Besides, I'm *totally* off men!"

Seb nods.

"We'll see about that, babe. That's exactly what you said when you tattooed Sam."

He winks, and I narrow my eyes at him. *I hate it when he's right.*

"Give me a shout if you need anything."

I nod, and he walks away, leaving me to punch in the correct size on the thermal copier. I wait for the stencil to come through the machine and take it back to my station where Nick is talking in hushed tones to the woman who came into the shop with him.

"Where are my manners, Peyton? This is my agent, Chastity Evangelina Chamberlain, she travels with me sometimes, to keep me out of trouble," he says with an amused tone to his voice.

I shake her hand as she regards me intently.

"You can call me Chas. Pleased to meet you, Peyton," she says in a prominent American accent.

We both smile, and I pull away from her firm handshake.

"Likewise, Chas."

She gives Nick a knowing look as she makes her way across the shop.

"Sorry about her, she's a tad protective. Likes me to steer clear of unsuitable women, but she's a pussycat really. She reins me in when I need it," he explains, and I nod.

He begins to unbutton his shirt and removes it, revealing his tanned, tattooed torso. His abs are covered in fine dark hairs, forming a trail down to the top of his boxers. I try not to stare, but he really is the whole package, good body, great personality, not to mention a great actor, which I found out after I watched the film that shot him to stardom last night on Netflix.

I move towards him and clean the area with antiseptic before I begin to place the stencil on his ribs. I pat his ribs and peel off the stencil with a steady hand, leaving the outline there for me to follow.

"Do you want to look in the mirror to see if the positioning is good?"

He looks at me and then looks down to check it.

"Perfect, love."

He winks, and I roll my eyes. *Shameless.* He stands up, and I fold the chair down flat, so it looks like a leather bed. I lock it into position and pat the bed.

"If you could lay down here for me?"

He grins wickedly.

"I didn't know you felt that way about me, I'm flattered."

He gets up onto the bed and turns on his side. I shake my ink bottles, set up my inks in small plastic pots on the table, pull on my black rubber gloves, and clip my hair away from my face before I begin. I start the tattoo machine and begin tattooing him.

After a few hours of tattooing, Nick steps outside the back of the shop for a break. I use the bathroom to freshen up, grab a bottle of flavoured water from the fridge, and check my mobile. I have a text from Sam.

We need to talk about what happened the other night, angel
Call me

S x

I sigh, ignoring the text, and tuck my phone back in my bag while I step outside to get some air. I stand back, observing Nick as he lights a cigarette. He inhales deeply and blows out a plume of smoke.

"Do you make a habit of ogling handsome men, love?" he says with a hint of amusement to his voice.

I chuckle softly and step outside next to him.

"Do you make a habit of charming the pants off tattooed women in back street tattoo shops?"

He laughs.

"You're quite the woman, Miss Harper."

I sigh.

"I'm glad someone thinks so."

He inhales on his cigarette deeply, and he looks at me with concern in his eyes.

"Those things will kill you, you know?"

I swiftly change the subject, before he gets to voice his concerns, and he chuckles softly.

"So, I'm told, but we're all allowed our vices, love. Mine happen to be a good smoke, a fine wine, and an extremely handsome, muscular man at my beck and call."

My eyes widen and I'm not sure if Nick is joking. He laughs and cocks his eyebrow.

"Lift your jaw off the floor, Miss Harper. Before you jump to conclusions, not just any man, one man in *particular.*"

He emphasises the word *'particular'* piquing my curiosity. I look at him, regarding him intently.

"Let me guess? I don't look the type to have...dabbled? I'm an actor, I'm extremely good at laying on the charm and convincing people of whatever I want them to believe. That's why they pay me the big bucks, darling," he says as he discards his cigarette and crushes it under his shoe.

"I have to say, I can see why Sam is quite smitten with you. You're ballsy and you're...beautiful. I would definitely be into you to, if you were my type."

He winks, and we both laugh.

"What *is* your type then, Nick?" I say sassily, and he cocks his eyebrow.

"Feeling brave, Miss Harper? If you're really interested, my type is tall, brunette, not fussy on eye colour, but I also have a soft spot for a muscular, American male...I'm not gay, if that's what you're thinking. I'm...*not* bi sexual, call me *curious*...actually, I'm not even sure what I am. It's just *him*, Lucas fucking Landon."

My eyes widen at his admission. It explains why Lucas is such a private person and keeps his business to himself.

"One night with him had me questioning fucking *everything* I ever believed in. He made me believe I was worthy of being loved, just like you made Sam believe he could love and be loved in return. Don't get me wrong, I *love* having a beautiful woman beneath me. What red blooded man doesn't? But he did something to me, and I can't get that night out of my head. I wake up with a painful erection, panting like a desperate fucking dog, wanting more, wanting him...*Just* him, *only* him."

He sighs and leans heavily against the wall.

"All these women, I bury myself in them, but all I really want deep down is Lucas. I need him like I need the air to breathe. My agent and my P.R team are pushing for me to do this fucking awful reality T.V show to find me a wife, but I can't. I just can't."

In the way he speaks, I can see the pain his eyes as he speaks about his feelings for Lucas. I wouldn't call it love, but there's definitely *something* there and my heart breaks for him.

"Don't pity me, love, I can see it in your eyes."

I shake my head.

"It's not pity, it's...beautiful, poetic, like star-crossed lovers."

He laughs.

"I'd hardly call it that. Is that what you and Sam are? Star-crossed lovers?" he asks curiously and my smile fades.

"Me and Sam are over," I say matter-of-factly and he nods.

"It's over when he says it's over, love. He's a man not to be crossed, and he always gets what he wants, *always.*"

Suddenly, I start to feel curious.

"How did you meet Sam?" I ask inquisitively, and he smirks, as if remembering the day he met Sam.

"Ah, the day I met Sam. Kind of a strange day, if I'm honest. Rancid Vengeance were doing the soundtrack to the movie I was in at the time and just after we'd finished filming, my agent got a call from J.D. He had this idea that the boys could shoot a music video, without *having* to star in it, that's where I came in. He wanted me to star in the video, think Robert Downey Jnr. in that famous Elton John video. Although, this video featured me running naked down a train track to a pre-recorded version of a Rancid Vengeance song, in near dark, in January. It was fucking freezing. The boys were holed up drinking hot coffee in a toasty warm trailer, watching on a monitor and I was jogging along a train track, stark bollock naked, freezing my nads off, listening to J.D order me around like I was nobody. After the tenth take, my teeth were chattering, my feet were killing, and I felt like I was going to die of hypothermia. I was so close to walking off the set, and I was starting to lose the will to live. Either that, or I was going to be put in prison for murder. That's when Sam stepped in; he roared at J.D for treating me like a dog, gave me his coat, and dragged me into the trailer. He introduced himself and the boys and went to deal with J.D personally. He was so angry, I could see just by the look on his face. I hardly knew him, but I already knew we were going to be friends, all of us. I'd never met such down-to-earth men like that before. I'd been around over privileged rich kids who had no sense of entitlement, and who thought the world owed them a living. But these boys, they were solid, friends, brothers. They had each other's' backs. It was...refreshing, new."

He gets this faraway look in his eyes, and I can tell there's more to his story than what he's told me so far.

"We chatted, we got to know each other, and we bonded, even after those few hours. They couldn't stop apologizing for J.D's awful behaviour, and we reshot the video. Ever since that day, we've kept in touch. Whenever I'm in town, we always make time to catch up, or when the boys visit L.A, they always come over to my place for beer and BBQ. It's become a thing for us. I feel like I belong, like I'm part of something...something good."

He smiles a genuine smile, and I regard him intently.

"Something wrong, love?" he asks softly, and I shake my head smiling.

"It just reminded me of the day I met Sam. He came in looking every bit the rock star I'd read about. He had this...air about him. He wore sunglasses and leather, it was all about the leather!"

We both laugh.

"As he walked into the shop, everything just...stopped for a few seconds. I couldn't believe that someone as...beautiful as him existed!"

I chuckle softly, and Nick brushes my arm.

"It was love at first sight, I can tell. I don't usually believe in all that crap, but I can see it in your eyes."

I smile shyly and drop my gaze to the floor.

"Don't be embarrassed, love."

We are interrupted by Chas.

"Nick, you're needed back inside."

He nods and gestures for me to step inside before him. He follows, and we make our way back into the shop. I pull my black rubber gloves on, settle back down, and begin round two.

A few more hours pass of tattooing, filming, harmless flirting, and easy chatter between Nick and me. I hardly notice the film crew, who seem to have a camera trained on our session. After almost eight painstaking hours of working on Nick's tattoo, it is finally complete. The brunette pin-up girl looks almost lifelike; the colours make her stand out, and the aces and the old school lettering add to the charm. I am extremely happy with the design and the way it turned out. Nick looks down and whistles.

"*Wow,* your work is amazing, love. I'm speechless."

His agent laughs.

"Nick Slade speechless, well God damn!"

They both laugh and the camera pans in close to Nick's finished tattoo. Seb comes over, and he nods, pulling me close as he kisses my forehead.

"Exceptional work as always, babe. You make me so proud."

He winks, and his smile is so wide I think his face might crack!

"If Nick doesn't mind, would you photograph it for the shop portfolio, and then we're done for the day."

Nick shakes his head.

"I don't mind at all, mate."

Seb nods and shakes Nick's hand.

"Cheers, man."

They exchange pleasantries and Seb walks across the shop to chat to the T.V crew, leaving me to photograph Nick's ribs on the shop's Nikon D3200 camera. Once I have the image, I spray antiseptic on his ribs, clean the excess ink off, rub Vaseline on the finished tattoo, and cover it with cling film. Nick begins to pull his shirt back on and buttons it up.

"Thank you so much, love. The tattoo is by far one of my favourites, Sam wasn't wrong when he said you were the best."

I smile shyly at his compliment.

"You're welcome, and thank you for requesting me, it was my pleasure."

He nods curtly, and I make my way to the back of the shop. I wash my hands, pull on my coat, and grab my bag. I pull out my phone, go back out into the shop, and hug Seb goodbye.

"See you tomorrow, babe."

He kisses my cheek and Nick wanders casually over with his hands tucked into his pockets. As he stops in front of me, he takes my phone out of my hand, swipes the screen, and begins to type. I narrow my eyes. *What is it with these famous types, thinking they can do whatever they want?* He gives me back my phone.

"I've programmed my number into your phone, love. Call me, and we can meet up for coffee next time I'm back in the U.K."

I nod.

"That would be nice. It's been a pleasure, Nick."

He reaches for my hand, kisses the back of it, and bows gracefully in front of me.

"It was an honour, Miss Harper. Until the next time."

He winks, and I leave the shop with a spring in my step. My step falters as Sam gets out of a car that is idling at the kerb.

Fuck me.

13

Peyton

He leans casually against the black Chevy Warrior at the kerb and tucks his hands into his pockets. His hair is perfectly mussed, and he is wearing a white vest, showcasing his 'My Angel' tattoo across his broad, muscular chest. He has on those faded, ripped jeans, which hang low on his hips, a black belt with a large skull buckle, a pair of motorcycle boots, and a black hoodie unzipped.

"Angel."

It takes a little while for my brain to catch up with itself, and I mentally chastise myself for staring at him.

You told him it was over, and you're standing there eye-fucking him like some sad desperate whore. Get a grip Harper.

"What are you doing here, Sam?"

He chuckles throatily.

"I'm wounded. I thought you'd be pleased to see me after I rocked your world the other night."

He smirks cockily, and that fucking dimple jumps into place.

"You didn't return my text, so here I am. I told you when we were in New York, you can't hide from me anymore, angel. I'll always find you."

I raise my hands in the air in despair and I'm actually mad as hell that he showed up here like this. *Way to mess up my head again, Newbolt.* I go to walk around him, but he steps in front of me, towering over me.

"Don't walk away from me."

He goes to reach for me, but I back away and walk down the street. The hairs on the back of my neck stand to attention, and I know instantly that he is following behind me. But all I feel right now is burning rage towards this frustrating fucking man behind me and all I want to do is slap his beautiful, smug, mother fucking face.

"Was that all I was to you? A fucking adventure? A challenge? Something to be conquered, because I didn't automatically open up my fucking legs to you?" I shout, attracting the attention of passers-by, and he smirks cockily.

"If I recall it didn't really take much for me to get you to open up those gorgeous legs of yours, *repeatedly,* did it, angel?" he rasps and cocks his pierced eyebrow suggestively.

I look at him, agape, and my temper spikes at his words.

"Oh God, Sam, please don't stop, oh yes, oh Sam, please fuck me harder!" He mocks, and that is when my hand shoots out as I slap him hard across his face.

His head snaps to the side, and he chuckles softly. I know we are in public view, but my reasoning seems to have abandoned me at Sam's appalling behaviour. *How fucking dare he.*

"Remember how good we are together, remember how I pleasured you until you screamed my name? How I fucked you so hard that I touched your fucking soul? And how I came so deep inside of you, I fucking put a baby in you?"

His voice is gruff and filled with such pain and torment that it makes my heart ache. We have reached a set of traffic lights and all I want to do is get away from him. I am about to step into the road to put some distance between us, when suddenly, I am flung back into Sam's arms as a car speeds past, beeping its horn at me. My heartbeat quickens, and he pulls me close to him. The scent of him invades my nostrils, and I am rendered speechless as I feel the colour drain from my cheeks. I start to shake violently from almost being killed.

"Hey, hey I've got you, angel. Look at me."

I look up at him and the look of concern in his blazing green eyes makes my heart skip a beat.

Remember that feeling Harper?

"*Jesus,* you're white as a sheet."

He strokes my cheek softly, and I swallow harshly.

"T...Thank you," I manage to stutter out, and he smiles his dazzling smile, disarming me once again.

"No need to thank me, you saved me from myself, once upon a time; I was just returning the favour. Besides, you're way too beautiful to be road kill!"

He smirks and before I know what I'm doing, I am spinning around and crushing my lips so desperately to his, as if I am a starving woman. The feel of his soft lips on mine instantly makes my pussy drip with desire. I relish the scrape of his stubble against my skin and the feel of his hand pressing the back of my head closer to his, as if he can't get close enough to me. The rest of the world ceases to exist in this moment and all I crave is *him*.

I feel his erection pressing into my thigh and his grip on me tightens. I suck his tongue into my mouth, and he lets out a deep growl from within his chest. I reach my hands up and tug the hair at the nape of his neck. He briefly pulls away from our kiss, and we are both standing breathless, as people continue to walk around us, the occasional person wolf-whistling and telling us to "get a room".

"Let's check into a hotel, let me show you what you've been missing. I'm beginning to forget what it feels like to be buried deep in that hot little pussy of yours, even though it was only two days ago," he rasps and my body shivers.

He smiles his famous dimpled smile, and I am overcome with desire for this man. It seems that no matter how much I deny him, I want more of him. He stands in front of me, all six feet four inches of hard, masculine perfection, and I can't say no to those blazing green eyes. I bite my lip piercing suggestively, and I nod. That's all the confirmation he needs as he takes my hand in his and strides with purpose down the bustling street.

We make it to the Hilton Hotel on Pentonville Road, close to the tattoo shop in Islington. He walks up to the receptionist, and she visibly swoons on the spot as she recognises him. Her face lights up as she flicks her long auburn hair over her shoulder and smiles brightly. She flutters her fake eyelashes and straightens her royal blue blouse, so her boobs are in full view. I roll my eyes at her blatant attempt at flirting.

"Good afternoon, Mr. Newbolt, welcome back to The Hilton Hotel. What can I do for you today?"

He smiles his dazzling smile and winks.

"Talia, good to see you again, babe. I'd like a room please, preferably a suite, if you have one available."

She nods and taps on the computer as Sam takes out his wallet, pulling out his credit card.

"Of course, Mr. Newbolt. I'm afraid the only suite we have available is the Presidential Suite."

Sam nods as I stand awkwardly off to the side, mentally talking myself out of being here with the one person I shouldn't be with.

"We'll take it, thank you."

Sam hands his credit card over.

"I expect your discretion, Talia. I don't want any nasty surprises. The press can't know I'm here, do you understand?" Sam says with an air of authority to his voice, and she nods almost robotically.

"Yes, Mr. Newbolt. We pride ourselves on our discretion here at The Hilton."

She swipes his credit card, and she pushes the receipt towards him. Sam signs it, and she hands him back his credit card and the key card to the room. He doesn't give her time to say anything else, because he reaches for my hand and pulls me towards the lift. He presses the call button and I sense all of his control draining from him as we wait in silence for the lift to arrive. The lift arrives in record time, and he pulls me inside. He waits for the doors to close and then he pushes me against the mirrored wall. I am instantly assaulted with Sam's reflection from all angles. He's all muscles, tattoos, and exudes pure strength and power.

"*Fuck,* I can't wait to get you naked, angel; I want you so fucking badly."

As soon as his hands roam over my body, I am instantly on fire for him.

"Sam," I whisper and every nerve in my body is tuned to Sam as he crushes his lips to mine.

I suddenly forget where we are; everything around me ceases to exist, all that exists is Sam and me. His hand finds my breast, cupping it in his large tattooed hand. I find his belt and start to frantically unbuckle it. I unzip his jeans and his hand shoots out, stopping me from going any further.

"Angel, you touch my cock and I'm going to fucking explode. I want to take my time with you; I want to worship and devour every fucking inch of your delicious body," he says gruffly as the lift reaches our floor.

The doors open, and he scoops me up over his shoulder cave man style and strides with purpose down the corridor with me giggling. I cheekily pinch his delectable arse, and he laughs.

"You little minx!"

He slaps my bum, and I yelp at the harsh sting that floods my pussy with need for him to be inside me. He makes it to our room and slips the key card in, unlocking the door. He kicks the door open with his boot, and I don't get a chance to take in the rooms interior as he flings me into the air and I land in the centre of the queen size bed. He pulls off his hoodie and discards it as he crawls between my legs like a hungry lion about to devour its prey. He undresses me slowly, nipping and caressing every inch of my skin as he goes. Soon, I am lying naked and exposed to his blazing green gaze.

"Fucking beautiful," he says huskily as I reach up to strip his vest off.

I fling it across the room and lick my lips at the sight of his tight tattooed abs, lean waist, his thick-corded arms, his hard-muscular pecs, and his washboard stomach.

"Like what you see, angel?" he says with a hint of amusement in his voice, and I nod.

"Always, you're...perfection, Sam."

He chuckles softly.

"I'll take that as a compliment."

He winks, and I reach for his already unbuckled belt, tugging him down so his body is pressed against mine. I wrap my legs around his hips and pull him in for a deep kiss, pressing my lips to his.

"Sam, I want you so badly," I say breathlessly.

"Patience, angel. I'll take care of you, I always do."

His throaty voice is filled with pure desire. He shoves his jeans down his legs, along with his boxers, until he is completely nude before me. His sculpted, statuesque body never ceases to amaze me; his abs look like they are made of stone. He smiles his panty-dropping, dazzling smile and I start to grind my hips against him.

"Sam," I purr seductively, and he presses his lips eagerly against mine.

He coaxes my mouth open wider and slips in his tongue. I suck on his tongue and he growls.

"Fuck," he curses, and I look up at him, his green eyes are hazy with desire.

He reaches down and swipes his long-calloused finger up my slit, causing me to cry out at the feel of his hands on me.

"*Christ,* you're soaking; you're always so wet for me. Tell me you want me, tell me you want me to fuck you."

I look into his eyes, and I swallow hard. The moment I set foot in this hotel room, I knew I wouldn't be able to resist him. He's like a drug, a *fucking addiction.* Every time I am near him, I can't help myself.

"God, Sam, I want you to fuck me like you used to. I need you, and I need your cock inside me," I pant out desperately, and I hate that I sound so needy.

"How do you want me to fuck you, angel? Tell me, I need to hear the words. I love hearing you talk dirty to me. I've missed your filthy mouth."

He grins wickedly.

"I want your big hard cock in my pussy now, Sam."

He snarls like an animal and presses his forehead against mine.

"Forgive me, angel, I'm skipping the foreplay. I need to be buried inside you, right fucking now."

He drives forward and buries his cock inside me. I moan out loud as his piercing rubs a spot inside me that I never knew existed.

"Sam, oh God, Sam."

He growls. I cup my breasts in my hands and mewl softly with every drive of his cock inside me.

"Oh God, Sam. Fuck me, fuck me harder," I cry out as I reach up and wrap my arms around his neck, loving the feel of skin on skin.

My cool skin against his heated skin feels almost too good. He roughly shoves forward, and with each thrust, he pushes me up the bed.

"God, you feel too good...so fucking good."

He throws his head back with pleasure. He increases his thrusts, and his piercing rubbing against my inner walls. His name is like a strangled sob as the first hard tremor of my orgasm hits me. It feels like an earthquake, and all I can do to ground myself is hold onto Sam's thick biceps. Seconds later, Sam growls out his release as he empties his cock inside me. The warmth of his semen inside me reminds me that he didn't use a condom. I shake that thought away as he pulls out of me and collapses on the bed next to me. He pulls me into him and wraps his tattooed arm around me.

I rest my head on his chest and his other hand softly runs through my hair. As my eyelids flutter closed, I start to shake with tiny aftershocks. Sam chuckles softly, and I don't think he understands the extent of what being with him does to me. He makes me lose all sense of control, and I can't say no. He's my weakness, my kryptonite, a habit I just can't kick. He came into my life like a hurricane, a totally unexpected tidal wave that turned my life as I knew it upside down. We both lie in absolute silence for what seems like an eternity, and I idly stroke my fingers down the ridges of his abs.

"I've missed you, angel. So fucking much."

I smile to myself, feeling content with just lying here next to him.

"I've missed you too, Sam."

He pulls me tighter against him.

"Don't run from me anymore, I can't fucking stand it. I need you. Tell me you don't feel the same way. It killed me when you told me it was over between us the other night. I know you think you're doing it to protect me, but I'm no good without you, angel."

He's right, I do feel the same way, but each time I'm with him I mentally talk myself out of being with him. The year I was gone, I was resigned to the fact that I would have to stay hidden permanently, for the sake of my son's safety. A lot has happened over the past few months: leaving Remy behind, returning to England and the life I had before.

"Say something," he says quietly, almost as if he is afraid of my answer.

"I...I'm sorry it has to be this way, Sam."

He sits up and perches on the edge of the bed, scrubbing his hands down his face.

"Just go, I can't keep fucking doing this."

I get up from the bed, dress in silence, and grab my bag.

"I'm so sorry, Sam," I whisper as I turn and walk away.

14

Sam

I've been voted sexiest man of rock in Core magazine. Amy, Cole's fiancée, is the editor and boss at the magazine. She built it up from nothing, and it is one of the most successful women's magazines in the country. She had such a smug look on her face when she announced I had won the poll and instantly bombarded me with ideas for a photo shoot. So here I am, about to be photographed after being primped and preened within an inch of my fucking life. I don't feel like Sam Newbolt, or even my alter ego Bolt. I look in the mirror after an hour in the stylists' chair, and I see a stranger staring back at me. My hair is the only part of me that hasn't had the stylist's treatment, it is styled in my signature soft spikes, which is the only redeeming quality.

I'm currently dressed in a tailored Armani suit, black shirt, and a black tie with a white skull on the bottom. *Very rock n' fucking roll.* I feel like a complete dick. I'm a rock star, *I don't wear fucking suits.* My tie feels like it is strangling me, and it should be fucking illegal to be up at the arse crack of dawn doing a photo shoot. The rest of the boys have a rare day off, and I'm here with the hangover from hell, which is nothing new, and my brain feels like it is trying to evacuate my skull. I got so fucking wasted last night after Peyton left me in the hotel room. I vaguely remember calling Cole to come and get me, because I couldn't see straight or remember where I lived. At one point, I couldn't even remember my own name. *It was one of those nights.* After we had sex in the hotel room, the way she looked at me, I thought there was hope for us. But she seemed to have other ideas.

Fucking women.

I wander aimlessly around the large, stark, black and white set as people fuss over me, and all I can do is fidget awkwardly with the cuffs on my jacket. *I could think of a million places that I'd rather be at than here.* All of my tattoos are virtually unnoticeable. I feel *way* out of my depth, and I'm so far out of my comfort zone that it's not even funny. Give me my leather trousers, biker boots, and a t-shirt and I'm happy as a pig in shit. Me in a suit? Not so much. I continue to fidget with my cuffs when I see a shadow in front of me.

"Here, let me help you with that."

I can't help but recognise the familiar voice and as I lift my gaze. I'm looking into the sparkling steel blue-grey eyes of Piper Gibson. The eyes of my first love, the girl whose heart I shattered into tiny pieces when I cheated on her.

Fuck me, could this day get any weirder?

"Piper Gibson, as I live and fucking breathe. Looking good, babe," I rasp, and she swallows hard as my gaze roams over her hot little body.

"Sam," she says flatly, and I smile devilishly.

"What's a beautiful girl like you doing in a place like this?"

I smirk as she rolls her eyes and takes the cuff of my jacket, fixing the skull shaped cuff links in place.

"I'm the photographer's assistant. Believe me, there's a million places I'd rather be than here with you, Sam," she says bitterly and busies herself with fixing my cuffs.

I place my hand on my heart and mock being injured.

"Ouch, you wound me, babe. And here's me thinking we could pick up from where we left off all those years ago."

I smile, bringing out my dimples, and she tries her best to appear unaffected.

"You cheated on me and ripped out my fucking heart, Sam. I wouldn't sleep with you if you were the last man on this bloody earth," she snaps in a low voice so only I can hear her.

"*Wow,* you got feisty. I like it."

I reach out and run my finger gently along her jaw.

"*Fuck me,*" I curse, and she looks up questioningly into my eyes.

"What's wrong?" she says with a hint of concern in her voice, and I smirk wickedly.

"I'm going to have to go through this whole photo shoot with a raging fucking hard on."

I adjust myself in my trousers and she tries to avert her gaze. She fidgets with the other cuff and clumsily drops the cuff link on the floor. We both bend down at the same time to pick it up from the floor. I lean in close to her as my hand brushes hers.

"Are you imagining what my cock felt like inside you, Piper? How I made you come, over and over again," I say seductively.

She loses her balance and falls flat on her arse. Her face starts to flame with embarrassment as the look on her face tells me she remembers. I try to suppress my laughter as I stand to my full height and offer her my hand. She takes it with a frown as I help her to her feet. As she stands and rights herself, she snatches her hand away from mine.

"You don't get to fucking do that to me, Sam. You and me, it was a long time ago. I'm over it," she says harshly, and I step closer to her.

"If you believe that, then you need to do a better job of making it a little more convincing."

As someone calls her name, Piper spins around and hurries away from me.

My day just got a whole lot more fucking interesting.

I pull my phone out of my pocket and check the time. It feels like I have been waiting here for an eternity; three fucking hours to be exact. I'm starting to get impatient and extremely fucking bored. I tug at my tie, and a stylist rushes over to me. She brushes the shoulders of my suit jacket and straightens my tie.

"Hopefully, not too much longer now, Mr. Newbolt. Is there anything I can get you?" She purrs, and I smile.

I know exactly what she can get me.

"Yes, actually. Could you tell Miss Gibson to meet me in my dressing room, please? We're old friends, and it would be great to catch up with her while I'm waiting."

She nods. I try to make my smile genuine and stride across the set. I make my way to my dressing room and leave the door ajar. I sit down on the sofa and put my feet up on the coffee table. A few minutes later, the door creaks open and in walks Piper. She tucks her black hair behind her ears and stops in front of me with her hands defiantly on her hips. She definitely wasn't like that when we were together...but fuck, if it isn't hot!

"Mr. Newbolt, Sasha said you requested I come to your dressing room?"

I cock my pierced eyebrow at her.

"You're addressing me as Mr. Newbolt, when you know my body just as intimately as I know yours? That birthmark underneath your left breast, the tattoo above your pubic bone."

I purposely speak in a gruff voice, and I visibly see her demeanour change. She runs her hand across her chest and lets out a breath.

"Look, Sam, it's been ten fucking years, I've moved on."

I get up from the sofa and tug my tie loose. I start to stride forward, and with my every stride, she takes a step back, until she hits the door. The door closes, and I flip the lock with a click. I cage her beneath me with my arms either side of her head.

"Admit it, you want me. As soon as I heard your voice, I knew it was you, even after all these years."

I stroke her face and move my hand down to caress her breast softly. She starts to pant, and her breaths come in shallow bursts.

"How much time do you think we have before they're ready for me out there? Honestly?" I ask, and she clears her throat.

"About twenty minutes or so," she says breathlessly.

"Enough time for me to make you come at least twice. Let me make it up to you."

I smile my panty-dropping, and I know I've got her.

"Tell me to stop, babe, and I'll walk away right now. But neither of us want that, do we?" I say cockily as she shakes her head.

"I can't, because I don't want you to stop, Sam," she says with a hint of desperation in her voice.

That is all the permission I need. As I lift her up, she automatically wraps her legs around me, and I shove her up against the door. I press my lips to her neck, and she shivers in my arms. I chuckle softly against her.

"Some things never change, babe."

She laughs softly and melodically, just the way I remember from all those years ago.

"Sam," she croons and runs her fingers through my hair. "Holy fuck, you're even more perfect now, than you were ten years ago," she blurts out, and I laugh throatily.

"*Wow,* compliments as well. I'm honoured," I rasp, and she tugs my hair sharply, causing me to growl.

"There's no need for violence. If you want me to fuck you, you only have to ask me, Pipe."

She narrows her eyes.

"No one's called me Pipe in years. I swear you used to do it to wind me up on purpose, you fucking fiend!"

I cock my pierced eyebrow.

"*Fiend?* Now I know you can do better than that, babe. You used to use some pretty colourful insults. If I remember right, you were quite fond of the term cockwomble."

She grins widely, and I don't think I've ever seen her smile like that.

"You've got such a pretty smile, babe."

She rolls her eyes.

"*Oh please.* Are those the lines you're using these days?"

I smirk and nip her neck with my teeth, causing her to yelp out loud.

"I'll have you know my lines work just fine, they worked on you for years."

She goes to shove me away from her, but I capture her wrists in one of my hands and hold them captive above her head.

"Yeah, they worked just fine until you stuck your cock in some other whore, like I meant nothing, Sam."

It's my turn to roll my eyes as she struggles in my grip.

"Let me guess, you tripped, and your cock happened to land in her vagina?"

I throw my head back and laugh.

"Nice," I say sarcastically as she looks up at me defiantly, and I crush my lips to hers. "You want to get that pent-up frustration out? Then fuck me like you hate me."

I let go of her hands and she tugs my hair hard as her lips nip mine. She reaches for the zip on my trousers and yanks it down. She starts to pant in my mouth, and I knead her breast in my hand. She pulls away from our kiss and moans softly in my ear.

"Sam, condom," she says breathlessly.

"In my wallet."

She reaches down and palms my erection in her hand. I let out a growl from deep within my throat and go to yank my tie off when the door I have her pinned to bangs sharply.

"Mr. Newbolt, we're ready for you now."

Talk about fucking shitty timing.

I clear my throat as I watch Piper trying to straighten herself out.

"I'll be out in a second," I manage to say coolly and press my forehead to Piper's.

"Until next time, Piper."

I straight my tie, wink, and zip my trousers back up. I nod curtly and leave the room to the sound of her quietly cursing to herself.

I enter the set and Amy is waiting for me. She beams as I approach her and pull her in for a hug.

"Aims, good to see you, babe."

She kisses my cheek.

"You too, babe. Looking sharp."

I shake my head.

"I told you, I don't do fucking suits."

I pull away from our embrace, and she chuckles softly.

"Are you pouting, Newbolt?"

I cock my pierced eyebrow.

"Really, Aims?"

She throws her head back and laughs.

"*You are.* You wait until Cole and the boys hear about this."

I narrow my eyes.

"You're a hard woman, Lightman."

She winks.

"That's why you love me, sugar. Is the barbeque at your parents' estate still on for the weekend?"

I look at her. I'd fucking forgotten about that. My mum and dad host barbeques in the summer months. It's like some sort of ritual. Me, my dad, and my brothers' man the barbeque, like it's some sort of dick swinging contest, and the women eat, drink, and incessantly bitch about each other.

"I hear Peyton's going to be there."

My eyes widen. *Peyton, at my parents' house?* I don't fucking think so.

"Peyton? Where did you hear that?"

Amy smiles.

"Your mum told me. She asked Ruby to invite her. They want to spend some time with their grandson, and what a better way to do that than to invite her to their annual barbeque? I'm sure it'll be fine, sugar. Look, I know you're having some issues right now, but you share a kid now. It's important that you get on."

I shake my head, unable to get my head around the fact that my ex, the mother of my child, the woman who I love more than anything else in the world, is going to be at my parents' house this weekend.

Fuck me.

15

Peyton

The next day, after my hotel encounter with Sam, I wake up, shower, and get ready for work almost on autopilot. Dexter is sitting at the breakfast bar with Freddie on his lap, wearing a grey vest, black jogging bottoms, eating cereal, and reading the newspaper. His hair is messy and still damp from the shower.

"Morning, sis."

He smiles around a mouthful of cereal.

"Morning, Dex. What are you looking so happy about this morning?"

He puts his spoon down and hands Freddie to me. I take him and inhale his unique baby smell, there's nothing like it.

"Good morning, handsome boy."

He blows a raspberry and claps his hands excitedly.

"Grace called me last night and said she's ready to talk."

I smile. I'm so happy that my brother's fiancée, Grace, has agreed to speak to him.

"That's great, Dex! I'm so happy for you."

Dexter continues to eat his cereal with a permanent grin on his face. It is the first time I've seen him smile properly in days. An hour passes, I've given Freddie his breakfast, dressed him, and I'm ready for work. I grab my denim jacket, pull it on, and grab my bag while checking my hair in the mirror. Today, I'm opting for ripped denim cropped jeans, red Converse, and a red racer back vest which has the word *#Selfie* on the front in large white letters.

"Ruby's coming over to watch Freddie in a little while."

He nods and salutes as Kai steps out of his room in his signature black suit.

"See ya later, sis."

He winks, and Kai nods curtly.

"Bye Dex, bye Freddie."

I kiss Freddie on his forehead and wave as Kai and me leave for work.

We make the journey to the tattoo shop in relative silence just like every morning. Kai parks the car, I get out and make my way to the shop with Kai following five steps behind. It still amazes me that I have a security detail.

When I get to the shop, the familiar calming smell of disinfectant greets me. Seb is there before me, as always, with my morning pick-me-up: a cup of Starbucks finest coffee waiting for me at my work station. My usual is a large espresso macchiato, one sugar, easy on the milk.

It really is like I've never been away.

"Morning, honey bunny."

Seb beams, and I smile.

"Good morning, pumpkin."

I wink as I take the lid off my coffee and take a welcome sip. Harlowe, our new temporary shop receptionist, waves enthusiastically from the front desk.

"Morning, pet," she says in a thick Geordie accent.

"Morning H."

I beam, and I'm instantly reminded why I love my job so much. The shop, the clients, and more importantly, the people I work with. They all contribute to making the days so much more worth it. I make my way to the back of the shop, take off my coat, and check my phone before I stow my bag away. I have a missed call from Ruby. I dial her number and call her back.

"Hey, babe," she says brightly.

"Hey Rubes, what's up?"

She laughs.

"Well...I was wondering if you wanted to meet for lunch? Maybe pick up a little something for the barbeque on Saturday, something that might bring a certain Mr. Newbolt to his knees? And I want to discuss something with you, me and Jax are having an engagement party...he popped the question."

She squeals.

"OH-MY-GOD!"

I find myself screaming enthusiastically, and my heart slams against my ribcage, reminding me of when it was Sam and me celebrating our engagement.

"That's amazing! I'm so happy for you, Ruby."

She giggles. She actually *giggles* like a schoolgirl. My best friend getting married to Jackson Chase. *Wow!*

"I couldn't wait to tell you! We'll talk more about it when I see you, but I've got a surprise for you too, babe. You'll love it, I promise. I'll come to the shop around twelve thirty, I'll bring Freddie, love ya."

"Right back at ya, Rubes. See you later."

"Byeeeee!" She says in a sing-song voice and hangs up.

I roll my eyes and smile to myself. I put my phone away and make my way back into the main vestibule of the shop. The film crew aren't in today, but we're still booked solid until the shop closes. I walk over to my workstation to get prepared and set up for the day ahead.

Today's going to be a busy one.

My extremely busy morning of tattooing goes by quickly, and before I know it, the door to the shop is opening. The bell rings, and Ruby struts in, her heels clicking across the floor. At five feet eight with long shoulder length, jet-black hair, flawless olive skin, and dark hazel eyes, she looks like she could model for Vogue, even at almost six months pregnant. She is wearing a black t-shirt with white hand prints on which says, 'Hands off the Bump', a pair of loose black linen trousers, and four-inch heels.

"Hey Seb, hey babe," she says in her familiar singsong voice.

She kisses me on the cheek, and I am suddenly filled with the sweet familiar scent of her *Ed Hardy* perfume and feel a calm confidence just from her presence.

"Hey babe, where's Freddie?" I say in a panicked voice.

"Relax, he's totally fine. Dexter's still at your place, and he told me he would look after him, so we could have some girl time."

I instantly relax as I wipe down my station after my last tattoo of the morning. Ruby is practically bouncing with excitement.

"Hurry up."

I roll my eyes and laugh at her impatience.

"Give me five minutes."

I finish wiping my station, rush to the back of the shop, wash my hands, and dry them on a towel. I pull on my jacket and grab my bag. I go back out into the shop and Ruby rolls her eyes dramatically.

"About bloody time!"

I smirk as Ruby links my arm and we leave the shop. We walk down the high street to a quaint little bistro called Swingin' Eli's Bistro. This place was a regular haunt and a particular favourite of Ruby's and mine. It is famous for its homemade, authentic Southern American food. The decor is old school swing, with paintings of old swing artists scattered on the walls. We are in there so often that we sit at the same table by the window and the owner, Eli, knows us by name as well as exactly what we're going to order. Eli is a tall Southern American man in his mid-sixties, with coffee coloured skin, greying hair, and a wide infectious smile. His eyes are warm, brown, and friendly. We walk in and he has our drinks ready: a strawberry milkshake for Ruby, and a caramel hot chocolate for me.

"Good afternoon, Peyton, Ruby."

He nods politely. He has written down our order and is smiling for us to take a seat at our usual table. We take our drinks from the counter and sit down opposite each other. I'm barely in my seat when Ruby practically squeals in my face.

"I've got so much to tell you, babe!" she says enthusiastically. "First, your surprise."

She looks over to the door and beckons someone to come in. I can't hide the shock on my face when I find myself looking into the familiar, deep hazel eyes of Remy Logan. The man who looked after me and my baby in the year I was gone. *My rock, my first love.* He looks so different to the way he did the day I left him. His long brown hair is now short and slicked back, his square jaw is stubbled, and he looks visibly thinner and more defined.

"Remy."

He smiles, and I stand up pulling him in for a hug. He instantly embraces me, and it feels familiar and safe. I step back and take him in.

"*Wow!* You look...different."

He smiles a boyish grin which lights up his whole face.

"Ah, it was time for a change, beaut," he says nonchalantly.

He is wearing dark blue jeans which cling to his muscular thighs, a red dress shirt with the sleeves rolled up and three buttons undone, and a pair of black Oxfords.

"*Fuck me*, Peyton Harper speechless, *wow!*"

He laughs, and I look up into his deep brown eyes. The love he feels for me clear in his eyes. I start to wonder what his reasons are for coming to England after he's built a life for himself back in the States.

"I came back for Ruby and Jackson's engagement party, just in case you were wondering. I booked the first available flight."

I nod, and he winks, as if reading my mind. Ruby looks from me to Remy, taking in our reunion. An awkward silence passes as Remy pulls up a chair from the table next to us and goes to the counter to order a drink. I turn to Ruby and narrow my eyes at her.

I'm so fucking mad right now.

"What the fuck, Ruby? Why didn't you tell me he was coming here? A little warning would have been nice," I snap in a hushed tone and she rolls her eyes dramatically.

"What, and give you a chance to make an excuse not to see him? He's my brother! You had sex with him and then left the country, for fucks sake! It was you who put the ocean between you this time! He was coming back for our engagement party anyway, which is next weekend by the way. He's in love with you, Peyton. By the way you're looking at him, the feelings reciprocated. Now I know why you're not with Sam, it's *so* obvious."

I shake my head.

"No, it doesn't hide the fact that you fucking blindsided me! He was my first love, Ruby. He took my virginity, and I'll always have feelings for him, but it *can't* happen with us. It was a one-time thing, never to be repeated."

She takes a sip of her milkshake and regards me intently.

"*Bullshit!* You're blushing, Peyton Leigh Harper. I do believe you're in love with my brother."

She claps her hands excitedly.

"Before you start planning the wedding, I'm still in love with Sam."

She cocks her perfectly groomed eyebrows at me.

"If you truly loved him, you'd be with him. And by the way, we're going to be discussing the two-page spread in today's newspaper, and you're going to give me all the gory details, you slut!"

We both laugh, and Remy puts his cup down and sits down to join us.

"So, how are my two favourite girls?"

His voice washes over me like a cool calming breeze as he looks at me with familiar hazel eyes. Eyes that he can't take off me. I drop my gaze, and his mouth forms a straight line. Ruby stands up abruptly.

"I need to pee; fucking pregnancy is a nightmare. I'll be right back," she announces as she winks at me, and I silently curse her as she struts away.

Bitch.

Remy reaches for my hand, and I let him hold it. It feels warm, safe, familiar and everything I've missed.

"That look in your eyes worries me, beaut," he says simply, and my eyes lock with his.

As I look into deep brown depths, my eyes fill with tears.

"*Fuck me*, come here."

He pulls me into his arms, and I cling to him, as if he is a life raft.

"Rem," I sob, and he runs his hands up my back, instantly soothing me.

"Hey, shhh, it's ok. I've got you. I'm here, beautiful."

I nuzzle my face into his chest, and he squeezes me tighter.

"The place is so quiet without you and the little guy. Santa Monica misses you."

I pull away and look up at him. He swipes his thumb underneath my eye, catching my tears.

"Coming back here was such a fucking mistake, Rem. Why didn't I listen to you?"

He smirks wickedly.

"Because, I told you, no one ever listens to the cripple!"

I frown, and he smiles, smoothing the frown line between my eyes.

"Not funny, Rem."

He rolls his eyes, and with that action, he reminds me so much of Ruby.

"We could have been happy. That night we spent together was one of the best nights of my life, then I woke up the next morning and you were gone. I knew exactly what you were doing, I have the ability to read you like a book, Peyton."

My name leaves his lips like a prayer. A feeling of utter regret washes over me and threatens to drown me in it.

"I take it the reunion with a certain Mr. Newbolt didn't go as planned then, beaut?"

I squeeze my eyes shut at the mention of Sam's name.

"Don't. It's all such a fucking mess, Rem. I should have fucking listened to you, I never should have come back here."

He moves his chair closer to mine. He tucks a strand of hair behind my ear and presses his forehead to mine.

"I lie awake at night longing to hear those words from your lips. Please, come back to Santa Monica with me, Peyton."

He moves away from me and curses, *"Fuck."*

My eyes widen at his question as Ruby chooses that moment to re-join us.

"Everything alright?" she asks, and I finish my drink in three mouthfuls.

I pull out my phone, pretending to tap the screen as I take out some money to cover my lunch. I place it on the table. *I have to get out of here.*

"I'm sorry, I have to get back to work, babe," I lie, and she looks at me questioningly.

"We need to talk about the engagement party, I wanted to ask you to be my maid of honour."

I take a deep breath.

"I'd be...*wow*, I'd be honoured, babe. Of course I'll be your maid of honour, thank you."

I smile, and she narrows her eyes, as if she knows something is wrong. But she doesn't say anything, which I am grateful for.

"Seb just called, and a walk-in client has been asking for me. I need to go, come to the flat tonight, and we'll talk more, I promise. I'm sorry."

I kiss her cheek, and Remy gets to his feet.

"Beaut, please, don't go," Remy pleads with me to stay, but I don't.

I just turn and rush out of the bistro as quickly as I can. Kai is standing next to his black 4x4 at the kerb.

"Everything ok, Miss Harper?"

I nod and try to catch my breath.

"Yeah, everything's...brilliant Kai, thanks. I have to get back to work."

He nods curtly, and I climb into the passenger seat. He gets in the driver's seat and pulls smoothly out into the traffic. I get back to the shop in record time and all I can think about is the reappearance of Remy. Seeing him again bought back old feelings, and I had to get as far away from him as possible.

I do not need any more complications in my life.

The afternoon goes by in a flash, and before I know it, it is time for the shop to close. I am finishing up cleaning and wrapping up my last tattoo in cling film, when Seb comes over to join me.

"Babe?"

He looks at me questioningly. I smile at my last client, a young boy of around nineteen with sandy brown hair.

"Thank you so much," he says enthusiastically, and I nod.

"You're very welcome, honey. It was my pleasure."

He stands up and shakes my hand.

"Harlowe will take care of you at the front desk."

I take off my black rubber gloves and throw them into the bin. I begin to tidy and clean my workstation. Seb stops me.

"Babe, stop. I'll take care of that." He brushes my arm. "Do you want to talk about it?"

I shake my head.

"I'll be fine, Seb, honestly."

He moves closer to me and towers over me. He tips my chin up so I am looking up into his worried eyes.

"Don't give me that bullshit, babe. You know me better than that, I know when something's bugging you."

The doorbell of the shop sounds, and that signals the end of our day.

"I've got some vodka in the back."

I smile. *I love how Seb knows me so well.*

"It's in the top drawer of the filing cabinet. H, will you break down and clean Peyton's workstation, please?" Seb asks Harlowe.

"Yes, boss," she calls out.

I go into the back and wash my hands. I open the top drawer of the cabinet and take out the bottle of vodka. I take a long pull from the bottle. The fiery liquid burns, causing a delicious warmth in my stomach. I screw the lid back on and take my phone out of my bag.

Change of plans

Wenlock and Essex for a well-earned drink
No more nasty surprises! ;)
P xx

I text Ruby, and she texts back almost instantly.

Promise ;)
Sam's coming over to take Freddie
Meet you @ 8
R xx

I smile to myself at the thought of Sam spending time with his son. Things might not be good between us, but he deserves to know his son. Seb comes into the back and wraps his arms around me.

"Now, do you want to tell me why you're looking so sad?"

We sit down on the sofa with the vodka, and I begin to tell him all about my time in Santa Monica, J.D, Remy, my identity change, giving birth to Freddie, all up until I found out Sam had been kidnapped and stabbed by J.D. Seb listens intently, and by the time I have finished, I feel like a weight has been lifted off my shoulders.

"*Fuck me,* babe, I had no idea."

His eyes widen, and he sinks back into his seat as he pulls me into his side.

"Why didn't you tell me all of this sooner? I could have helped, I could have been there for you!"

He moves slightly away from me and scrubs his hands down his face.

"I haven't been myself for this past year, Seb. It was my burden to carry, and I've had to be strong for my little boy."

He shakes his head.

"That's no reason why you shouldered all that on your own, babe. It wasn't your call to make. This Remy bloke sounds like a...knight in shining fucking armour, and I'd love to shake the bloke by the hand."

I laugh.

"Well you might be able to do just that, he's back. That's why I came back early from lunch. Ruby kind of just sprung it on me, he showed up at Eli's."

Seb's eyes widen, and he smiles.

"*Fuck me,* it's like a bloody soap opera!"

We both laugh.

"Do you want to join Ruby and me for drinks at the Wenlock? Bring Willow, it would be great to see her."

He nods and looks at his watch.

"Yeah, we'd love to. I'll give her a call."

I get up from the sofa, pull on my coat, and grab my bag. In the time it takes me to get ready to leave, Seb has called Willow and they're both going to meet us there at eight. I kiss Seb on the cheek, promising to see him in a little while, and leave the shop.

After getting back home to an empty flat and a note from Dexter in his familiar scrawl, which reads:

Peyton
Gone for that chat with Grace
Sam's got Freddie
Wish me luck!
Don't wait up sis!
Dex xx

I roll my eyes and smile to myself as I read his note which is stuck to the fridge with a fridge magnet. I shower in record time, tousle my short hair into loose waves, apply my usual natural make up, and opt for a short sleeveless purple dress, with leather panels running down either side. I team it with leather accessories, feather earrings, and my purple leopard print peep toe heels. I slick on some lip gloss and grab my skull clutch bag. I check my reflection one last time in the mirror before I head downstairs to meet Kai, who is waiting to drive me to the bar.

The Wenlock and Essex is a large bar with an urban bordello and a unique burlesque style. Its ruby-red ceiling, tassel lampshades, and candelabras showcase its solid Wild West saloon-style bar. It is one of my favourite bars and the food is to die for. It's just what I need to unwind after today. I step inside and there is a decent crowd for a week night. Ruby is perched on a bar stool and waves enthusiastically. I walk over and join her, with Kai an acceptable distance away.

"Hey babe."

She jumps off her stool and throws her arms around me. I hug her back and kiss her on the cheek. I pull away and take her in. Her long dark hair is pulled into a high ponytail, she is wearing a cream Peter Pan style collar dress, her bump protruding in front of her, and she is wearing nude heels, and simple diamond stud earrings. She looks even more pregnant now than she did earlier, which makes me smile. We both perch on two free barstools and I order some drinks: A soft drink for Ruby and this place boasts the best cocktails, my favourite is called a Pont berry, vodka, cranberry, and cassis liqueur, so I order one of those for myself. I reach into my bag, and before I can pull out some money, a familiar voice has my head snapping up.

"I'll get those, baby cakes."

Callum, my ex. He stumbles from one side to the other, he's clearly more than a little drunk. I look up into light brown smiling eyes, and I instantly feel sick. I can't believe I ever dated this drunken moron. His usually blonde hair is darker than it was the last time I saw him. he is wearing tight black jeans, a black t-shirt, and a black blazer with the sleeves rolled up. He pulls out a twenty-pound note from his pocket and throws it on the bar.

"Whiskey please, bar keep, and whatever these beautiful ladies are having."

I look at the bar man and smile.

"We'll get our own, thanks, mate."

Callum pushes his money over the bar.

"I insist, baby cakes. I wondered how long it would be before I saw your beautiful face again," he slurs, and I roll my eyes.

Ruby jumps off her bar stool and jabs her finger in Callum's chest.

"What did I tell you the last time I saw you, you pathetic little fucking worm? I told you I'd cut your balls off and feed them to you, although that's not what Brody said to you, is it?"

Callum's face turns a ghostly shade paler as he remembers.

What the fuck did Brody say to him on the night of Sam's birthday all those months ago?

"We'll catch up when your guard dog has disappeared, baby cakes."

He winks, and Ruby's eyes widen.

"He did *not* just say that to me, Peyton? Oi! Fuck face!"

She goes to go after him, until I step in.

"Leave it, Rubes, he's not worth it."

I placate her as Callum takes a step forward, and Kai moves in front of me.

"I suggest you leave well alone, if you know what's good for you," Kai says menacingly in his American twang.

Callum cocks his eyebrow.

"And who's this fucking clown, baby cakes?"

Kai squares his shoulders and puts his hands on his hips in a move that Arnold Schwarzenegger would be proud of.

"This clown is my bodyguard. Kai, this is my dickhead ex. I'm sure you've been filled in on our history?"

He nods.

"Yes ma'am. Now, you've got two choices, either walk away, or I can take you outside and teach you a fucking lesson you'll never forget. Which is going to be?"

Callum holds his hands up defensively and stumbles backwards.

"Now apologise to the ladies."

Kai lifts his head and narrows his eyes in Callum's direction. The look on Callum's face is priceless, he actually looks like he's going to shit himself!

"I'm sorry," Callum says sheepishly, and Kai nods curtly.

"Now fuck off."

Callum stumbles off across to the other side of the bar. Ruby kisses Kai on the cheek, and I swear he actually blushes!

"There's perks to having a security detail! I wonder if I can get Jax to hire one for me!"

Ruby and I both laugh as Seb and Willow arrive. I smile at Seb and hug him. He pulls me in for one of his famous bear hugs and Willow squeals excitedly. She looks exactly the same as she did the last time I saw her. She is average height, slim, with black hair short on the one side and long on the other. She has Sam's green eyes and a warm dimpled smile. She is wearing a green skater dress and green knee-high Converse.

"Peyton!"

She shoves Seb playfully out of the way and hugs me tightly as she bounces up and down.

"It's so good to see you."

Ruby smiles, and Willow pulls away from me to hug her. We spend a few hours drinking, dancing, chatting, and catching up. Ruby tells me that Jax proposed with the help of a guy he used to busk with. He sang will you marry me, and Jax dropped down on one knee outside Brent Cross tube station. She accepted instantly, and my heart slams against my chest when I think about how Sam proposed to me in Vegas. It seems like a lifetime ago.

I finish my drink in one mouthful and put the glass down on the table.

"I need to use the loo, I'll be back in a sec," I say in a sing-song voice, and I suddenly feel a little drunk.

Ruby stands up.

"I'll come with you, babe."

We gossip all the way to the toilet, and it's good to be out with two of my best friends. I do what I need to, wash my hands, and re-apply my smudged make up. I smack my lips together and finger comb my hair. *That will have to do.* I fling open the toilet door and leaning against the wall waiting for me is Kai, and next to him is Callum. They are having a heated discussion. *Shit.* Callum has his hands tucked casually into his pockets.

"Baby cakes," He slurs and smiles.

He is tall, but his lean frame is nothing compared to Sam's, and I curse myself for thinking of him. Ruby narrows her eyes.

"Didn't Captain America make it clear enough for you?" Ruby snaps and points to Kai with her perfectly manicured fingernail.

"I just want to talk to Peyton, alone, for five minutes. That's all."

Kai steps forward, but I stop him by holding up my finger. I look from Ruby, to Kai, and back to Callum.

"How have you been, baby cakes?"

Ruby and I go to walk around but he stops me. Kai steps between us.

"I won't fucking tell you again," Kai says with a threatening edge to his voice, and I step around him. "Peyton, what are you doing?" Kai questions, and I move closer to Callum until we are practically nose to nose.

"You don't deserve even five fucking seconds of my time, Callum."

I lift my knee up and knee him as hard as I can in his balls. He lets out a high-pitched yelp and drops to his knees, clutching his crotch area.

"You come anywhere near me again and I swear to God, it won't be your fucking balls next time," I say with a hint of warning to my voice.

I spin on my heel and head back to our table with the sound of Ruby whooping behind me.

16

J.D

All the months of watching her all over him, the way he looked at her, as if she was the only person in the world. Lying awake at night on the tour bus, listening to the way he pleasured her, the raw, carnal, animalistic noises he made as he found his release.

It should have been me.

She had to die, it was the only way. He will love me the way I love him, the way I have always loved him. Ever since I first laid eyes on him all those years ago. His boyish charm, his smile, his dimples, and his sweet, introverted nature. The way he trembled when we made love, the way his body felt pressed against mine, the softness of his luscious pink lips on mine. In the ten years I have known him, he has blossomed from a lanky, awkward, shy boy into a muscular, tattooed, confident man. I will never stop wanting him, no matter how much time passes.

That age-old Newton theory of 'every action has an equal and opposite reaction'. That is the reason I am in prison. I was so blinded by my feelings for him, that I hurt the only man I have ever truly loved. I took the life of his fiancée and his unborn baby, but I am not sorry for that. I would do it all over again in a heartbeat if it meant that I got to spend just one more day with him.

The truth is, no one knows what it's like to be me, not even Sam. No one has walked my path, no one has walked a mile in my shoes. No one in here cares what or who I once was out there. I am just a number, a faceless anomaly, *a fucking filthy criminal*. But my only crime was committed out of love. It was a crime of passion.

In here, all I have is time, time to think and time to reflect. I keep to myself, taking solace in the silence of my cell. The only thing I have to look forward to in here are my phone calls with the only person that truly understands my feelings for him. We are allowed out in the yard and I take comfort from those minutes I spend with the blazing sun on my skin. For a moment, I forget I am incarcerated for murder, kidnapping, and injuring the man I love. He haunts my dreams as I go over and over the hurtful words he said.

"How could you ever think I had fucking feelings for you? What happened between us all those years ago was purely for my career. I did it for the boys, and I took one for the team. I wanted my music career so badly I fucked my manager. And you know what? It wasn't even that good, you fucking sick, pathetic pervert!"

I understand totally that he was angry, and I will never forgive myself for hurting him, but I *have* to explain. I have to make him understand that my actions were justified; all of it was for him and only him. I might have acted a little irrationally, but love makes everyone irrational, right? I am always in quiet control; I am rarely careless and reckless, but he has this adverse effect on me. Those sparkling green eyes of his, the tattoos, those rock-hard abs, the tight curve of his arse, all have my mind turning to jelly. I can't think rationally when he is near me, I am assaulted and tortured by the scent of him. I am devastated that I will never experience his touch, his intoxicating scent, and that I will never get to drink in the sight of his perfect body again.

As I am sitting in my cell, contemplating, I am struck with an idea. I will write him a letter. I open the drawer next to my bed and pull out the note pad and a pencil, which are next to the bible that I have found solace in.

Dearest Sam,

Before I carry on know this, I am sorry for hurting you, but I had to make you understand that all of this was for you and for you alone. I know you will never forgive me, but I have to try to make you understand that my actions were carried out purely out of my love for you. I believe that 100%. That night we spent together, all those years ago, I know you felt it too. All these years I have protected you, protected your assets from the gold diggers, and waited patiently for you to realise your true feelings for me. In here, all I have is time to think about you and us, what could have been. We could have been happy, Sam. Please know, I never meant to hurt you. Know that one day we will be together. I will love you always, and that thought is what keeps me warm at night.

All my love

John xxx

The only redeeming quality of being in here, confined to a cell, is you get to think about the things that didn't seem important before and the insignificant things that are just...*meaningless*. Like, what defines a freak? Am I a freak for falling in love with Sam? Is Sam a freak for denying his sexuality? Am I a freak for killing the woman he loved and their baby? For denying him his happy ever after? Is Peyton a freak for falling in love with a man so out of her league and who is, in short, broken? The answer to that question is like attempting to answer the meaning of life. There is more than one answer. It's complex, complicated, and fucked up beyond all recognition.

When I was a boy, I always used to think there was monsters hiding under my bed. As I've grown older, I believe that sometimes monsters and demons lurk in the shadows. Sometimes they hide in plain sight, waiting to strike when we least expect them. My demon was chained up for ten years, craving and yearning its drug of choice. *Sam Newbolt.* My addiction, my own personal unique brand of cocaine. An addiction I cannot break, a habit I just cannot quit.

I know absolutely nothing about the American prison system, all I know is that I'm awaiting trial, which could take months. After being refused bail, I am being held in Washington State Penitentiary, which is a medium security prison. Also, because of my high profile, I am at risk from the other prisoners. Therefore, I have been placed in segregation. I have only been incarcerated for a few days, but it feels like so much longer.

I sit in my cell, eating my breakfast in relative silence. The door to my cell is open and the only noise I can hear is the T.V from the guards' station across the hallway.

"Peyton Harper, tattoo artist and former fiancée of Rancid Vengeance front man, Samson Newbolt, has been found alive and well after being allegedly murdered by the band's then manager, John Dalton a.k.a Johnnie Diamond. Police are questioning Miss Harper, following up on their line of enquiry. Nevertheless, the question on everyone's lips is, was this a genuine incident, or a cruel trick to fool Newbolt and the world into thinking she was dead? Only

time will tell. Harper's family refused comment, and we are eagerly awaiting a
statement from Rancid Vengeance."

My head snaps up as I hear the news report and the mention of my name.
How the fuck can she be alive? *I killed her!* I drove a knife through her
chest; I watched the life fade from her eyes. I *fucking* buried her! I launch my
breakfast tray against the wall in a fit of rage, and I perch on the edge of the
excuse they call a bed. I am trembling with such anger. *What the fuck?* I have
to talk to Anna. It can't be true. It can't be. I pace my cell, running my hands
frantically through my hair. *Fuck, fuck, fuck.* I need to speak to Anna, *now.*

I make my way out of my cell and down the corridor to where the phones
are. I take my phone card out of my pocket, put it into the slot, and I dial the
number, which I have memorised. It rings twice before she answers, and I've
never been so relieved to hear her voice.

"Hello, Anna? It's me," I say with an air of panic to my otherwise calm
voice.

"John, how are you? It's so good to hear your voice," she says cheerily.

"You too, Anna. I've just seen the news, is it true?" I blurt out, and she
sighs heavily.

"Yes, unfortunately, it's true. I wondered how long it would be until you
saw the news. I thought you eliminated the problem, John?"

My shoulders sag as she says those words.

"I did, at least I thought I did. Are they together? Is he fucking her?" I
ask curiously.

"She's been to see him at the hospital, that's all I know so far. I'm sorry I
can't tell you anymore. I know how you feel about him," she says sadly, and I
sigh.

"There's not a day that goes by where I don't think about him, Anna."

There is a slight pause.

"I'm so sorry, John, I know this must be hurting you."

I squeeze my eyes briefly shut as she speaks again.

"After everything you did for me, after what happened, I fucked up the
one thing you needed me to do, and now you're in prison. I'm so sorry," she
says with such emotion in her voice. "I wish there was a way I could make this
right."

I take in her words, and I shake my head.

"What's done is done, there's no changing the past, Anna. It's over," I say, with more than a hint of defeat in my voice.

I've accepted my fate, only God can judge me now.

17

Peyton

The week ended pretty much as it begun, uneventful. Before I know it, Saturday has rolled around. Today is the day of the barbeque at the Newbolt's house in Kent. Ruby has assisted me in getting ready and today. I'm opting for a fifties prom dress, it is white with black polka dots and it has a halter neck, which accentuates my boobs. The skirt is full and sits at my knees, showing off my leg tattoos. I am wearing a pair of white Converse, my usual natural make-up, and a white rose in my hair. Ruby finishes applying my lip gloss and places her hands on her hips, admiring her handiwork.

"You look gorgeous, babe."

She smoothes my hair, and I suddenly feel butterflies forming in my stomach. I place my hand on my stomach and puff out my cheeks.

"Why do I feel so fucking nervous, Rubes?"

She smiles softly.

"It's the first time you've been around any of them properly since you came home. It's natural, babe, you'll be fine. I'll be right there with you, I promise."

She kisses me on the cheek and gives my hair one final fluff. She smiles with satisfaction and links my arm with hers.

"Ready?"

I nod and manage a weak smile. *I'm ready as I'll ever be.*

As we approach the Newbolt's estate in Ashford, Kent, I find myself once again awestruck at the looming property in front of us. It is a detached five-bedroom house, with a double garage, stables, and around three acres of land. I remember Sam explaining to me, all those months ago, that it was built in the style of a traditional Kent barn.

Ruby, Jax, Freddie, and I make our way to the front door. We are greeted by Lori Newbolt, who looks exactly the same as I remember her. She is a tall, slender, striking older woman, with dark brown jaw length hair. She has blue-green eyes and a bright red lipsticked smile. She is wearing a soft pink and white floor length maxi dress, with white Jackie O style glasses perched on top of her head.

"Ruby, Jackson, how lovely to see you both."

She pulls Jax in for a hug and air kisses Ruby on both cheeks. Her face seems to lose its softness as she takes me in.

"Peyton, good of you to come."

She pouts and nods curtly. Her face lights up as she catches sight of Freddie.

"Hello Freddie, aren't you a handsome boy? Just like your daddy," she croons and plucks Freddie from my arms.

"Come to nana, come inside."

He squeals with delight, and I happily let her take him inside the house. We all head inside, and I hang back to talk to Ruby as Jax strides off to find Sam.

"This was a bad idea, Ruby," I whisper, and she clutches my arm.

"Don't be silly. It's going to be fine, babe, I promise. At least stay for a few drinks, for me."

She sticks out her bottom lip, and I roll my eyes as she leads me through the house and into the garden. As we step into the large garden, it feels almost normal. Except it isn't, not really. Sam's family are all there: Marlowe, Lori, Brandon, Elijah, Willow, and a visibly pregnant Savannah. My face drops as I catch sight of Callum with his arm casually slung around Savannah's neck. I spot the Lightning Bolts, Milo and Seth, as well as Cole, Amy and Addison. Nearby are the boys, Lucas, Jax, Brody, as well as Seb and the bands new manager, Alistair, his wife Lexi, their twin girls, Autumn and Bella, and Alistair's six-year-old son Alfie. It is quite a gathering, and it seems like a lot has changed since we last came together.

The weather is warm and sunny, but I feel awkward being here. Ruby convinced me to come here, but I'm already regretting the decision. Ruby breezes around the garden, saying hello to everyone as if it's second nature, and I hang back like the new kid in the school playground.

Someone shoot me now.

My skin prickles as I catch sight of Sam with Jax, Brody, and Lucas. He is wearing tight denim cut-off shorts, a white vest with a blue, white and black checked shirt over the top with the sleeves rolled up. His raven black hair is longer, but still it's usual mussed up spiky style, with a pair of aviator sunglasses sitting on top of his head.

"Look at him, Peyton; he can't take his dreamy greens off you," Ruby whispers, interrupting my thoughts.

I turn around, and I see Sam's intense green eyes lock with mine.

"Rubes, don't," I warn, looking away from him.

Even though I have been here less than ten minutes, I know I can't do this. Being here amongst his family, the boys, and our friends. It's difficult, and it's fucking awkward. The only thing that's keeping me from going insane is Freddie, our little boy, who is currently being handed around by Lori. I catch his bright green, wide, inquisitive eyes, which remind me so much of Sam. His eyes are so full of unconditional love and innocence; it makes my heart swell and ache all at the same time.

"Come on, Peyton, go and talk to him. What have you got to lose?"

I shake my head. It is like everything my mum said has just gone completely out of the window.

I shouldn't be here.

"Rubes, I can't. I just can't," I say softly as Ruby brushes my arm reassuringly.

"Let's get a drink, Lori makes the best punch you've *ever* tasted. I'm gutted I can't sample it."

She leads me off to a large white tent towards the back of the garden, which is being tended to by waiting staff.

"Two glasses of punch, one alcoholic, one virgin, please?"

Ruby nods to the waiter, and he quickly pours both drinks into two high ball glasses. I look at the pink liquid and cock my eyebrow at Ruby.

"Are you sure this isn't poisoned?" I say, with an air of cynicism to my voice, and Ruby throws her head back and laughs.

"Don't be so dramatic. There's only room in this friendship for one drama queen, and that would be me!"

She takes a long sip of her non-alcoholic cocktail and swallows.

"See, I'm not writhing around in agony."

I follow suit and take a sip. It is really refreshing, until you get the burn of the alcohol. After a few glasses of this, I'll be spilling all of my deepest, darkest secrets, which is something I don't want to do. A few minutes passes and an extremely excitable Addison comes rushing towards me, followed by Amy, Cole's fiancée. She skids to a stop in front of me. She is as adorable as I remember her. Addison Benedict is Cole and Amy's daughter and Sam's god daughter. Like her mum, she has flawless coffee coloured skin, bright wide inquisitive brown, almost black eyes, and her curly black hair framing her face. She is wearing a purple polka dot sundress and matching purple Converse. She narrows her eyes and places both hands on her hips.

"You made my Uncle Sammy sad!"

She points her finger at me accusingly and my mouth forms a perfect 'O' shape at her hostility. She might only be five years old, but she seems to have the mind of someone a lot older.

"You made him sad and I hate you!" she says with such an unfriendly tone to her tiny voice that it takes me aback.

My eyes widen, and I can feel hot tears stinging the back of my eyes.

"Addison Rose Benedict!" Amy chastises her. "Apologise to Peyton right now. That wasn't nice was it?" Amy says firmly.

Addison frowns and narrows her eyes at me.

"Apologise now, Addison Rose."

Amy raises her voice an octave and she mouths '*I'm sorry*' to me.

"NO!" Addison shouts and stomps her feet.

All eyes turn to our altercation as Sam strides over with purpose and crouches down next to Addison.

"What's wrong, Princess? Come on, you can tell Uncle Sammy."

She throws her arms around his neck and he swings her up into his arms. She points her finger at me and her bottom lip starts to quiver.

"*She* made you sad Uncle Sammy. You cried and drank lots of party juice, and it was all her fault."

Sam looks from Addison to me and I hang my head.

Even a five-year-old knows I messed up. Great.

"It's not Peyton's fault, baby girl. She was just doing what was right for our little boy. Do you see him over there with Aunty Lori? I'm his daddy and Peyton's his mummy. She wasn't with the angels' princess, she was making sure our little boy was safe and looked after."

Addison nuzzles her nose against Sam's and it's adorable to see them interacting. She is protective of him, and I understand that.

"Now, are you going to say sorry to Peyton?"

Addison's deep brown eyes are wide and full of remorse as she looks at me.

"I'm sorry, Peyton," she says in a small voice and I nod.

"It's ok, Addison. Excuse me, I...I..." I stutter and rush off into the kitchen.

I lean against the worktop and take a few deep breaths. I am interrupted by the gurgling of Freddie and the click of heels against the kitchen tiles.

"Peyton."

Lori's soft American voice cuts through the silence, and she hands Freddie to me.

"Hello, precious boy."

His face lights up and he grabs hold of my necklace with such fascination in his intelligent green eyes.

"I don't want to cause a scene or an argument with you Peyton, but you should know something. The year you were gone, he fell apart. Do you know what it's like as a mother seeing your child so broken? Watching him torture himself day after day and not being able to do a damn thing about it? I hurt for him. He was good at pretending, but a mother's instinct is never wrong."

I look at her, and I see the fierce protectiveness in her eyes.

"He was so full of grief and self-loathing, he wasn't thinking clearly. When Freddie gets older, you'll understand that as a mother there's nothing worse than seeing your baby boy on his knees and crying because the woman he was going to spend the rest of his life with...is gone."

She brushes a stray tear away from her perfectly made up eye, and for the first time since I met her, I see a human side of Lori Newbolt. She's a mother who watched her son go through the worse time of his life, and there wasn't a thing she could do about it. I suddenly see things from her perspective. If Freddie were to go through the same trauma, I would have the same reaction. If my boy hurts, I hurt too, and I get that now.

"You'll do anything to protect your kids and I understand why you stayed away. I don't blame you, Peyton, but please see it for what it is. I know you're still adjusting, but respect that Sam is too. He went from a grieving fiancé, to a father in such a short period of time. Give him some space. I know he's still got feelings for you. Give him time to adjust, he'll come around."

Her heartfelt words cut me deep and I can think of nothing other than to run as far away from here as possible. I hold Freddie's hand in mine and kiss his knuckles. Lori watches us intently for a few seconds.

"You're a great mother, Peyton. I can see that. I know it must have been hard for you, bringing him up on your own for the first six months of his life, but we're his family now too. If you need any help at all, you can come to us anytime. He's part of us now."

I smile warmly, and she moves closer to me, brushing my arm reassuringly.

"Take care, Peyton."

She nods curtly at me, kisses Freddie on the top of his head, and exits the room, leaving me with Freddie. I let out the breath I didn't know I was holding and take a moment to reflect on Lori's words.

"Every time we're near each other you act like we're strangers. Why, Peyton?"

My thoughts are interrupted by Sam's familiar rasp, and I flinch, startled by his presence.

"*Fuck* Sam, do you have to creep up on me like that?" I snap, and he holds his hands up defensively.

"I'm sorry, I didn't mean to scare you, angel," he says softly as I stand up straight and look at him.

His green eyes are at their sparkling best, but his masculine beauty is marred by the presence of dark circles underneath his eyes. He strokes Freddie's cheek.

"Hey, rock star."

He smiles, and the corners of his eyes crinkle. He turns from Freddie to me; my skin starts to prickle at his presence. I hate and love the effect he has on me.

"*Christ*, you look fucking stunning."

He tucks an errant strand of hair behind my ear, and I take in all six feet four inches of him.

"I didn't think you would come."

I look away from his mesmerizing green eyes.

"I wasn't going to. It wasn't until Ruby practically railroaded me into it. She's still hard to say no to."

Sam smirks and tucks his hands in his pockets.

"Yeah, she is. Jax is a lucky man."

He smiles, revealing his trade mark dimples.

"I'm glad you did though, angel. I really mean that, it's really good to see you."

He steps forward, and we are interrupted by Ruby's sing-song voice.

"Hey babe, hey Sam."

She takes in the situation unfolding in the Newbolt's kitchen.

"Do you want me to take Freddie?"

I nod and smile, handing Freddie to Ruby, relieved at her intervention.

"Are you sure you don't mind?"

She shakes her head.

"Of course, I don't mind, babe. I'm his Aunty! It's fine."

She smiles knowingly.

"Thank you. Go to Aunty Ruby, Freddie. Mummy will see you in a little while."

I kiss him on the end of his adorable button nose, and she breezes out with him as Freddie squeals excitedly in her arms, leaving Sam and me alone. He takes a step forward and presses me back into the worktop. He places his hands either side of me, caging me against his hard body.

"Sam, please don't," I whisper, and he presses his groin against my stomach.

He is so close, I can smell his familiar Sam smell: Joop, mint, and he also smells faintly of beer.

"I can't stop thinking about last week. I want you so fucking badly right now; feel how hard my dick is for you," he rasps.

I feel the familiar slick heat pool between my thighs, and I inwardly curse my body to hell for betraying me. He tilts my chin up to face him.

"Look at me," he commands, and I look into his blazing green eyes. "Angel, stop fighting it, stop fighting me."

He holds my gaze, and I take advantage of the gap he has left by moving his hand from the worktop. I go to make my escape, and he grabs my wrist, spinning me round to face him.

"*Christ*, stop running from me, please. I'm a fucking mess, angel," he admits.

His raised voice sounds pained. It makes my heart ache, and I shake my head.

"I can't do this, Sam, I can't. I shouldn't even be here. I can feel everyone's eyes on me, silently judging me," I whisper, and he pulls me tightly against his chest.

"No one's judging you. Please, never think that, not for a second," he says softly, then curses harshly.

"*Fuck!* Look, I know you had sex with Logan and Jack fucking Scott, ok? I tried to pretend I was ok with that, but I'm not. I'm not ok with other men having their filthy fucking hands on you when you should be with me!" he says through clenched teeth.

I can tell by the tone of his voice, and his stance, that he is furious, but he seems to be holding back.

"Maybe I want their hands on me, maybe I want their cocks buried so deep inside me it erases the fact that you were there in the first place!" I blurt out angrily and he growls, letting me loose from his grip, as if I've burned him.

I know I have got to him, and it came out harsher than I intended. He punches the cupboard door in a rage, shattering the glass panel, with a loud crash.

"*FUCKKK!*"

I make my escape through the back door and out into the garden. I stride over to Ruby, who is sitting down with Freddie in her lap, and Jax jumps up from his seat, striding into the kitchen to investigate where the loud noise came from.

"Everything alright, babe?" she enquires, and I shake my head.

"I need to leave now, Ruby. I can't be here anymore, I just can't," I say shakily, trying desperately to hold back the torrent of tears that are threatening.

She nods, and I take Freddie from her, settling him on my hip.

"We're going home, my gorgeous boy. What do you say to a night in front of the TV? You, me and Monsters Inc. yeah?"

He giggles excitedly, and I smile at his enthusiasm.

"Good boy, it's a date."

I tickle his belly, and he lets out another giggle.

"Are you sure you're ok, babe? You know you can talk to me."

Ruby's voice is filled with concern, and I nod.

"I know, babe, but everything's fine, honey. I promise. I'm just really tired that's all."

She gets up and hugs me.

"Bullshit. You know better than to lie to me, Peyton," she whispers so only I can hear her, and I shake my head.

"Not here, not now, Rubes, please. I'll talk to you tomorrow, I can't face it right now."

She nods in understanding.

"Ok, but please text me as soon as you get in. Let me know you're both ok."

I nod and leave through the back gate, not taking the time to say my goodbyes to everyone. I know it's rude, but I can't be here. Kai is sitting in his large black Land Rover 4x4. I tap the window, and he winds the window down.

"Peyton? Is everything ok, darlin'?"

I swallow the lump that's forming in my throat and manage to nod.

"Could you take us home, please, Kai?"

He nods curtly and helps me strap Freddie into his car seat in the back. I climb into the back and Kai gets into the driver's seat. He starts the engine and begins to pull out of the Newbolt's drive just as Sam flies out of the front door with Jax and Brody hot on his heels.

"Please, Kai, just drive," I plead, and he catches my gaze in the interior mirror.

He speeds out of the gravel driveway as fast as he can. Sam's looming figure running his hands through his hair frantically is the last thing I see.

18

Sam

Why the fuck do I let her have this effect on me? Why does my common sense abandon me, every time she's near me?

I've just watched her run from me, again. The look of pure panic and conflict in her eyes as Kai drove her away tore and ravaged at my insides. I lean heavily against the door frame; my hand is dripping blood from punching the glass cupboard door, but the adrenaline and the effects of the alcohol make it so I can't feel anything. A hand squeezes my shoulder in a gesture of reassurance and pulls me from my racing thoughts.

"Sam, mate, come back inside. Let's get fucking wasted, yeah? We don't have to talk if you don't want to," Jax says softly, and I shrug him off.

"You've got no fucking idea have you, Jax? Just leave me the fuck alone."

I shove past him, and he blocks my path.

"I get that you're hurting, I get that you love her man..."

I cut him off.

"Spare me the fucking pep talk, Jax," I say icily, and push past him, this time he doesn't stop me.

I stride through my parents' house and head into the living room. I route noisily through my dad's drink's cabinet, the clatter of the bottles grating on every last nerve in my body. I need to get wasted, I need to obliterate the thoughts of her running away from me again, I need to block out the empty feeling I feel every time she shuts me out and tells me it's over.

"Sam, what's going on?"

My sister's soft, melodic voice fills my ears and I squeeze my eyes briefly shut.

I don't need this shit.

"I'll tell you what I told Jax, Sav, leave me the fuck alone," I rasp, and I run the hand that isn't bleeding through my hair.

"Sam, you're bleeding."

I shrug.

"It's nothing," I say nonchalantly. *A bit of blood is the least of my concern.*

"She's not worth all this. You know that, don't you, Sam?"

I turn around and my big sister is a sight to behold. Her long, straight, black hair trails down her shoulders in a thick, glossy cascade. Her big brown eyes, with flecks of green, are a mixture of our mum and dad. Her small bump is visible underneath her floral maxi dress, and the familiar smell of her Escada Island Kisses perfume fills my nostrils.

"Sav, I know you mean well, and you probably drew straws with Brand, Eli, and Willow on who was going to come talk some sense into me, but it's really not fucking necessary," I say a little more harshly than I intend.

She brushes my arm, and her large eyes are filled with concern.

"We're all worried about you. Why can't you see that? Let us help, let us be there for you, Sam. Please, we all just want what's best for you."

I shake my head and jab my finger in her direction, my temper getting the better of me.

"I don't need your fucking pity or your concern, Savannah. Stop acting like you give a shit!" I snap and pull a full, unopened bottle of vodka from my dad's drinks cabinet.

I turn around and stride out of the living room to the sound of Savannah yelling my name.

I walk out into the garden and pace purposefully towards Ruby. She stands up as I approach.

If anyone knows what's going on with Peyton, it's her.

"What the fuck did you say to her this time, Newbolt?" Ruby retorts and narrows her eyes at me as she stands there with her hands on her hips.

I unscrew the lid from the vodka bottle and take a long pull. The fiery liquid burns and instantly quiets my racing thoughts.

"Why does everyone fucking assume it's my fault? I'm sick of being painted as the bad guy in all this. She fucking told me she'd rather have *your* brothers' cock in her than mine!" I roar crassly, and all eyes turn to us.

I see my dad march towards me, his eyes full of fury.

"Sam, a word," he says sternly and grips my arm.

"Take your hand off me, old man," I say venomously.

"Inside now," he says frostily, and I snatch my arm away from him, feeling more out of control than I've ever felt.

My dad's bottle green eyes soften and as he is about to speak. I suddenly feel so full of resentment towards the man whose blood runs through my veins.

"You don't get to fucking treat me like a child, dad! So, spare me the lecture. I'm Samson fucking Newbolt, no one tells me what to do, or how to fucking feel!"

I am trembling with such rage. I feel like a ticking time bomb, and I'm about to fucking blow.

"You're causing a scene, Sam, and you're bleeding. Please, come inside."

He tries to pacify me, and I take a few steps away from him.

"What, come inside so you can put something in my drink again to shut me up? I don't fucking think so!" I say bitterly, and he visibly balks at my words.

"Sam, son, you're upsetting your mother."

I hold my finger up.

"You know what? *Fuck this!*"

I turn and walk into the kitchen. I grab a towel from the towel rack beside the fridge, run it under the cold tap and wrap my hand in it. I stride through the house, into the living room, grab another bottle of vodka, and head up the stairs. I walk around the mezzanine and down a short corridor until I am stood outside my old bedroom. I shove my shoulder into the door and push it open. It is like stepping back in time, before I was famous, to the time when I was no one, before I was Bolt. When I could walk down the street without being hassled, when I was just ordinary Sam Newbolt.

I close the door behind me, and the silence envelopes me. I let out the breath I didn't know I was holding, and my shoulders visibly relax. I look around and take in my surroundings. I might not live here anymore, but this will always be my sanctuary away from the world outside, my safe place, my sanctum sanctorum. The room hasn't changed a bit, and the decor is still the same as I remember.

The walls are an alternating pattern of white, royal blue, and a deep red. There are three guitars mounted on the wall, adjacent to my bed. My first guitar from when I started playing, my dad's guitar from when he first started in The Lightning Bolts, and a guitar that belonged to Milo Lightman, my dad's band mate and one of my musical heroes. The feature wall behind my bed is a mural of the first time The Lightning Bolts played their first gig live on T.V. The lifelike images of the audience reaching out to them and the look of pure awe on each of the band's faces. It's what I aspired to be when I was growing up.

My bed is still the red, white, and blue of the Union Jack. Underneath the large window, that spans the rear of my bedroom, is my desk. I run my fingers across the engraved graffiti, which reads 'Hope big, dream bigger, fame beckons'. It was a quote that Milo said to me on endless occasions when we were chasing the dream of becoming famous. It is a phrase that I have tattooed on my right bicep. It reminded me that no dream was too big, and no matter how many knock backs we had, no matter how many shitty gigs we did, it would all be worth it in the end.

I kick off my flip flops and drop down heavily on my bed. My head is spinning from all the vodka I drank, and my stomach is churning from lack of food. My mind starts to race with thoughts of today's events. They say that a drunk man tells the truth, but did I truly mean what I said? I take another pull on the vodka and scrub my hand down my face.

I'm not sure how much time passes, but my vision is starting to blur, and my drunken mind is working overtime. I start to think how the fuck did we get here? How did we get to the point where all we do is hurt each other? In my drunken, fuzzy brain I somehow convince myself that I have to go to her and ask her. I have to know why she's doing this to me, to us, to our son.

I manage to sit upright and swing my legs out of bed. I stand up and find that I'm a little unsteady on my feet, but I manage to jam my feet into my flip flops and make my way out of my bedroom. My vision is hazy, and I'm struggling to focus. I carefully putting one foot in front of the other. *I can do this.* Somehow, I get down the stairs and walk through to the garage, without closing the door behind me. I pull the keys to my Chevy Warrior truck from the key hook and jab mindlessly at the fob to unlock the door.

Fuck me, I wish I could see straight.

"Dude, what the fuck?"

I hear Brody curse, and he steps around me. I close one eye to focus on him, without seeing two of him.

"*Fuck me*, you're drunk. Were you seriously going to fucking drive?" He snaps, and I scrub my hand down my face.

Fuck me running, my head is all over the place right now.

"I have to go s...she Peyton," I slur, and he rolls his eyes, snatching the keys from my hand.

"I'm not sure that's a good fucking idea, man. You're drunk and you're in no fit state to see her. Sober the fuck up and see her tomorrow."

I jab my finger in his general direction.

"You...You don't get to tell me to fuck...that's not right...you don't get to tell me what to do!"

I sway back and forth, and Brody helps me to stand up straight.

"*Fuck me*, dude, how much have you had?"

I close one eye and look at my hands. I hold one finger up, then two, and narrow my eyes.

"I don't fucking know."

I start to laugh childishly, and Brody bites his lip to stifle his smirk.

"Come on, soppy bollocks, I'll make you some coffee."

I shake my head, and the room starts to spin. *Shit.*

"I don't fucking need coffee. I need to see Peyton."

Brody shakes his head in exasperation, and Jax joins us.

"What's going on, man?"

Brody looks from me to Jax.

"This fucking prick was trying to drive drunk to Peyton's. Look at him, he can barely fucking stand up straight."

Jax growls.

"For fucks sake, dude. You need to get your head on straight before you do, or say, something you'll end up regretting."

I roll my eyes.

"Since when did you turn into my fucking dad? Spare me the fucking lecture, Chase. I have to see her now. I need to know why she's fucking doing this to me, because I can't take any more. I'm a fucking mess."

Jax looks at Brody and rolls his eyes with a look of exasperation on his face.

"Come on then, you prick, I'll fucking drive you."

Looks like we're going to Peyton's.

19

Peyton

We pull up in our usual parking spot over an hour later, and I will be forever grateful to Sam for keeping my apartment. I take Freddie out of his baby seat and pick him up. Kai jumps out of the car, locks it, and follows us back up to the flat. All the time he's fully alert and keeping a vigilant eye on us both. I unlock the door, kick it open, turn on the lights, and lock the door behind us. Kai salutes and takes his jacket off.

"Goodnight, Peyton."

He smiles, and I nod.

"Night, Kai."

He goes into his bedroom and closes the door behind him.

"We're home, baby boy."

I take Freddie's tiny hand in mine and kiss his chubby fingers. I grab a few cushions and set him down on the sofa. He looks so comfortable and content. I kick off my shoes and take the rose out of my hair, setting it down on the counter in the kitchen. I grab my phone and text Ruby.

Me and Freddie are back home safe

Stop worrying :)

Just about to set the Disney Plus up

Monsters Inc. here we come :)

P xx

A few minutes later, she replies.

Sam's pissed

He's on his way to yours and he's really drunk

Brody and Jax are with him

Just giving you a heads-up, babe

Call me if you need me

R xx

Oh shit, that's all I need. Hurricane Sam.

I quickly change into my black yoga pants and a grey t-shirt. I grab a bottle of rose wine from the fridge and a glass from the cupboard. I go into the living room, and Freddie has fallen asleep. *Bless him.* I'm glad he isn't going to witness his dad being a complete prick. I pick him up and take him into the nursery, settling him down in his cot. He doesn't stir as I pull a blanket loosely over his tiny body; I turn on his mobile above his cot, kiss the top of his head, and leave the nursery, closing the door quietly behind me.

I flop down on the sofa, place the baby monitor beside me on the table, pour myself a glass of wine, and flick on the TV.

A few hours pass and I am settled, watching re-runs of *The Walking Dead,* when I hear a loud pounding on the door.

"Angel."

Sam's familiar rasp comes through the door.

"Open this fucking door right now, or I'm going to break it the fuck down!" he roars as I get up from the sofa and fling the door open.

Sam's stance is loose. He is breathing hard and swaying from side to side. He looks menacing and his green eyes are hooded.

"Could you knock any fucking louder? Your son is asleep," I hiss angrily, and he backs me unsteadily into the apartment.

"Sam," Brody warns, and Sam holds his hand up.

"I'm fine! Why the fuck are you two dickheads here, anyway?" He slurs, and Jax narrows his eyes.

"Because you were adamant you wanted to come here, and you were too fucking drunk to drive. That's why, you prick!" Jax snaps.

Sam doesn't take his eyes off me as he stumbles further into my flat. Kai comes bounding out of his bedroom in a white vest and long black basketball shorts, ready to strike.

"Is everything ok, Peyton?"

I nod, and he visibly relaxes.

"Everything's fine, Kai, I can handle it."

Kai looks from me to Sam and takes in the situation unfolding in front of him.

"*Leave,* now," Sam orders Brody and Jax. The tone of his voice says it isn't a request.

"No chance. We're not fucking leaving you here alone with her, dude. Not fucking happening."

Brody's tone is harsh.

"I'm not going to hurt her; she's already ripped my *fucking* heart out, what more damage could she do?"

Sam laughs bitterly, and I feel like I have been slapped. The pain I feel in my heart is like a thousand knives, and I wince at his harsh statement. Brody steps closer to me, his face marred with concern.

"Are you ok, sweets?"

He brushes my arm, and I nod, swallowing back a lump in my throat.

"I'm good, babe. Honestly, I'm fine."

Sam narrows his eyes.

"Are you two fucking?" he accuses, and Brody looks from Sam to me.

"You are, aren't you? You fucked my girl? You prick!"

Sam's nostrils flare, and he pulls Brody away from me, pinning him to the wall.

"What the fuck! Not this shit again!"

Jax tries in vain to pull Sam off Brody, but he doesn't budge. Kai steps in and grabs Sam in a chokehold.

"Get off me, you cocksucker!"

Sam rages and Brody straightens.

"Of course, we haven't fucked! Brody is one of my best friends', you idiot!" I explain in a vain attempt to try and placate him, but Sam's drunken brain doesn't register it.

He somehow manages to get free of Kai's grip, and he lunges for Brody. He pins him to the wall, and he tightens his grip on Brody's throat. Before I know what is going on, Sam's fist has connected with Brody's jaw, spraying blood everywhere.

"Will you just fucking stop?" I scream.

"Sam, dude."

Jax tries to appease him, and as Sam is about to punch Brody again, Cole steps through the door, catching Sam's fist as he cocks it back.

"*Jesus fucking Christ,* Sam. Can you not go anywhere without getting into trouble? Kai, it's not in your job description to get involved in domestics. I got this, man," he growls and pulls Sam off Brody without effort. Kai nods and retreats back into his room.

"For fucks sake," Cole mutters, grabbing Sam and shoving him down on the sofa.

"You need to sober the fuck up; I don't need this shit. Peyton, sugar, do you have some coffee and a first aid kit?"

I nod and go into the kitchen. I open the cupboard, take out the first aid kit, and turn on the coffee machine. I spin round, and I am greeted by Brody's blood-stained face.

"*Fuck,*" I curse and gesture for him to take a seat at the breakfast bar. He sits down.

"I don't know what you said to him, sweets, but he's...well you've seen the state of him. He's a fucking mess without you. He's off his meds, he's self-medicating and taking drugs, he's getting into fights, he's drinking heavily, and pushing everyone away, refusing help."

His voice is filled with concern for his best friend, and I know what is coming next.

"He's having another episode, isn't he?"

Brody hangs his head and nods.

Fuck, fuck, fuck.

"Yeah, they're happening a little too frequently these days. He's refusing rehab, he's refusing medical attention. Even Marlowe can't get through to him. He was fine until you left his parents' house, then he just disappeared to his old bedroom with a bottle of vodka."

I can't help but feel responsible for all this, after I let my mouth run away with me. I open the first aid kit and tend to Brody's wounds, cleaning him up as best as I can. He winces in pain as I swipe an antiseptic wipe over the cut on his nose.

"Stop being such a girl," I joke.

We both smirk, and he rolls his eyes, the mood momentarily turning serious.

"He fucking needs you, sweets."

I shake my head.

"I can't, Brody. I just can't."

He takes my hand in his.

"Why not? What are you so fucking scared of?"

I snatch my hand from him and walk across the kitchen, ashamed to look him in the eyes.

"Sweets, talk to me."

He hops off his barstool and rounds the counter.

"What's so bad that you're pushing away a man that loves you?"

He cups my face in his hands, and I shake my head. A tear escapes from the corner of my eye, and I squeeze my eyes closed to stop the dam from breaking.

I will not cry, I will not cry, I chant in my head.

"Sam loves the fuck out of you, sweets."

Brody pulls me in for one of his famous bear hugs, and he wraps his muscular arms around me. I try to resist, but he doesn't allow it.

"Stop fighting it, everything's going to be ok."

I wrap my arms around him, and in that moment, I am so overwhelmed with grief that the sadness envelopes me, and it feels like I can't breathe. Gut wrenching sobs overtake me, and Brody's hands roam over my back, soothing me.

"Shhh, I've got you, sweets. It's alright, shush, I'm here," he pacifies.

I don't look up, but I feel Brody's head move, and I know that Sam is standing in the doorway; my skin prickles as I feel his presence, even though I don't look up to see him. I pull away from Brody's embrace and straighten myself out. I swipe my tears angrily away from my eyes and look up at Sam. His eyes are a dull forest green, and the dark circles underneath his eyes look out of place on his hotter than hell face.

"I think you should leave," I say, but something in the tone of my voice tells me I don't mean it.

"Say it with a little more conviction, angel. You don't really want me to go. The way you're looking at me is the total opposite. I know that look, that look is...I want you to scatter my inhibitions all over the kitchen floor, along with the buttons on my dress, and fuck me like you hate me."

I'm not sure his voice could get any sexier. The deep, husky timbre washes over me and causes my whole body to involuntarily shudder with lust. He seems a little soberer as he strides closer to me with purpose. He runs his calloused finger down my neck and across my collarbone. I briefly close my eyes, bite my lip, and a small moan escapes from my lips. My eyes fly open as I slowly realise that I can't let him do this to me. I can't let him have this effect on me. I swallow hard and blink a few times, as if to gather my scattered senses.

"You need to leave, Sam."

My voice is small, and I don't recognise it as my own. A cocky smirk spreads across his face, as if he knows the effect he's having on me.

"I'll do as you ask, just this once, angel, but I'll keep my phone on in case you change your mind."

He winks smugly, tucks his hands into his pockets, and leaves.

Well that wasn't what I was expecting.

Brody looks from Sam's retreating back, to me.

"Well fuck me running."

We both laugh. He hugs me and kisses me on the forehead.

"I'll call you in the morning, sweets."

He turns to leave. I hear the hushed conversation and the door closing. With that, the peace in my flat is restored. I let out the breath I didn't know I was holding. Suddenly, an unexpected feeling of loneliness washes over me, and I give in to the crushing guilt and sadness I feel.

20

Sam

I am silent on the journey back to my place, and my mood plummets the further we get from Peyton's. I fucked up, I'm such a fucking idiot. *Shit, shit, fuck, BOLLOCKS!* Why the fuck did I think it was a good idea to turn up at her flat drunk off my face? I slam my head back against the headrest of the car and curse softly as my phone starts vibrating in my pocket. I pull it out and look at the screen. It's Vance Stryker, our solicitor. I swipe the screen and answer it.

"This better be fucking good, Stryker," I half growl and half slur.

There is a slight pause.

"Ah, nice to hear from you too, Mr. Newbolt."

I roll my eyes and lean my head back. *I don't need this shit right now.*

"Get to the point," I snap, quickly losing my patience with the man who calls himself our solicitor.

Vance Stryker is our solicitor and has been for almost eleven years.

"I'm afraid you're going to want to hear this, Sam."

I stare at the ceiling of the car and sigh.

"What's up, Vance? Give it to me."

It takes a few seconds for him to continue.

"A date has been set for J.D's trial. I thought you should know."

I sit up straighter, and my eyes widen. Great, this is all we need. Dragging up a time that Peyton and I would rather forget. *FUCK!* I scrub my hand down my face, and all I want at that moment is oblivion.

"Cheers for the heads-up, Vance, I appreciate it. Call me when you've got more details."

"You can count on it, Sam. Take care and enjoy the rest of your night."

I end the call without saying goodbye and toss my phone on the seat next to me.

"Everything alright, dude?" Brody says with concern in his voice.

"Everything's fucking peachy, mate."

I plaster a fake smile on my face, and by the look in Brody's eyes, I can tell he doesn't believe me.

"Cole, can you drop us at Lust and Redemption? I feel like getting wasted."

Cole catches my stare in the interior mirror, and he looks at me questioningly. He goes to speak but thinks better of it and nods curtly. Twenty minutes later, we are pulling up outside Lust and Redemption, the strip club that Lenny, Brody's sober sponsor, owns. As I get out, I hear Cole talking to Jax in hushed tones.

"Are you coming or not, Chase? Or do you need Ruby's permission these days?" I retort and Jax flips me the bird.

I throw my head back and laugh as I throw my arm around Brody's neck.

"I'm in the mood for a blow out, man!" I say brightly, and he stops us from walking any further.

"Look, are you sure this is what you want, mate? I get that you're pissed..."

I halt him from speaking.

"I'm fine! Look, man, I'm on top of the fucking world! Let's get wasted, maybe a cheeky little blow job for good measure?"

I cup Brody's face in my hands.

"Come on, Hart, you've never needed this much fucking persuading before! Are you with me, brother?"

His eyes regard me with quiet unease.

"I'm fine! Seriously!" I reassure him with all the enthusiasm I can muster, and he eventually nods.

"YEAHHHH!" I roar as Lenny catches sight of us.

"B, this is a nice surprise. I wasn't expecting you, son."

He grins dazzlingly and gives Brody a hug.

"Thought I'd surprise you, old man!" Brody quips.

I enter the club and the music is pumping. I recognise the song as, *'Zombie' by* Bad Wolves. The slow, pulsing beat flows through my veins as a brunette with short cropped hair who is covered in tattoos approaches me. Her eyes are an unusual shade of amethyst, she has a nose ring, and she is wearing two leather belts crossed over each breast, barely there leather, studded hot pants, and black knee-high boots. She is holding a silver tray.

"Good evening, welcome to Lust and Redemption. I'm Zena, what can I get you?"

I flash her my dimpled grin, and I see her swallow hard.

"Depends, I'm feeling...a little rebellious tonight, babe. What would you recommend for that?" I say low and gravelly as I move closer to her.

I tower over her, and I'm so close to her I can feel her breath coming out in sharp gusts.

"I think you need loosening up a little bit, lover."

I cock my pierced eyebrow as I see Brody and Jax carefully observing our exchange.

"Sounds like a plan, sweetheart. Do you want to rebel with me?" I rasp low and seductively.

I offer her my hand and she takes it. I spin her around and crush my lips to her soft, plump lips. She's the first to pull away, and we're both rendered breathless.

"Well, aren't you a fast mover?"

She giggles nervously as a balding man approaches us. He is overweight, average height, and has sweat beading on his forehead. He is wearing an ill-fitting suit and his shirt buttons look as if they are about to pop as he grunts in our direction.

"Is everything alright here, Zee?"

He looks from her to me and her demeanour changes from a flirty, carefree woman to a meek, timid one.

"Everything's fine thanks, Nigel."

She smiles a fake smile as Nigel narrows his eyes at us both.

"Is this dickhead giving you grief?"

His eyes flash as he sees her hand in mine, and he snatches her hand away.

"Get your fucking hands off my girl, knob head," he says low and threatening, as he grabs her arm roughly.

Before I know what is happening, he throws a punch and manages to land a blow to my chin, knocking me a little off balance. He goes to hit me again, and that's when I lose it. I charge at him and slam my large body into his, tackling him to the floor. I kneel over him as I pound my fists into his pathetic fucking face. He tries to block my punches with one hand as he rears his fist back and thumps me square in the eye, causing a blinding pain to tear through me. Every ounce of control and every modicum of anger I feel, the news from Vance about J.D, Peyton, everything that's happened between us since her return, and the crushing guilt I feel for fucking Lyla, comes pouring out. The moments that pass are hazy as I register Brody and Jax spring into action.

"SAM!"

I vaguely hear Brody's voice, and as he goes to grab me, I send him hurtling backwards across the club floor. I refuse to listen to reason as this fat fucking prick takes the brunt of my rage. I continue to rain blow after blow down on this sad, feeble fucking excuse of a human being. His face morphs into J.D's and every vein in my body starts to pulse, causing my blood to feel like it is scalding me from the inside out. I can't stop myself, the sickening sounds of every slug, the crunching of bones, and the spray of blood, until he stops moving. That's when Brody, Jax, and at least three of Lenny's security men lift me up. I am restrained with my arm up my back and dragged away.

I'm in a daze as I'm shoved into a chair in one of the clubs back offices.

"What the fuck were you thinking, you fucking idiot!" Jax barks, and I struggle to focus.

"Are you even listening, fuck nut?"

Jax paces the office furiously. I take in my surroundings and suddenly feel a little bit more drunk than I did earlier. *Fuck me, the room is starting to spin.*

"I swear to Christ, I'm going to fucking twat him!" he says threateningly, and Brody pulls his phone out of his pocket.

"Yeah, it's Brody. We need you to come to Lust and Redemption. I know it's late, and I'm fucking sorry, mate. We've got a situation, we need you to clean it up and take care of it. I'll explain when you get here. Cheers man, we owe you."

I shift in my seat and put my head in my hands as Lenny comes striding with purpose into the office.

"What the fuck?" he roars gruffly as he drags me up from the chair.

"Give me a good fucking reason why I shouldn't let my men take you round the back and teach you a lesson?"

I don't know what comes over me, but I start to laugh hysterically.

"You think this is fucking funny? Do you, boy? I'm going to have the filth come crawling over this club in less than five fucking minutes!"

Brody steps in.

"Len, I'm so sorry. Look he's just had a bit too much to drink, that's all. I'll take him home. I'm sorry for bringing him here."

Lenny looks from me to Brody and let's go of me, shoving me back down into the chair.

"I should be shaking your fucking hand, boy. I've wanted to nail that scumbag for months."

He laughs throatily, and he pulls out a handkerchief from his jacket pocket. He throws it and I catch it.

"Here, clean yourself up and sober the fuck up. You owe me, B."

He winks at Brody, and Brody smirks.

"Have I ever let you down, Len?"

Brody laughs as Lenny exits the room. I'm not sure how much time passes, but all thoughts of self-pity are halted by the entrance of Tate Jackson, our P.R guy.

"What the fuck have you done this time, Newbolt?"

Oops!

21

Peyton

The next morning, I am woken at six forty-seven a.m. to Freddie crying. It is Sunday morning, and even though I had a decent night's sleep, I feel exhausted. I pad out of the bedroom, grabbing my robe and pulling it tightly around my body. I walk into the nursery, pick Freddie up, and cradle him in my arms, soothing him until he stops crying.

"Good morning, handsome boy," I whisper and take him out into the kitchen.

I pick up my phone, and I have six missed calls and five text messages. Three of the calls are from Ruby, two are from Brody, and one is from Sam. I sit down at the breakfast bar, rocking Freddie in one arm and scrolling through my phone with the other.

Call me, babe

Let me know you're ok

I'm worried

R x

I scroll down to the next message.

Is everything ok, sweets?

Call me if you need me

Brody xx

I smile at my friend's concern and scroll down to the next message.

Angel,

I'm so fucking sorry

S x

I roll my eyes at Sam's attempt at an apology and scroll down.

Angel,

Forgive me

Call me, please

We need to talk

It's important

S x

I get up from the barstool and set about making Freddie a bottle. I scroll to the last message.

Sweets,

It's Sam

He got into a fight

He had an episode

Just thought you should know

Please call me as soon as possible

He's not in a good way

He needs you

Brody xx

Fuck. I knew something like this was going to happen. I rock Freddie in my arms.

"What's your daddy like, eh? Shall we call uncle Brody?"

Freddie gurgles, and I dial Brody's number.

"Morning, sweets," he says softly.

"Brody, is he ok?"

He sighs audibly.

"He's sleeping it off, babe. Tate cleaned it up as best as he could, to limit the damage on the band's reputation, but he's in a bad fucking way, sweets."

I close my eyes.

"Ok, I'll drop in on him, honey. Thanks for calling."

He pauses, and I can't help but worry about Sam's current state of mind.

"No worries, sweets. Call me when you're on the way, I'll let the security team know you're coming; drive right up to the gates."

I hear footsteps.

"Ok, look I have to go. I'll see you soon, bye."

I end the call and tuck the phone in the pocket of my robe as Kai steps out of his room.

"Mornin', darlin'," he says sleepily, and I smile.

"Morning Kai. Could you drive me to Sam's, please? I know it's Sunday, and it's early, but I'd really appreciate it."

I hate having to rely on other people, and I suddenly feel really bad for asking him.

"Sure, doll, it's not a problem. Give me half an hour and I'll drive you."

He smiles, and I return his gesture before setting about getting ready for the day ahead.

An hour later, I am showered and dressed. Today, I opt for a pair of black skinny jeans, a red Guns n' Roses t-shirt, black Converse trainers, and black military jacket. I have on my natural make up and my hair is straight secured in a black hair band. I am in the middle of dressing Freddie when there is a knock at the door. I pick him up and pad out into the living room. I swing open the door. Standing there looking fresh is Ruby. Her bump is growing bigger by the day yet she still looks like she could still model for Vogue. She breezes in and gives me a one-armed hug, her scent enveloping me. I take her in; she is wearing a black and white striped maternity vest, which accentuates her bump, black velour trousers, and black Converse.

"*Bleurgh*! My feet are so fucking swollen, I can't get my feet into my heels," she says melodramatically, and I chuckle softly as she pulls away from our embrace.

"Thank God you're ok. I heard about Sam."

She holds me at arm's length, as if she is taking me in.

"*Jesus*, that boy is a fucking mess, babe."

I sigh.

"So, everyone keeps telling me."

She takes Freddie, and his face lights up as he catches sight of her.

"Good morning, beautiful boy. Aunty Ruby's here," she says in her familiar singsong voice, and Freddie giggles.

"You're going over to Sam's, aren't you?"

I nod.

"Brody texted me last night, but I didn't get his message until this morning. I called him straight away. Was it bad?"

She worries her lip between her teeth and nods.

"Pretty bad, babe."

I scrub my hand down my face.

"*Fuck,*" I curse, and she brushes my arm reassuringly.

"He needs you; you need to go to him. The boys are losing patience with him, and I have a feeling you're the only one he'll listen to."

I nod and kiss Freddie on his chubby cheek.

"Love you, baby boy," I croon and Ruby kisses my forehead.

"Take as long as you need. Call me when you can, babe?"

She winks, and I smile as I leave the flat with Kai. We make the ninety-minute journey to Sam's new place in Sawbridgeworth in relative silence, both left to our thoughts. Security is expecting us and buzzes us straight through the wrought-iron gates. We pull onto the gravel driveway, and I get out of the car, leaving Kai waiting in the driver's seat. Brody greets me at the door. He is wearing a black beanie hat, a pair of combat shorts, a black skull t-shirt, and a pair of khaki Converse trainers. He envelopes me in one of his bear hugs, and I squeeze him tightly.

"Hey, sweets," he whispers, pulling away from our embrace and leading me inside Sam's house.

The house is as opulent as his old apartment, with black and white tiled flooring throughout the hallway, and gold and platinum discs lining the walls.

"Where is he?" I say quietly.

"I'm here."

I hear his familiar rasp, and I look up. He looks magnificent making his way down the oak staircase, wearing a pair of black silk pyjama bottoms. He is shirtless, and his hair is sleep mussed. His hard-tattooed chest is just as I remember it, with the addition of his *'My Angel'* tattoo. As he reaches the bottom, he runs his hand through his hair. His one hand is heavily bandaged.

"You didn't have to come."

He moves closer to me, and I look up at him as his six-foot four frame towers over me. I am silent, but he tilts my chin up to face him. He has a purple bruise on his right cheek, a black eye, and a split lip; even with a beaten and battered face, he is still breath taking.

"Look at me, angel," he says huskily. "Thank you. I'm glad you came, you look gorgeous."

He smiles, bringing out those adorable dimples, and I feel the familiar slickness between my thighs. Brody observes the exchange between us and cocks his eyebrow.

"I'll leave you two to it."

He smirks and strides out of the room, leaving Sam and me just staring at each other. A few moments of silence passes between us.

"Say something, angel."

He moves closer to me, and he reaches out to cup my chin.

"I'm not sure what to say, I...I'm sorry about what I said yesterday. It was in the heat of the moment. I was angry, and I shouldn't have said it."

He shakes his head.

"I'm the one who should be apologising. I acted like a complete prick, I shouldn't have shown up drunk on your doorstep, shouting my mouth off. It was a dick move on my part, I'm sorry," he says softly.

He moves hand away from my face, and I feel bereft from the loss of contact.

"How's Freddie? Is he ok?" Sam enquires, and I smile.

"Yeah, he's great, thanks. He's with Ruby."

He smiles a genuine smile and nods.

"Do you want some coffee?"

I nod, and I suddenly feel awkward in his presence. I have never experienced this awkward feeling with Sam since I met him, and I'm unnerved by it. He strides into the kitchen, and I follow him, watching his sexy gait and his perfect arse.

"I can feel your eyes on me, angel."

He chuckles softly, as if to lighten the mood, and I bite my lip. We enter the kitchen, which is a deep orange colour, with orange appliances, black marble worktop, and black and orange tiles on the floor. It shouldn't look stylish, but it does. He turns on the coffee machine; he pulls two cups out of the glass-fronted cupboard and I stand awkwardly off to the side, viciously biting my nail. He moves around the kitchen and strides over to me. He moves my hand away from my mouth and backs me into the worktop.

"God, you're so fucking beautiful. I want you so badly, standing there all vulnerable and innocent," he says huskily and thrusts his groin roughly into me. I moan softly at the delicious pressure he creates. "You want me too, admit it."

He leans down and nips my earlobe between his teeth while his bandaged hand roams my body. His hand comes to rest on my breast, and he cups it in his large hand, kneading it softly.

"*Christ*, make me fucking stop, angel."

His voice sounds pained, and I bite my lip. *Do I really want him to stop?* My head is screaming at me to run for the hills, but my heart is telling me that I want this just as much as he does, if not more. I cup his erection, which is straining in his pyjama bottoms, and he growls.

"I can't stop myself when I'm around you, Sam. My body craves you. You're my addiction."

He lifts me easily onto the worktop and nudges my legs apart with his muscular thighs.

"I won't share you with Logan, or anyone else. Once I have you, this time, you're mine again, angel. Do you understand?" he rasps.

I bite my lip and nod.

"Answer me, I need to hear the words."

Our eyes lock.

"Yes, I understand. Oh God, Sam, please take me," I plead, and a lazy smirk crosses his handsome face.

"I need to be inside you," he rasps as he rids me of my coat and t-shirt, until I am sitting in my bra in front of him.

My heart is thundering at his close scrutiny, and J.D's evil words crawl to the forefront of my mind.

"Sam doesn't do damaged goods."

I feel my breathing start to quicken. He pinches my chin between his thumb and forefinger, jolting me back to the here and now.

"Stay with me. I've got you, you're safe."

His lips graze mine, and he looks down at me. He examines the top half of my body, which is marred with scars. He runs his finger over the thick white scar, which runs from collarbone to collarbone. He curses, and my eyes begin to swim with tears.

"You are still the most beautiful woman in the world to me, Peyton. I'll take whatever I can get with you, scars and all."

He rests his forehead against mine.

"We don't have to...we..."

I silence him by placing my finger against his lips.

"I need you to take it away, Sam. Please, take it away."

He crashes his lips to mine, feverishly, and he slips his hand into the cup of my bra, softly stroking my sensitive nipple. I run my hands over his chest and his broad shoulders.

"God, I've missed having your hands on me," he says against my lips.

I let my hands roam over his tight backside and down to his erect cock. He growls.

"That's it, angel, Mmm," he rasps and lifts me up onto the kitchen counter, the coldness of the marble causes my skin to break out in goose bumps.

In one lithe move, he leans down and pulls my nipple into his mouth. I gasp softly at the pinch of pain that the nip of his teeth causes. He looks into my eyes; his blazing green eyes are filled with lust. I grab hold of his soft hair and close my eyes.

"I need those eyes, look at me. Look how good I make you feel."

My eyes lock with his, and my nipple leaves his mouth with a pop.

"Tell me what you want, angel. Tell me."

His voice sounds as if he's swallowed a bag of gravel, and I shiver as my pussy floods with pure pleasure.

"Oh, Sam, please. I want you to lick my pussy. I want you to lick me until I come all over your tongue," I pant out desperately, and he smirks cockily.

"Good girl, I love it when you tell me exactly what you want."

I look down, and I blush crimson.

"*Wow!* Peyton Harper blushing? Fuck, that made me hard!"

I stifle a smirk and bite my lip. His blazing green eyes turn smoky with desire.

"Don't do that. I'm trying to control myself, but all I really want to do is ram my cock so deep inside you that you'll be begging me to stop. I want to punish you for letting those other men inside this delicious pussy."

As he says those words, he shoves his long-calloused finger inside me. I gasp at the intrusion as he moves it leisurely in and out. I moan out loud and throw my head back in ecstasy.

"Sam."

He pulls his finger out of me and sucks his finger into his mouth, licking my juices clean.

"You taste so good, angel. Now, where was I?"

He looks so mouth-watering standing nude in front of me; he looks like a perfectly sculpted Greek God. His raven black hair is mussed and falling haphazardly in his eyes.

"Stop looking at me like you want to devour every inch of my body," he growls and buries his head between my legs.

The moment his tongue touches my swollen clit, I feel like I'm free-falling head first back into the world of Sam Newbolt.

22

Sam

I've missed her taste, the soft moans of pleasure, the bounce of her beautiful tits, and the way her eyes change from vivid blue to steel blue when she's turned on. The curve of her waist, the feel of her soft skin against mine, and the scent that is uniquely Peyton Leigh Harper. After last night, after the barbeque, turning up at hers, the fight at the club, all of it. That wasn't me, I never lose control over a woman. Or at least I didn't until I met her. She makes me want to be better, a less broken version of me.

As I swipe my tongue up her wet folds, she cries out and tugs on my hair. "Sam, Oh God!"

She writhes beneath me, and I continue my luscious assault on her pussy. I expertly lap and relentlessly thrust my tongue up inside her. She clamps her legs around my head and screams.

"SAM! SAM! OH SAM!"

I look up at her and the look of pure pleasure on her face makes me realise how compatible we are sexually. I know what she wants, I know what she craves. She likes it rough, she likes it gentle, she loves it when we fuck, and she loves it when we make slow gentle love.

"SAM!" she mewls, and I stop what I'm doing for a second.

"What do you want, angel? Tell me," I say with a dominant edge to my voice.

"Oh God! Sam! I want you to make me come! Please, make me come," she pants out feverishly, and I stand to my full height.

I stroke my cock a few times and she eyes it, as if she's never seen it before. I push her legs open wider, and she cries out loud as I thrust my cock deep inside her. Her inner walls contract around my cock as she adjusts to my size.

"Only I belong in this pussy. Do you understand me, angel? Only me," I rasp, and her eyes gloss over. "Do you fucking understand me?" I practically growl, and she looks up at me.

The look she gives me makes her look so vulnerable. She bites her lip and nods.

"Only you, Sam," she whispers, and as she says those words, I thrust deeper inside her.

I slide my hands underneath her bum and lift her up. My cock slides easily out of her wet heat, and she mewls softly at the loss of contact.

"We're continuing this in my bedroom."

I carry her up the stairs with her clinging to me, as if she's scared I'm going to let go at any moment. I hold her tighter as my way of reassuring her, and as I reach the top of the stairs, I make my way to my bedroom. I kick the door open with my foot and stride towards the bed with purpose. I deposit her gently in the middle of the bed. I crawl up the bed and settle between her legs.

"Now where were we?"

I wink, and she shivers. *I love that after all this time I still have the effect on her.*

"I think I need you to remind me, angel."

She reaches up and pulls me closer to her by my neck.

"Your cock was deep inside me, Sam."

She is husky with desire, and I smile at the fact that she is no longer afraid to tell me what she wants.

"Good girl. Spread those gorgeous legs for me."

She spreads her legs wider, and I can see her pussy dripping with want. I stroke my cock, and as I thrust forward to enter her, she screams.

"OH GOD! SAM! SAM! SAM!"

My name leaves her lips like a love song, and I increase my pace.

"*Jesus! Fuck!* You feel so good around my cock, angel," I say gruffly, and she moves her hips to meet me thrust for thrust.

"*FUCKKK!*" I curse, and she wraps her arms around me, pulling me closer to her.

"Harder, I need you to fuck me harder, Sam!"

I rear back and thrust forward. My cock is so deep inside her, I'm not sure where I end and she begins. Her hands start to roam over my back and shoulders. I love the way her tiny hands feel on me; I crave her touch. I lick my lips and gasp as she rakes her nails across my back. My pace quickens, and I ram my cock in her.

"Oh God! Don't you dare fucking stop!" she pants, and I smile lazily at the effect I have on her. "Make me come, please, make me come."

I shove her up the bed and grab her legs, lifting them over my shoulders. At this angle, every time I push my cock into her I feel my piercing bump her cervix. I build up a punishing pace as my cock rams in and out of her slickness. I can feel her pussy rippling around me and I know she's close.

"I can feel you around my cock, angel. You're close."

I let go of one of her legs and reach down to find her swollen nub. I rub it in small circles, and with one sudden movement of my cock, her orgasm detonates from deep within her.

"*Fuck*, Sam...Oh God! I'm going to come."

I drive my cock into her to the hilt with an expert swivel of my hips.

"I've got you, come for me."

She screams out as her orgasm floods through her like a tidal wave.

"FUCK! I'M COMING! OH GOD! I'M COMING!" she cries out, and she quivers as I explode into her at the same time.

"FUCK! PEYTON! JESUS! I'M COMING!"

I tremble against her as we both ride out our orgasms. I empty my seed inside her, and her legs fall limply either side of me. I collapse on top of her, trying not to crush her.

We are both spent after our sex session. She nuzzles her face into my neck and inhales my scent, as if reminding herself of what we once had. I roll to the side and flop down next to her, pulling her closer to me. She rests her head on my chest and she starts to trace her fingers lightly over my *My Angel* tattoo. She follows the lines and sighs audibly.

"Are you ok, angel?"

She nods slowly. We lie there in complete silence, and I couldn't think of another place I'd rather be.

23

Peyton

We lie there for long minutes in silence. My head is on his chest, and I snuggle closer to him, listening to the sound of his strong heartbeat. Sam is attentive, loving and gentle. It feels almost like the past year never happened.

We order takeaway. He orders my favourite Chinese of chicken and king prawn curry, with mushrooms and egg fried rice. We eat together at the kitchen island, me in one of his t-shirts and him shirtless. He is wearing a pair of grey jogging bottoms, which hang low on his hips and reveal a perfect *'V'* on his lower abdomen, which I find to be the most delicious part of him.

We spend the evening snuggled on Sam's sumptuous sofa and watch a few episodes of *'Mindhunter'* on Sam's huge T.V. It's times like these that I have missed, it almost feels like we are just a normal couple, enjoying each other's company. But I know that in reality, we'll never be normal, not as long as Sam is in the public eye.

I let my thoughts drift to all the reasons why we can't be together. Am I just using them as an excuse? Am I jeopardising my own happiness because of my insecurities and my need to protect him? Have I built a wall around my heart to keep Sam Newbolt out, to protect our son? The back and forth of my thoughts make me dizzy. He seems to sense my contemplative mood and doesn't question it, which I am grateful for. We head to bed around midnight and make slow, sweet love in his king size bed. After we make love, I start to feel that maybe we could have a fighting chance, and with that thought at the forefront of my mind, I drift off into a blissful sleep.

I'm not sure how long I have been asleep, but I am woken by the soft, haunting melody of what sounds like a piano. I reach over; expecting to find the warmth of Sam's body next to me, but all I am greeted with is cold sheets and an empty space. Judging by the coolness of the sheets, he has been gone for a while. I look at the digital clock next to the bed and the glowing blue numbers tell me it's 2:54am. I swing my legs out of bed and shiver as my feet hit the cold floor in Sam's bedroom. I make my way over to the chest of drawers, pull open the top drawer, and take out one of Sam's Rancid Vengeance t-shirts. I pull it over my head and I inhale deeply, it smells of him. The musky, masculine smell of Joop and pure Sam Newbolt.

I follow the sound of the piano, and I know I must be getting closer, because the sound gets louder. The melody is so haunting, it is truly heart breaking. As I get closer to finding Sam, I hear his raspy voice try out some lyrics. Every nerve in my body is locked on to him, and it seems to be attuned to him. I turn the corner into his den, and that's when I spot him. He looks delicious sitting at his black leather piano bench, shirtless and barefoot, wearing a pair of loose grey jogging bottoms. He is tinkling the piano keys with one hand and scribbling in his notebook on top of the piano lid. The moonlight casts a glow over his solitary figure, drawing my eyes to the bunch and flex of the muscles in his back and shoulders. The glow highlights the large Phoenix across his broad back.

I lean in the doorway, observing him unnoticed. He places both hands back on the piano keys, his hands dance effortlessly and rapidly across them. It creates the most heartfelt melody which reaches the depths of my soul and causes the hairs on the back of my neck to stand on end. I feel somewhat voyeuristic, as I continue to silently watch him, giving me a glimpse of the Sam Newbolt I met all those months ago. I notice a half full glass on top of the piano filled with amber liquid.

"Some nights I get so fucking wasted, I don't see you in my dreams."

His powerful, husky voice washes over me as he slams his hands down on the piano keys.

"Fuck!" he growls out in frustration.

I chuckle softly to myself, making him aware of my presence.

"*Shit*, I'm sorry, angel. I didn't mean to wake you. I couldn't sleep."

I move gracefully through the den and sit down on the piano bench next to him. The cool leather of the bench making me shiver as my bare bottom gets acclimatized to the temperature. He turns to look at me and the glow of the moon lights up his eyes, making the green blaze. He strokes my cheek and kisses my forehead.

"How long were you standing there?" he enquires, and I feel my face burn with embarrassment at being caught watching him.

"Long enough," I say vaguely and bite my lip piercing suggestively.

He chuckles throatily and takes a long sip from his glass.

"I'm not angry, angel. I find it...*hot* that you were stood there watching. You're quite the voyeur, you little minx! I'll have to remember that."

He winks, and we both laugh. I am reminded that the sound of Sam laughing is my favourite sound in the world. He senses a shift in the mood and turns to me.

"What are you thinking, beautiful girl? What's going on in that gorgeous mind of yours?"

I drop my gaze suddenly feeling shy.

"Angel, look at me," he rasps and tilts my chin up so I have no choice but to look into the green pools of his eyes.

"The sound of you laughing has to be my favourite sound in the world. You sound so young and care free, it almost makes me forget what I put you through," I say apprehensively, and I briefly close my eyes, glad of the reprieve of his intense gaze.

When I open my eyes, his gaze has softened, and a warm smile spreads across his face, bringing out those adorable dimples I love so much.

"Don't do that, let's not ruin it. I don't want to talk about the past, just you and me, here and now."

He reaches for my hand and brings it up to his lips. He kisses the back of my hand, and the stubble on his face scratches my skin, but it feels divine.

"Today reminded me of how we used to be," I say thoughtfully, and he cocks his head to the side.

"Me too. Let me take you to work. Can pick you up afterwards and I can take you to dinner?"

I look away shyly and try to make a joke.

"Like a date, Mr. Newbolt?"

He smiles.

"Exactly like a date, angel."

I know he's subtly trying to get me to agree to be with him, and I casually try to distract him by getting up from the piano bench. I walk over to the opposite side and climb onto his lap so I'm straddling him.

"I want you to fuck me, Sam," I purr, and he chuckles softly.

"You don't play fair, Miss Harper."

I grind my bare pussy against his crotch, and he growls.

"*Fuck!* You're insatiable," he curses.

"You're such a tease," he says gruffly as he gets to his feet.

He lifts me up, and I wrap my legs around him. He sits me on top of the piano and crashes his lips to mine. He haphazardly grasps the hem of his t-shirt and pulls it over my head, throwing it over his shoulder.

"It's not nice to tease."

He pinches my oversensitive nipple between his thumb and forefinger. I gasp, and he smiles wickedly. His large calloused hands caress my skin and roam gently over my body. Every nerve in my body is lit up and is in tune with everything that is Sam Newbolt. My blood is singing at the feel of his hands on me. He takes my face in both of his hands and presses his lips ravenously to mine. His kiss is intense, and his tongue explores mine. When he pulls away, his eyes have gone from blazing green to a dark forest like green.

"You belong to me, angel. You are mine," he grinds out with a clenched jaw and drops his trousers unashamedly.

He steps out of them; his erection is standing loud and proud between his legs.

"I told you before, every fucking inch of you belongs to me and only me. Now lie back for me."

I lie back on top of the piano, the coldness causing goose bumps on my skin. I feel suddenly exposed and I cup my breasts in my hands. The light from the moon highlights Sam's profile, he is truly beautiful. All hard lines, muscles, and everything that should be illegal.

"Don't ever hide your body away from me. You're fucking beautiful, every inch of you is...perfect."

He moves my hands away from my breasts, and he shakes his head.

"How did I get so lucky?"

He steps between my legs and slides me forward so my bum is hanging off the edge of the piano.

"*Fuck,* I need to be inside you again, right now."

His voice is a rough whisper, and he grasps his rigid erection in his hand. He enters me urgently, and I shriek out at the invasion. His pace is rapid and unrelenting. I whimper softly and writhe beneath him as he is pumping in and out of me in frantic strokes.

"Sam," I cry out softly, and he places his finger against my lips.

"Shhh, quiet, angel. I've got you, I feel the same."

He slows his pace, and his green eyes lock with mine.

"Look at me, don't take those gorgeous eyes off me. I want you to feel what I feel."

I gaze longingly at him, and I am captivated by the feelings he induces in me. The rhythm he sets is slow, measured, and sensual. He leans forward and pins my wrists above my head. I curl my one leg around his waist and he thrusts forward with an expert swivel of his narrow hips. He kisses my neck and nips my earlobe while tirelessly pumping in and out of my soaking wet pussy.

"Peyton."

He lets out a low growl and with each languorous thrust; I feel my orgasm rising.

"You're close, angel, I can feel you."

Sam pants.

"So close, baby."

With each plunge of his cock, I can feel him deep inside me, rubbing my g-spot with his piercing. An intense orgasm builds with each drive and he lets go of my wrists.

"Peyton, get those fucking beautiful eyes on me; I'm so close," he rasps, and my eyes lock with his.

As he says those words, I feel my orgasm wash over me so powerfully that it feels like the earth has spun right off its axis and I'm free-falling. A second later, Sam finds his release, and he growls as his hot seed spurts deep inside me. As I come down from my orgasmic high, I am left breathless and spent on top of his piano. Sam pulls out of me and stands to his full six-foot four height.

"*Jesus!*"

He puffs out his cheeks and I chuckle softly. Sam strides forward and grasps both of my wrists. He pulls me up effortlessly and launches me over his shoulder, as if I weigh nothing. I squeal and giggle like a school girl. I love playful Sam, and it's times like this that I can't deny that I'm irrevocably in love with him.

***

The next morning, I wake in Sam's bed, and as I roll over sleepily, I feel a delicious soreness deep inside me, reminding me of our marathon love making session yesterday. The silk of his sheets feel cool against my skin, and I almost forgot how soft and decadent they feel. I reach out and find Sam's side of the bed empty. I sit up, and he chooses that moment to step into the bedroom with a white towel wrapped around his lean waist. His hair is still damp from the shower, and he looks glorious with beads of water running down his tattooed torso. I lick my lips as I catch sight of him, and his dazzling smile temporarily disarms me.

"Good morning, angel," he rasps, and my eyes shamelessly roam over his almost nude body.

He cocks his pierced eyebrow and smirks.

"Don't mind me, I'm quite happy for you to lie there and eye fuck me. As long as I can return the favour."

He winks and sits down on the edge of the bed. I crawl closer to him, and he rips the cover away from me. I go to grab it to conceal my modesty, but he shakes his head and slaps my bum. He pulls me in for an earth-shattering kiss, and I'm left breathless when he pulls away. I will never get used to the effect he has on me. I suddenly think of Kai and how I left him waiting outside on Sam's driveway yesterday.

"*Shit*, where's Kai?"

Sam narrows his eyes.

"Should I be worried that you're thinking of another man while you're lying naked in my bed, angel?"

I smirk devilishly.

"No, I left him outside in your driveway. I was just concerned that he was still there."

Sam throws his head back and laughs.

"Relax. He stayed over, had a few beers, and played Xbox with Brody. I called Cole and told him I'm driving you to work today, so he's given him the morning off, angel. It's fine, I'm more than capable of taking care of you."

He kisses me on the end of my nose and starts to dry off. *He's nothing if not thoughtful.* I kick my legs up behind me and rest my chin on my hands.

"I know it's Monday morning, but all I'm craving is pancakes and sex," I purr seductively.

He cocks his pierced eyebrow and smirks that delicious smirk of his, his dimple jumping into place.

"Demanding this morning aren't we, angel?" he rasps playfully and traces his fingers down my cheek. "You go and shower, and I'll go make you those pancakes, angel. Bathrooms through there, and there are fresh towels under the sink."

He kisses me chastely on the lips, pulls on a pair of black boxer briefs and a pair of loose, ripped blue jeans, leaving the fly unzipped. He runs his fingers through his damp hair and leaves the room. There's something about the way he moves gracefully around the bedroom, and I can't help but watch him.

Are you completely out of your ever-loving fucking mind? This man clearly wants to be with you.

I shake away that thought as I make my way into the en-suite bathroom. It is every bit as luxurious as the other rooms in Sam's house; it screams luxury, wealth and style. Everything in the bathroom is *so* Sam. The walls are made up of black rectangular tiles, the floor is white marble and it gleams as I move further into the room. One wall has a large flat screen T.V across it and there are speakers in each corner. There is a large vanity unit with a glass egg shaped sink and a large rectangular mirror above it. There are a series of cube like cupboards underneath the sink, a large egg-shaped bath and a large shower cubicle, which is so huge you could literally fit a football team in it. I step in the shower, and after a few attempts, I finally work out how to turn it on and I relish the feel of the hot water from the seven jets cascading over my body.

I take a little longer in the shower than I normally do, and by the time I am finished, I feel refreshed, relaxed, and ready to face a brand-new week at work. I step out of the bathroom, and as I rub the towel over my highly sensitive skin, every nerve in my body is on high alert. I shouldn't be here, I need to be as far away from Sam Newbolt as possible. I shouldn't be anywhere near him. My heartbeat starts to quicken, and I have this sudden urge to run. The rational part of my brain tries to convince me, that I should stay, at least give us a chance. But the other, less rational side, tells me it is all kinds of wrong for me to even be in the same room as him.

I finger comb my hair and give my hair a quick blast with a hairdryer that Sam left out for me. *How thoughtful.* I look in the mirror at my reflection. My skin is still flushed pink from the shower and my blue eyes are sparkling back at me.

Get it the fuck together, Harper.

I take a deep breath and route through Sam's drawers for a t-shirt. I pull out a distressed grey t-shirt with the words 'Rehab is for quitters' in large white letters and pull it on. The cotton brushes over my skin like a gentle caress.

Pull up those big girl pants and go to him, Harper.

I make my way downstairs and I can hear music coming from the kitchen. The dulcet tones of The Script are coming through the speaker system, Danny O' Donoghue is singing about a man on a wire. Sam is quietly humming to himself and making pancakes as I enter the kitchen. He is bare chested, his hard, tattooed, muscular chest is on show. His hair is perfectly mussed, and I'm itching to run my fingers through his raven softness.

Danny's rich, velvet voice fills the room, and I chuckle softly to myself as Sam moves gracefully around the kitchen, as if he was born to cook. He has a look of such concentration on his face as he picks up the spatula and lifts out the perfectly cooked pancake. *Is there anything this man isn't good at? Fucking show off!* He places it on the already growing pile and ladles more mixture into the pan. He lifts his head and his green eyes lock with mine.

"Angel," he rasps and begins to move closer to me, until he is standing in front of me.

He reaches out and gently grips my wrist. As his hand makes contact with my wrist, I feel the all too familiar electricity spark between us.

I can't do this, I can't allow myself to want him.

I snatch my hand away from him and start to back slowly away from him. The smile on his face fades and his face softens. The look in his eyes crushes me, but it gives me the strength and resolve to run back the way I came. I run up the stairs as fast as my legs can carry me and burst into the bedroom. I start to frantically gather my clothes from yesterday and peel off Sam's t-shirt. I quickly pull on my bra and decide to go without knickers. As I pull my vest over my head, Sam is leaning casually against the door frame.

"*Fuck!*" he curses and runs his fingers idly through his already mussed hair.

"What are you running from, angel? Did I do something wrong?" he rasps softly.

I close my eyes briefly and shake my head.

"I want you too much, Sam," I admit reluctantly, and a dazzling smile washes over his face.

"Please, don't fight this anymore; don't fight me. I fucking love you, I need you, I'm nothing without you. You can never want me too much, it's not possible."

He's standing in front of me now and his six-foot four frame towers over me.

"Don't overthink it, just...*go with it*. Let's start with eating breakfast together, then I'll drive you to work, and if you decide you don't want me, then I told you when we met: I'm a patient man, I can wait."

He tips my chin up to face him, and the green in his eyes is so intense, it's almost hypnotising. I find myself nodding and agreeing all too easily. The smile he gives me in return lights up his whole face, and I have a feeling this is the first time he's smiled like that in a while.

"You don't have to wear yesterday's clothes, angel. There are some fresh ones in a wardrobe in the room at the end of the hallway. You'll find everything you in need there. Get dressed and meet me in the kitchen, that's an order."

He winks, and I find myself smiling at his dominant side.

Maybe I'll find myself agreeing to forever a little more easily than either of us could anticipate.

We eat breakfast together of homemade pancakes, maple syrup and bacon. We sit at the kitchen island and the dynamic between us is easy and flirty, reminding me of how we used to be. We talk about everything and nothing, all at the same time. I don't think I've smiled this much in a long time. After we eat breakfast, I go into one of Sam's many spare rooms to change my clothes. It is like any woman who's obsessed with fashion's wet dream. I don't have time to peruse properly, so I just opt for a denim skirt, a black halter neck top with a white candy skull print on the front and matching black Converse. I grab my bag and Sam gestures for me to get into my car. My purple Chevy Camaro ZL1, which Sam gave me as a present for my twenty-seventh birthday. *I can't believe he kept it.* I smile at the memory.

"Your chariot awaits, m'lady!"

He winks, and I climb in the passenger seat with a permanent smile on my face. The seats are bucket seats, which feel as though they hug you. They are a gunmetal grey colour and the leather is so soft and comfortable. Sam climbs into the driver's seat, the flex of his muscles causing the all too familiar ache between my thighs. Sam smirks as I take him in. He is wearing a pair of faded ripped jeans, which hang low on his hips, a black and white striped My Chemical Romance vest, and a pair of black motorcycle boots. His hair is styled into soft spikes, and he has a pair of aviator sunglasses perched on top of his head.

"See something you like, angel?"

I bite my lip, and he growls.

"You're asking to be fucked on the bonnet of this car, angel, but I don't want to make you late," he rasps and winks, knowing the effect he has on my raging libido.

Handsome bastard.

He starts the engine and pulls out of the driveway smoothly. Sam handles his car the way he handles every aspect of his busy rock star life. With precision, and quiet control. The way his muscles bunch with every turn of the steering wheel has me rubbing my thighs together like a woman starved of sex.

"Do you need something, angel?" he says playfully.

I turn my head towards the window, embarrassed that I'm so turned on.

"Don't turn away from me. Open those gorgeous legs for me."

My head whips back round to face him. *He can't possibly be serious.*

"Don't look so shocked; relax and live a little. The windows are tinted, no one can see, although I think the thought of someone watching you climax turns you on. The danger, the thought of almost getting caught; admit it, the thought makes you wet."

His voice drips with seduction and pure sex. I bite my lip at the rasp of his voice and press my thighs together anxiously.

"You're desperate to come, aren't you? I can smell your arousal; you smell...*fucking delicious*. How would you like it if I pushed my finger deep inside you and circled your swollen clit until you couldn't take anymore?"

He nips my earlobe and moves one hand from the steering wheel. He walks his fingers down to rest between the apex of my thighs.

"I can feel the heat between those gorgeous thighs."

I swallow hard, and a small moan escapes from me. He removes his hand and places it back on the steering wheel.

"How does it feel knowing that I own every fucking inch of you, Peyton? I can play your body like an instrument. I know which buttons to press to satisfy your every need, your every desire, and every dirty little fantasy."

His gruff voice washes over me, and I rub my thighs together more furiously, desperate for the pending climax I can feel deep within me. Sam chuckles softly and runs his rough calloused finger down my neck. His touch feels like electricity, like my skin is burning for him to take me.

"Sam," I whisper, aware that my voice sounds breathy and full of need.

I chance a look in his direction and his eyes are focused firmly on the road, seemingly unaffected. But when I look down at his crotch, I find his hard-on is straining against his jeans, and I know that look is a facade.

"*Jesus*, I'm so fucking hard, it's painful. You look so hot right now, angel. All hot and desperate for my cock to slide deep inside you. I'm craving to have you beneath me. I should have fucked you this morning and then every time you moved today, you'd be sore and remember that it was me who made you that way. That you belong to me and *only* me; all the other men will pale into insignificance."

His voice is low and hoarse as I turn my head to face him. His green eyes are blazing with lust.

"I...I need you," I manage to pant out.

"I wish I could lay you across the bonnet of this car and fuck you like I need to."

The atmosphere in the car is charged with sexual energy.

"Take off your knickers and touch yourself."

I lean the seat back and quickly, but awkwardly, slide my knickers down my thighs until I pull them off. The gust of cold air from the air conditioning brushes over my bare sex, causing me to shiver and goose bumps to break out all over my body. I slowly move my one hand down my abdomen and down to my pussy. I press one finger into my slit and surprise myself at how slick I am. I gently rub and tease my wet folds. Sam growls whilst trying to pay attention to the road.

"Fuck me," he curses.

I push a finger inside myself and moan aloud as I begin to quicken my pace, moaning softly at the slow build-up of my orgasm deep within me.

"Mmm, you've got no fucking idea how hot you look right now."

I introduce a second finger and a third. I gasp at the feeling of delicious fullness. I can feel my orgasm cresting to the surface, my heart beat quickening, my breath coming in sharp pants.

"Don't stop," he says gruffly and smiles his panty-dropping smile, as I continue to fuck myself with my fingers.

"Fuck me, you're so beautiful," he whispers seductively, and the sound of his voice makes me shiver with lust. "Even after all this time, my voice still affects you doesn't it, angel?"

He chuckles softly, and he takes his eyes off the road briefly. Suddenly we are shunted violently forward. The scrape of metal on metal makes my stomach roil. Sam curses long and loud.

"W...what the fuck was that?" I say anxiously, and Sam shakes his head.

"I have no fucking idea."

Sam pushes a button on the steering wheel, as I straighten myself out.

"Benedict."

Cole's rumbling voice comes through the surround sound system.

"Cole, it's me. I'm driving Peyton to work, but I think we're being followed, man. The car behind just bumped into the back of us," he says firmly, and Cole growls.

"For fucks sake, you really can't go anywhere without getting into fucking trouble can you, Newbolt?" Cole chastises, and Sam laughs nervously, desperately trying to keep the worry out of his voice.

"What can I say, dude, I like to keep you on your toes."

Cole chuckles softly.

"Alright, try and calm down, yeah? I need the make and model of the car and the registration plate if you can."

Sam turns to me.

"Have you got your seatbelt on, angel?"

I nod.

"Good girl, buckle up and hold tight."

Sam puts his foot down on the accelerator, and I am thrown back into my seat. My heart beat starts to quicken, and my fingers grip the seat tightly.

"Relax, angel. It's going to be fine, I promise."

We come to a roundabout and he takes a sharp left turn, causing the tires to squeal. His eyes flick from the interior mirror to the road and puffs out a sharp breath.

"Are they still following, Sam? I need you to tell me exactly what's going on," Cole asks, his anxious tone from earlier replaced with a calm one.

"Black Audi A3. I can't tell if the driver is a man or a woman, I can't see their face. Whoever it is, they're wearing a hoodie, a baseball cap and sunglasses. Still following, I tried to lose them, but they're not fucking giving up, Cole."

Sam presses the accelerator again and the car's V8 engine purrs like an angry kitten. Unexpectedly, the car bumps the back of our car a little more forcefully this time, causing Sam to briefly lose control of the car. He steers into the turn and regains control.

"FUCK, FUCK, FUCKING FUCK!" Sam roars.

"Sam, talk to me. Don't you dare do anything fucking stupid," Cole barks.

"*Shit!* I'll call you back."

Sam abruptly ends the call, and he signals left into a side road. He continues driving for a few minutes, with the car behind us in hot pursuit. Without warning, he pulls up the handbrake and expertly turns the car around, heading straight for the Audi.

"SAM! WHAT THE FUCK ARE YOU DOING?" I scream.

Sam stares fiercely ahead at the Audi, his eyes ablaze with anger. He roars, slamming his hand down on the steering wheel and causing me to flinch in my seat.

"COME ON, YOU WANKER!"

He tightens his grip on the steering wheel and my heart starts to pound in my chest. My stomach roils, and I feel like I need to throw up. *Fuck.* The rumble of the car's engine is the only sound I hear as we hurtle towards the Audi in a game of chicken. The driver of the Audi seems to take us heading straight for them as game on. As we edge to the Audi, Sam shouts 'FUCK!' and wrenches the steering wheel to the right, causing the Audi to clip the back end of our car. Sam loses complete control of the car, and the crunch of metal and the squeal of tires, fills my ears. The low sound of Sam cursing is the last thing I hear.

24

Sam

FUCK! What the fuck was I thinking? Heading straight towards a car that was following us is like holding a used tampon to a vampire. *Stupid fucking idiot.*

"Angel, angel, talk to me."

When she doesn't respond, I bump my head back on the headrest in frustration.

"BOLLOCKS!" I curse and a sharp pain lances through my shoulder. I roar out in agony and turn to Peyton.

"Angel," I rasp as I reach over to check for a pulse.

She groans softly and the feeling of relief that washes over me, causes me to let out the breath I didn't know I was holding. The sound of my phone ringing fills the eerie silence, and I push the button on the steering wheel with a trembling hand.

"Sam, don't *ever* fucking hang up on me like that again, you cocksucker."

Cole is about to continue, but I cut him off mid-sentence.

"We fucking crashed," I say flatly and Cole curses.

"*Shit!* Are you ok? Are you hurt? Sam?"

I growl in frustration.

"Dude, we've fucking crashed," I repeat, as if I can't believe what just happened.

Cole sighs heavily.

"Kai's on the way and so is an ambulance. I tracked your GPS on the car, but I need to know if you're injured, Sam? Talk to me, mate."

I turn to Peyton, and she moans as her eyes flicker open.

"*Motherfucker!* I think my shoulders dislocated. Peyton was unconscious, but she's coming around. I can't tell if she's injured. Angel?" I reach for her hand. "Angel, it's ok. We've been in an accident."

She lets out a strangled sob.

"I need you to tell me where it hurts."

Her terrified blue eyes lock with mine.

"Sam," she whispers hoarsely as I squeeze her hand.

"Shhh, I'm here, angel. Everything's going to be ok, but you need to tell me where it hurts."

She starts to sob uncontrollably. I think she's in shock. *Shit.*

"My head and my neck hurts," she says hoarsely, and Cole seemingly takes control of the situation.

"Help is on the way, I need you both to keep calm for me. Sugar, listen, everything's going to be alright. Freddie's safe, he's with Ruby, Jax and a few of the guys from my team. I've tracked the GPS system in the car, I know exactly where you are. We're going to find this motherfucker and nail him to the fucking wall," Cole says with an icy edge to his voice.

The sound of Peyton's soft sobs pierce my heart like a thousand knives. At that moment, the sound of sirens fills the silence and all I can think is, *this is all my fucking fault.*

25

Peyton

I wake up in an all too bright room with blinding fluorescent lights above me. I struggle to focus my eyes on my surroundings while a blinding pain in my head rips through me, and I feel like I've been hit with a shovel.

Fuck me, that hurts.

I try again to focus, and that's when I see him, Sam. He is sitting in the large beige coloured chair next to my bed, wearing a black sling and worrying his lip between his perfect white teeth. His raven black hair is mussed and looks as if he has been constantly running his hand through it.

"Angel," he says gruffly, his familiar striking face marred with worry. "You're in the hospital, you've got a concussion and mild whiplash."

I nod as a dull throb settles itself in my frontal lobe. *Ouch, that really fucking hurts.*

"Where's Freddie?" I say with a panicked edge to my voice.

"He's fine, he's safe. He's back at my place with Ruby and Jax."

My shoulders sag with relief.

"What the *fuck* were you thinking?" I say through gritted teeth, and the look in his green eyes almost destroys me.

He swallows a few times before he speaks.

"Angel, I..."

We are interrupted by a soft rap on the door. Sam opens the door and I hear Cole say.

"Can I have a word, Sam?"

Cole's deep timbre fills the eerie silence.

"Anything you have to say, you can say it in front of Peyton," Sam says hoarsely, and Cole enters the room, nodding curtly in my direction.

He is wearing a black suit, a black tank top and a shirt and tie underneath, with black shoes, a black flat cap, and a black pea coat. He pulls out a card and walks over to me. He hands me what looks like a business card, what is written on the card, causes a cold chill to run down my spine and settle in my gut as I feel the colour drain from my face.

Next time, bitch

X

"It came with a bunch of white lilies, which arrived about half an hour ago. We have to treat this as a serious threat."

Cole folds his arms across his broad chest, and I can't fight back the tears anymore as a sob escapes from my mouth. There was a time when I felt safe with Sam and nothing could hurt me while he's around, but at this moment, I start to doubt whether I am truly safe. Before I know what, I'm saying, I blurt out.

"Please leave."

A look passes between Sam and Cole.

"You don't mean that, angel."

Sam's voice is laced with hurt, and Cole tries to placate him.

"Come on, Sam, don't fight her on this one. I'll drive you home, mate."

Sam steps forward.

"This isn't fucking finished, angel."

With those words, he turns around and leaves. I don't doubt that it is far from over, not by a long shot.

***

In the week that passes, security is doubled, and I now have another guy called Trey guarding me in addition to Kai. Trey is an ex MMA fighter, and he has long black hair pulled back into a ponytail. He has cafe au lait skin and is of Native American descent. He has broad shoulders, dark brown eyes, a goatee beard, and he looks menacing, but he is the nicest person I have ever met. I recovered from concussion after a few days of bed rest and TLC from Remy, who has become a welcome fixture to our lives again. It really is like old times and he has fitted back into our lives as easily as he did for all those months we stayed with him in Santa Monica.

Also, the week was filled with endless concern from my family, Ruby, Seb, Danny, and the boys. The endless phone calls and text messages from Sam remind me that I'm never far from his thoughts. I understand why he drove straight for that car. Sam is a fighter, but I don't know if I can ever truly forgive him for putting both our lives in danger through sheer recklessness and stupidity. The messages of apology came thick and fast, but faded out by day three, after I told him in no uncertain terms that I needed some time to think.

After a busy few days back at work, Friday has rolled around, and tonight is Ruby and Jax's engagement party. It is being held at Neon Nights, a regular haunt for the boys from the band and where a lot of their after-show parties are held. Ruby is staying at my place and it feels just like it did when we lived together. We are getting ready side by side in the mirror in my bedroom. The dulcet tones of Adam Levine singing about Lost Stars, is playing softly in the background as I'm applying my mascara and Ruby is putting the finishing touches to her ice blonde wig.

"Sam's been walking around like a bear with a sore arse all week, when are you going to stop fucking about and forgive him, babe?" Ruby says nonchalantly, and I cock my eyebrow.

"Really, Rubes? He almost got us both killed, and you're asking when I'm going to forgive him?"

She sighs.

"I have my happy ending, you deserve yours too, and Sam is clearly still in love with you."

I roll my eyes. *Ruby is the eternal romantic.* I have a feeling tonight is going to be eventful.

Ruby has a penchant for everything dramatic, and somehow, she managed to talk Jax into making their engagement party themed. The theme is fairy tales and superheroes. Ruby is dressed as Elsa from Frozen, with an ice blonde wig in a fishtail plait and Jax is dressed as Thor. I'm dressed as a sexy Red Riding Hood, complete with a black and red corset, a full black and red net skirt, and black stockings with red bows at the top, black Christian Louboutin heels, a red cape, and hood. My hair is styled into a neat bob, I'm wearing my usual natural makeup, with heavy eye makeup, and striking red lipstick.

It doesn't take us long to get to the exclusive venue, Neon Nights, which in the heart of the West End, near to Leicester Square. Jax, Ruby, and I arrive in a black limo. As we step out, we are immediately blinded by flashbulbs from the waiting paparazzi. Jax and Ruby walk hand in hand down the waiting red carpet, and I follow close behind them, my heart beating a frantic tattoo at the surreal feeling of being photographed.

It never gets easier, no matter how many times it happens.

We get to the clubs' entrance and a doorman, who I don't recognise, lets us through the velvet red rope with a curt nod. Everyone erupts into a round of applause as Ruby and Jax enter the room. He slings his arm around her protectively and kisses her gently on the forehead. She looks at him as though it's just him and her in the room; they look so in love. As I watch them interacting with each other, they are swept up in greetings from the crowd.

The club is filled with familiar faces. I see Brody, who is dressed as Superman, and Lucas is dressed as Captain America, complete with his signature shield. There is Cole, who is dressed as Batman, his fiancée Amy is dressed as Cat Woman, and their little girl Addison is dressed as Cinderella. The rest of the people in attendance are all dressed as various superheroes and characters from fairy tales. My mum and dad were invited too, but my dad is in Milan on a high-profile aftershave ad campaign, so my mum offered to babysit Freddie to give me a break, which I am extremely grateful for.

The club is exactly as I remember it, the walls decorated with opulent black and aubergine wall-coverings. The main area of the club is open, with purple plush sofas all around the edges and the tables are black granite and chrome. The fully stocked black granite bar takes up the whole back of the venue. A waiter wearing a tuxedo is instantly at our sides, handing us flutes of champagne. I take one and that's when I see him. *Sam.* He is dressed in a deep purple shirt, open at the collar, the sleeve of his shirt is rolled up to reveal his large bulging muscles and his heavily corded and tattooed arm. He has his other arm in a black sling. He is rocking a pair of black trousers, that make his arse look delicious, black Doc Martens, a black trilby hat and he finishes his Gambit from X Men outfit off with a black pinstripe waistcoat. He takes off his hat to reveal his hair, which is now cut short, but still long enough for him to spike and run his hands easily through. He looks exactly the way he did when we first met.

I feel his presence before I see him, the sparkle of his blazing green eyes, the dazzle of his brilliant smile, and the intensity of his eyes focused solely on me. I am instantly left breathless and reminded of the day we met. I can almost hear him rasp "Hey beautiful". The way he looks at me is as if he wants to devour me whole. The way he holds himself, the flex of his muscles, the way he holds his bottle of beer, the crinkle of his eyes as he laughs at something someone in his group says. I know I am staring, but I can't take my eyes off him.

"Quit staring and go talk to him, he misses you."

My thoughts are interrupted by Sam's sister, Willow. She stands in front of me and she looks the same as she did the last time I saw her. Her black hair still short on one side, long on the other side, and she is dressed as Wonder Woman. I smile warmly at the young woman who I became good friends with, during mine and Sam's relationship. I'm glad she is dating Seb, they are good for each other.

"Did he tell you what happened?" I say with a hint of malice in my voice.

Willow nods and takes a sip of her drink.

"If it's any consolation, he's sorry. Some men are lovers, some men are fighters and Sam's definitely a fighter. He would walk through hell for you, Peyton, don't be so hard on him."

My eyes choose that moment to lock with his, and he winks cheekily at me. I shyly look away, and Willow rolls her eyes.

"Come on, Peyton, you're practically eye-fucking each other from across the room. I can literally feel the sexual tension between you."

I drop my gaze and avoid looking her directly in the eye.

"He's a mess without you," she says softly, and I shake my head.

"He seems to be doing just fine without me, honey."

She rolls her eyes dramatically.

"*Oh please*, you're even more of a fucking fool than I first thought if you believe that crap."

I look over to where Sam was standing, and he is gone.

"I thought my ears were burning, angel."

His familiar is rasp so close to my ear that he startles me and causes goose bumps to break out across my skin. I look up into his eyes and shiver at his closeness. I inhale his intoxicating scent.

"I could feel your eyes on me from across the room, is it the suit? I always knew you couldn't resist me in a suit."

He smirks cockily. The look in his green eyes has me transfixed, and I can't look away. Willow clears her throat and brushes my arm.

"I'll leave you two to it," she says smirking and winks as she walks away, leaving Sam and me alone.

My eyes roam over his muscular body, and he chuckles throatily

"I would be more than happy to stand here and let you eye fuck me all night, but we both know we've got unfinished business, angel."

He takes a long sip of a glass of amber liquid, and his eyes shamelessly wander over my body.

"The unfinished business that almost got us both fucking killed?"

He winces at my icy tone but quickly recovers, cocking his pierced eyebrow.

"I thought you got off on the danger? I seem to remember you shamelessly touching yourself right before the crash."

My face flushes with embarrassment as I recall the way he commanded me to touch myself in the passenger seat of the car.

"Hold that thought, angel, I'm sure I can arrange a repeat performance, minus psychopaths in Audi A3's."

He winks, and I scowl at him.

"How can you even joke about that? You're fucking unbelievable, do you know that, Sam?"

I hiss as he throws his head back and laughs, putting his empty glass down on a nearby table.

"So, I've been told," he says cockily, and I go to walk away from him.

He grabs my wrist and I feel the familiar spark of electricity as his skin makes contact with mine.

"Don't fucking walk away from me, angel. I'm done waiting. I've apologised for what happened, and I'm sorry for keeping things from you, but you have to know that every single one of my actions was carried out because I'm trying to protect you and our son."

We are interrupted by the instantly recognisable voice of Ruby's mum. I turn around and she beams at me, throwing her arms enthusiastically around me.

"Peyton! Sweetie!" she says breathily.

Pearl Logan is the same as I remember her. She is an older, more sophisticated version of her daughter. Her waist length dark hair is twisted into an elegant chignon, her make-up is flawless, and her figure is to die for. At fifty-four, she looks like she could be a movie star; she has an understated elegance to her demeanour.

"You look fabulous, darling! Let me look at you!"

She pulls away from our embrace and holds me at arm's length.

"You're too thin, sweetie! Too thin, you need to start eating," she states dramatically, and I smile softly.

"It's been too long, Pearl, how are you?"

She nods.

"I'm good darling, how are you?"

I nod, and she turns her attention to Sam, watching our interaction intently.

"This must be the famous Sam, I've been dying to meet you."

He steps forward and kisses the back of Pearl's hand.

"The very same, often imitated, never duplicated. Pleasure to meet you."

Cocky bastard.

I swear Pearl swoons on the spot, and I shake my head in exasperation.

"I'm Pearl, Ruby's mum."

He flashes his dimples, and Pearl giggles like a teenager.

"Ruby's mum, *no*. You don't look old enough, I would have said you were sisters!" Sam compliments, and Pearl giggles like a teenager.

"*Oh, stop it!* Peyton darling, in't he handsome?" she gushes, and I roll my eyes.

I don't how Ray puts up with her antics sometimes.

"*Oh please!* Don't encourage him, Pearl, his ego is large enough."

Sam throws his head back and laughs.

"Darling, that boy is sex on a stick and you've been keeping him hidden and all to yourself. Didn't Sophia ever teach you how to share?" Pearl jokes, and I laugh.

Pearl Logan is incorrigible and a shameless flirt.

Sam leans in close, whispering in my ear.

"There's that jealous streak again, angel. Keep it up, you're only making me harder," he rasps so only I can hear him, and I feel my cheeks flame at his seductive words.

Ruby's dad chooses that moment to join us. Ray Logan reminds me of an older, more distinguished version of Remy. His dark hair is streaked with grey, and the russet brown of his eyes is identical to Remy's. He is visibly thinner than the last time I saw him, and he is wearing a tuxedo. I'm assuming he is dressed as James Bond.

"Peyton, sweetheart, so good to see you," Ray says in his gruff East London accent and sweeps me up in a bear hug.

"Ray, it's good to see you too, it's been forever! I was just telling Pearl that I've missed you both."

Ray kisses me on both cheeks and narrows his eyes in Sam's direction.

"Ray Logan," he says curtly, and Sam takes his outstretched hand.

Ray was always like a father to me and extremely protective of me and Ruby while we were growing up. Like my mum and dad, Pearl is the strong, dominant matriarch of the family, and Ray is the quiet, protective patriarch.

"Sam Newbolt, pleased to meet you, Ray. If you would excuse me, I have some business to attend to. It was nice to meet you both."

He nods, winks at me, and strides off to the other side of the club. Pearl fans herself with her hand.

"Is it me, or is it hot in here? That boy is mad about you, darling."

She chuckles, and Ray rolls his eyes. I shake my head exasperated as my phone vibrates. I take it out of my handbag and swipe the screen to open the message.

Car park

5 minutes

S xx

I finish my drink and put my phone away.

"I'm sorry, Pearl, Ray, but Ruby needs me. We'll catch up soon, I promise. We can arrange a girly day at the spa, you, me, and Ruby."

I kiss her on the cheek and go to walk away, but I collide with a hard-muscular chest. I look up into the amused russet eyes of Remy, and he wolf whistles.

"I must say, you're looking very hot tonight, beaut."

He winks as I take him in. He looks gorgeous and is dressed head to toe in leather as Guy of Gisborne from Robin Hood. He is wearing leather trousers, which mould to his lean frame, as if they were made just for him. He is also wearing a long leather jacket, a leather shirt open at the collar, black leather gloves, a bow and arrow slung across his back, and calf-length boots.

"Not so bad yourself, Logan."

We both laugh, and he kisses me softly on the forehead.

"Where were you off to in a hurry?" he asks curiously, and I shift my gaze to the floor.

"Ah, Newbolt's clicked his fingers, so like the good little woman, you're running to him. What happened?"

I look up at him and bite my lip.

"It's not like that, Rem," I say defensively.

He cocks his eyebrow and tips my chin up to face him.

"Then enlighten me, Peyton. He put your life in jeopardy. What's it going to take for you to see that he's bad news?"

I take a step back from him.

"I...I...need to go."

Before I give him a chance to speak, I flee across the club and make my way down to the stairs to the underground car park. My heels clicking across the concrete floor is the only sound to be heard. As I turn the corner, that's when I catch sight of Sam. He looks mouth-wateringly delicious leaning up against the wall with one hand tucked casually into his pocket. He looks up and his eyes lock with mine, they are instantly smoky with lust. I approach him cautiously, and as I inch nearer to him, he grabs my wrist, pulling me to him. I stumble into him, and he catches me easily. He spins me around and pins me to the wall.

"I can't keep my eyes off you dressed like that, angel. You look...*fuck*...every man in there wants you. Do you know what that does to me?" he says gruffly.

He leans down and lightly nips my neck with his teeth.

"It makes me feel..." he growls and lifts me up with one arm, throwing me over his shoulder.

I yelp as he slaps my arse and strides across to a deserted section of the car park. It is shrouded in shadow. The only car parked in this section is a sleek, pearlescent blue, McLaren P1. He deposits me on the bonnet until I am spread out for him. He steps between my legs and the look in his eyes is hungry, as if he wants to devour me. I lean back on my elbows and he makes quick work of getting me naked from the waist down. He disregards his sling and Sam is in front of me looking magnificent, like a sculpted Greek God. His body is ripped, his bulging tattooed biceps, his thick, heavily corded arms, and his broad chest on show in his deep purple shirt. His hair is tousled, and his green eyes are blazing with lust, as he looks down at me.

"Look how swollen your clit is, angel, always so pink and ready for me," he rasps in that seductive way that turns me on so much and makes me ache with pure want. "*Fuck me,* you are so damn beautiful."

I bite my lip.

"God, Sam I want you so badly, I need you to fuck me hard, please, fuck me."

I try not to sound desperate but fail miserably.

"Good, because I certainly can't promise that I'll be gentle."

He smiles that dazzling smile that has haunted my dreams every night.

"I don't want you to be gentle."

My voice is barely a whisper, and Sam growls. He unzips his black trousers and frees his impressive erection.

"I need your cock buried deep inside me."

He chuckles softly.

"Oh, sweetheart, I'm going to fucking bury myself so deep inside you, neither of us will know where you end, and I begin," he whispers huskily and roughly shoves two fingers inside my shamelessly soaked pussy.

I cry out in pure pleasure as his fingers fuck me thoroughly.

"SAM!"

His calloused fingers expertly twist and move deep within my hot channel. I am writhing on the cool metal and grasping my breasts.

"I've got you, angel."

He introduces another finger, and I scream out.

"OH FUCK! SAM!"

He looks at me with pure want in his eyes.

"Come for me, Peyton, come now," he commands, and with one swift movement of his fingers, my orgasm tears through me, like an explosion of pent up sexual energy.

I scream out in pure ecstasy as Sam wrings every ounce of pleasure from my body.

"God, you are so hot when you come," he rasps.

As I come down from my orgasmic high, he roughly enters me with a sharp shove forward. He fucks me so hard, I feel the slap of his balls with each thrust.

"*Jesus!* Your cunt is so fucking tight," he grunts, and he continues to fuck me hard.

He lifts my leg over his shoulder, and he thrusts so deep I can feel him bump my cervix with each plunge of his hard cock. I arch my back in ecstasy and moan loudly.

"*Oh Sam!* I need it harder, fuck me hard," I cry desperately, and he increases his deep drives, fucking me like a mad man.

"Do you like it hard, angel?" he growls.

"*Oh Jesus yes!* Yes! I love it when you fuck me hard."

He reaches out and pulls the cup of my corset down and rolls my sensitive nipple between his thumb and forefinger. The combination of pleasure and pain causes me to scream.

"YES! OH GOD YES!"

As I cry out, he grips my throat tighter and increases his deep thrusts, fucking me harder each time.

"Let it go, Peyton, *fuck,* I can feel you throbbing around my cock. Come for me NOW!" he demands, and my orgasm washes over me like a tidal wave of pleasure.

I scream out and Sam muffles my cries by putting his hand over my mouth as he finds his release.

"*FUCKKK!*" he growls as his hot seed spurts deep inside me.

As both of our orgasms subside, we both lie in silence, the only sound is our laboured breaths. I shudder with tiny aftershocks as he pulls out. He chuckles wickedly and zips up his trousers. He crushes his lips to mine, and I am lost in everything that is Sam Newbolt.

After dressing and straightening ourselves in relative silence, we head back inside separately. As I enter the main vestibule of the club, Ruby rushes towards me and throws her arms dramatically up in the air.

"There you are! I've been looking everywhere for you, babe."

She hugs me and scrunches up her nose.

"You smell of sex."

She narrows her eyes and as she takes me in, her mouth forms a perfect 'O' shape. She claps her hands animatedly and bounces on the spot.

"OH-MY-GOD!" she shrieks, attracting everyone's attention, and I flush with embarrassment.

"Ruby!" I chastise her, and she shrugs.

"You and Sam?"

She makes a sexual gesture with her hands, and I cover my face.

"Yes, and please never do that, ever again!"

We both laugh as her face suddenly turns serious.

"I want all the gory details, you filthy little slut! But first, I need your help, babe."

I narrow my eyes, and the anxious look in her eyes sets me on edge.

"What's wrong, Ruby?"

She grabs my hand and drags me in the direction of the toilet. Jax is standing guard at the door and we enter the men's toilets. Remy is cowering in the corner with his hands over his head. He looks like a frightened animal, his head whipping from side to side. He covers his ears.

"NO!" he shouts, and the look of worry on Ruby's face breaks my heart.

"What's wrong with him, Peyton?"

I recognise the signs, Remy is having a post traumatic episode. It is an anxiety disorder and is common in ex-military. Remy's soft whimpers cause my heart to break all over again, as if I'm witnessing it for the first time. He scrambles back across the floor, with wide, glossy eyes.

"ON YOUR LEFT, SOLDIER!" he shouts.

I crouch down and gently touch his arm.

"Rem, Rem, you're not in Afghanistan anymore, you're in London with me. It's Peyton, remember? Remy? Come back to me."

I take his hand and stroke his knuckles, trying desperately to soothe him.

"Remy, listen to me, babe, you're safe now, I promise. It's me. Nothing's going to hurt you, I won't let it," I say softly, and I see the moment when his eyes clear.

His russet brown eyes lock with mine and a frown line appears between his eyes.

"Remy."

His eyes dart around the room and then focus on me alone.

"It happened again didn't it, beaut?"

I nod and stroke his face as he quietly curses to himself.

"It's ok, it's fine, Rem. Look at me."

The look in his eyes destroys me. He used to tell me back in Santa Monica, that every time he had an episode, he could hear gun fire, smell burning flesh, and the stench of rotting corpses. He has nightmares and flashbacks of when he was out in Afghanistan, which affect his day to day living. He manages it by taking antidepressants and going to a weekly group meeting for wounded soldiers. I can't even begin to imagine what he went through over there.

"Look at me, Rem. It's alright, everything's going to be fine, I promise. I'm here."

I pull him into my chest, and he sobs softly. I rub my hands up and down his back soothingly. It breaks my heart to see someone I care deeply about go through this. We spend long minutes on the floor in the men's toilets, until Remy pulls away and gets to his feet. He offers me his hand and pulls me up with him. He yanks me to his chest and squeezes me tightly.

"Thank you, for being there...for always being there for me."

I breathe him in and snuggle closer to him.

"You don't have to thank me, but you're welcome."

He pulls away from our embrace and splashes his face with cold water. He dries off with some paper towels and straightens himself out. He briefly speaks to Ruby in hushed tones, kisses her on cheek, and leaves the toilet. I lean against the sink and let out the breath I didn't know I was holding.

"Does that happen a lot?" Ruby enquires, and I nod sadly. "Thank you. Jax walked in on him freaking out, we didn't know what the fuck to do, babe," Ruby says with a panicked edge to her voice, and I brush her arm reassuringly.

"It was a regular occurrence back in Santa Monica. It was a little difficult to deal with at first, waking up to him screaming in the middle of the night, but I learned to cope with it."

Ruby throws her arms around me.

"I had no idea. He's my brother, and I knew nothing about it. What kind of person does that make me?"

I squeeze her tighter.

"He didn't want you worrying. You know what he's like, he's stubborn, just like your old man."

We both laugh. I pull away from her and cup her face in my hands.

"Now, let's get this party started, babe!"

26

Sam

I've been watching him all night. He can't take his eyes off her, and the rage I feel inside is threatening to consume me.

Remy fucking Logan.

Even the name sounds bitter on my tongue. I couldn't help myself, I *had* to take her to the car park and fuck her; because in my twisted mind, it marks her as *mine*. How fucked up is that? As I make my way through the throng of people to the toilet, I catch him coming out of the gents. I step in front of him and he comes to a halt.

"Ah, Newbolt. I'd say it's nice to see you, but I'd be lying."

Cocky motherfucker. I cock my eyebrow and back him against the wall. He lifts his chin defiantly, as if to goad me into doing something I'll regret, but I don't take the bait. I fold my arms across my chest and look him straight in the eye.

"You're in love with her, aren't you?" I say, with an icy tone, and he is silent.

He mirrors my body language and folds his arms; his stance is loose as his steely gaze locks with mine.

"Answer the fucking question, Logan. Are you in love with Peyton?" I say glacially, with a clenched jaw. I feel so out of control and this *isn't* me.

"YES! YES, I'm in love with her, and I'm not ashamed to admit it. I've been in love with her since we were fucking kids! It's only *ever* been her, but I never stood a chance."

He runs his hands through his dark hair and at that moment, I actually feel sorry for him.

"I haven't set foot in the U.K. in ten fucking years, but I came back for *her,* in the vain hope, that she would finally have moved on and be over you. That year she was with me in Santa Monica, I'd never felt more alive, she bought me back to life. Since she left, it's like the lights went out."

He scrubs his hand down his face, and even though I am listening to another man tell me he has feelings for my girl, *I understand*. That's exactly how I felt when I found out she died and again when she said she didn't want to be with me anymore. *I was truly fucking crushed.*

"Walk away, Logan. It's only a matter of time before she realises she wants to be with me."

He stands up straighter and rolls his shoulders. He takes a step forward and places his hands on his hips.

"You have no right asking me that. I walked away from her before and it was the biggest mistake of my fucking life," he says, and at that moment, I admire his raw honesty.

"I put a whole ocean between us because I was terrified of the way I felt about her, but by the time I finally realised, it was too late. I'd signed up to the army, and I was being deployed. The day I left, I kept hoping she'd come to me, to say goodbye. I waited for her, but she never came. I knew then it was over between us."

He sighs and laughs bitterly.

"I have no fucking idea why I'm telling you this."

We are interrupted by heels clicking across the floor. I look up and see Remy's mum, Pearl, heading towards us.

"Sam! Darling!"

She stops in front of us and pinches my cheeks.

"You're so bloody handsome! If only I was ten years younger!"

She winks, and Remy rolls his eyes.

"Mum! Please! You're embarrassing yourself."

Remy tries to drag her away, but she digs her heels in.

"Remy, darling! Have you met Sam? In't he handsome?"

I can smell the alcohol on her breath, and I can feel the tension hang thick in the air.

"Me and Sam have met mum. Come dance with me, and leave Sam to it, yeah?"

I can tell Remy is trying desperately to get his mum away from me. I can't say I blame him. *I like the older woman, but the only woman I want is Peyton.*

"Peyton is a lucky woman," Pearl states, and I see Remy silently bristling at his mums' side.

"Come on, mum."

He manages to drag her away, and I wave awkwardly.

"See you later, Sam darling!"

She blows a kiss in my direction, and I let out a sigh of relief. *Now I need to go and find Peyton.*

27

Peyton

After Remy's near meltdown, I take Ruby back into the club and we dance. I let my inhibitions go, and I dance like no one is watching. As one song blends into another, the room is filled with the unique sound of *Uptown Funk* by Mark Ronson and Bruno Mars. The funky drum beat and the distinctive voice of Bruno Mars lights me up from the inside. *I love this song.* I see Remy out of the corner of my eye and playfully grab his hand. I mouth the words *'Dance with me'.* He nods, smiles, and twirls me around. I laugh as he pulls me close to him. The heat radiates between us and he moves fluidly against me. *Remy is an extremely good dancer.*

We move in harmony with each other, and with each grind of our hips, it makes us both breathless. He takes both of my hands in his and creates distance between us. The look in his eyes is one I remember well, it tells me exactly how he feels about me. We continue to move in perfect rhythm, he twisting his hips while he twirls me around then catches me in his arms. We look in each other's eyes and my skin starts to prickle. I know Sam is near, I can feel his presence. Before I know what is happening, I'm snatched from Remy's hold, and Sam towers over me.

"I'm cutting in," he rasps, and I snatch my hand away from his.

He narrows his eyes.

"Angel," he says in warning, and I shake my head.

"Don't."

Unexpectedly, I feel a sharp pain in my stomach. *Shit, that hurts.* Then I remember, I'm due on my period. The pain feels like stomach cramps and I start to feel like I need to throw up.

"Beaut? Are you ok?" Remy says with a hint of concern to his voice.

"I don't feel too good, Rem."

I blink my eyes a few times, and he steadies me.

"I'll take you home."

Sam goes to protest, but the look in Remy's eyes tells him not to argue.

"Get the fuck out of my way Newbolt, or I swear to God, I will fucking end you," Remy says with a menacing edge to his voice.

Sam's green eyes blaze with anger and he clenches his fist at his side. He looks as though he wants to argue, but he just finishes his drink in one large gulp and slams the glass down on a nearby table. His eyes lock with mine, and he nods tersely.

"I hope you feel better soon, angel; this isn't finished. I'll have Cole come and get you tomorrow."

He turns on his heel and strides away before I can give him an answer.

Fucking men.

***

As we arrive back at my flat, I've started to feel marginally better and I kick the door shut behind me. Before I know what is happening, Remy spins me around, pins me to the wall, and kisses the life out of me. He knocks the breath straight from my lungs as he introduces his tongue, softly, stroking and teasing mine. He suddenly stops kissing me and rests his forehead against mine, his breath coming out in sharp gusts.

"*Fuck,* I'm so sorry, beaut, I...I don't know what the hell I was thinking."

I cup his face in my hands and look at him, his brown eyes are filled with such turmoil.

"Don't apologise, Rem."

I am about to crush my lips to his, when a cramp tears through me, almost taking my legs out from beneath me. Remy scoops me up in his arms.

"Right, where do you keep your hot water bottle? Go lie down, that's an order. I'll make us some hot chocolate, I've been dying to get my hands on that fancy coffee machine."

He winks cheekily, and I point him in the direction of the kitchen cupboard.

"As much as I like you in leather, Dexter left some clothes behind in my spare room. You're about the same size, you're more than welcome to them if you want to change into something more comfortable."

He nods, and I undress for bed, climbing gingerly underneath the covers. Ten minutes later, Remy returns wearing a pair of loose grey jogging bottoms and a plain white t-shirt. *I still can't get used to him with short hair.* He has two mugs of hot chocolate with marshmallows in his hands and a hot water bottle underneath his arm.

"I improvised. Hope you don't mind?"

He looks boyish as he says those words, and I chuckle softly.

"Course not, thank you. You're so thoughtful."

He smiles boyishly. He hands me the hot water bottle, and I place it on my stomach. He places both mugs down on the table next to my bed, and he perches himself on the edge.

"How are you feeling now?"

I nod.

"Better, thank you."

He nods and takes out a box of paracetamol from his pocket, placing them on the table.

"Here, I found these. They should help with the pain."

I smile.

"Thank you. Lie with me for a while?"

I open the duvet, inviting him into my bed. He climbs in next to me, pulling me into his side. I snuggle up to him, and soon, I am drifting off into a dreamless sleep.

***

My breathing comes in short, sharp, erratic bursts. My lungs are burning, and my body is trembling with such crippling fear.

"Did you really think I would allow you to have your happily ever fucking after, slut?"

J.D laughs maniacally as I start to sob hysterically. He looks the same as I remember him, and I know I won't survive, not this time; he won't allow it.

"FUCKING ANSWER ME, WHORE!"

I shake my head no as he scratches his head with the butt of his gun, which I didn't realise he was holding. The action makes this all too real and I wish this was all a bad dream. I struggle against the metal handcuffs, which have me shackled to the bed. The bite of the metal against my wrist reminds me I'm not going anywhere. How the fuck did I get here? I realize I am naked as he steps closer to the bed. He sits next to me and runs the gun down my sternum. J.D traces a line down my abdomen and stops as he gets to my pubic bone.

"I think it's time for us to have a bit of fun, don't you? Although my mother used to remind me all the time, it's not good manners to play with your food."

J.D chuckles bitterly and I feel helpless. My legs are spread and bound as I see the familiar red light of the camera set up in the corner.

"Samson fucking Newbolt is going to curse the day he ever met me!"

His eyes wide and crazy. He presses the gun lower and without warning, shoves the barrel deep inside my pussy. The burn of the invasion stings as he starts to move the cold metal in and out, increasing his pace. I am screaming so loud, my ears ring with the sound.

"NO! NO! PLEASE STOP!" I scream, but it seems to urge him on as he is pumping it faster and faster. "STOP! PLEASE STOP!"

He laughs hysterically.

"I love it when you beg me, you little slut. I heard you on that tour bus begging Sam to fuck you harder. You sounded just like the rest of those sad, desperate groupies," he taunts as he thrusts the gun harder into me.

It feels like something bursts inside of me and he looks down at his hand, which is covered in blood. My blood.

***

I wake up with a sharp gasp and sit bolt upright in bed. My breathing is laboured, and I am covered in a thin sheen of sweat while my heart thunders in my chest. I gulp in lungsful of air, and I pull back the duvet. The sight that greets me has my stomach roiling. The bed covered in a pool of dark crimson. I look down and the bottom half of my body is soaked in blood. I let out a strangled sob.

"Oh God, oh God, oh God."

I start to feel myself panic and shake Remy, who is asleep next to me.

"Rem! Rem! Help me, oh God...Rem, please, help me."

My voice is verging on hysterical as he sits up, rubbing the sleep from his eyes. He turns to me and takes in the sight before him, his deep russet eyes widen.

"*Fuck me,* beaut."

I shake my head and I let out a sob. I go to swing my legs out of bed, but I am crippled by a blinding pain that shoots through my abdomen. Remy moves quickly up out of bed and he places his hands under my thighs, scooping me up in his arms, seemingly not caring that he's covered in my blood. He lifts me up and carefully maneuvers me towards the door.

"Shhh, I've got you. It's going to be ok. Look, I'm going to take you to the hospital. You're ok, shhh, I'm here," he soothes, and I bury my nose into his neck, taking in his calm woodsy scent.

The scent that is uniquely Remy Logan. I cry out as another crippling pain rips through me.

"*Shit,* I'm going to ring an ambulance. I'm going to put you down for a minute."

I clasp my hands tighter around his neck.

"No, Rem, please don't leave me, please," I plead desperately, and he nuzzles his nose against mine.

The only thing I can focus on is the blinding pain in my lower abdomen.

"I'm going nowhere, I promise. I promise I won't leave you, I'm right here."

He places me down on the bed and I faintly hear him speaking into his phone when everything goes black.

28

Sam

I'm still at Ruby and Jax's engagement party. After I watched Peyton leave with Remy, I just lost it. I snorted some coke and drank a fuck load of vodka. *I'm suitably wasted.* When I heard Peyton was alive, I stopped taking my medication, and ever since, I've been self-medicating. Not the best idea I've ever had, but I feel in control for the first time in my life. I don't have J.D keeping a constant eye on me, so no one knows, not this time. Not my family, not the boys, no one. My phone starts ringing, and I see Peyton's number flash up on my screen. I toy with the idea of rejecting it, but morbid curiosity wins out, and I swipe the screen to answer the call.

"Hello? Angel?"

The sound of Remy Logan's panicked voice instantly tells me that something isn't right.

"Sam, this is Remy. Look, I'm at the hospital…it's Peyton, she needs you."

A look of pure confusion crosses my face. *What the fuck?*

"What happened?" I ask, and he lets out an exasperated sigh.

She was fine when she left the party, well she had stomach cramps, but I put that down to all that girly shit.

"Look, just…please, get here as soon as you can; I'll explain then. She's at the Royal London Hospital."

With those words, I feel all the colour drain from my face as he hangs up. *What the fuck is going on?* A frown line jumps into place between Brody's eyes.

"You look like your fucking puppy just died, dude," he tries to joke, but I don't smile. "Mate, you're freaking me the fuck out, what's up?"

I swallow a few times.

"It's Peyton, she's in the hospital. Logan just called me."

His eyes widen.

"Come on, let's fucking go. What are we waiting for?"

The next hour passes in a total blur, and I'm not sure how I get from Neon Nights to the hospital, but I find myself in the corridor outside her room with Remy, Ruby, and Brody. We look oddly out of place still in our fancy-dress outfits. I am dressed as Gambit from X Men, Brody is dressed as Superman, and Ruby is dressed as Elsa from Frozen. As soon as I set eyes on Remy, I know something isn't right. His arms and his clothes are covered in blood.

What the fuck happened?

"Is someone going to tell me what happened?" I say with a panicked edge to my voice, and as Remy is about to speak, we are joined by a doctor.

The doctor is a tall, lean woman of around mid to late forties, with long ice blonde hair down to her shoulders, light blue eyes, wearing a white lab coat. She has a stethoscope around her neck and a grave look on her face.

"I'm Doctor Fallon Fontaine. I've been informed you're down as Miss Harper's next of kin, is that correct?"

I nod.

"That's right, would someone please tell me what's going on?" I say as calmly as I can manage, and she takes me to one side.

"Miss Harper has suffered a miscarriage, Mr. Newbolt. I was informed by Mr. Logan that you were the father? I'm so sorry for your loss."

Her voice is filled with sympathy, and as she says those words, the bottom drops out of my world.

Peyton was pregnant with my baby? What the fuck?

It takes everything I have not to break down right in front of her.

This can't be happening. I didn't even know she was pregnant.

"Would you like a moment, Mr. Newbolt?"

I clear my throat, and I suddenly feel stone cold sober.

"No, no, I'm fine. Can I see her?"

She smiles kindly and nods.

"This way."

I follow her, and I step into the stark, sterile hospital room. An unwelcome feeling of helplessness washes over me as she lies there looking tiny and so fragile. There are wires coming from all directions, and the dull beep of the machines fills the room.

"I'll leave you to it, Mr. Newbolt."

The doctor nods, leaving me standing awkwardly next to her bed to come to terms with what I've just been told. Peyton was pregnant, she had a life growing inside of her, a life that we created together. *Now it's gone.* My head starts to spin, and I drop down into the chair next to her bed as the enormity of the situation hits me like a fucking brick.

We've lost our baby.

29

Peyton

My eyes flicker open and I recognise the familiar bright fluorescent lights that greet me. *I'm in hospital.* This is the second time this week I have found myself here. I turn my head and I see Sam pacing the room like a caged animal.

"Sam?" I say softly, and he stops pacing at the sound of my voice.

He turns to me, and his eyes are red rimmed.

"Angel."

His voice is thick with unshed tears, and he moves fluidly towards the bed.

"I'm so fucking sorry, this is all my fault."

What the fuck is he talking about? I think back to the last things I remember: the nightmare about J.D, blood-soaked sheets, and Remy. My thoughts are interrupted by the appearance of a tall, female doctor with blonde hair.

"Miss Harper, I'm Doctor Fallon Fontaine."

I nod and manage a weak smile. The expression on her face is grim, as if there's something she isn't telling me.

"Miss Harper, you've suffered a miscarriage."

As she says those words, my head starts to spin, and I feel like I need to throw up.

A miscarriage? How? I didn't even know I was pregnant.

"H...how?"

I manage to choke out, and she schools her features.

"You were six weeks pregnant, but there was a chromosomal abnormality."

I look blankly at her, then at Sam. *What the hell does that mean?* Sam steps closer to the bed and reaches for my hand. It's unexpected, but I don't reject it; I am more than happy to let him. The feel of his warm, calloused hand around mine comforts me.

"Can we get that in English, please?" Sam asks.

His voice sounds almost robotic, as if it doesn't belong to him. Doctor Fontaine nods curtly.

"Of course. Chromosomes are the tiny structures in each cell that carry our genes; basically, blocks of our DNA. We each have twenty-three pairs of them, one set from the mother and one set from the father. Sometimes, when the egg and sperm meet at the point of conception, the foetus receives too many, or not enough chromosomes. The reasons for this are often unclear, but if one or the other is faulty, the chromosomes can't line up properly. In that case, the resulting embryo has a chromosomal abnormality, this means that the foetus will not be able to develop normally, and the pregnancy usually results in a miscarriage."

I let the tears flow freely as I listen to her explain the reason why.

"I'm so sorry for your loss, both of you. If you both require counselling, don't hesitate to let me know, and I can arrange it for you."

She smiles sympathetically and leaves the room. The silence in the air is almost suffocating as Sam pulls up a chair and drops down into it. He doesn't let go of my hand.

Why is this happening?

"Tell me one thing, angel, was that baby mine?"

I breathe in through my nose and try to swallow back the lump that's formed in my throat. I'm struggling to process everything that's happened, and I can't speak. *After all we've just been told, all he cares about is if the baby was his?* I scramble to try and work out the dates in my head. *Six weeks?* It was Sam's, he's the only person I've slept with in the past six weeks. I can't say the words out loud, because I'm so overcome by grief, so I just nod. He looks up to the ceiling and rakes his hands harshly through his hair. He nods and curses to himself.

"*Fuck.*"

I lean my head back into the pillow, and a tear silently slips down my cheek.

"I'm so sorry, Sam," I whisper.

"Hey, none of this is your fault. You've got nothing to be sorry for, angel, nothing at all."

I sob, and he lifts my hand to his face.

"*Fuck*, you're tearing me apart, angel."

I gasp out heart rendering hiccupping sobs, and he squeezes his eyes shut. When he opens them, a lone tear rolls down his cheek. He swipes it away quickly and sniffs.

"I'm so fucking sorry," he says gruffly and runs his hand through his hair.

He kisses the back of my hand and stands to his full height.

"I can't do this, *fuck,* I'm sorry."

He shakes his head and those are the last words I hear, from Sam Newbolt's lips as he turns and walks away.

30

Sam

This is all my fault.

Seeing her so broken, so...overcome by grief at the loss of our baby, it overwhelmed me, ripped me the fuck open. I know I'm a selfish bastard for leaving, but I can't watch the woman I love falling apart like that. I stride out of the room to the sound of her gut wrenching sobs. Remy, Ruby, and Brody are waiting outside, Brody pacing up and down the corridor like a man possessed.

I know that look, he wants to get high.

"You need to get high?"

He nods, and the look of shame on his face lets me know he's hurting too.

"I get it, dude, I do, but you're stronger than that."

He is about to speak as Remy laughs bitterly.

"You're out here while she's in there breaking down? Please tell me, you didn't just walk out on her?"

I hang my head in shame, and he paces towards me his fists clenched.

"YOU'RE FUCKING UNBELIEVABLE, DO YOU KNOW THAT? YOU'RE A SELFISH BASTARD, SAM NEWBOLT!" He roars and grabs his t-shirt in his clenched fist.

"Do you see this? That's your baby! Her fucking blood! Where the fuck were you? She needed you!"

Ruby steps closer to him and places her hand on his shoulder.

"Rem," she says softly, and he jabs his finger in my direction.

"This is all your fucking fault, Newbolt! She deserves so much better than you, you prick!" he says coldly, and I don't flinch, because I know every ounce of hatred he spits at me is deserved.

"Aren't you going to say anything?" he says a little too calmly, and Ruby steps in front of him, cupping his face in her hands.

"Stop, that's enough, Remy."

He steps around her and strides towards me. Before I know what is happening, Remy's fist connects with my face and knocks me off balance. I swipe my hand across my nose and find it is bleeding.

"Next time, it won't be just your nose. I'll fucking end you, Newbolt, and that's not a threat, it's a promise."

The chill in his voice is evident as Remy turns around, and with a slight limp, strides off down the corridor.

"You really can't go anywhere without causing trouble, can you, Sam? Acting like a prick seems to come naturally to you these days, doesn't it?" Ruby says furiously, and for once, I don't disagree.

31

Peyton

Watching Sam walk out of that door shattered my already broken world into a million more tiny pieces. This feeling of utter despair, this deep ache I feel, makes me think that no amount of glue can fix this mess. This...wreck, this carnage is irreparable, *we* are irreparable. Each gut wrenching sob and each tear that falls is a cruel reminder that a part of us is gone. What I feel right now is beyond words. I feel that somehow this is all my fault. I'm to blame, this is my punishment for behaving so recklessly.

"Penny for 'em, sweets."

Brody interrupts my thoughts and for once, I'm grateful for the distraction. As I continue to sob softly, Brody moves silently and stealthily across the room, until he is standing next to my bed. He leans over and places a gentle kiss on my forehead. He hops up onto the bed.

"Budge up."

He smiles, and I manage a weak smile in return at his gesture. I move up to make room for him, and he tucks me under his arm. He wriggles to get himself comfortable and softly kisses the top of my head.

"*Fuck me,* these beds are tiny!" he mutters as he stretches out his long legs, clad in blue tights.

He looks ridiculous still dressed as Superman, and I smile inwardly. I snuggle into him. He smells of apples, beer, and all things Brody Hart. I find myself snuggling closer to him, desperately craving comfort. He wraps his thick, sinewy arm around me, and I cry silently.

"Shh, shh, I've got you, sweets. I'm so fucking sorry," he says so quietly I barely hear him.

I'm not sure how long we lie in complete silence, but we are interrupted by a soft tap on the door. I look up and my eyes meet Remy's.

"Am I interrupting, beaut?" he says softly, his brown eyes are tender and glossy.

Brody lifts my hand to his lips and places a kiss on the back.

"It's fine, mate, I was just leaving. You need anything at all, sweets? Just holler and I'll come straight back. I'll go and find Sam, I'll talk to him."

He winks, and I nod. He leaps off the bed and salutes Remy as he leaves the room.

"Later," he calls as he leaves the room.

Remy moves further into the room, closing the door behind him. I look up at him and his appearance makes me sob harder. He has dried blood all over his t-shirt and his trousers, as well as blood smeared on his left cheek and up his arms. The blood that remains on Remy is all that's left of our baby. He moves quickly over to my bed and scoops me up in his arms.

"*Jesus,* if I could take the pain away, beaut, I would in a fucking heartbeat. I'm so sorry."

I cling to him, as if he is a life raft, and I sob hard into his shoulder. He runs his hands up and down my back soothingly, whispering softly in my ear how sorry he is, how he wishes he could take away the pain, how he's going to be there for me, and I don't doubt him, not for one second.

***

I'm not sure how much time passes, but I wake to find an empty space next to me. The room is shrouded in darkness, and as I look around the room, my eyes come to rest on Sam sitting in a chair in the corner of the room. His hands are resting on his stomach, and he looks deep in thought. I take a brief moment to collect myself before I notice tear stains down his face. I can see the sadness etched there.

"Sam?" I whisper, and he seems to momentarily snap out of his trance.

"Angel."

His voice barely sounds like his own. He leans forward and rests his elbows on his knees.

"I'm so sorry."

The raw emotion in his voice causes my heart to slam violently against my rib cage. I suddenly realise that it's not just me, he has experienced a loss too.

"I should never have just left you like that. It was unforgivable, and I can't apologise enough. It was selfish...I'm not good at dealing with stuff like this."

The agony I feel is mirrored in his clear green pools, and before I can gather my thoughts, I find myself blurting out.

"Boo hoo, you pathetic cunt!"

I don't know where the sudden anger comes from, but I see him flinch as he hears the venom in my voice.

"Angel, I..."

I cut him off abruptly. I am unexpectedly boiling with such rage and every single bit of it is directed at the man in front of me.

"Shove it up your arse, Newbolt. Fuck off, I don't want you here."

Even as I say those words, I know they aren't true. I do want him here. He stands up and begins to pace, running his hands through his hair.

"What can I do, angel? Tell me what I can do to make it right."

As he paces closer to me, I notice he has dried blood under his nose.

"You have blood under your nose, what happened?"

I briefly change the subject, and he laughs bitterly.

"Remy punched me after I walked out on you. I don't blame him, I fucking deserved it."

I roll my eyes.

"*Oh please,* stop fucking feeling sorry for yourself, and take responsibility for your own actions for once in your bloody life!"

I raise my voice, and he blanches at my more than irate tone.

"You fucking left me when I needed you the most, Sam. How do you think that made me feel? I expected it from Callum, but never from you. I thought you were different, but you and him, you're exactly the same," I say icily.

Something flashes in his eyes and his nostrils flare.

"I get that you're angry at me, but don't ever fucking compare me to that cock sucker, angel. I'm nothing like him," he says with an edge to his voice.

He folds his arms, and I try not to let myself get distracted by the flex of his muscles.

"You're a selfish prick, Sam. I needed you and all you cared about was yourself. All you fucking cared about was how it was affecting you. You didn't, not once, consider *my* feelings."

I swallow the lump that has formed in my throat, and the frown line between his eyebrows is firmly in place.

"Seeing you cry, watching you break down like that, it shreds me, angel. I'd rather rip out my own heart than see you like that."

My eyes widen at his blatant selfishness. *Fucking arrogant arsehole.*

"You're unbelievable, you're doing it again! You think this is all about you. You're a selfish prick, Sam Newbolt!" I scream, and he growls.

He runs his fingers frantically through his hair.

"What the fuck do you want from me, Peyton?" he says with a clenched jaw.

"Just get the fuck out, Sam."

I turn my head away from him, and it takes everything I have not to burst into tears.

"Go," I say a little louder as I hear his footsteps across the floor. I feel his presence, even though I don't look in his direction.

"Tell me what I can do to make it right, angel, please," he says softly, and I squeeze my eyes shut.

"Please, just go."

I let out a strangled sob, and before I know what is happening, he envelopes me in his arms. I try to struggle free, but the truth is, I need this, *I need him.* I need him here to comfort me, and I cling to him tightly. I sob hard into his warm chest as he gently rubs his hands up and down my back in a soothing motion. He rests his chin on top of my head.

"Shhh, I've got you, angel. We'll get through this together. You're not alone anymore; I'm here, and I'm not going anywhere."

As he says those words, I'm hopeful that we will find a way to reconcile and finally have our happily ever after.

32

Peyton

I place my hand on my stomach, and I don't know what I expected to feel, but I feel...*empty*. I feel as if I have no right to feel this way since I didn't even know that he or she existed. I know it's messed up, but I can't help feeling that way. After I was released from hospital a week ago, I called my mum, and after much persuading, I talked her and my dad out of coming up here. Even though I feel like I have a limb missing, I asked them to keep Freddie for a few more days. I feel like a terrible mother, but deep down, I know it's the right thing to do.

Every day for the past week Sam has been ever present in my life. After our reconciliation at the hospital a week ago, he has been attentive, flirty, and his usual charming self. Even through the grief I feel for our baby, I look forward to his calls and texts and find myself strangely looking forward to his nightly phone calls before I go to sleep. Hearing his voice before I drift off has been oddly comforting and has become part of my nightly routine. Even though he has been really busy with the band, he's managed to find time for me, and it really does feel like this past year never happened.

Today is Monday, and it's my first day back at work. I'm looking forward to getting back to the shop, to tattooing, and doing what I love. Tattooing is my passion, and my form of therapy. It centres me, and it's a part of who I am. The flat is so quiet without Freddie. I miss him so much, but I need some time to heal and to get over this terrible tragedy we've suffered.

After my morning shower, I dry off, dry and straighten my hair, and get dressed to begin my day. Today, I'm opting for a purple t-shirt with 'Keep calm and get tattooed' across the front, a purple black and white checked shirt with the sleeves rolled up, a short, distressed denim skirt, black tights, and I finish my look with purple Converse. I apply my natural make up and slick my lips with a light coating of lip gloss. I grab my black hoodie, pull it over my head, and roll up the sleeves. I grab my bag, and as if he's an expert in my morning routine, Kai steps out of his bedroom wearing his signature black suit, white shirt, black tie, and a new feature to his attire, a clear earpiece which curls behind his ear. He nods his usual greeting and we leave the flat.

The journey to work is filled with the familiar awkward silence. We pull into the shop car park, and I jump out of the car. As I turn the corner, I glimpse the familiar yellow and black sign of Saint Sinner Ink. I plaster a smile on my face and push the door open. The familiar smell of disinfectant instantly calms me, and I find a cup of Starbucks finest coffee waiting for me at my work station. It's my usual large espresso macchiato with one sugar, easy on the milk.

"Good morning, honey bunny," Seb says brightly as he looks up from a tattoo magazine and smiles his familiar crooked smile.

"Good morning, pumpkin."

I wink and go into the back to put my stuff away. There is a huge bunch of black dahlias on the counter. I take off my coat, hang it up, and peer around the door frame.

"Who are the flowers for, babe?" I inquire, and Seb rolls his eyes.

"Do you really need to ask? You, of course. They came around half an hour ago. I'd literally just opened the door and they arrived."

I nod and go to the counter to look at the card.

Angel,
Just so you know, you're never far from my thoughts.
We have a gig tonight
The info is on the back
All my love
S xx

As I read the words, I bite my lip. What Sam wrote in the note brings those familiar butterflies to my stomach. I haven't felt those in a while, and I welcome them. I almost feel exactly the way I did when he bought me flowers all those months ago, after our first date. I pull my phone out and dial Sam's number. He answers on the second ring, almost as if he was waiting for my call.

"Angel," he rasps, and he sounds like he's just woken up.

I imagine him spread out across his king size bed, his hair sleep mussed, his muscular, tattooed body a contrast to his sheets. I bite my lip at the thought. *Now is not the time to act like a wanton hussy who's lacking a man between her thighs.*

"Hey," I say, my voice is small and apprehensive.

"Did you get my flowers?"

I can hear the smile in his voice.

"Yeah, they're lovely, thank you. It's been a long time since anyone bought me flowers."

He chuckles softly.

"I'm glad you like them, angel. A beautiful woman like you deserves flowers every day."

I melt at his words and smile to myself. *I feel like a fucking teenager again.*

"The gig tonight is at The Roundhouse. It's a small, intimate gig for a bunch of competition winners. We can meet after the show, and maybe I can take you for dinner?"

As he says those words, I find myself smiling and readily agreeing to his offer.

"Ok, I'll be there."

He breathes audibly down the phone.

"That's great, babe. Ruby will be there too. Security already know you, but I'll put your name on the guest list just in case, I'll see you later."

"Ok, see you later, Sam."

We say our goodbyes and I press the end call button by swiping my finger across the screen. I put my phone away and go back out into the shop to prepare for the day ahead. Throughout the day, I feel a sort of nervous energy at the thought of seeing Sam again. I know I should hate him for the way he behaved, but the truth is, I still love him. I've always loved him. Ever since the day I set eyes on him, it's been him and only him. I know I tried to stupidly convince myself he would be better off without me, but I know now that's not true.

The rest of the day goes by in a blur of tattoos and the usual banter between me and Seb. As Seb flips the closed sign, I am wiping down my station.

"Go on, get yourself off home, babe. I'll finish doing that."

I wipe my brow with the back of my hand and look at him.

"Are you sure?"

Seb cocks his eyebrow.

"Do you really need to ask me that? Go. I'm assuming the shit-eating grin you haven't been able to wipe off your boat all day has something to do with Sam?"

I smirk.

"Now, that would be telling. Don't you know that ladies never kiss and tell?"

Seb snickers.

"Yeah. Show me the lady and I'll ask her, shall I?"

He winks, and I throw my head back and laugh.

"Cheeky, you're lucky I love you, Henry."

He snatches the cloth from my hand.

"You wouldn't have me any other way, honey. Now go, and don't do anything I wouldn't do!"

He winks cheekily and swats my bum as I make my way into the back to grab my stuff. I pull on my jacket, sling my bag on my shoulder, and hug Seb.

"It's good to see you back to your old self, babe," he says into my neck and I cling to him tighter.

He kisses the top of my head and pulls away from our embrace.

"Now go, that's an order!"

He smiles his crooked grin, and I blow him a kiss as I leave the shop. Kai is waiting at the kerb leaning against his black 4x4 with his hands tucked casually in his pockets. As he catches sight of me, he nods curtly.

"Peyton."

I smile.

"Hey, Kai."

He returns my gesture and opens the back door for me. I climb in, and he closes the door after me. He jumps in the driver's seat, closes his door, and does one final sweep of the area with his eyes as he starts the engine and pulls smoothly away from the kerb. The journey back to the flat is uneventful and in our usual awkward silence. He pulls up outside the building, and I climb out.

"I need to go to the office to check in with Cole, but Trey is covering me, He's sitting right across the street, he's got your back, doll," he says.

I look over at the man machine that is Trey. He is sat in a gunmetal grey Bentley with a pair of sunglasses shielding his eyes. He salutes me from across the street, and I nod as I climb the steps into the building. I wave a greeting to Jimmy as I make my way up to the flat in the lift. I unlock the door and lock it behind me. I am greeted by Ruby, with her feet up on the sofa, and a cup of tea resting on her large bump.

"Hey!" she says brightly, and I chuckle softly.

"Is there a reason that you're in my flat on my sofa, babe?"

She rolls her eyes dramatically.

"Yep, I'm here to make you look gorgeous for a certain Mr. Newbolt. He hasn't been able to wipe that grin off his face all day, it's bloody sickening!"

We both laugh.

"There's wine open in the kitchen, and I've bought my box of tricks. The limo is coming at six, so we've got plenty of time."

She gets up awkwardly and puffs out her cheeks.

"This baby needs to move off my bladder, little fucker," Ruby complains, and I roll my eyes at her usual dramatics.

I toe off my shoes and hang my coat up as there is a soft tap on the door. Ruby starts clapping her hands excitedly.

"I called in reinforcements!"

I narrow my eyes suspiciously and open the door. Danny is leaning casually against the door frame, wearing a pair of black hot pants, slippers, a white vest which sets off his golden tan, and a black trilby. He is holding a bottle of wine, and there is a metal case at his feet.

"Aunty Debs, has arrived!" he shrieks theatrically as I throw my arms around him and he lifts me off the ground.

It's been a few weeks since I last saw him, and it's so good to have the old gang back together.

"Hey baby girl! It's been too long! Someone's got a lot of catching up to do, start at the beginning. I haven't seen you in *forever.* Aunty Debs wants *all* the gossip on that gorgeous rock star! Meanwhile, me and Ruby will be your fairy godmothers and help you look even more beautiful than you do now!"

He winks, and with those words, I know things are well on their way to being back to normal.

A few hours pass, and after a lot of gossiping, wine, primping, and preening, I don't recognise the woman staring back at me in the mirror. I look totally different to the way I did when I came home from work. Danny, in addition to being a drag queen, is a fully qualified hair stylist. In between working at the club, he moonlights as a mobile hair dresser. My usually short brown hair is now long thanks to Danny's hair extensions. It's glossy and falling down my shoulders in loose waves. My natural make up is replaced with dark smoky eyes and red lipstick. My outfit consists of a short black dress with white stars all over the front. The front dips low, and it makes my boobs look amazing. My outfit is finished off with simple silver jewellery and a pair of black Iron Fist heels with a black bow and a white skull in the middle. Danny stands in my living room with one hand on his hip and the other clutching a glass of wine, admiring his handiwork. He turns to Ruby and high fives her.

"I think our work here is done, baby mama."

He winks, and Ruby grins. She looks gorgeous as always; her dark hair is pulled up into a high ponytail, and she is wearing a red polka dot dress, with a white belt around her waist which accentuates her bump.

"Those gorgeous rockers are in for a treat tonight, ladies. You're both looking foxy. If I was straight, I'd definitely hit on both of you!" Danny compliments and we all giggle.

I've had a few glasses of wine, so I feel relaxed and ready to go. Danny hands us both our bags, and right on time, the door buzzes. Ruby and I take turns at hugging Danny, thanking him for tonight. He waves us off.

"Don't be silly. Where else would I be but with my girls? You're my sisters from another mister!"

He laughs.

"Now shoo, I'll be round tomorrow with wine for all the gory details!"

He blows us kisses as we leave and head down to greet Trey at the kerb.

"Ladies."

He nods coolly and we both climb into the back of the black limo on route to the Roundhouse.

33

Peyton

Ruby taps softly on the dressing room door.

"Sam Newbolt, get your moody arse out here, right now!"

I giggle at Ruby's bluntness. Sam swings the door open, and the sight that greets me almost knocks me off my feet. *Fuck me*, he looks even more delicious than the last time I saw him.

"Hi," I say, almost unsure of myself.

The look of awe on Sam's face as his eyes roam over me renders me speechless. *Do I have something on my face?* I feel like an awkward teenager on a first date. Is it possible that Sam feels the same, or has he changed his mind?

"Hey yourself," he rasps, and I let out the breath I didn't realise I was holding.

The glint in his emerald green eyes almost reduces me into a quivering mess at his feet. He leans his large body against the doorjamb, and his tattooed muscles flex as he continues to stare at me.

"Do I have something on my face?" I blurt out, and he laughs wickedly.

"Quite the opposite, angel. You look...*fuck*...you looking absolutely stunning."

I feel my cheeks flush pink at his compliment, and he reaches over to idly twirl a strand of my hair in between his fingers.

"You changed your hair."

He smiles, and his dimples jump into place. I nod, in awe of this man in front of me.

"Every time I look at you, angel, you take my fucking breath away."

We stand there holding each other's stare for what seems like forever, and I allow myself to get lost in Sam's clear green pools. We are interrupted by what sounds like a school bell.

"This is your five-minute warning. Five minutes to show time, five minutes to show time."

We both laugh at the timing. I hear heels clicking along the floor, and Ruby is instantly at my side. She takes me by the hand.

"Sorry to interrupt your intense staring contest, kids, but we need to go."

Sam reaches over to stroke my cheek gently.

"Until later, angel. I'll be waiting."

He winks as Ruby leads me away.

"What the fuck was that, babe? It's been a long time since I've seen him like that, what did you do to him?"

I chuckle softly.

"I have no idea what you're talking about!"

Ruby throws her head back and laughs.

"You little slut! Come on let's go and find our seats."

Ruby practically drags me off down the corridor and into the main vestibule of The Roundhouse. The venue is small, and intimate compared to some of the other larger venues Rancid Vengeance have played; its capacity is one thousand. It is one of the most architecturally astounding and unique spaces in the whole of London. The structure reminds me of an old nineteen thirties dance hall with an up-to-date twist. It has modern brickwork and ultra-trendy strobe lighting. The circle balcony framing the main space below delivers a fantastic vantage point that overlooks the breath-taking space below. The main space is the beating heart of The Roundhouse. The low stage is situated in the centre of the room and the boys are sound checking as the competition winners mingle excitedly with each other at the circular tables which are evenly spaced throughout the venue.

"I thought I was going to have to break out the fire extinguisher, the sexual tension between you two was off the fucking chart, babe!"

Ruby fans herself dramatically, and I roll my eyes.

"Oh come on, Peyton, you're either deaf or fucking blind if you can't see how that boy feels about you. I haven't seen him like this in such a long time; he's happy, don't take that away from him."

I smile at her, and I know what she's saying is spot-on...but I can't help thinking that it's too good to be true, and at any moment all this - Sam, me, Freddie, the whole happy ever after - is going to be taken away.

"We've been through so much, I keep thinking that it's going to get taken away from us again. I went through hell when J.D kidnapped me. I thought

I was going to die. After that, I vowed I'd never let anyone do that to me ever again, but Sam can break me, Rubes. He's got the potential to rip my heart out, and I can't allow that to happen; I've got my son to think of now."

Ruby narrows her eyes.

"Why do you do this? You constantly second guess yourself. You deserve to be happy, Peyton. You and Sam deserve your happy ending, the boy is fucking smitten with you!"

Ruby finds our table in front of the stage, and she sits down.

"*Fuck me,* I feel like a beached whale."

She puffs out her cheeks, and I chuckle softly. Jax spots her and flashes a cheeky grin at her. He winks, and Ruby giggles like a school girl. She blows him a kiss, and he pretends to catch it. I'm so happy that my best friend found someone she can settle down with. Her and Jax are a perfect match.

"Look how he watches you, babe. It's like he sees nothing but you."

I look up from beneath my lashes and my eyes lock with Sam's. The green in his eyes is illuminated by the lights, making him look almost ethereal and otherworldly. He stands to his full height, and he looks especially sexy tonight. His stage outfit consists of a pair of dark jeans with a chain hanging from his belt loops, a white vest, a black leather waistcoat, and black motorcycle boots. His hair is styled into his signature messy, spiky style. He positions himself in front of his microphone, and the lights are dimmed. The crowd goes wild as he growls into the microphone. The stage is shrouded in darkness as Lucas pounds out a drum beat. The spotlight illuminates a shirtless Lucas as he throws his drumsticks up in the air and elaborately catches them with effortless ease. He taps his sticks together, and Jax joins in with a complex guitar solo as a second spotlight lights him up. Brody moves fluidly across the stage and stands back to back with Jax, accompanying his solo. The spotlight is on both men now. Ruby wolf whistles and shouts to Jax.

"WOOOOOOO, FLASH! YOU SEXY BEAST!" she screams, and we both giggle.

I can see the mischievous grin on Jax's face. Suddenly, all the music stops, and the stage goes completely dark. Sam's liquid velvet voice fills the venue, and the spotlight is on him alone. He stands proud and tall on the stage with the microphone in his hand. His eyes are closed as he sings the lyrics.

"The night is the hardest time to be alive, 4am knows all my secrets. I can't erase the void, the ill divide, between make believe and reality. The vitriolic agony I feel reminds me I'm still here. Digging a little deeper, into my already fragile, twisted mind."

As Sam's gravelly voice washes over me, the haunting sound of Jax's guitar accompanies Sam, the familiar pounding beat of Lucas' drums, and the driving thrum of Brody's rhythm guitar. I start to listen to the lyrics and it feels as if I am reliving the last year through his eyes, his voice, and his music. It is truly heart breaking.

"Some nights I get so fucking wasted, so I don't see you in my dreams. Even in sleep, I'm never at rest."

As I listen to the emotion in Sam's voice, a tear slips down my cheek. Ruby reaches for my hand and squeezes it. I catch her gaze, and she smiles softly with glossy eyes. Sam steps to the front of the stage and looks out into the crowd. He continues to sing and his green eyes lock with my blue ones, as if he singing only to me.

The song draws to a close and the tears are streaming freely down my cheeks. Now I understand, I understand the pain he went through when he thought he had lost me. He removes the microphone from the stand, and the crowd goes wild, cheering, screaming, and stomping their feet.

"Good evening, London! You're all looking beautiful out there tonight. How the fuck are we doing?"

The crowd goes crazy.

"Yeahhh! You all know who we are by now, so no introductions are needed! We all want to say congratulations to you competitions winners and welcome you all to The Roundhouse. It's so fucking good to be here."

He moves back to his microphone and puts it back on the stand.

"Now, we're going to do something a bit different to what we normally do."

Jax hands Sam his guitar and a piano is wheeled onto the stage. Jax takes his seat at the piano bench, and the crowd await anxiously as to what is going to happen next.

"Here's the thing, the boys and me, we strictly don't do cover versions, but I felt this was fitting with where we're all at right now, so I hope you like it."

They all scream in encouragement, hanging on to his every word. Sam turns to Lucas and nods curtly. He strums the opening chords and I instantly recognise the song as Apocalyptica *Not Strong Enough*. He plucks the strings in perfect rhythm for the introduction and bangs his hand on the guitar. Jax joins in with the piano, and Sam begins to sing acapella style.

Sam's eyes lock with mine, and I instantly know the song choice was deliberate. Sam's voice is gruff and so full of emotion, my heart slams against my rib cage. Brody steps to the front of the stage and begins to strum an improvised guitar solo. Sam closes his eyes and loses himself in the music as the crowd become totally enraptured by their performance. It is truly breath taking. Sam's voice and the lyrics light me up from the inside. I can feel each lyric deep in my bones. *Neither of us were strong enough to stay away from each other.* Ruby nudges me, briefly breaking our eye contact.

"That boy is so in love with you, it's fucking sickening!" Ruby whispers, and we both giggle.

Sam cocks his pierced eyebrow and smirks as he continues to sing. The song finishes, and he moves fluidly to the front of the stage.

"There's actually another reason why we're performing this song tonight. I want to invite my girl up onto the stage."

Sam reaches his hand down, and I look at him questioningly.

"Come on up, angel."

I look at Ruby, and she shrugs, shooing me.

"Go get him, tiger!"

She giggles as I get up and curiously make my way onto the stage to a chorus of cheers from the crowd. Sam takes my hand and looks to the side of the stage.

"Can I get a stool, please?" he asks Donovan, one of the bands roadies.

He quickly grabs a stool and rushes onto the stage to place it in the centre. Sam gestures to me to sit down, and my every nerve is tuned to him.

"This is nowhere near as smooth as the first time I asked you, so you're going to have to make do with just me, straight up."

The look in his eyes is so sincere, it makes me want to cry.

"I loved you the minute I saw you, the day I walked into Saint Sinner Ink...that day changed my life. Not only are you the most beautiful woman I've ever laid eyes on, you're the mother of my son, Freddie. You're my best friend, my lover, my rock, and my soul mate. You own me, angel. Every fucking inch of me. I'm probably going to walk out of this place with my rock star reputation in tatters, but I don't care."

The crowd starts to laugh, and I chuckle softly as I swipe away a stray tear.

"You tie me up in fucking knots. I know things haven't been easy for us lately, but I want to spend the rest of my life making up for that. Once upon a time, I was an arse hole, and I can't tell you how sorry I am for that. You're my angel, Peyton."

He drops down on one knee, and I start to sob softly. He reaches into his pocket and pulls out a small square box. The ring inside takes my breath away.

"Peyton Leigh Harper, I asked you once before, but now I'm asking again. Will you do me the honour of being my wife? Marry me?"

The crowd gasps and starts to cat call. I am so shocked at his proposal, I find myself nodding. He moves closer to me, and his eyes are glossy.

"Is that a yes?" he rasps, and I nod.

"Yes! Yes! A thousand times yes!" I manage to say, and he lifts me easily off the stool.

He takes the ring out of the box and places it on my ring finger. The crowd erupts into rapturous screams and the whole place vibrates with the noise. The boys start cheering noisily, and Ruby gets to her feet, bouncing excitedly. Sam presses his lips to mine, and his kiss is hungry as his tongue explores my mouth. He pulls away and looks into my eyes.

"You've got no idea how fucking happy I am right now, angel," he whispers and seems to forget that he still has a show to perform.

"I love you so much, Sam."

I sob, and my tears are happy ones. After everything Sam and me have been through, this moment alone makes up for the year of hell we've both been through. With one last mind-numbing kiss, Sam pulls away.

"I love you. I'll come and find you afterwards, we've got some celebrating to do!"

He winks cheekily, and I blush fiercely as I make my way back to my seat, still in shock from Sam's surprise proposal. Ruby grabs my hand enthusiastically.

"OH-MY-GOD!" she squeals as Jax begins an epic guitar solo.

"You know what this means? Double hen do!"

She starts to clap excitedly as I admire my ring. It is a platinum band with an infinity knot and a huge, princess cut diamond encased in the centre. Right now, my heart feels almost too big for my chest, and I'm so deliriously happy that nothing could possibly ruin this moment.

After the gig finishes, Cole escorts both Ruby and me backstage. As we stop outside Sam's dressing room, he unexpectedly kisses me on the cheek.

"Congratulations, sugar. Look after him."

He winks and knocks on the dressing room door. Ruby nudges me with her elbow.

"Told you he was a big teddy bear!"

We both giggle as Sam swings open the dressing room door. He is shirtless with a towel around his waist. His hair is dripping wet, and Ruby rolls her eyes.

"Is it too much to ask for you wear a fucking shirt, Newbolt?"

Sam throws his head back and laughs.

"Is someone jealous, sweetheart?"

She huffs.

"In your dreams."

She chuckles softly and pushes past him, straight into Jax's arms. I fidget nervously with my new engagement ring, and Sam lifts my hand to his lips. He places a gentle kiss on my ring, and I stroke his face.

"Angel," he rasps, and I smile softly.

"Hey," I whisper, and he steps out of the doorway, gesturing for me to go into the dressing room.

I walk in, and he closes the door behind me. He stalks forward and pins me to the door.

"*Fuck,* it's taking everything I have for me not to just pin you to this door and fuck you until neither of us can see straight," he says gruffly, and I shiver at the sound of his voice.

"How romantic! You could at least wait until we're all out of earshot, you fucking animal!" Ruby quips and I laugh as Sam tries to suppress his smirk.

Sam kisses my forehead and drops his towel, flashing everyone in the room.

"*Fuck me,* dude, put it away!"

Brody yells, and Lucas shakes his head.

"The size of that thing ain't normal, man! It's the size of a baby's arm!" he says drily, and we all laugh.

"Do you mind not flashing your dick in front of my woman, Newbolt, I'll get a complex!" Jax jokes and covers Ruby's eyes with his hand.

"My cock is like a work of art! It should be in a fucking art gallery!"

Sam picks up his towel and bows gracefully as he goes off into the small bathroom towards the back of the dressing room.

"Are you sure you want him to be your future husband, sweets? It's not too late to change your mind!" Brody asks cheekily, and I roll my eyes.

"It's not the size of the boat, babe. It's the motion of the ocean, and boy does he know how to use it!" I say wryly, and Brody sticks his fingers in his ears.

"La-la-la-la-la! TMI sweets!"

I laugh hysterically and sit down next to Ruby on the sofa. We gossip while I wait for Sam to finish up getting ready. Ten minutes later, he emerges from the bathroom looking like he could literally be on the cover of a magazine. He is wearing black skinny jeans with a skull belt buckle, a red, white and black checked shirt with the sleeves rolled up and three buttons undone, revealing his '*My Angel*' tattoo across his collarbones. He is wearing black motorcycle boots and finishes off his look with a black beanie hat. I stand up and move towards him. He offers me his arm.

"We have a table reserved, angel. I'm taking you to dinner, we've got some celebrating to do."

I take his offered arm, and the room erupts with applause.

"Congrats, to both of you." Jax says sincerely, and Sam shakes his hand.

"Thanks, man".

Jax kisses me on the cheek, and we say our goodbyes as we head out on our date.

The drive to the restaurant is short, and Sam doesn't let go of my hand the whole way there. I feel safe with my hand enveloped in his large, tattooed one. We soon arrive at our destination. We pull up outside and Sam helps me out of the car. He takes my hand and leads me down a hidden path along the Regents canal to a stylish and unique restaurant called 'The Cave', complete with a bright conservatory. We are greeted at the door by a tall, muscular man wearing camouflage combats, a black apron, and a black vest which shows off his full sleeve tattoos on both arms, and black Doc Martens. He is wearing a black and white checked bandana. He has dark olive skin, deep brown eyes, and a goatee on his chin.

"Sam! My man! When my Maître D said *the* Sam Newbolt was gracing us with his presence, I couldn't pass up the opportunity to come and greet you myself. It's been a while, mate!"

He beams brightly, and I instantly like him, his enthusiasm is infectious. Sam gives him a one arm hug and slaps him on the back.

"Kit, so good to see you, mate. Yeah, it's been a while. You know how it is, being on the road and all that. How's it going?"

Kit nods.

"All good, Sam, all good."

He regards me intently.

"Kit, this is my fiancée, Peyton. Peyton, this is an old friend of mine, Kit Roman. He's the chef and the owner of this fine establishment; we went to school together."

He takes my hand and cheekily places a kiss on the back of it.

"Pleased to meet you, Peyton. You kept that quiet, man! Congratulations!"

Sam smiles, flashing his dimples, and he looks almost shy.

"Do you have a sister?" Kit asks, and I laugh.

"As a matter of fact, yes I do!" I banter back, and he winks.

"If she's as beautiful as you, put in a good word for me."

I nod.

"I will do, she also happens to be single."

I cock my eyebrow, and he looks from me to Sam.

"I like this one, Sammy. Keep hold of her."

He winks and shows us into the restaurant. The restaurant is filled with what look like paper lanterns as the main source of light. The bar is made of stone and the round tables are covered in black and white striped tablecloths. The walls are decorated in a mid-grey colour, with a selection of different beachscapes. The table he seats us at is towards the back of the restaurant in the corner, shrouded in the privacy of four exotic looking trees that are covered in colourful foliage. Sam pulls my chair out for me as I sit down, and he takes his seat opposite me.

"You need anything at all, holler me. My staff have been briefed not to bother you unless you need them. I know how you get!"

Kit chuckles, and Sam smirks.

"Anyone would think I'm some high maintenance rock star!"

Sam jokes, and we all laugh.

"Cheers, man, I really appreciate it."

Kit nods curtly.

"I'll leave you two to it. It was nice to meet you, Peyton. We'll catch up soon, I'll dish the dirt on this one."

He points at Sam, and I laugh. He leaves, and I find myself idly twirling my new engagement ring around my finger. Sam reaches across the table to tip my chin up to face him.

"This is day one, angel. Just for one night, can we pretend we just met, we don't have any history, and we're two ordinary people getting to know each other?"

I smile at his sentiment, and my eyes lock with his.

"It's a little difficult when I've just agreed to marry you, and we have a child together."

Sam laughs.

"Fair point. But please, just try, for me," he rasps, and he knows I can't resist that husky voice.

I nod, and his face relaxes.

"I'm Sam, it's a pleasure to meet you."

He offers me his hand, and I take it.

"Peyton, pleased to meet you too, Sam."

He smirks as a waiter comes over to place two champagne flutes and an ice bucket on the table with a magnum of champagne in it. Sam nods his thanks, and the waiter scurries away nervously. Sam takes out the bottle of Cristal, pops the cork, and pours the champagne into the glasses. I watch the pull and flex of his muscles as he completes the action; I involuntarily lick my lips. *Even doing the most mundane of actions, he gets me hot.* He places the bottle down, lifts his glass, and hands me mine. I take it, and we clink our glasses together.

"To us, to our engagement, and laying to rest this past year. I know I said this is day one, but it needs to be said, angel. When you came back, I felt like we were given a second chance. Then to find out you'd given birth to our son, it was like...I was finally alive. My world was bright again after living a year in the dark. So this is a toast to us, our engagement, and to second chances."

I clink my glass with his and we both take a welcome sip of the cold, bubbly, liquid. Sam looks at me, his eyes smouldering with want, and all I can think of is him taking me across the table. He smirks, as if he reads my mind.

"Keep thinking those thoughts, because I'm thirty seconds from taking you into a toilet cubicle."

His voice is gruff with seduction, and I squirm in my seat, remembering the last time we had sex in a toilet cubicle. I anxiously rub my legs together to satiate my pussy's wanton needs. *Slut.* He puts his glass down and hands me a menu. I pretend to peruse it, but I'm distracted by the more than perfect specimen of a man in front of me. *He really is perfect.* Sam summons the waiter with a curt nod of his head, and he is instantly at our table.

"Two steaks, please. Both with homemade chips, both rare, one with stilton and mushroom sauce, one without please?"

Sam smiles, and I smile at his skills. The waiter scurries off with the order, leaving us alone once again.

"How do you do that?" I say, with a hint of awe in my voice.

"You forget I spent almost a year with you, angel. I know all your little tells. I know you better than you know yourself. I know that you pushed me away because you thought you were protecting me, but deep down, you wanted nothing more than to be with me. That's how well I know you. I know I might have over reacted, but I had to make you see for yourself. I know your favourite foods, your favourite colour, your favourite song, favourite film...I know it all."

He takes a sip of his champagne, and I narrow my eyes.

"That's the look you get when you can't work something out. I'm just good at reading people, and I told you once before, you fucking own me. You know every corner of my heart, just as I know every corner of yours, angel."

He smiles smugly at his deduction skills, and I smile, almost feeling ashamed that I hardly know anything about him.

Before I know what, I'm saying, I blurt out, "Did you always know you wanted to be in a band?"

He laughs, and his face turns thoughtful, as if contemplating my question.

"Pretty much. I know it's a cliché, but it's in my blood. I grew up in awe of my dad and his band mates. I didn't speak my first words, I literally sang them! While my mates were practising football, I was practising guitar and piano until I pretty much perfected both. Then I moved onto drums, and then started to exercise my vocal chords."

He smiles as he reminisces, and it's good to see him so animated, almost passionate about his chosen profession. I am suddenly struck by the fact that this is the first time we have actually sat down and just got to know each other since we met all that time ago.

"Did you always know you wanted to be a tattoo artist?"

I smile and take a sip of my champagne. I nod and swallow the liquid, feeling the bubbles burst on my tongue and the warmth as it settles in my stomach.

"Yeah, I'd always been creative from an early age. I'd start to daydream and get bored easily. I'd start doodling on anything I could get my hands on. My teachers always used to tell me I had my head in the clouds, but my art teacher, Miss Ferguson, saw something in me. She said I was naturally gifted when it came to art and sketching. I can sketch from memory, I remember every little detail. I knew I was different from the other kids, creative...a tom boy. I never really had any female friends, until I met Ruby; she bought me out of my shell. When I left school, I had no idea what I wanted to do with my life, then I heard of this tattoo artist who was opening up a shop in Islington high street. I knew then, I think, that I wanted to be a tattoo artist. I dropped out of school at seventeen, and I had a year of my mum and dad on my case about getting a job. Then Ruby had an interview for an apprenticeship at this big shot advertising firm in London. She got it, obviously, because she's a natural flirt and knows how to talk the talk. She asked me if I wanted to move to London with her, and I jumped at the chance. The rest you probably know."

He laughs.

"Of course! Like your favourite colour is purple, your favourite film is *Lock Stock and Two Smoking Barrels*, but you also love *The Hangover*, *21 Jump Street*, and the *Fast and Furious* films, mostly because of the cars. Your favourite actor is Leonardo DiCaprio, favourite actress is Kate Winslet. Your favourite TV show is *Supernatural*, but you also love *The Walking Dead*. Your favourite book is *P.S I Love You* by Cecelia Ahern, but you preferred the book to the film. Your favourite food used to be chicken and mushroom pasta Alfredo, but you went off it after you gave birth. Now your favourite food is steak, cooked rare."

Sam leans back in his chair and regards me intently. I sit there in awe of this man in front of me, the man who seemingly knows me better than I know myself. The waiter comes to serve our food at that moment, and we both nod our thanks as he leaves. The food looks and smells delicious, my mouth instantly starts watering. I pick up my fork and wipe it on the napkin provided, and Sam chuckles softly at my actions. We are about to tuck into our meals when Sam's phone chimes. He takes it out of his pocket, and his eyes widen at whatever is on the screen.

"Is everything ok, babe?"

He clears his throat and nods.

"Message from Cole."

He takes a moment to gather his thoughts before he speaks again.

"J.D's dead, he committed suicide in prison."

The look of relief that washes over my face is evident, and I feel like I can breathe again, for the first time in a long time. The genuine smile that Sam flashes me causes me to almost melt in front of him.

I hope he never stops having that effect on me.

He reaches over and takes my hand in his.

"Let's go to Vegas tonight, let's get married. J.D's dead, it's over. There's nothing stopping us now, angel, marry me."

I smile at his childlike enthusiasm and find myself agreeing all too easily. Even though I was taken, kidnapped, and almost killed in Las Vegas, I made it through, and I rose like a phoenix from the flames.

This is mine and Sam's second chance at our happy ever after.

34

Peyton

Two nights ago, after we left the restaurant, Sam set up the bands private jet, and we flew to Las Vegas. After making a few calls, we gathered all our close friends and family, and Sam flew them all out yesterday to witness our big day. It wouldn't feel right if they weren't there to celebrate with us. We are staying in one of nine exclusive private villas at The Bellagio. It is the height of luxury, with a twenty-four-hour butler service, and a spacious marble foyer with glass chandeliers that add opulence to the room. The living room has a fire place, a forty-inch plasma TV, and home theatre entertainment system with surround sound. We also have access to a full-service bar, a formal dining room for eight people that is separated by a private entrance, and a private kitchen that looks like something out of a movie. We have lavish his and hers marble bathrooms that sport whirlpool baths, rainforest steam showers, and a fifteen-inch built in LCD TV.

Ruby and I have been taking full advantage of the private salon and massage room. We have a personal workout room, a steam sauna room, and a private courtyard with a fireplace, pool, spa, and manicured gardens.

Today is our wedding day and I'm being pampered and preened within an inch of my life. I am sipping champagne when the nerves suddenly begin to kick in.

Fuck me, I'm getting married today to Sam Newbolt, one of the world's most famous rock stars.

Never in a million years, did I think that we would be here a year ago.

"You look like you're about to throw up, babe. You're marrying the man of your dreams; this is your happy ever after. Enjoy it, you deserve this," Ruby says sincerely and takes my hand in hers.

She squeezes it reassuringly as my hair is being curled and styled by the bands hair stylist and make-up artist, Blu. Sam paid a wedding planner a ridiculous amount of money to make sure everything was perfect. We are getting married in a chapel aptly named The Angel Wings Chapel of Love. We ditched everything traditional and have gone for an alternative style. After Sam made a few calls and pulled a few strings, I have the most beautiful wedding dress. It is a simple, strapless, white tea length dress with a full skirt and a black sash around the middle. It also has a black rose in the centre and is embellished with diamantes and skulls. I have a black rose in my hair, instead of a veil, and my make-up has been kept natural. Ruby, Addison, my sister Eden, and Willow are my bridesmaids. They are all wearing simple, black, bridesmaid's dresses, and each of them have white roses in their hair.

Half an hour passes, my hair is finally done, and I have my dress on. As I look in the mirror, the reflection staring back at me is far from the woman I was. I have my glow back, my cheeks are rosy, and my hair is glossy and falling down my shoulders in loose curls. *I feel beautiful.* My mum lets out a strangled sob as she moves closer to me, holding Freddie in her arms. Freddie is dressed in a little suit, with a white shirt, a black clip-on tie, and a tiny trilby hat. He looks the mirror image of Sam. He giggles and claps his hands.

"Doesn't mummy look, beautiful, Freddie? You look stunning, my darling girl."

I smile, and my eyes are glazed. A heavily pregnant Ruby waddles towards me and points her finger at me.

"Don't you dare bloody cry! You'll set me off, my hormones are already all over the fucking place!"

We all laugh.

"We'll be fine, as long as you keep your legs closed, babe!"

Ruby pouts at my joke, and I chuckle softly. I turn to my mum and hug her.

"Love you, mum."

She kisses me on the cheek and strokes my hair.

"I love you too. The most important thing is that you're happy, my darling. I know I told you to get to know each other again, before rushing into things, but I can see you love Sam. Now's your time, Peyton, grab life by the balls and live it, with that handsome rocker of yours!"

I laugh, and the door taps softly. My dad, my brother, his fiancée Grace, Sam's mum, and all of my bridesmaids come in. My dad stops in his tracks, he looks so handsome in his traditional black tuxedo.

"You look beautiful, sweetheart."

He kisses me on the cheek, and Dexter nods with an impressed look on his face.

"You scrub up well, sis!"

I roll my eyes, and Grace hits him playfully.

"Don't be so mean, Dex! She looks stunning!"

I laugh at her chastising him and straighten his crooked tie.

"Is that your way of telling me I look ok?"

He nods and bats my hands away.

"You look knockout, sis."

He winks, and I smile at his compliment. Everyone greets me, and Addison bounds up to me and throws herself into me, almost taking my legs out from under me.

"Aunty Peyton! Aunty Peyton!"

I swing her up in my arms, and she idly twirls my hair in her fingers.

"Hey Addison. Wow, don't you look pretty?" I say enthusiastically.

She plants a wet kiss on my cheek, and I find myself laughing. She flashes me a toothy grin and points to her teeth.

"Look, my tooth fell out and mummy said the tooth fairy is going to visit me! But if I'm not at home, how will she know where to come?"

I look at her, and I'm about to speak when Lori enters the room. She looks almost regal in a champagne trouser suit, with a matching fascinator in her perfect brown hair. I put Addison down, and Ruby takes her hand.

"Peyton, you look breath taking. My son is an extremely lucky man."

She hugs me and air kisses me on both cheeks.

"Take care of him, Peyton," she whispers, and I nod.

"I intend to," I reply, and she smiles softly.

"You ready then, sis?" Eden says, and I take a deep breath.

This is it, the moment I'm about to become Mrs Peyton Leigh Newbolt.

35

Sam

I'm waiting inside the chapel with my older brother Brandon as my best man by my side. I never get nervous, but right now I'm shaking like a shitting dog.

"*Fuck me,* you look like you're about to be thrown to the lions, little brother."

I wring my hands and narrow my eyes.

"*Prick,*" I mutter, and Brandon chuckles to himself.

"You're about to marry the most beautiful girl in the world, which I have to say, is a fucking injustice by the way. Is she sure she's marrying the right brother?" he jokes, and I shake my head.

"I knew it was a mistake asking you to be my best man," I mutter sarcastically, and he shrugs.

"You secretly wanted to torture me by making me wear a suit!"

We both laugh as he tugs on his tie. I am wearing a traditional black wedding suit, with a white shirt, black tie, black waistcoat, trousers, and black Doc Martens. Brody wanders over and slaps me on the back.

"You do realise you look like a fucking penguin?"

I fidget with my cufflinks which my dad gave me; they are shaped like old style microphones. I grab Brody playfully in a headlock.

"Is someone still wounded that you lost our stag night bet?"

On my stag night, which Brody and the boys organised, we took an overnight trip to Prague. After a night of drunken debauchery and '*what goes on tour, stays on tour*', Brody and I made a bet. We bet that a girl in a bar we were in was a guy, and it turns out 'she' had a bigger cock than all of us put together. His forfeit was to get a tattoo saying, 'Emergency exit' and an arrow above the crack of his arse. Ever since that night, which was now two nights ago, we've done nothing but rib him about it. He narrows his eyes at me.

"I'll get you back for that, you prick! But seriously, from the bottom of my heart, good luck man. You deserve it, both of you."

I smile and nod.

"Cheers, dude."

He goes back to take his seat next to Jax and Lucas as I turn around to look around the room, which is filled by our close friends and family. Even though I'm nervous as hell, I couldn't be happier. I'm marrying the mother of my child, the woman I love, my best friend, and my soulmate.

Today is the start of our forever.

Peyton

After arriving at the chapel on the back of a Harley Davidson V Rod Custom, which is driven by my dad, we are met in the foyer by Marlowe. He looks handsome and distinguished in a grey suit, with a white shirt and silver tie. His green eyes, a mirror image of Sam's, are framed by thick black-rimmed glasses.

"Peyton, you look absolutely ravishing, love," he says, with more than a hint of awe in his voice.

He kisses me on the cheek and informs me that there is going to be a slight delay with the ceremony. I nod and walk into the main vestibule of the chapel. I smile my greetings to our close family and friends, who are gathered in small groups, talking amongst themselves. As I catch sight of Sam in his wedding suit, I fall in love with him all over again. All six feet four of him, dressed in a three-piece suit, with tears in his eyes as his green eyes lock with mine. I can't take my eyes off him, and as I reach the altar, Sam wraps me in his strong, muscular arms.

To hell with tradition.

"*Fuck*, angel...I can't find my breath...you look... incredible," he rasps and his breath catches as he takes me in.

Our moment is interrupted by my phone vibrating inside the cup of my dress. I pull it out and I feel the colour drain from my face as I read the text message. The message is from an unknown number.

J.D didn't cut your brakes

It was me

You're going to fucking pay for this, bitch.

My vision is blurry from tears and my world starts to spin as I look up to see a mysterious figure who emerges from the chapel entrance. They are dressed from head to toe in leather and are wearing a motorcycle helmet. The figure is holding a box, and before I get a chance to register what is going on, the figure pulls out a gun and opens fire, spraying the room in a rain of bullets.

***

Breaking news just coming in. The wedding of Samson Newbolt, lead singer of the popular rock band Rancid Vengeance, and tattoo artist Peyton Harper, was today interrupted by a hail of bullets in a Las Vegas chapel. The bloodbath claimed the lives of eight people and left more than twenty injured. Close friends and family of the couple were gathered in the Angel Wings Chapel of Love, when a figure wearing a motorcycle helmet entered the chapel and opened fire. Newbolt and Harper both suffered serious injuries but are said to be stable in a nearby hospital. The names of the fatalities are yet to be confirmed. The reason behind this horrific act is still unclear at this stage. Our thoughts and prayers are with the families and victims of this tragic incident. More details to follow.

36

Sam

What the actual fuck is going on?

I can't seem to come to terms with what has just happened and the sheer fucking insanity of it all. I can't feel any one single emotion because of all the shit that's steamrolling its way through my shell-shocked brain. The one thing that won't leave my fucking mind is that sickening, wet, thudding sound of bullets ploughing into the people I care the most about. The metallic smell of blood permeating my nostrils makes my stomach roil. Every time I close my eyes I can hear it, and I can feel my mind trying to spiral out of control. It feels like I am reliving that single moment over and over again, on a constant fucking loop. The deathly silence that followed will forever haunt me, until the day I fucking die. The one feeling I find myself able to cling to, is one of pure numbness and disbelief. As I listen to the dull beep of hospital machines surrounding me, it's then when the sudden realisation hits me like a ten-tonne fucking truck.

Our lives will never be the same again.

The door taps softly, and my head snaps up from my reverie. My dad enters the room, looking older than I've ever seen him.

"Cole has just come out of surgery. He's stable, but the next forty-eight hours are critical. Peyton is still in surgery...they're doing their best, but it's not looking good, son".

As he says those words, my world turns on its axis, and I can't comprehend the scale in which this whole fucked up situation has impacted our lives in such a short space of time.

I can't fucking lose her again.

Suddenly, the door swings open and Jax almost falls through it, but my dad manages to catch him in his arms. The strangled wail that rips from deep within him rocks me to my fucking core. He doesn't speak, he just falls apart in my dad's arms.

"It's alright, son, I've got you," my dad soothes, and Jax looks up.

The look in his eyes says it all, he doesn't need to say the words for me to know what's happened.

Ruby's dead.

Jax's fiancée, Peyton's best friend, and welcome addition to the Rancid Vengeance family, is gone. This isn't happening, this isn't fucking real...it can't be. *This is a dream, a fucking sick joke, it has to be.* I subtly pinch myself, and I'm definitely not dreaming. *Shit.*

Watching my best friend, *my brother,* fall apart in front of me took on a whole new perspective. He had watched as I fell apart, because I thought I had lost my fiancée and my baby. Now, I truly know how it feels...to feel helpless, useless, and knowing there isn't a fucking thing you can do to make it right. I can't find the words, I'm at a loss for what to say to the broken man in front of me. He looks up, and the pained look in his eyes cuts me deep.

He swipes angrily at his tears, and he unexpectedly blurts out, "I'm a dad, Sam."

My eyes widen in shock.

"Ruby...died, but they managed to save our baby...I've got a daughter."

The impact of his words renders me speechless.

Jax is a dad.

***

I'm not sure how much time passes, but I am woken by another soft tap on the door. I look up, and the doctor enters the room.

"Mr. Newbolt, I'm Doctor Simon Etienne."

He nods curtly.

"Call me Sam."

I try to sit up straighter, but the pain is too much. *Fuck me.*

"Your fiancée is out of surgery, and we managed to repair her stomach. The next twenty-four hours are critical, but we're positive that she'll make a full recovery. You're both very lucky."

My shoulders sag with relief.

"Thank you. When can I see her?"

He moves further into the room to check my chart.

"I'll have someone come with a wheelchair, and they can take you to see her."

He smiles, and I nod my thanks as he leaves. I am left alone for a few seconds before Kai enters the room. He has a graze on his head, but otherwise he looks unscathed. His tie is missing, and he is clutching an iPad in his hand. He looks as if he has the weight of the world on his shoulders.

"Sam," he greets me.

"Kai, how's it going?"

The look in his eyes is grim, and I know the news he has come to deliver isn't going to be good.

"There's been a video posted online, it's gone viral. I think you should see it."

I beckon him into the room and gesture for him to take a seat beside my bed. He taps the screen a few times and turns it towards me, so I can see.

Peyton

I hear the sound of muffled voices speaking in hushed tones, but I can't make out what they're saying or who the voices belong to. I almost feel like I'm in the middle of a dense, heavy fog. Everything around me is unclear as I give in to the blackness.

I'm somewhere in between unconsciousness and wakefulness when I hear Sam's familiar gruff tone.

"Please wake up. I can't lose you a second time...I won't survive it this time. The way I feel for you, it scares the living shit out of me. The year you were gone, I morphed back into the self-obsessed arsehole I was before I met you. I wasn't a nice person. *Fuck,* if I met me, I wouldn't have liked myself. Those first six months were the worst, I was an absolute wreck. I was so overwhelmed by grief, it consumed me. Everywhere I went, it was all people wanted to ask me about. In the end, I shut myself away and hid. I lost myself in writing lyrics, and I barely functioned most days. After I attempted suicide, they watched me more closely. The boys took turns watching me, making sure I was never alone. But all I wanted was to be alone. J.D was my rock through it all yet all along it was him; this is all his fucking fault. I should have ended him when I had the chance. I should be sad that he's dead, but I'm fucking glad. I'm glad he's dead. Wake up, angel, I need those beautiful blue eyes of yours."

I feel him grip my hand and the feather light touch of his lips to the back of my hand. I struggle to open my eyes, to let him know that I can hear him, that I heard every word he said to me. My body won't cooperate. My eyes feel as if they are glued shut, my limbs feel like lead, and my voice feels as if it is trapped somewhere deep within me.

"I need you, angel. Everything's falling apart. Please, wake up, I can't do this without you."

The desperate need in his voice is apparent, and it breaks my heart. I want to reassure him, I want to look in his clear green pools and tell him everything is going to be ok. Inside I am screaming, I'm calling out to him, but no matter how loud I scream, no one can hear me. I need all the people

I care about to know that I'm ok, that it's going to take more than a psycho with a gun to finish me off.

"I'm struggling...this whole thing is too much to take in."

Somehow, I manage to make my brain cooperate with my limbs, and it takes every ounce of strength I have in me, but I squeeze Sam's fingers.

"Hey, it's me, I'm here."

I feel the fog begin to clear, and the weight that was crushing my chest begins to lift. The dull beep of the machines rings in my ears, and as my eyelids flutter open, the bright light stings my eyes. It takes a moment for me to adjust, before I look into the eyes of the man I love.

"Angel."

His husky voice breaks through my consciousness, and the relief is evident.

"You're in the hospital. You're going to be fine, I promise you. I'll get the nurse."

He pushes a button, and almost instantly my hospital room is a hive of activity. The doctor's crowd around my bed, shining lights in my eyes, removing tubes, checking my wounds, and administering pain medication. Soon, the room has cleared, and we are left alone. I take in the sight before me, Sam is dressed in Batman lounge pants, a black v-neck t-shirt, and he is sat in a wheelchair. His hair is mussed, and he looks as if he hasn't slept in a while.

"Sam."

My voice is barely a whisper

"I'm here, angel."

He squeezes my hand in reassurance, and I'm not sure where it comes from, but a tear slips down my cheek. All of this, being in hospital, the events leading up to this moment, is all a little overwhelming.

"You're safe now."

Suddenly, everything that happened in the chapel hits me like a Boeing 747, and it feels like I am reliving it all over again. The gunshots, the bloodcurdling screams of terror coming from the people I love, the mysterious, chilling figure wielding the gun like something out of a Hollywood movie sequence. The remember moment I felt the bullet rip through my stomach and the moment I fell to the floor and my whole world went dark.

"Sam," I sob.

"Shhh, it's ok. You're safe, no one can hurt you now."

He gets to his feet, and he winces in pain.

"You're hurt," I whisper, and my voice sounds foreign in my throat.

He shakes his head as he smiles his dazzling smile. *It feels like a lifetime since I saw him smile.*

"It's just a scratch, angel. I'm fine."

He kisses my forehead and I reach up to grip his t-shirt in my hand, pulling him closer to me. I need him. I need him like I need air to breathe. I bury my face in his chest, and the masculine scent of him instantly soothes me. I know at that moment, we'll get through this, as long as we have each other.

Sam

How the fuck do I tell the woman I love more than life itself that her best friend is dead? How can I be the one to blow her world apart like that? How can I be the one to put that look of pure heartbreak in her eyes? I can't, I just can't.

I held her for a while, softly soothed her, and told her everything was going to be alright until she drifted off to sleep. Both of us are lucky to be alive. The physical damage is always repairable, but the mental and psychological damage is irreversible. I'm lying in my hospital bed in near dark, almost drifting off to sleep, when the door taps softly. The door opens, and I'm greeted by the last person in the world I expect: Remy Logan. He is walking with a crutch and is wearing loose, grey, jogging bottoms, a white vest, and a dark grey, chunky knit cardigan.

"Newbolt."

I nod curtly. He enters the room and closes the door behind him. He drops down heavily onto the chair next to my bed. He leans his crutch against the wall and scrubs his hands down his face.

"How are you holding up? I'm so sorry to hear about Ruby," I say, breaking the heavy silence.

He looks up at me with such pain in his eyes that I actually feel genuinely sorry for him.

"Thanks, I can't fucking believe she's gone...my baby sister."

His voice breaks as he says those final three words.

"It seems so...surreal, it feels like a bad dream. My mum and dad are in bits, I bet Peyton is devastated."

I half turn my head away and avert my gaze elsewhere.

"She doesn't know, does she?" he states matter-of-factly, and I shake my head.

"She's just come around, I couldn't hit her with that. Call me selfish, but I can't do that to her, not yet."

He looks me square in the face and nods in understanding.

"Maybe I should be the one to tell her. She was my sister, after all, and I feel like I owe her that."

The emotion in his voice is too much for me to take in, and for once, I don't argue.

Peyton

I wake, and it takes me a few moments to gather my bearings. When I do, I turn to look into the eyes of Remy. He looks pale and older than his thirty-three years. His deep, hazel eyes look sad and troubled.

"Rem".

He reaches over and clutches my hand in his.

"Beaut." I squeeze his hand tighter. "How are you feeling?"

I nod.

"Sore, but I'm ok."

I manage a weak smile, and the look Remy gives me tells me that there's something that he's holding back.

"Rem, is something wrong?"

He briefly closes his eyes, and when he opens them, they are filled with tears.

"Ruby didn't make it...she's gone, beaut."

As he says those words, my whole world collapses around me. It has to be some sort of sick joke. Ruby can't be dead, she can't be. It takes me a moment to process what Remy has just told me, and as I do, the dam breaks. I sob hard and uncontrollably. Remy stands up, and I move gingerly to make room for him. He climbs up onto the bed and holds me while I cry for my best friend and the baby she was carrying.

I'm not sure how much time passes, but I wake with a damp face and I feel exhausted.

"Beaut," Remy says sleepily.

"What happened, Rem? I have to know."

He turns his head away and looks up to the ceiling.

"She was shot in the head, it was...*Jesus,* words can't describe it. There was so much blood."

He swallows hard, and I can't imagine how difficult this must be for him.

"The ambulance got there, and it was kind of hazy after that. We got to the hospital, and the doctors told us that they could keep her alive long enough for the baby to survive. We had to make the decision to save her baby...she was eight months pregnant. She had a daughter, beaut. Jax is a dad, and I'm an uncle."

He lets out a sob, and I squeeze him tighter as I sob softly.

Ruby had a daughter?

37

Sam

I'm still trying to find the courage to tell Peyton the real reason why this is happening to us.

"Grow some fucking balls, Newbolt," Brody growls.

"You have to tell her, you can't keep it from her. She has a fucking right to know, and you're being a prick for keeping her in the dark. This has impacted us all. We've lost people who have been with us for over ten fucking years, man. Cole might never walk again."

He runs his hand over his head. He's more than a little agitated; he hates hospitals.

"She doesn't deserve this. She almost fucking died, so did you. Jax lost the woman he loved, and he has a child to take care of now," he says, and I still can't wrap my head around the fact that Jax is a dad.

"Eight people are fucking dead, Sam, people we cared about!" he says, with a clenched jaw. "Now, would be the perfect time to get fucking high, *shit*. I have to go, I can't fucking be here."

He curses and storms out of the room. A few moments later, the door knocks once, and I wonder who the fuck it is this time.

"Come in," I rasp, and as I look up, my eyes meet those of Seb Henry.

He gestures to the chair next to my bed.

"May I?"

I nod, and he sits down.

"I know what you're going to say, mate," I say to Seb, and he nods once curtly. "Tell me what happened," I ask out of morbid curiosity, and he leans forward to rest his arms on his knees.

"When I heard the shots, my military training kicked in. All I saw was a target that had to be taken down, it was just instinct. By the time I got there, she'd already shot so many people. We're not trained to think, we're trained to take out the threat, and she was a threat. I was near the back of the room, so I was out of her peripheral vision. I managed to sneak in behind her, and I took her down."

Listening to his account of how he killed my sister, I can't put into words how I feel. She murdered innocent people that were close to us, and injured so many others, but she was still my sister. She was still my flesh and blood.

"How?" I murmur, as if I could possibly torture myself more.

He briefly squeezes his eyes shut.

"I broke her neck."

I look up to meet his eyes.

"I don't know how the fuck I'm supposed to feel about this...Thank you for telling me personally. Now...I just need some space to process."

He nods in understanding, and he stands up. Before he leaves, he moves closer to me and squeezes my shoulder.

"I'm sorry, mate, genuinely I am," he says sincerely as he turns and leaves the room.

The few minutes that pass after he leaves allows me to process the true extent of what has happened, and I don't know how the fuck I'm going to tell Peyton that it was my sister that caused all of this...mindless slaughter.

Get it together, Newbolt, you have to tell her.

I manage to manoeuvre myself into the wheelchair at the side of my bed.

A fucking wheelchair, I inwardly curse as I drop down into it, wincing at the pain in my side.

I wheel myself down the corridor, nodding to Kai as he helps me with the door and places the iPad he has in his hand on my lap. I navigate my way through her door, and Kai closes it behind me as my eyes lock with hers. She looks so upset, so devastated.

"She's gone, Sam. Ruby's gone," she sobs, and I move towards the bed.

I clutch her hand in mine and plant a kiss on the back.

"I know, angel. I'm sorry, I'm so sorry," I whisper.

I know that once she knows what I have to tell her, all hell is going to break loose. *Fuck.*

I can't hold back any longer. Brody's right, she has to know. I'm a dick for keeping it from her. I take a deep breath, and I know it's now or never.

"Angel, there's something you need to know."

She lifts her head and the look in her eyes says, 'what more could you possibly have to tell me?' I tap the screen on the iPad a few times and turn it towards her as the person on the screen begins to speak.

***

"If you're watching this video, it means I'm either dead or in prison. J.D was the only one who believed me, and you took him away from me, that's why you all had to fucking pay. I was nine years old, the first time Jed Dalton raped me. At the age of eleven I told my mother, who told me I shouldn't tell such vicious lies and that people would stop loving me if I kept on lying. I didn't say anything to anyone again, until I was fourteen years old and John walked in on me crying in my bedroom. I told him everything. He was the only person I could ever truly trust, and we formed a bond thicker than blood. You see, John and me, we had the sort of relationship that Sam and me should have had. He had my back, and I had his.... I always felt like an outsider, even in my own family. There was never a connection, not like I had with John, it was unbreakable. He never felt good enough in his family, and I understood that, because I felt the same. Our bond was so strong that he even killed his dad for me. He did it to make him pay for what he did to me, all those years ago. John made it look like Jed died of a heart attack, when in fact John poisoned him with ricin, which is untraceable."

The tears roll freely down Peyton's cheeks, and every tear feels like a knife to my fucking heart. I can't stand to see that look in her eyes, it shreds me. I softly stroke her knuckles in a gesture of reassurance as we continue to watch.

"I knew he was in love with Sam, I've known for years. When I saw what his relationship with Peyton was doing to John, I had to do something to protect him. I cut the brakes on Peyton's car, but the bitch survived. Then, after what happened in Las Vegas, John seemed happier. He had the relationship with Sam he'd craved for so many years. They were close for the first time in a long time, but he went off the rails after Sam tried to end his own life. He fell deeper and deeper into drugs, until he couldn't see a way out. The night before he took Sam, he called me. He was out of his mind on cocaine, babbling about how he was going to make Sam love him. I had no fucking idea what he was going to do, I swear. After that, my true brother was arrested and died in prison, all because Sam fucking Newbolt fell in love with the wrong person. John would have gone to the end of the fucking earth for Sam, that's why I have to avenge his death. I have to show every single fucking one of you that there are consequences."

Peyton can't hold back the sob that escapes her as she pushes the iPad back towards me. The look in her eyes fucking destroys me, and she doesn't speak for a few moments. After what feels like a lifetime, she swallows a few times and her eyes, full of tears, lock with mine.

"Savannah was working with J.D all this fucking time?"

Her voice is shaky, and it is as if her saying it out loud brings it home. My sister, Savannah Newbolt, was working with J.D, and she was the one who was behind this. She was the one behind the shooting, she was the one who cut Peyton's brakes, which started the wheels in motion. She was the one who tried to run us off the road...all of it, with the help of J.D, was her. My flesh and blood.

I can't get my fucking head around any of it.

Peyton

Seeing Savannah's confession on the screen in front of me...it doesn't seem real. Sam's sister was working with J.D all along, and none of us had a clue. As if we haven't been through enough with the shooting, this happens.

How much more can we take?

"Is she...?"

I can't say the words out loud. What I want to say is *"Is the psycho bitch dead?"*, but she's still Sam's sister. It is as if he knows what I want to say, and he simply nods.

"Seb killed her," he says flatly, with no emotion to his voice, and I reach for his hand. "Eight people died and twenty-three people were injured, Peyton. No matter if she was my sister, my blood, I can't fucking forgive her for that," he rasps. "Cole may never walk again, he was shot in the hip. Ruby, Alistair, Lex, and Blu are all dead."

Words can't describe how I'm feeling right now. My best friend is gone as are a number of people from Sam's entourage. They were people I got to know through my association with him and are all gone, lives cut short because of some psycho bitch with a fucking grudge. I can't comprehend the enormity of this.

It's too much.

"My mum and both of my brothers were injured, and my baby sister, Willow. How could she fucking do this to us?"

He puts his hand to his head and tugs his hair hard. I can't imagine how difficult this must be for him. We are interrupted by an abrupt knock on the door.

"Come in," Sam says gruffly, and the door opens.

Marlowe enters the room, and the look on his face is grave and ashen.

I know this isn't going to be good news.

"Sam, it's your mother...she..."

He sniffs and takes a moment to compose himself. Sam manages to get his feet, clutching his side.

"Dad? What's happened?"

Marlowe places his hand on Sam's shoulder.

"She's gone, son."

Sam sinks down to the floor and starts to sob hard.

"No! No! No!" He wails.

I feel helpless as I lay in my hospital bed, watching the man I love crumble because his mum is dead. A tear slips down my cheek, and I wipe it away quickly. Marlowe drops to the floor and pulls Sam into his arms. He reminds me of a small child, and my heart breaks watching the scene unfold before me. Sam's right, our lives will never be the same again.

Sam

Just when I thought things couldn't get any worse, I find out my mum is dead. Another victim of my sister's killing spree. My head starts to spin, and the enormity of this whole thing strikes like a bolt of lightning.

My mum is gone.

The woman who bought me into this world and nurtured me into the man I am today. Something inside me fucking snaps, and the strangled sob that finds its way out of my mouth doesn't sound like my own. I sit on the floor, letting my dad hold me and soothe me for the longest time. The overwhelming sense of grief and loss cripples me until I feel like I can't be here any longer. I need to leave, I need to deal with this the only way I know how, and that is to beat the living shit out of anything I can lay my hands on...just so I can feel anything other than this gut wrenching agony.

I pull away from my dad's tight embrace and manage to get to my feet. My dad stands up at the same time, and the look in his tired green eyes mirrors mine. I lean over to kiss Peyton on the forehead and leave the room in silence. I stride down the corridor, with purpose, ignoring the pain that tears through my chest, and stop in front of the coffee machine. I pull a dollar out of my pocket and insert it into the machine. I press the button for coffee, and as the cup pops out, I notice a tea bag in the bottom of the cup.

Fuck me.

White hot molten rage rushes through my veins, and I smash my fist into the keypad, on the machine.

"FUCKING COFFEE MACHINE!" I roar, and I can't seem to focus on anything other than tearing this machine apart, piece by fucking piece.

I continue to smash my fists against the machine, repeatedly, in a fit of pure fury. I grab the top of the machine with both hands and tip it forward until it collapses with a loud crash to the floor. I feel all the anger drain from me as I lean against the wall and slide down it, until I am sitting on the floor. As the adrenaline rush starts to subside, my knuckles throb and the feeling of pure anguish engulfs me once again. The names of the people, who died start to flash through my mind on a constant loop.

Lori, Ruby, Alistair, Lex, Blu, Riley, Callum, Grace, Joel.

My mind starts to slowly begin to process the extent of this fucked up situation. Almost everyone we care about is dead or has a life changing injury, and it's all because of my sister.

Savannah Newbolt. *Anna.*

38

Peyton

Las Vegas is plagued with bad memories for us. Two of the most horrific events of our lives have taken place there. Sin City has become a place of nightmares, a place that haunts my dreams and plagues my every waking moment. This is the very reason we have decided to return to London.

The days that followed were spent going over and over that fateful day in minute detail. Reliving every gun shot, every scream, and the dull cacophony before everything faded to black. Even after everything she did, I have some kind of empathy with Savannah. It doesn't excuse her actions, but an innocent child was brutally abused and then her mother refused to believe a child's words over that of a sick fucking man who was old enough to know right from wrong. I can't imagine the torment and hell that she went through, or maybe, I just don't want to. Lori Newbolt is as responsible for all of this as Jed fucking Dalton. I suppose fucked in the head runs in the Dalton family. Jed was a sick fucking pervert, and his son turned out to be a psychotic, kidnapper. I think the saying is true, the apple never falls too far from the tree.

We've been back in London for two weeks now, and I have given up my flat in Camden. Freddie and I have moved into Sam's mansion in Hertfordshire. In the week that followed our return, I could feel Sam withdrawing further and further away from me; so much so that he went into his studio, and I've hardly seen him. The boys have holed up in there with him, and I know not to disturb them while they're making music. Seb closed the tattoo shop for the foreseeable future, due to the death of his sister, Riley, in the massacre. So, I'm staying home with Freddie and helping Jax with his daughter, who has officially been named Thea Ruby Chase.

For the past couple of weeks, I have felt so alone while dealing with the loss of my best friend and the people that were closest to Sam. Sam has become so withdrawn. I hardly recognise him as the man I fell in love with.

We sleep in the same bed, but I feel so far away from him, and I'm terrified I'm going to lose him. I decide there and then that I am going to make an effort to reconnect with him, to show him that I'm here for him, no matter what.

I dress in a knee length black skater skirt, a black ribbed vest, a denim waistcoat, and my black and white checked Vans. My hair is styled in thick, brown, glossy waves down my shoulders. I make my way up the stairs and down a short corridor with framed album covers and gold discs hanging on the walls, until I get to Sam's soundproof studio. It is larger than the one he had back at his apartment in Greenwich. It has a full-size drum kit with the Rancid Vengeance logo on the front of the main drum, two electric guitars, and a microphone stand behind a wall of thick, soundproof, glass. There is a full mixing desk with two Mac computers on the table. Off to the side, there is a fairly large office, which is used for conducting band business.

As I enter the room quietly, I see Sam lying back in a gun metal grey, oversized Captain's chair. He is shirtless, which distracts me from my original plan. His hard, muscular, tattooed chest is on full display. He has a visible scar on his shoulder from where J.D stabbed him, and a large wound on his chest, which is healing nicely. He has one thick, corded arm resting above his head, and the other is resting on his flat, toned abs. He has his long legs, which are encased in a pair of devastatingly tight leather trousers, and his booted feet up on the glass desk in front of him. There are empty bottles of vodka scattered around along with the white powder remnants from his drug fuelled antics. He has a Bluetooth headset in his ear, and he sighs.

"For fucks sake, I told you I'm busy. No, I don't wish to give them an interview about what happened in Vegas. I really don't give a shit, D. We pay you to be our P.A, nothing more, nothing less. Got it? No, no, listen to me. It's no one's fucking business, and leave Peyton out of it," he growls, and my curiosity is piqued at the mention of my name.

I step further into the room, and he suddenly moves his legs down from the desk and sits up straighter in his chair. It is as if he senses me without having to turn around to register my presence.

"D, just sort it, please. I have a visitor, I need to go."

With those words, he touches his ear to end the call and throws the headset onto the table with a loud clatter. He stands up to his full six foot four height and turns around. Our eyes lock, green to blue, and he runs his hand through his wild, untamed, raven black hair.

"Angel," he rasps as I take him in.

He looks as if he hasn't slept in a while, and he has large dark, circles underneath his eyes. He has at least a weeks' worth of stubble on his chin, and he looks pale.

"Can I help you with something?" he says gruffly.

I feel my inner vixen stir as I step towards him, until I am within touching distance. I run my finger down the centre of his chest and stop at the waistband of his trousers.

"I'm not sure, but I have something that needs...tending to, as a matter of importance," I whisper enticingly.

He growls as I slowly unbuckle his belt and unbutton his trousers.

"And what might that be, angel?"

The low seductive tone of his voice causes my pussy to flood violently, and I've never wanted him inside me as badly as I do right now. He reaches down underneath my skirt and swallows harshly.

"*Fuck,* you're not wearing any underwear."

The grin I flash him makes his cock jump in his deliciously tight trousers, and I cup him in my hand. His eyes turn smoky with desire, and he grips my hand tightly.

"Angel," he says with warning in his voice, and I look up at him.

"Take me to bed and make love to me, rock star."

He doesn't say another word, he just backs me into the wall and presses his lips to mine, desperately kissing the life out of me. He kisses me breathless, and by the time he pulls away, we are both panting with need for one another. Sam lifts me up in one swift motion, and I lock my legs tightly around his waist as he carries me out of his studio. He strides with purpose down the corridor, and the only thing that is fuelling me is my pure unadulterated lust for this virile man holding me in his arms.

I cling to him and nip his earlobe between my teeth as we make it to our bedroom. He enters the room and kicks the door shut with his boot. He lays me down on the king-size bed we share and straddles me, his muscular thighs on either side of me. He takes both wrists in one of his hands and pins them above my head. He presses his body against mine, and I love the feel of his weight on top of me. He kisses my neck, and the feel of his stubble against my bare skin causes goose bumps to erupt on every inch of my body.

"*Jesus,*" he rasps as he kicks off his boots and begins to pull off his trousers and his boxer briefs.

He is naked in record time, and I take a moment to admire his rippling physique. I will never get tired of seeing him naked in front of me; it is a remarkable sight.

"I need you naked," he says with a rough edge to his voice, and I do as he says.

I take off my skirt, my vest top, waistcoat, and kick off my shoes. Soon, I am lying on the bed in my bra. He hasn't taken his eyes off me once, and the look of admiration in his blazing green pools makes my heart slam against my ribcage.

"*Fuck,* you're so...fucking beautiful."

His voice is a low purr, and the admiration is evident as I feel my arousal slick between my thighs.

"Sam," I say desperately as he releases my hands from above my head.

I take that as a green light, and I let my hands roam shamelessly over his body, feeling closer to him than I have in weeks.

39

Sam

The feel of her hands on me is welcomed, and I am suddenly filled with such an overwhelming regret at my behaviour since our return from Las Vegas.

"Sam," she mewls as she runs her hands through my hair.

I press my erection into her stomach.

"Do you feel that, angel? You have no comprehension of the effect you have on me."

I flash her my dimpled grin, and she bites her lip between her teeth.

Fuck me, does she not realise that she's it for me? She always has been.

All I want to do is to apologise for my shitty behaviour, but words aren't needed right now, so I guess I'll have to show her.

"Tell me you belong to me, tell me you're mine."

She writhes beneath me, and she wraps her legs around my waist.

"I belong to you, Sam. I'm yours, always yours."

I nod.

"Good girl. There's no one here, the boys are out, so it's just you and me. I expect you to take full advantage of that; make sure you scream my name when you come," I say huskily.

Her touches become more frenzied as I grasp my erection and slide it gently into her. Her pussy is like a vice around my cock as she pulls me deeper inside her.

"Oh God," she moans softly, and I thrust my hips forward.

The rhythm I set, is unhurried and punishingly sedate. As I plunge my cock into her, at a slow pace, tears begin to stream down her cheeks, and the look in her eyes breaks my fucking heart.

"What's wrong, angel? Do you want me to stop? Am I hurting you?" I say with a panicked edge to my voice, and she shakes her head as she continues to sob softly.

"I don't want you to stop, Sam. Please don't stop," she says with desperation in her voice. "Make love to me like you used to, Sam, please," she pleads, and I agree without saying a word.

I lean down and kiss each and every one of her tears away as I continue to drive my cock into her, quickening my pace with each measured thrust.

"Sam, Sam, Oh, Sam," she whispers.

"Are you close, baby?" I ask as I feel the familiar flutters, and she nods.

I place soft kisses down her neck, shoulder, and across her collarbone. I knead her breast in my large tattooed hand while keeping up my gentle tempo. I reach down and find her wet, sensitive nub and stroke her in leisurely circles while she detonates violently around me. She screams out in unadulterated pleasure and tightens her legs around my waist, squeezing me between her silky thighs.

Fuck me, I've missed this.

"I'M COMING! FUCK! SAM! OH GOD! SAM! SAM!"

I find my release seconds later as I spurt my hot seed into her.

"OH, JESUS FUCK! SHIT! PEYTON! PEYTON!" I roar, and it feels as if both of our orgasms last longer than usual.

I let out a staggered breath as our orgasms dissipate. A few moments of silence passes as our breathing returns to normal. She winces as I pull out of her sensitive pussy, and I lie down next to her. I tuck her under my arm and pull her close to me. I idly trace random shapes on her arm, and she snuggles against me, as if she can't get close enough. The connection that has been missing for the past few weeks has returned, and even though the post orgasmic haze between us is still lingering in the air, I can't help the guilt that washes over me.

The reason I've withdrawn and distanced myself from her for past few weeks, is because I feel like this is all my fault. That if I hadn't met Peyton, none of this would have happened. I know that the only person to blame for this was my sister, Savannah, but I can't help feeling partly responsible. As I feel her breathing even out, I feel like a complete prick for withdrawing from her when all she ever wanted was to be there for me, to comfort me in my time of grief. In my own way I'm grieving, for the loss of my mum and my sister, but I also hold them both equally responsible for this entire situation.

I can't forgive either of them for setting this chain of events in motion, and I probably never will, but I've made peace with that.

As I turn to face Peyton, I find her sleeping next to me. She looks like a Goddess with her hair fanned out on the pillow. The distressing whimpers that escape from her cause my heart to shatter a little bit more. I slowly get up out of bed, without waking her, after sleep has evaded me for the past five hours. I pull on a pair of loose grey jogging bottoms, which hang off my hips, and pad silently out of the bedroom. I make my way into my recording studio and I quietly observe Jax singing softly to his daughter. I recognise the song, as *Daughtry Life after You* and the sad, melancholic tone in Jax's voice causes my heart to slam against my ribcage. It brings back awful memories for me.

"I need you, Ruby. I have no fucking clue what I'm doing here. She's this helpless little thing who reminds me so much of you every time I look at her. I feel so much love for her that it overwhelms me; this wasn't part of our plan, buttercup."

He puts his hand to his head, and as I continue to watch the touching scene unfolding in front of me, I feel like I'm intruding on an extremely intimate and private moment. At that moment, a flash of inspiration hits me like a freight train. I've spent two weeks in the studio writing and composing with the boys, but this...*this is something special.*

I can feel it deep in my gut. I can almost hear the melody and the arrangement, the lyrics are flowing like a torrent in my head. I have to get this down. I make my way further into the studio and sit down on the low, brown, buttery leather chair. I pick up my acoustic guitar, begin to strum out a melody, and hum softly. As I close my eyes, I lose myself in the music. All sense of time abandons me, and everything else is insignificant. All that exists in my head is the music and the lyrics.

Unexpectedly, I hear a steady drum beat and the accompaniment of an electric guitar. A few moments later, I hear the haunting melody of a piano, and I look up to see that Jax, Brody, and Lucas have joined me in the studio. I smile, and Brody flashes me an encouraging wink.

"We will weather the storm and dance in the rain, we'll raise a glass to numb the pain," I sing as my fingers dance up and down the fretboard.

The boys keep in time with every riff, and in that moment, I'm grateful that they know me so well.

"We'll break down the walls, risk it all, stand tall, when the angels come to call. Stitch by stitch, stone by stone, we will never be alone. Fly free and we will be, dancing in the rain."

The grin that spreads across all of our faces is the happiest we've been in two weeks. We continue writing and jamming well into the night, doing what we love best.

40

Peyton

Time is never finite. Time is precious, and I cherish those treasured moments between sleep and wakefulness. For those few minutes, everything, is as it was before. *Normal.* As soon as I open my eyes, it hits me like a double-decker bus. My best friend, Ruby, the scared girl from the climbing frame, turned tough, ballsy woman...*she's gone.* It is like my heart breaks all over again, and the pain threatens to choke me, drown me. Life is fragile, like the little girl with the big, expressive, hazel eyes, who is the mirror image of Ruby. She is a part of Ruby that will live on, with her blood running through her veins. There isn't a day goes by where I don't think of her and miss her, the treasured memories we made together and, the unbreakable bond we had.

She wasn't just my best friend, she was my sister.

The rain is pouring as I stand a solitary figure at the floor length window of our mansion, looking out across the acres of green land that seems to go on for miles. I watch the rain pound on the window and follow a lone drop as it tracks its way down.

Life isn't fair.

I clutch a mug of coffee in one hand and hold my son in the opposite arm. Today is the day we bury my best friend, Jax's fiancée, and beloved member of the Rancid Vengeance family. I am wearing a figure hugging, lemon yellow dress, with a black belt around my waist which accentuates my slight frame. Ruby and I once talked about what we would like at our funerals during one of our many alcohol fuelled nights. She said that she didn't want anyone to wear black, she wanted everyone in bright clothes and uplifting music playing. I smile to myself as I think of that moment, which seems so far away now. My thoughts are interrupted by Sam sliding his hands around my waist and nuzzling his face into my neck.

"Angel," he rasps in my ear and pulls me closer to him, my back to his front.

I nestle my face into Freddie's chubby cheek, and he giggles.

"Hey, how's daddy's little rock star doing today?"

Sam spins around and plucks Freddie from my arms. The sight of him in a suit with a mint green shirt temporarily disarms me, and I bite my lip. He growls, and I roll my eyes. The weeks that have passed have bought Sam and me closer together. We're closer than we've ever been before, and our relationship is solid.

"Carry on looking at me like that, and see where it gets you," Sam says in warning, and I cock my perfectly plucked eyebrow at him.

"Hopefully beneath you, baby," I sass him, and he flashes me his dimples in that way of his.

Jax storms into the room with Thea in his arms. His suit is crumpled, his tie is crooked, his hair is mussed, and he looks like he hasn't slept.

"I'm glad you two are finding this amusing. I'm burying the love of my fucking life today, and all you two can do is grope each other and laugh like this is just a normal fucking day!"

He raises his voice as our faces grow serious, and he scrubs his free hand down his face.

"I haven't fucking slept because Thea wouldn't stop crying, and I have to get up in front of all of her family and read a eulogy when I have no clue what to fucking say."

The tone of his voice breaks my heart, and I step away from Sam to take Thea from Jax.

"Hey little lady, have you been keeping your daddy awake?" I coo as I cradle her in my arms.

My heart slams against my ribcage as her likeness to her mum is glaringly apparent.

"Did your mum not teach you how to dress yourself, dude? Because she would tear you a new one if she saw the state of you right now!"

Sam rolls his eyes as he attempts to straighten Jax's tie. Jax bats him away with his hands and shakes his head.

"I don't even know why I'm wearing a fucking tie, she hated ties!"

We all manage to smile as he tears his tie off, discarding it over the back of the chaise lounge in our bedroom. He then undoes the top two buttons of his baby pink shirt.

"*Fuck it!* I'm not wearing a tie! You hear me, buttercup?"

He looks up to the ceiling, as if he expects her to answer, and I smile softly as his eyes fill with tears.

"*Shit,* I fucking miss her."

Sam gives him a one-armed man hug.

"I know you do, man, we miss her too," he says sincerely, and he smiles tenderly at me over Jax's shoulder. He pulls away and turns to face him. "I have to ask, dude, are you wearing that shirt for a fucking bet?"

Jax smirks and shakes his head.

"It was a private joke between me and Ruby. Even from beyond the grave, she's laughing at me, little firecracker."

We all share a moment, united in grief for Ruby Logan.

***

As we make our way into The Parish of Old Saint Pancras, in Camden, Pearl, Ray, and Remy Logan, are standing on the grass outside. Pearl is wearing sunglasses and has a handkerchief in her hand. She is sobbing softly and dabbing her eyes at intervals. Ray's face is sombre, but the look in Remy's eyes...I've never seen him look like that in all the years I have known him. He looks pale, drawn, and tired. He has one hand tucked casually in his pocket, and as Pearl and Ray greet us in turn, Remy pulls me into him. He squeezes me tight, and I feel him trembling against me.

"I can't do this, beaut. I can't bury my baby sister," he says so quietly I barely hear him.

I pull briefly away from our embrace, but he clings tightly to both of my hands.

"Listen to me, Rem, you *can* do this. I bet she's up there having a right old laugh at us, because that's how I remember her. She was a moody cow in the mornings, but she was always smiling, always laughing. Jax is wearing a pink fucking shirt, so who do you think got the rough end of the deal here?"

He smiles weakly as he averts his gaze to Sam, who is observing our exchange with a silent wariness.

"I'm going back to Santa Monica, Peyton," Remy blurts out, and my eyes widen at his admission.

Remy's going back to America?

"I've already lost my best friend, Rem. I can't lose you as well."

My voice cracks as Remy lets go of my hands.

"You lost me the day you walked out and left Santa Monica, beaut."

I wince at the acerbic, virulent tone to his voice.

"I can't fucking stay here."

I am about to speak, when we are interrupted by the rest of the boys joining us. Lucas casually salutes me and smiles.

"I fucking hate funerals," Brody grumbles softly, and he kisses me on the cheek as we all begin to make our way into the church.

Sam puts his arm around me and kisses me on the forehead.

"I'll see you inside, angel."

He winks, and Pearl links my arm with hers as we make our way inside. I sit in the front row next to Pearl, and as the haunting voice of Chester Bennington, as he sings *One More Light* fills the small, intimate church, a tear slips down my cheek as Jax, Sam, Remy, and Ray carry Ruby's coffin down the centre aisle. As Pearl catches sight of her daughter's pink and black polka dot casket, she reaches for my hand, and I let her take comfort in the simple gesture. They reach the front of the church and lay her coffin down on a raised platform. The boys make their way into the front row, but Remy is stood stock still over his sister's coffin. He places his hand on the top and breaks down in gut wrenching sobs. The sound causes my heart to slam against my ribs, and my breath catches in my throat at the sight of Remy's lean frame hunched over the casket. Pearl squeezes my hand and leans close to my ear.

"Go to him, Peyton, darling. He needs you."

I get to my feet and make my way over to him. I stand behind him and cautiously place my hand on his shoulder. It takes me by surprise when he reaches back and places his hand on top of mine. He slowly turns around and takes my hand in his.

"Don't let go of my hand, beaut. I can't do this without you," he whispers so only I can hear him, and I nod in acknowledgement.

We make our way back into the pew, and I find myself sandwiched between Sam and Remy. My past and my present are colliding in a spectacular fashion. The priest gives a brief speech, and then it's time for Jax to say his eulogy. His long blonde hair is styled perfectly, his eyes are glazed over, and the top two buttons on his baby pink shirt are open. He is wearing black skinny jeans and black motorcycle boots. He takes out a crumpled piece of paper from his pocket and flattens it out, as he clears his throat.

"I…I spent hours trying to find the right words to say, to sum up Ruby Logan, and now that I'm up here…I've got nothing."

He laughs nervously.

"Words will never be enough to describe Ruby. We met at Saint Sinner Ink when she breezed in with her heels and her attitude. She took my breath away then, and she continued to take my breath away up until the moment she took her last. As she took her last breath, our daughter, Thea, took her first."

He puffs out his cheeks and swallows hard. He looks up to the ceiling.

"I'm…struggling with using the past tense, because I keep expecting her to come teetering up that aisle in her heels, cursing like a sailor."

I smile through my tears as Jax continues.

"We all knew Ruby in different capacities, daughter, sister, best friend, fiancée, and when I sat down to write my eulogy, I came up blank. There was so much I wanted to say, but something inside me wondered if it was enough to do the Ruby I and everyone else knew justice. I feel like a bit of a fraud standing up here when you all knew her a lot longer than I did. I knew her for just over a year, but in that year, she taught me a valuable lesson: life isn't about waiting for the storm to pass, it's about learning to dance in the rain, and as a couple, we weathered the storms life threw at us. If she hadn't learned to dance; she may have remained dry, but unfulfilled. She was fulfilled, she lived life to the full by colouring outside of the lines and on her own terms. Never, never stop dancing in the rain, buttercup."

A tear rolls down Jax's face, and he swipes it away. The fortress that has been holding my tears at bay suddenly gives way under the pressure. The tears fall freely down my cheeks, like a torrent. Sam runs his hands up and down my back in a soothing motion, whispering words of comfort in my ear.

"Shhh, I've got you, angel. It's going to be ok, I promise."

We somehow manage to make it to the end, and I feel emotionally drained as we move from the church to the graveside. We all gather round

Ruby's final resting place, and as I throw a handful of dirt onto the coffin of the best friend I've ever had, I say a final farewell.

41

Sam

Summer turns into autumn, autumn turns into winter, and the six months that pass have been some of the hardest, darkest months of our lives. The months that passed saw a lot of changes in the Vengeance family. We buried the people we lost in the Vegas massacre and tried to piece our shattered lives back together. News spread of what my sister had done and my mother's part in it.

Our private lives were now front and centre, and everything we did that followed the events of Las Vegas was under intense scrutiny. Our fans continued to support us, and as a band, we made the brave decision to break away from Diamond Records. We put on a united front and launched our own record label called Vengeance Records. We now have a new manager, Michael James Richmonde III, or M.J for short. M.J is a flamboyant, American, ex member of a seventies rock band, called The Scarlett Jetts. At almost fifty-eight years old, M.J retired from the music industry, choosing instead to manage up-and-coming acts and become a judge on the panel of a popular American talent show. We hired M.J, because of his experience in the industry and his chilled out, devil may care attitude.

Also, we have a new tour bus driver, who is a welcome addition to the Rancid Vengeance family. George Roche, or Gorgeous George as everyone calls him, is a six foot seven force of nature. He never fails to make everyone smile with his quick wit and dry sense of humour. Two other additions to our team include our new hair stylist, Danny, who was Peyton's next-door neighbour in Camden. He gave up his role as a drag artist after he sustained facial injuries from the shooting. Also, we have Otis, our new make-up artist, who reminds me of RuPaul. Even though we will mourn the loss of the people who died in Vegas for years to come, life *has* to go on. Although the threat has been eliminated, our security has doubled in size, especially now that Cole is on limited duties due to his injuries. Cole was shot in the hip, and after he has endured a number of operations and intense physiotherapy, he now walks with the aid of a cane.

As a band, the events that occurred, have bought us closer together, and in the six months that passed, we recorded a new album, *Vengeance Resurrected*. We are just weeks away from releasing it.

We have a well-earned two weeks off before we embark on the album launch and a worldwide tour, which is going to keep us busy and on the road for a whole year. We have flown to The Cook Islands, which are the best kept secret in the Pacific Ocean. The fifteen islands are scattered over a vast expanse of seductive and sensuous ocean and boast of an idyllic climate and rare beauty.

Peyton, me, Freddie, the boys, Cole, Amy, Addison, our security guys, George, Danny, and Otis are all staying in M.J's luxurious beach lodge, which is located directly on the beach. We flew out on our private jet, Air Vengeance. The lodge, boasts its own housekeeper, cleaner, and chef to tend to our every need, all courtesy of M.J. This is exactly what we needed to get away from it all, relax, recuperate, and recharge our batteries before we get back to the crazy world of Rancid Vengeance.

The view of the crystal-clear ocean, and almost turquoise sky, is absolutely breath-taking as I step out onto the sand and sit down on a lounger with my guitar. I strum out a few chords and hum softly as I'm interrupted by Peyton. She looks like a fucking angel, wearing a long flowing white skirt and a black bikini top. Her tan makes her tattoos look even more striking. Her dark hair is pulled up into a messy knot on top of her head, and she has sunglasses shielding her eyes. As I look at her, I wonder how I got so lucky, and I'm thankful for her each and every day that passes. She has Freddie in her arms; he's just turned two, and every time I look at him, he takes my breath away. He's starting to walk awkwardly, and his expressions remind me so much of me when I was a child. His clear green eyes light up as he catches sight of me, and he starts clapping his hands.

"Daddy!"

I smile and stop playing for a few moments.

"Hey rock star. Are you being a good boy for mummy?"

Peyton walks further onto the sand, and I pull her down into my lap.

"Angel," I rasp, and she cocks her eyebrow.

"Not in front of our son, you beast!"

We both laugh as Amy comes out wearing a purple and orange cover up with sunglasses perched on top of her head. Her hair is in a French plait, which hangs down her back.

"Do you want me to take Freddie, so you guys can spend some time together, hon?"

Peyton nods.

"If you don't mind, babe?"

Amy shakes her head and smiles.

"Course not, hon, he's no trouble. Come to Aunty Amy."

She plucks Freddie from Peyton's arms and goes back inside, leaving us alone on the sand.

"Now that we're all alone, what am I going to do with you, angel?" I say gruffly, and she wriggles in my lap.

"I can think of a few things," she says sassily, and I cock my pierced eyebrow at her.

"Don't start something you're not going to finish, play fair."

She winks wickedly.

"You know I don't play fair, Newbolt."

She grinds on my growing erection, and I lean my guitar against the lounger.

"Do you need me to take care of something, angel?"

I pull her closer to me and nip her earlobe between my teeth, causing her to throw her head back and moan softly.

"I need you, Sam," she says breathily.

I cup her breast in my hand, and she gasps out loud.

"Tender?"

She nods and bites her lip.

"I'm due on my period, so we better make the most of it, while we still can."

I move my hand underneath her skirt to find she isn't wearing any underwear.

"You little minx! Do you enjoy teasing me? I think you do, you fucking unman me. Do you have any idea how hard it is for me to keep my hands off you when you stand there looking like a fucking goddess?"

I stroke her clitoris softly and knead her breast in my other hand, until she is writhing on my lap.

"Sam," she pants out and I quicken my pace, teasing her wet nub with my index finger.

Suddenly, we are interrupted by a loud bang on the window.

"Get a fucking room! You're like a pair of horny fucking teenagers!" Brody shouts, and I flip him the bird as I lean in to whisper in her ear.

"Let's take this to the bedroom."

I lift her up effortlessly in my arms and carry her inside. The boys all start applauding as we enter the living space.

"Do you have no shame, dude?"

Jax rolls his eyes and Brody snickers.

"*Fuck me!* I got hard watching that! I need to get fucking laid! I'm going to have to take a cold shower!"

He adjusts his cock in his loose board shorts, and I smirk as we head for the bedroom to the sound of the raucous laughter of the boys. I kick the door closed with my bare foot and launch Peyton into the air, until she lands in the middle of the bed in a fit of giggles. I crawl between her legs, like a predator stalking its prey, and trap her beneath me with my arms either side of her.

"Alone at last," I rasp, and she reaches down to cup my erection with her hand.

I squeeze my eyes shut and growl low in my throat.

"You don't know how good that feels. *Fuck!*" I curse and make light work of getting us both naked in record time.

"I need to bury my cock inside you, now, angel."

I fist my cock in my hand a few times and the head of my pierced cock finds her entrance. I shove forward, impaling her on my waiting firmness.

"*Oh Jesus,* fuck, you feel like heaven."

I pick up my pace, moving in and out of her slick heat and fuck me, it feels so good...*so right*. She wraps her arms around my neck and tugs the hair at my nape. She moans softly into my ear as my pace starts to quicken. I feel her orgasm cresting to the surface, and she squeezes her inner walls around my cock.

Fuck me, this woman is definitely going to be the death of me.

I growl at the feeling.

"*Shit,* that felt...*FUCK*!" I bark as I continue to piston in and out of her as she explodes around me.

"I'm coming, *fuck*, Sam. Oh God, I'm coming," she yells, and I move my hand over her mouth.

My orgasm is right behind hers as my hot seed jets inside her, causing a second orgasm to detonate from deep within her. She cries out around my hand, and as we come down from our orgasms, the only sound is our breathless post orgasmic pants. I pull out of her, roll over, and lie down on the bed next to her. My mind starts to wander as the events of Vegas flash through my head at two hundred miles an hour. *Fuck.* I squeeze my eyes shut, and she crawls into my arms, as if she knows what I need. I pull her close to me, and I look into her mesmerizing, clear, blue eyes.

"I would burn the fucking world for you, angel. There's nothing I wouldn't do for you or our son. Knowing I couldn't protect you on our own wedding day...*Jesus*, that fucking destroyed me, beyond recognition. Something happened outside of my control and that never sits well with me. I'm sorry, I'm so fucking sorry."

The fierce determination in my voice is evident, and her eyes are shining with tears as I wrap her in my arms.

"I'll never let anyone hurt you ever again, I fucking promise you," I say gruffly and plant a chaste kiss on the top of her head.

As I lie here, with my girl in my arms, I think of everything that we've been through in our relationship. We've endured more than any other couple I know, but we've come out stronger, and I'll spend my life dedicated to no one but her.

I'm one lucky motherfucker.

42

Peyton

There was a time when J.D first kidnapped me that I finally accepted my fate and made peace with it. I made peace with the fact that my fate had been sealed, and that me and my baby were going to die at the hands of that sick, twisted, depraved freak who had me bound and at his mercy.

Now, as the orange hues of the sun rising over the Pacific Ocean in M.J's sumptuous beach lodge in The Cook Islands, I am lying awake, watching Sam sleep next to me. He looks so peaceful in his slumber, and after our marathon sex session last night, we both slept soundly for the first time in months. There wasn't a nightmare in sight.

There isn't a day goes by where I don't think of the terrible suffering and loss we all endured at the hands of Savannah Newbolt on that fateful day. My brother Dexter lost his fiancée, Grace, and Seb lost his sister, Riley. Everyone who was present on that day, whether it serious or minor, suffered an injury.

As I watch Sam sleep, my thoughts start to wander to how far we've come, since we met at Saint Sinner Ink; it seems like a lifetime ago. It seems like forever since I first heard Sam utter the words *"Hey beautiful"*, the words that would change the course of my life, completely.

My thoughts are temporarily interrupted by the sound Freddie's tiny whimpers. I swing my legs out of bed and enjoy the feel of the cool, tiled floor beneath my feet. I go over to his cot to find him still sleeping, and my heart feels almost too big for my chest as I look down at the little boy that Sam and I created. I pad across the large opulent bedroom and into the en-suite bathroom. The bathroom is decorated in serene aquamarine colours, and the floor is clear, which gives me a view of the ocean beneath us. I don't get to enjoy the tranquillity of the fishes and the low sound of the water lapping as my stomach roils. Unexpectedly, I feel like I need to throw up. I drop to my knees and empty the contents of my stomach as I vomit violently into the toilet bowl. It feels like it's never ending, until the roiling of my stomach finally ceases, and I'm dry heaving. Abruptly, the door handle rattles and there's a light tap on the door.

"I don't like locked doors, angel," Sam rasps softly.

"I'm fine, babe. I'll be out in a second."

He sighs audibly.

"Don't make me take the door off its hinges, sweetheart," he growls, and I can sense the underlying panic in his voice.

My sweet mercurial rock star is gracing me with his presence.

I get to my feet, wipe my mouth on some toilet paper, and flush the toilet. I unlock the door as Sam crowds into the bathroom, gloriously naked, with a look of pure anguish on his handsome face. I make my way over to the sink, and he stands in front of me, tipping my chin up to face him. It is as if he is inspecting me, to make sure I'm ok.

"Are you ok, angel?"

I nod and smile.

"Babe, I'm fine, honestly. I've been sick, that's all. I think it must have been something I ate. Go back to bed, I'll come and join you in a sec. I just need to brush my teeth, I have vomit breath."

He frowns and regards me intently as I turn on the cold tap, run my toothbrush underneath the water, and apply some toothpaste.

"Are you sure everything's alright?"

The gentle concern in his voice causes my heart to slam against my rib cage. I reach up to gently caress his lightly stubbled cheek, and he leans into my touch.

"Everything's perfect, I promise."

He places his hand on top of mine.

"It fucking shreds me to think of losing you again, angel. You've ruined me for all other women, no other woman will ever come close to the way I feel about you."

I smile tenderly up at him, and the look in his crystal clear green eyes tells me all I need to know. I belong to Sam Newbolt. He owns me, just as I own every inch of him. No one will know the real Sam Newbolt, not the one I see in private. They get to see glimpses that he lets them see, that he wants them to see. They don't get to see the way he gets this faraway look in his eyes when he's inspired. They don't get to see him in the mornings looking sleepy and

God-like. I get to see every facet of Sam Newbolt, the fiancé, the father, the lover, the son, the best friend, the showman, and the shy, unsure, vulnerable, normal man he is when we're together.

After I put my toothbrush in the holder next to Sam's, I open the mirrored cabinet above the glass topped sink. I take out some Pepto-Bismol to help with my sickness, and the thought that crashes through me as I catch sight of the unused box of tampons almost knocks me off my feet.

Shit, my period is late.

Sam and I have never discussed the prospect of another baby. I had been more than surprised when I found out I was pregnant with Freddie. It's times like these when I really miss Ruby. Having a best friend, who happened to be female, always helped put things into perspective for me. I treasured the shoulder to cry on, and I valued her advice and opinions, even if they were a little harsher than she intended. That was just Ruby's way.

The six months that have passed has seen some additions to the Rancid Vengeance family, and George, the band's tour bus driver, has become a really close friend, confidant, and ally for me. George, or Gorgeous as he likes to be called, is thirty-eight years old, six feet seven, average build, with long, shoulder length, blonde hair that reminds me of a lion's mane, blue-grey eyes, a beard, and he speaks with a strong Bristolian accent.

He has been a roadie for various different bands for the past fifteen years and has done everything from moving stage equipment venue to venue, to driving tour buses. He was married but is now divorced and came out as gay shortly after his marriage ended. He has a ten-year-old daughter, called Daisy, and has the dirtiest laugh I've ever heard. He's no replacement for Ruby, but along with Seb, Brody, and Danny, I consider him one of my best friends. Over the six months he has been part of our lives, I have got to know him well. His razor-sharp wit, his penchant for telling it like it is, and his dry sense of humour are what makes him unique.

After the initial feeling of panic has subsided, I go back out into the bedroom to find Sam sprawled out naked across the bed, with the sheets pooled at his feet. I lick my lips at the sight of him with his hand resting on his hard, tattooed abs. I decide to leave him to sleep, and I pull on his discarded white short-sleeved shirt and head to the kitchen to get a glass of water. I get a glass from the cupboard, and as I turn around to fill my glass, I am startled by George leaning his hip against the fridge. I jump and place my free hand on my chest.

"*Jesus Christ,* Gorgeous, you scared the shit out of me!"

I hit him playfully as I take him in. He is wearing a black silk kimono with an impressive dragon stitched into the back. It's over the top, and it suits him.

"Sorry, my love, I didn't mean to frighten you. Say you forgive me?"

I narrow my eyes, and he bats his eyelashes at me, causing me to giggle out loud.

"Of course I forgive you, you tart!"

I roll my eyes as George laughs dirtily, and I find myself laughing right along with him.

"That laugh gets me every time, honey."

He folds his arms and narrows his eyes as he points his index finger at me in a circular motion.

"Something's wrong, isn't it, my love?" he says in his soft Bristol lilt. "You can tell me. You know I'm here, if you ever need to talk."

Something about his gentle, calming nature makes me sag against the fridge.

"My period is late, and I think I'm pregnant."

His mouth forms a perfect 'O' shape.

"*Shut the front door!* That's fantastic, love!" he says dramatically, and I smirk at how much Ruby would have loved him.

Those two would have got on like a house on fire.

He stands there, with a shocked look on his face for a few seconds, then he throws his arms around me, lifts me up, and spins me around. I giggle, and I feel like I'm five years old again.

"You two make such beautiful babies! You make me fucking sick!" he says with an elaborate sweep of his arm and rolls his eyes.

There's never a dull moment with George around.

"Come on, spill, I can sense there's something more."

I smile at his intuitiveness.

"Sam and me have never discussed having more kids. What if..."

He moves closer to me and places his finger on my lips.

"Stop right there. The two most pointless words are 'what if', love. Sam adores you, anyone can see that. So what if it wasn't planned? Life would be boring if everything was planned. My motto is, spontaneity is the spice of life," he says with a wink.

I laugh as we are interrupted by the appearance of Sam. I swear George swoons on the spot as he catches sight of Sam wearing just his boxers.

"Angel," he rasps, his voice thick with sleep. He looks from me to George and nods.

"Gorgeous," Sam says with a cheeky smirk.

"Sam," George says nervously.

I take in all six feet four inches of pure Sam Newbolt, as if I am committing him to memory. He's all hard, clean lines, sculpted muscles, and his boxers sit low on his hips, revealing the perfect V on his lower abdomen. I never get tired of looking at his masculine perfection. George clears his throat, breaking the silence.

"I'll...erm...leave you two lovebirds to it."

George winks, turns around, and leaves. Sam steps closer to me and wraps me in his strong arms.

"Come back to bed, angel. I want to worship you some more," he says huskily, his voice dripping with seduction, and I decide not to tell him about the possible pregnancy yet.

I follow him to the bedroom and I let him worship me.

***

The next day, the boys are putting some finishing touches to their new album, and I'm left to my own devices. I decide to take a boat to the mainland and go shopping with George. While we're there, I buy a pregnancy test, and by the time we get back to the lodge, I am a bundle of nerves. I stand at the floor length window and watch the scene that is playing out in front of me. Sam is on the sand wearing a straw trilby hat, a white vest, red board shorts, and his guitar in his hands. Addison is on his lap, and she is giggling girlishly as Sam plucks the strings of his guitar. Freddie is playing at his feet and clapping his hands excitedly. I'm suddenly wracked and ravaged with an overwhelming sense of guilt.

How the fuck could I doubt what Sam's reaction would be, when he's so good with his son and Addison?

I quietly observe the scene for a few moments longer and the love I feel for the two men in my life makes my heart feel almost too big for my chest.

"I always knew you were a voyeur, sweets."

I smile, and as I spin round, I'm greeted by Brody eating a bag of cheesy puffs.

"You and that little boy are his life. You know that, don't you? In the year you were gone, one of his major food groups was vodka. I'm surprised he wasn't pissing it fucking neat."

I am taken aback by Brody's revelation, and in that moment, I know what I have to do.

I have to take the test, I have to know for sure.

I smile softly, kiss him on the cheek, take one of his cheesy puffs from the bag, pop it into my mouth, and head for the bathroom. I go into the bathroom and sit down on the toilet. I take the test out of the box with trembling hands, briefly read the instructions, and I pee on the stick before I wait for the results develop.

A few minutes pass and I look at the result, 'pregnant'. Instead of being shocked by the result, I find myself smiling and place my hand on my stomach as I look in the mirror at my reflection. I don't know why I didn't realise I was pregnant. As I stare at myself in the mirror, I notice the subtle differences. My hair is glossy and falling down my shoulders in tousled, glossy waves. My sapphire eyes are sparkling, and even though they are extremely sore and tender, my boobs look incredible. This time around, I'm no longer terrified of what Sam is going to say.

This life that is growing inside me, is the next chapter of our forever.

43

Sam

Today is our last day in The Cook Islands, and after everything that's happened within the past six months, I haven't been this relaxed in a long time. Today is also Peyton's twenty-ninth birthday, and I've spent the day spoiling her. She deserves to be treated like a fucking queen. In the time we have spent together, she has taught me that life is precious, and no matter how badly we fuck up, everyone deserves a second chance.

To celebrate her birthday, and to end the holiday on a high note, we are all going out to dinner. I catch sight of her through the floor length window as she is looking out at the sun setting over the crystal-clear ocean, and she looks like an angel. She is wearing a black and turquoise maxi dress, and her hair is in a side ponytail. She looks contemplative as I step out onto the sand to join her. I slide my arms around her waist and rest my stubbled chin on her bare shoulder, pulling her back to my front.

"Angel."

I nuzzle her neck and she chuckles softly.

"Hey handsome," she says quietly and turns in my arms.

As she takes a step back, I notice she has a long, black rectangular shaped box in her hand.

"I know it's my birthday, but this is my gift to you, Sam."

I glance at her with a puzzled look on my face and take the box from her. She watches me nervously as she bites her nail. I open the box and the sight that greets me makes me gasp out loud. A pregnancy test, with the word 'pregnant' in the small, oblong shaped window. The smile that lights up my face almost makes my jaw ache.

Fuck me, I'm going to be a dad again.

"Angel...*fuck*," I curse, and I lift her up in my arms.

The smile she gives me in return melts me instantly, and her blue eyes sparkle. The look on her face...I wish I could freeze the moment and keep it until the day I die.

"I never knew I wanted kids until I met you, Peyton. I never even knew I wanted the whole girlfriend thing. I was content with just using sex to get over the fact that my life was so empty and incomplete. When we first started out in the music industry, we were starry eyed, snot-nosed kids who thought the world was our oyster. After eleven years in the industry, our view on things has become somewhat jaded. The fame, the fortune, the attention, the women. Then you came along, and you changed everything. Finally, after all those years I spent feeling...*nothing,* I felt more love for you than anyone I'd ever met. I look at you and Freddie every single day, and I'm so fucking blessed to have you both. And now, we're going to be parents again, I...I can't believe it. I'm the happiest fucking man to walk this god damn earth. We got our second chance, and I'm so lucky I walked into Saint Sinner that day. It seems such a long time ago now, but it was the day my heart started beating again. I love you so fucking much. I want to spend every day showing you how much. I'm going to look after you, Freddie, and our little jellybean, because you deserve it."

I crush my lips to hers and taste the salt of her tears. In that moment, it's just us watching the sunset, and I couldn't be fucking happier.

Epilogue

Peyton
1 Year Later

As I stare at my reflection in the mirror, I hardly recognise the woman staring back at me. Today is our wedding day, and it feels like a lifetime has passed for us to finally get to this point. This past year has been a total whirlwind, from touring with the boys, managing Saint Sinner, and juggling being a mum to Freddie.

Over this past year, the band have been on a worldwide tour, and I travelled with them for a few months, in the early stages of my pregnancy. We moved to a new house, a purpose built, three storey, eleven-bedroom property in Chislehurst, Kent. I also continued to tattoo at Saint Sinner Ink, part-time, with Seb.

I adjust my veil, and my mum comes up behind me to help me.

"Here let me, darling girl."

I catch my mum's gaze in the mirror, and her eyes are glossy with tears.

"Don't you bloody dare, mum!"

My voice shakes, and we both laugh.

"You look absolutely breath taking, darling. That boy is a bloody lucky bastard!"

I laugh at my mum's cursing, and she kisses me on the cheek as Dexter enters mine and Sam's bedroom. The wedding will be taking place in the twelve-acre grounds at the back of our house. He has our son, Zachary Marlowe Newbolt, in his arms. Zachary was born on the fifth of July, and Sam never left my side throughout the birth. He was with me through the pain, the contractions, and the moment our son arrived into the world.

"I think someone needs a nappy change, sis! How can something so smelly come out of something that adorable!" he says with an exaggerated eye roll and a charming smile as he hands Zachary back to me.

The smile on his face looks genuine, and he has the sparkle back in his blue eyes, which was snuffed out the day he lost the love of his life. He has a golden tan, his dark hair is styled in a neat slicked back quiff, and he has grown a goatee beard on his chin. He is wearing a white shirt, a purple waistcoat, black trousers, and a purple and silver striped tie. His sleeves are rolled up, and he stands there with his hands on his hips.

"Are you just going to stand there like a spare prick at a wedding, or are you actually going to do something?" I quip sarcastically, and he cocks his eyebrow.

"Just because you're marrying a rich and famous rock star, don't go forgetting your roots!"

I hit him playfully, and my sister Eden enters the room in her purple bridesmaids' dress. She kisses me on the cheek.

"You look amazing, Peyton."

She is closely followed by Addison and the man who looked after me all those months ago, Remy Logan. Eden grabs his hand and thrusts him in front of me.

"Look who I found lurking outside, sis."

She smiles deviously, and my mum looks from me to Remy.

"Let me take Zachary, darling girl. I'll get his nappy changed, and we'll clear out to give you a few minutes alone."

I am grateful for her intervention, and she kisses me on the cheek.

"Love you, mum."

She takes Zachary and blows me a kiss.

"Love you too, darling."

The room is cleared within minutes, and Remy and I are left alone. I haven't seen Remy since the day of Ruby's funeral, almost a year ago.

"How have you been, Rem?" I say to break the awkward silence.

He stands there, looking all boy next door with his hands casually tucked in his pockets. His dark hair is brushing the collar of his white shirt, and his familiar russet eyes regard me intently.

"Can't complain, beaut. It's been a while...you're looking gorgeous as ever."

I smile shyly at his compliment. *You're still a charmer, Logan.*

"Congratulations on the birth of your son, he's beautiful."

I nod, and he chuckles softly.

"Since when did this get so awkward between us?"

He gestures from me to himself, and I laugh.

"I don't know, it's never been like this with us, Rem, ever. How's life treating you back in Santa Monica?"

He frowns.

"You're seriously asking me that when you're standing there looking like that? You look...*fucking stunning.*"

He steps a few inches closer to me and tucks a strand of my hair behind my ear.

"Sam is one lucky motherfucker," he curses and rests his forehead against mine.

"I lost a part of myself the day Ruby died, but you got me through it. You were my rock, and I'll be eternally grateful to you for that, but I'm not sorry I went back to Santa Monica. I had to get over you, and I did. It took me a long time, and a lot of bourbon, but I got there in the end. I'm ok with it. I've made peace with the fact that I had my chance, and I fucking blew it. I came back here today to say I'm happy for you."

He smiles tenderly and takes my hand gently, kissing the back of it.

"You look nothing like the fearless five-year-old I remember. You've turned into an equally beautiful woman, and I'm proud to call you my friend. I know you wish Ruby was here, and I do too, but she's with us."

My eyes gloss over, and I will myself not to cry.

"Hey, none of that, beaut. Today is about you marrying Sam. It's been a long time coming, and after all you've been through together, you deserve this."

He tips my chin up and kisses me softly on the lips as a tear slips down my cheek. He catches it with his thumb and puts it in his mouth, licking my tears off his thumb.

"Be happy, beaut," he whispers, and I narrow my eyes at him.

"Why does this feel like you're telling me goodbye, Rem?"

He smiles and shakes his head.

"Never."

He is about to speak again as the door taps softly.

"Are you decent, sweetheart?" my dad shouts.

"Yeah, just give me a minute, dad."

Remy adjusts my veil and wipes my tears with the sleeve of his jacket.

"Perfect, now go."

He winks, and I smile, kissing him on the corner of his mouth.

"Say you'll stay, Rem?"

He nods.

"Try and stop me."

He winks as I open the door to my dad.

This is finally it.

Sam

I'm standing at the make shift altar in the grounds of our house in Chislehurst, Kent. The people closest to us, our family, close friends, and a select few from the music and movie industry, are gathered here today for mine and Peyton's wedding.

"Are you sure this is what you want, little brother? There's always time to back out now!" my older brother, Brandon, quips, and I narrow my eyes at him.

"Very fucking funny, bro. You're not helping," I say quietly so Freddie doesn't hear me.

He is at the age where he's picking up on things, and he already used the word 'bollocks' a few days ago.

If Peyton found out, she'd have my balls.

"Daddy," he calls, and he looks so fucking cute in his little man suit to match mine.

His hair is sticking up in all directions, and every time I look at him, I couldn't be happier to call him my son. He comes bounding towards me, giggling loudly, and I swing him up into my arms.

"Hey, rock star."

He idly plays with my tie, and Brandon chuckles.

"That kid has you wrapped around his little finger."

I roll my eyes at him.

"You won't be saying that when you have kids."

He lets out a *'pfft'* sound, and I laugh.

"I practice safe sex. I'm not a fool, I wrap my tool!"

Freddie giggles.

"Tool! Uncle Brandon, tool!"

I laugh. *My son is nothing if not honest even at two years old.*

Brandon folds his arms and starts sulking. My dad, who is dressed in a white suit with black shirt and a make shift dog collar - he was ordained online - is going to be marrying us today. It is an honour to have the man I've looked up to for so many years marry us in front of our loved ones. After the loss of my mum, my dad threw himself back into his band. For the past year, the Lightning Bolts reunited and toured with us as our support act. Our relationship has become solid as father and son.

"Today's the day you get your happy ever after, son," my dad says proudly, and he gives me a one-armed hug. "I'm so proud of you, Sam," he says with awe in his voice.

I grin wider than I've ever grinned, in my life. Then, his gaze shifts over my shoulder, and he nods curtly as the strains of Nickelback *Gotta Be Somebody* fills the air. My heartbeat starts to quicken, and the steady da-dum-da-dum feels so loud that I'm convinced that everyone can hear it. I've performed on stage in front of hundreds of thousands of people over the years, but never in my life have I been this fucking nervous. I swallow hard and I start to wring my hands.

I think I'm going to throw up. Jesus fucking Christ.

"*Fuck me*, little brother, you're getting married, not facing the firing squad!" Brandon retorts, and I'm regretting asking him to be my best man.

Prick.

I hear snickers from the boys, but the sound becomes white noise as I turn and catch sight of her. Peyton.

Fuck me, she looks like an angel. My angel.

It takes everything I have to stay on my feet and not to drop to my knees in front of her. She looks ethereal, *radiant*...and words can't fucking describe what I'm feeling right now. A stray tear tracks its way down my cheek as her eyes lock with mine. Blue to green, green to blue.

Her bridesmaids, Addison, Eden, and Willow, are following close behind her, all wearing matching purple dresses. She is clinging to her dad, Max, for dear life, and I can clearly see her focussing hard on putting one foot in front of the other. I flash her a cheeky wink as she gets closer, and the smile I get in return unmans me in front of our closest friends and family. I literally burst into tears. I've never been this emotional or overwhelmed with happiness in my life, I feel like I could fucking explode.

I wipe my tears with the backs of my hands as I feel a firm grip on my shoulder. I turn to see the shining eyes of my dad.

"You deserve this, son," he whispers softly and kisses me on the forehead, like he used to when I was a kid.

Our moment is interrupted by Freddie turning to point at Peyton.

"Mummy, pretty."

I nod.

"Mummy is very beautiful, isn't she, Freddie?" I manage to choke out through the tears.

At long last, I get to take her in, all five feet three inches of her. She really is...mesmerizing. My heart stutters in my chest, and I gasp out loud at how beautiful she looks. Words can't describe the way I feel right now; I'm struck dumb at the sight of her. *My Peyton.* The woman I am going to spend the rest of my life with.

Her white dress is strapless, and the delicate neckline makes her tattoos stand out, and it compliments her curves. The sparkling silver embroidery dances down to the skirt and the dress blossoms into layers and folds of pure white silk. The way the light catches on the smooth fabric makes it look like it is dancing, making it look almost magical, and as if it was made just for her. The diamond encrusted angel wing necklace, which I bought as her something new, sits at her throat and sparkles in the summer sunlight. As her dad escorts her closer to me, my chest feels tight, and when she reaches me, I can't help the sob that escapes me.

Fuck me, since when I get so soppy in my old age?

Max hands her over to me, and the look he gives me is full of warning. I nod curtly in understanding, and he winks. As she takes her place next to me, Peyton grips my hand, and I lean in close to her.

"You look fucking breath taking, angel."

She smiles softly with glossy eyes, and she whispers in my ear.

"You don't look too shabby yourself, rock star."

She winks and hitches her dress up from the bottom, revealing white patent Doc Martens underneath with the words 'Mrs Newbolt' delicately stitched on the sides. We both laugh as my dad begins to speak.

"Friends, family, and everyone in between, we are gathered here today to celebrate the marriage of my son, Sam, and my soon to be daughter-in-law, Peyton."

We turn to face each other, and as I look into her sparkling blue eyes, I can see nothing else, no one else but her. That's the way it's always been, and that's the way it will always be.

This time it's forever.

Peyton

"I take you, Peyton Leigh Harper, to be my lawful wedded wife, to have and to hold from this day forward. I promise to protect you, with everything that I am. I choose you to be my wife, my partner in life. I chose you the day I walked into Saint Sinner Ink, hungover and feeling unsatisfied with life on the road. I promise you my unconditional love, and my fullest devotion through the pressures of the present and the uncertainties of the future."

A tear tracks its way down my cheek, and he wipes it away with the pad of his thumb.

"I call you 'My Peyton' because you are my everything. You are my light, and you've shown me more love than I've ever known. You gave me the most precious gift of all, in our sons Freddie and Zachary. From this day forward, I promise to give you the best of myself and to ask of you no more than you can give. I promise to accept you the way you are. I fell in love with you for the qualities, abilities, and outlook on life that you have, and won't try to reshape you in a different image. I promise to keep myself open to you, to let you see through the window of my personal world into my innermost fears and feelings, secrets and dreams. I promise to grow along with you, to be willing to face change as we both adapt to keep our relationship alive and exciting. And finally, I promise to love you, in good times and in bad, with all I have to give and all I feel inside, in the only way I know how. Completely and forever."

As I listen to Sam brokenly rasp out his vows to me on the happiest day of our lives, I feel my pussy clench and grow unwantedly damp at the sound of his voice. I know deep down that it's highly inappropriate, but with Sam, I can't seem to help myself. Every look, every rasp, every fucking facet of him, deeply fascinates and captivates me. It just emphasises that I have always belonged to him, just as much as he belongs to me.

Our eyes lock as he completes his vows, and he places my simple white gold wedding band on the fourth finger of my left hand. I smile warmly as the silence descends, and they expectantly await my vows to Sam. I swallow hard and suddenly feel an overwhelming wave of nervousness. He squeezes my hand and leans into me. He smells of his familiar Sam smell, and it instantly reassures me.

"Pretend it's just us, angel. Do you know how I manage to perform on stage? *You.* You're my reason, Peyton, remember that," he whispers so only I can hear as he stands up straight and shoots me a panty-melting wink.

I'm his reason.

My stomach does a somersault, just like it did the day he walked into Saint Sinner Ink. I take a deep breath and laugh nervously.

"I take you, Samson Newbolt, to be my lawful wedded husband, to have and to hold, from this day forward. On this day, I give you my heart, even though you had it the day you walked into Saint Sinner."

Soft laughter comes from our guests, and as I take a deep, steadying breath, I start to relax.

"I give you my promise that I will walk with you, hand in hand, wherever our journey leads us, living, learning, loving. I promise to be your lover, companion, and friend. Your greatest fan, and your toughest adversary, your comrade in adventure, your consolation in disappointment, and your accomplice in mischief. This is my sacred vow to you, my equal in all things. It's you, me, and our boys now, forever, Newbolt."

I let out the breath I didn't realise I was holding, and as I hold his stare, I notice, that his eyes are glossy with unshed tears. His Adam's apple bobs as he swallows hard. I squeeze his large tattooed hand in my small one as a gesture of reassurance, and he flashes me his signature Newbolt dimpled smile.

"I love you," I mouth, and he winks.

"Right back at ya, angel," he mouths back.

Marlowe smiles warmly as he pronounces us man and wife.

None of this seems real...any moment now I'm going to wake up, and it's going to be a dream.

"I now pronounce you, Mr. and Mrs. Newbolt."

Everyone erupts in rapturous applause as Marlowe says those words with a tremendous sense of pride and satisfaction in his voice.

"You may now kiss your bride."

Sam takes me in his arms and he kisses me with reckless abandon, and I lose myself in him. It is as if he can't believe we're finally married. His velvet tongue is gently probing and caressing mine. He is kissing me as if it is the last kiss we'll ever share, and it leaves me light-headed with desire. It shows him and the world around us that he is mine. I now bear his name, and I belong only to Samson Newbolt.

"Put her down, ya fucking animal!" Brody heckles, and Sam flips him the bird over my shoulder as we both pull away breathless and panting with uninhibited lust.

"Shall we, Mrs. Newbolt?"

I test those words out on my tongue, and it definitely has a ring to it. He offers me his hand, and we interlink our fingers together, the sunlight glimmering off both our wedding rings.

"Yes, Mr. Newbolt," I reply.

We both smile so wide, and my jaw starts to ache.

After all we've been through together, this moment has been a long time coming. We are finally Mr. and Mrs. Newbolt and are about to start our happy ever after.